The Secrets of Eronis 8

Tracey Canole

John,
Thank you for
your continued support!
Canole

KORBEN SKIES PUBLISHING

Korben Skies Publishing

Acknowledgements

F or many reasons, I was not convinced this novel would ever come to fruition. I had to put it down for medical reasons, thinking I would never write again. But with the support and love of those around me, I healed and continued on.

Thank you first to my family and friends who took care of me; who built me up and kept me sane in the darkest time of my life. To the Sac who supported us. My girls who brought us meals, kept me company, and told me everything was going to be okay. I can never repay you. My husband, Quinn, who slept on the couch next to me for months. I love you more than anything.

For my kids, Tristan and Aenea who've shown me the most empathy and care. You've been through more than anyone should ever have to, and I'm proud of the people you've become. You stand by me, ask me about my progress, and give me high fives and hugs with each accomplishment. You cheer me on more than anyone else. I am so lucky you're mine.

Finally, a special thank you to the writing community who put me back together and showed me I could still do this, even if they didn't know that's what they did. My amazing writing group, Michelle Darnell, E. Marie Robertson, Marc B. DeGeorge, J. Logan Rice, and Rhiannon Gurcuis. And my editor, Erin Zarro. Thank for the laughter, honest but critical critique, and constant support. I continued because you would not let me give up.

Chapter One
Captain Mitchel Remian

P ain. This was the first true sensation. All-consuming as the invisible tether holding me to the world I thought I'd lost was yanked violently. The ether which had encapsulated me for who knew how long dug its grip into my very being. It was as if space itself were unwilling to let me go, but whatever force pulled me back from the dark refused to release its hold.

I'd lived in this emptiness for so long. Time had passed without my knowledge, but as I came back into the world — as the agony of life took hold once again — I felt the years I'd floated press down upon me. Had I been adrift forever? It was a heaviness I was not convinced I'd survive. And if the images that flashed through my mind were correct, nothing would ever be the same.

A shock ran through me, reconnecting my consciousness to what I now knew I'd been missing. My body. It was unpleasant, but I was grateful for the anchor to the universe because it meant I was no longer adrift. Then, a rhythmic pounding resonated through the air, and I focused on the sound I somehow knew was my heart. With each steady beat, I rose from the dream, questions of who I was answered with each life-altering contraction. It was as if they told the story of who I'd been so that I could remember who I was now.

Lub-Dub. Your name is Mitchel...

Lub. Your favorite fruit is strawberries. *Dub.* But you will never taste one again.

Lub. Your sister died on the homeworld. *Dub.* Now, far away and long ago.

Excitement of knowing something, anything, rose within me as more and more of my memories returned. But as my body congealed around me, I realized that the wake-up wasn't over.

A distant tingling caught my attention — multiple points so far away. Wait, those were my fingers and toes. It started at the tips and spread up the digits in an unhurried pace. Over the knuckles, across the palm, to the wrist. When it reached my hands, the tingling changed, becoming a burn that followed the same path as before. First, mild and comforting, as a campfire is against the skin, then rising ever slowly until it felt as though a hot iron was pressed against the nerves themselves.

Lub. Marshmallows cooked over a fire with Tasha. *Dub.*

The wave continued, revealing my body one inch at a time, then lighting it aflame.

Lub-Dub. Flying sucks, but starships are your dream.

Had I remembered how to scream, I would have. If my body had allowed it, I would've dived back into the abyss. But it refused — my chest rising without my control. Air filled my lungs and, as it did, the burning subsided and the wave of sensation rolled up my limbs once again.

Calves, knees, then groin. Forearms, elbows, and then biceps. With each inch, the voice of memory explained this was normal. Tingle, warmth, then burn — this was expected. My body was waking up from a long sleep, and it was time to live again.

What did that mean?

Deeper, it delved into bone, muscle, and sinew. Farther it reached until it hit my torso, spreading like wildfire as if the veins there held secret paths directly to my cells.

Lub. Schematics of a massive ship where I now slept. *Dub.*

A bed? I could feel the bed!

My bones cracked in relief; the gasses built up released with the movement. It hurt. I tried to scream but couldn't. There was something in the way.

I attempted to swallow and instead choked. The muscles in my throat could not contract. Nor could they relax. My lungs were not under my control, and my breathing was not mine because there was something in my throat!

I strained. The pounding in my chest picked up, the images becoming more jumbled as my focus was pulled to a new agony shooting through my chest, back, and neck. Terror mixed with panic, and I attempted to reach for my face. I was too weak. My limbs, still too far away.

Think, damn it!

Eyes. I'd once had eyes. If I could see, maybe I could figure out what was happening.

I tried to blink, but my eyelids were heavily covered with a layer of something sticky. I peeled them open, groaning as the seal pulled at my skin. With all my effort, I forced my arm to lift and wipe away the goo smeared over my lids. The movement burned, my limb shaking violently, but I managed to clear it away. Opening my eyes was more successful this time. But as the bright light hit my pupils, a new pain stabbed through me. I slammed my lids shut once again.

Light. There was too much light. The back of my eyes burned, a spike being driven into my brain. I squeezed them closed, somehow knowing they'd need time to adjust. I took a moment to calm myself.

This is normal, the voice in my memory reminded me again.

Okay, calm. I could do that. Especially considering I recognized where I was. In the instant my eyes had opened, I'd seen the glass which wrapped me in a cocoon of warmth. Upon the surface was an insignia

I remembered. The sign of the fleet. The mark of the traveler that had labeled me for years. That one sight had brought everything back.

In my pod — the capsule that would allow me to pass years in simulated sleep. It explained my confusion and the sensation of time lost. Which meant it must be time to awaken.

The memory of the physician explaining the process ran through my head, and I flinched. Some steps I had already experienced, but... Oh, what came next would not be pleasant.

With a shocking snap, sound — which I had not realized was missing until that moment — bombarded my very being. It was like a switch flipped in my head. I covered my ears, the sensation too much to bear. The rush of blood mixed with the frantic wheeze of my breaths, terrified moans, and the indistinguishable hum, clicks, and pings of the pod. They were so loud, it felt as though the walls of my cage had suddenly begun to close in. I began to shake. I'd been deaf. The world had been entirely and absolutely devoid of sound. Now, I could hear everything, and I wished I could go back to the silence.

Yet, oddly, the noise calmed my panic. With each of the systems that turned on inside me, I could understand more of where I was — the pieces of who I'd been and what I'd known coming back.

The burning beneath my skin had receded, my attention drawn now to an itching as something soft and cold blew over my body.

A breeze...that was the word. I cringed away from its caress but sighed as my skin grew in around me, finally covering my arms, legs, chest, and face. Then gooseflesh spread, and I had the urge to laugh. I could feel it all now. I opened my eyes to see the lid to my pod had opened.

Tears sprang to my eyes. I was completely back in my body, and it was a miracle. This would all be over soon.

Muffled words of the artificial intelligence controlling the pod filled the air. *Relax...Not....Pleasant...*

Then, suddenly, there was a violent tugging on my mouth. I swear, my heart stuttered at the sliding sensation as the plastic tube was yanked from my throat. My body arched. As it left my trachea, I rolled to my side and retched. I coughed, the bile following the tube out, painting the cloth pad beneath me.

I threw my head back and sucked in a breath. But instead of fresh, clean air calming me as expected, my lungs seized. A spasm rolled through my entire body as I tried to understand what was wrong.

Oxygen. There was no oxygen. My medical training clicked in.

I had medical training?

The words of the tech who'd put me in here appeared in my mind. *"In case of failure..."* I reached for the smart mask hanging next to my head. I placed it over my face and inhaled deeply. Cool and clean, my chest rose, then fell.

Sweet air...

Eventually, my convulsions stopped. My forehead was pressed to the side of the pod, my body curled into a ball. I stayed like that for a long time. Breaths in. Breaths out. My throat ached from the extubation, and I cursed the medics who'd said the wake-up process would be easy. If they'd been nearby, I would have made it clear how wrong they were.

Wait...the doctors. Where were they?

Holding the mask to my face, I pressed a shaky hand to the bed beneath me and pushed to a seated position. Glancing around, I took in the space.

"This can't be good," I croaked.

Two hundred plus people slept here, and from the look of it, my group of about thirty was beginning their re-animation procedures, but nothing was how it should have been. The room was dim, the lights barely illuminating the large space. Where there should've been a crew of welcoming faces there to wake us, there was only empty space. Flashing red lights cast ominous shadows across the pods surrounding me.

As my gaze found the two pods nearest to my left, it became hard to breathe all over again. They were already open. One held a woman — her body limp, flopped over the edge, her fingers tracing the floor. A smart mask hung down beside her, but her lips were blue, and her eyes empty. A second body lay in the walkway, halfway to the control panel on the far wall. It was still. It reached for the wall of panels, and I instantly knew what he was trying to do.

He. I knew him. That was Samson, the engineer I'd worked closely with back home. I looked down and away from my friend.

The hiss of the glass casing opening on the pod next to mine stole my attention. Glancing over, I watched as another long-time friend was extubated. The sight of the automated process had me turning away, the sting in my throat amplified by the sight alone.

But Lieutenant Geron Richards recovered far quicker than I had. After his first inhale failed, he immediately reached for the smart mask. As it slid over his mouth, his eyes met mine.

"Air," he croaked, then winced. His throat must have been as sore as mine.

"Life support. Down," I said roughly. I gestured to Samson on the floor.

With shaky arms, Richards pushed himself upright. His lip curled at the sight of the bodies and, though I couldn't hear it, I knew which expletive slipped from his lips. It was his favorite.

"Fix," he said, meeting my gaze again.

Nodding, I forced my legs over the edge of the pod and placed my feet on the floor. My body was recovering — slowly, but still. My mind was clearer. I knew who I was, and I knew what I had to do. The rest of my body function and coordination would return with time. Should everything go right, within forty-eight hours, I'd be at full strength. Until then, I'd have to make it work.

I tried to push to my feet, bracing myself on the sides of my pod and using my body weight for momentum. The first time I over adjusted, almost flinging myself to the floor. Had that happened, I would've been crawling as Samson had. Luckily, I caught myself, and, trying again, I managed to stand.

Pain radiated from my feet, up my legs, and into my back. I swayed. I gritted my teeth as the line connecting my mask to the pod tightened, pulling me back and causing me to lose balance. Damn, I wouldn't be able to take the mask with me. So, I'd have to make it to the panel and fix life support before I ran out of oxygen.

Gasping hit my ears from the pod on the other side of Richards. I turned to find him leaning into the space. With shaky hands, he grabbed the mask and pressed it to the inhabitant's face. I couldn't see them fully, but I had a vague inkling about who it was.

That was it. If life support wasn't fixed, everyone on board who awoke would die. I could not let that happen.

Breathing steadily, I shifted from foot to foot, forcing my body to remember the sensation of standing and then walking. After a few moments — and once I felt steady enough mentally and physically — I faced my objective. Every station in this room could link into life support with the correct code. Mine. Not only that, each module of the ship held separate life support systems to verify if one went down, all areas didn't go down. I just had to figure out if this was system-wide or just this hub.

As if I were about to swim across a great pool of water, I sped up my breathing. Maybe, just maybe, it would give me enough to get to the panel before I passed out. I glanced at Richards and found him standing on shaky legs, testing the muscles still coming back to life.

"Follow in five," I croaked, the words coming out more like a whisper. "You finish when I pass out."

Richards nodded, but I didn't miss the worry lining his brow.

I inhaled one last time, expanding my chest as far as it would go. Then, I yanked off the mask and stumbled one tormented step at a time toward the console. My knee gave out ten steps in. As I fell, I grabbed onto the desk, barely managing to stay upright. Ten more agonizing feet, and I was at the panel. I braced one hand against the wall, then swiped the screen. Lights illuminated diagrams I recognized from my past life: ship statistics, air levels, alarms, and errors.

There were so many errors.

My chest burned. My eyes watered, and I fought against the urge to release my breath. I searched for the proper controls. At least my memory seemed intact once again. Second after second, I prayed to find them, but they seemed buried far deeper in the system than they should've been. Or perhaps it was due to the volume of warnings littering the screen.

My vision blackened at the edges.

When I found the correct system, I nearly collapsed from exhaustion. The good news was the problem was clear. Someone had shut all life support down to minimal levels.

What the absolute hell?

The more concerning issue was the alarms that blazed, indicating where sections of the ship had failed entirely. If anyone was outside their pods in those areas, then they were already dead.

Identification Verification appeared on the screen. It took me a moment to remember. Never before had my ten-digit password seemed so long. I pressed my head against the wall for support and fought against the agony in my chest. Using my code, I overrode the last command and navigated to the screen I needed. With each entry, I slipped farther down, my arm weighing a thousand pounds by the time I lifted it to press the button that would turn life support back online.

But before I made contact, everything went dark. The world disappeared, and my body collapsed to the floor. The blackness was back. I wondered if it would take me this time, and how I really felt about that.

Chapter Two
Captain Mitchel Remian

F eet were the first thing I saw when my eyelids lifted this time. They were mere inches from my face, the cold floor pressed to my cheek. A hand gripped my shoulder, and I was rolled to my back.

Richards's mouth lifted in a relieved grin when his eyes met mine.

"Captain?" he said, voice raspy.

My chest expanded, air rushing into my lungs the way it should have the first time. It was fresh, and the best thing I'd ever smelled. I relaxed my head back against the linoleum and sighed.

"Captain," Richards said, expression concerned.

Another face appeared next to Richards, and relief spread through me. I lifted a hand to my forehead. "Thank the gods. Montgomery. Richards. You did it." The dizziness was finally clearing, so I pushed to a sitting position.

"No, sir," Commander Patrick Montgomery said, helping me to my feet. He was the Head of Engineering and the smartest man I'd ever met. He was also one of the few I trusted with my life. "You did. You restarted the systems. Once that happened, I was able to get to the panel and re-calibrate life support. But Captain, systems are failing all over the place. We need to get to the Bridge, and then I need to be in Engineering. Complete diagnostics must be performed, and we need to figure out where the Elemental Crew is."

I stumbled over to the desk, then pulled a chair from the nook beneath it. I sat, spun to face the screen, and scanned the data covering it.

"They should've been here," Richards said, joining me.

The Elemental Crew. Their absence was a serious issue. Upon leaving home, it was understood that, while most passengers on board would sleep, twenty-four families with a few extra stragglers would stay awake. They would live their lives on the ship and be the guardians of those asleep. As such, they would be in charge of maintaining the vessel, verifying all wake-up procedures were completed safely, and that approach protocols were in order.

"Were we the first to wake? How many did we lose?"

"Yes. We lost two, Samson and Nielson," Richards said. "Shame, too. Neilson was a hell of a pilot. It looks like she was the first pod to open."

I cursed under my breath. They were both fantastic crewmembers. Even better people. Clearing my throat, I asked, "How many have begun re-animation? Are we on schedule?"

"There are breaks between groups to verify recharge of the Alementra System." Patrick leaned in and used the glass keyboard to type something. A diagram of the four sleep bays appeared. "Our group was the first to be initiated. Thirty-five in total. From this schedule, it looks as though the next forty will initiate in three hours. Once those are awake, two groups would be activated at a time."

"Yes, but we need to do a full analysis of all Stasis Bays." Richards pointed at the screen, indicating a few warnings flashing a bright red. "Section Nine has been damaged. We need to verify the severity and activate the process as soon as we can. If we don't, we might lose them all." He ran a hand through his messy golden hair. "For that, we'll need some help from the specialists in group two."

"Doctor Brackett's team?" I asked, and Richards nodded.

Just then, a very haggard-looking Connie Brackett, stasis expert and medical liaison, appeared with four others trailing her. Her normally vibrant, golden-brown complexion was ashen, pale from the stress of reanimation. Behind her, I could see the remaining members of our group slowly getting to their feet. They were all worse for wear, but they were alive.

"Captain," Dr. Brackett said, her dark blue eyes questioning, "where's the Elemental Crew?"

"We're not sure. Looks like they haven't been here for a while. Normally we'd be allotted time to recover, but I don't think we have that option given the damage I'm seeing."

It wasn't just the life support system that was down. There were warnings indicating breaches, downed engines, water leaks, overheating sections, and more. *The Aspire* was in trouble.

Brackett nodded. "I heard what Lieutenant Richards said. I can get started on Section Nine, but I'll need some help. Most of my team is in group two."

My respect for Brackett grew in that instant. It didn't matter that she looked about to fall over. She was a soldier, and she would do what was necessary to save the crew under her protection.

She stepped to the console beside mine and pulled up the manifests of both group two and Section Nine. With a grimace, she ran long dark fingers through her short, cropped hair. She exhaled through her teeth.

"I need my team," she said without looking up. "The damage to Section Nine is bad, and there are over three hundred people in that bay. I can get the process started here and then head down to evaluate a new timeline, but I'll need at least four to stay here and manage the wake-up process. I can show them everything they need to do. Plus, I'll need at least two Engineering staff to help with failures."

"There are crew we may need to initiate sooner too if their experience is deemed necessary," I said.

Patrick agreed. "Tasha Evans and Russel Cruz, for example. They'll be integral in getting the ship up to speed."

"They're in group six," Richards said.

Of course he would know. Commander Tasha Evans was his oldest friend — her older brother having been his best friend since childhood. Since Tasha's brother's death, he'd taken on the role of protector.

"Get a list together," Dr. Brackett said, nodding. "Once I have some extra hands, I can identify a new schedule and split our resources appropriately."

With a sharp nod to her, I pushed to my feet and faced the group as a whole. A groan nearly escaped my lips at the movement, my muscles protesting, but my pride refused to allow it.

"That we can do. All right, everyone," I said to the group at large. As was expected, all eyes fell to me — their Captain. It was funny how, minutes ago, I hadn't remembered who I was, and yet now, I'd fallen back into that role without hesitation. It felt good. Right. "We don't know where the Elemental Crew is, and we can't worry about that now. Our first priority is getting life support and all other vital systems back online. We also need those in Section Nine woken up. I'll be assigning a few of you to Dr. Brackett. Please help her with anything she needs. Doctor, can you please also watch over anyone who requires additional time to recover?"

Brackett nodded succinctly, her eyes scanning the crowd and landing on two who swayed on their feet. They'd need a full work-up. Even from here, I could see something was wrong.

Glancing away, I continued, "The rest of you, I'll give you fifteen minutes to get yourselves together. Then, we reconvene on the Bridge to figure out what happened."

Everyone nodded, but no one moved. I think, like me, they were still too sore. However, that wasn't an option; it was time to get to work.

Patrick stepped forward and clapped his hands. "We've got a lot to do. Let's get started."

I managed to bite back the scoff at that understatement. The number of alarms littering the screen was concerning. The systems and areas of the ship they affected were even more important. This could be disastrous.

I forced myself to hide the exhaustion and headed for the door, my back straight and head held tall. My limbs felt heavy, my feet trudged forward as if I were walking through mud, but that didn't matter. We didn't have the option to rest.

Where was the Elemental Crew? What the bloody hell had happened to the nearly sixty people who'd taken the job of protecting the ship and its occupants?

Something terrible must've happened. That was the only explanation. And whatever had caused this? I'd figure it out, but not before the ship was back in order, my crew was safe, and we knew if this mission had already failed or if we still had a chance of making it to our new home.

I entered the Bridge and headed straight for where our navigation expert normally sat. The lights automatically brightened, illuminating the empty space. It was strange to see the Bridge this way — quiet and so devoid of movement. I pressed a few keys on the display next to the Navigation Station, and the screen on the wall lit up. My jaw dropped, and it felt like the floor disappeared from beneath me. Using the desk for balance, I steadied myself.

"What is it, Captain?" Richards asked from my left. I'd known both he and Patrick had followed me, but I hadn't realized how close they now stood.

"Oh, shit," I whispered.

This couldn't be right. If these calculations were correct...

Richards's eyebrows rose. He elbowed Patrick in the side as he said, "Well, we know it's bad if it got him to break his pristine commander persona and curse."

Not acknowledging the jab, I explained, "We're less than four months to Merocius."

I ran both hands through my hair, linking my fingers behind my head. The pull on the strands was painful — the nerves still waking up — but I didn't care. It was necessary to solidify me in this moment and confirm I wasn't still dreaming.

"But that means —" Richards started.

"That means," Patrick repeated, rubbing his face, "we're nearly six months late to wake up! And even further behind in preparations. If not more."

I nodded, gaze still locked on the screen.

He was right. The preparations to slow a ship the size of *The Aspire* from these speeds, reach geosynchronous orbit, and then land on our new home required at least eight months to complete. There were phases that had to be taken to verify that the ship wouldn't break up during such a specific maneuver. Then there was separating the modules and verifying each was in working order to land. Checks upon checks had to be completed, as well as timed burns, evacuations, reanimations, weight distributions... Some of which could only be done months out. While others only while we were in orbit around our new planet. That's one of the reasons why the Elemental Crew existed. They would start the process.

"Fuck me," Richards said in an exhale.

"Yeah," I said, managing to keep my curse internal this time. How, I wasn't quite sure.

"What the fuck?" Patrick said, scanning the screen as well. From his expression, I could tell he was starting calculations that would take us days to sort out.

I rushed to the main workstation that chronicled system status and listed all malfunctions currently requiring immediate attention. "We have some work to do. I'll start prioritizing."

Richards slid into the seat next to me. "You take primary systems, and I'll manage external breaches."

Patrick snorted and cursed far more colorfully — and loudly — than I had, then stomped toward the door. "I'll be in Engineering. And Captain, please get Tasha and Russel awake and to Engineering immediately!"

Just to rile Patrick up further, because it would actually calm him down some, I said, "I'll have Dr. Brackett wake up Commander Evans and Master Sergeant Cruz immediately. Until then, I'll split up those awake and send some down to you."

With a roll of his eyes and a grunt, he disappeared. As his footsteps traveled down the hall, we heard his continued grumbles. The level said they were meant more for himself than us. "Really, Mitchel? You're gonna correct me on Command etiquette now? Ugh! We are so screwed! Why did I agree to this crap again? Six months late, seriously?"

Richards glanced to the door, then met my eyes. "You did that just to annoy him."

I chuckled, then dug into the never-ending list of problems littering my screen. Patrick may be the Head of Engineering, but he had a laid-back rapport with his staff. Especially Tasha and Cruz. Unlike me.

Chapter Three

Commander Tasha Evans

T he overhead lights flickered, sending the room into darkness. I glanced up, glared, and then looked down at the tablet in my hands. I pulled up the schematics for this sector and flipped through the power grid to see where the issue was. When I'd left Engineering, everything had been fine. I'd spent the last twelve hours resetting this section, but of course that meant absolutely nothing if we didn't know the root cause of the problem.

Screen after screen, I dug through the linkages that controlled this area and, with each pass, I added a new task to my workday. Then I found it, and icy dread seeped deeper into me.

"Holy mother of a crap shoot," I whispered to no one. This wasn't an issue that affected just this section, but all four of them! Which meant eventually, every one of *The Aspire's* Divisions would fail. "When I find the Elemental Crew, I'm gonna kill them."

I tossed the tablet on the bench next to me and pressed my palms to my eyes. It didn't help, but for a moment, I could pretend that this was all a dream, and the real world would appear with the light. But as the room came back into focus, my hope drifted away.

Because the truth was, someone had fucked up. Badly.

"You're gonna need Cruz's help on this one, Tash," I told myself, rubbing the back of my neck. "But not until after your break."

With a few selections on my armpad, I pulled up one of my team's lyncs.

"Commander?" Technical Specialist Veronica Aridas said simply.

"Aridas, we're still having power surges in Section Three. I have identified the potential cause. It's a three-step repair. Can you send a team down and have them begin on the initial work? I sent you the repair parameters."

"I thought you were on break."

"I am. I'll be there within the hour," I said, grinning. She'd been the one to push me out of Engineering and force me to rest.

"Cruz?" she asked, and I knew what she was asking.

"No. I'll get him on my way."

"Understood. Enjoy the view." With that, Aridas closed the connection.

I scanned the stark room. The dark gray walls and dim illumination of simulated night added to the coldness. It was such a contrast from the last time I'd been here — the noisy activity of an over-filled observation deck. It had been packed, people crammed into seats or standing along the walls. A young family had decided it wasn't worth the fight and plopped down right on the floor in front of me. It had made me smile at how grateful they were to be there even while others had looked at them with disdain. Good thing I could see the distaste was due more to the tension of the mission than anything else.

Luckily, the voice of calm reassurance had filled the space, and I'd watched those in the crowd relax. Captain Mitchel Remian always had that effect. Their shoulders dropped, expressions softened, and even a few sighs echoed around me. For the longest time, I'd debated if there was something innately different about the captain, or if it was all related to his pretty face and smooth accent. Probably a bit of both. At my low chuckle, his eyes had met mine, and — even through his professional mask — I'd seen the humor-filled glare he held back. He knew me too well.

The joy I'd felt that day should've been the same when I awoke, but no. Instead, my fingers combed over the fabric of the couch that was now more than eighty years older, and I felt lost. There was little wear and no fading to the fabric. It was fascinating how space could keep things so pristine, especially when there was no one to use it.

The longer I did this, the more I stared down, my brow furrowing. I took in the sensations, only then realizing how strange they were. Where I expected smooth, light pressure, I felt heat against a hard surface. That was the complete opposite of what I remembered. My fingers caught on a stray thread whose edge had broken loose, and I played with it, hoping the small motions would help my dexterity.

I needed them functioning normally again. Especially with a ship falling apart. I was forty-eight hours awake, and still nothing felt right.

Granted, nothing was going as we'd expected.

I shifted, pulling my legs from beneath me to place them on the floor. My muscles no longer protested as I pushed to my feet. For that, I was grateful. Slowly, I strolled through the bench seats and headed down the stairs toward the front. The click of my boots on the tile, though strange, was a welcome reminder that for right now, I was alone. Since awakening, this was the first time I'd been so. Finally, no one was asking me to make monumental decisions or figure out complex problems while my mind fought to go back to the fog it had lived in for nearly eighty years.

Eighty years. A lifetime of nothingness.

The memory of the captain speaking was the day we'd left. The day I'd voluntarily walked on board and agreed to take the chance at a new life. To me, it had only been days, but I could see how time had passed around me. My ship had felt it; that was for sure.

Chipped paint in the most-used areas, two overgrown greenhouse modules, and systems requiring serious maintenance was just the beginning. The ship had undergone three meteorite showers, two engine failures, and some strange anomaly which we had yet to figure out the cause. So many systems needed repair, and that was before the required preparations for orbit and landing. The fact that I'd been able to sneak out for a break with everything going on was a miracle.

I approached the thick panes of the window which separated me from the darkness beyond. Tiny pinpricks of white marked far-off stars. The blackness of space was both beautiful and overwhelming. Thicker patches of stars glowed a pale pink, indicating that the nebula was far more extensive than I could have imagined. It also whispered of our location and the ever-spinning timeline of the mission. The knowledge caused that sense of loneliness and fear to swirl faster through me. The weight of the truth sitting on my chest made it hard to breathe. So much was unknown. So much had to be done. Suddenly, the room felt even more desolate than before.

"Tasha! There you are."

I jumped at the voice and pressed a hand to my chest as I turned.

A man stood by the entryway, his long, lean frame no longer as muscular as I remembered. He wasn't sickly by any means, but there was a difference. I took a deep breath, praying for patience. Master Sergeant Russel Cruz tended to press my buttons.

"Cruz," I said, placing my hands on my hips. "What are you doing here? I thought you were helping Commander Montgomery get the reentry procedures of the shuttles verified. Have all connections between the shuttles and *The Aspire* been completed in the fifteen minutes since I left?"

His golden eyes narrowed at my tone.

"I was, but we came across something that needs your specific expertise," he said, stepping into the room. He ran a hand through his coiffed brown locks and continued, "It looks like the Elemental Crew did something to two of the shuttles. They altered them, and Patrick wants to review them with you before we make any changes. There's concern they won't be able to handle the calculated burns, nor reentry, if we don't."

"Damn it all," I said under my breath. My palms were clenched as I dropped them to my sides.

Two of those calculated burns should have already happened by the hands of the Elemental Crew, but instead we were rushing to get the first one completed within the new timeline Patrick had calculated yesterday. If we didn't have them to help with the burns, I wasn't sure how our path would be affected.

The thought of *The Aspire* being so quiet for so long sent shivers down my spine. The first group to awaken had said it felt almost ominous. Dead.

My thoughts strayed to the crew we'd lost that first day. I would miss both Samson and Nielson. Neilson for her loyalty and friendship, and Samson for his poker skills.

I pushed the thought away.

"Not a problem," I said, turning back to the window. "Tell Patrick I'll be there within the hour."

"He asked —" Cruz started, tone sharp. The sound of his steps approaching came first, and then the scent of his noxious cologne. It made my nose crinkle in disgust.

"I don't care what you say his demands were." With a quick glance behind me, I took in his puffed chest and clenched jaw. I continued before he could, focusing again on the sparkling nebula. "I've been awake less than forty-eight hours, and I have yet to stop working. Merocius will be visible in less than ten minutes. I want to see our new home, and I do not appreciate you questioning me, Sergeant!"

Cruz opened his mouth to speak but was cut off by another voice. "You heard her! Back down, or you will have to deal with me."

I grinned but didn't look back at Geron Richards, best friend and pain in my ass, as he entered the room. In truth, I didn't need to. We'd spent enough of our lives together that I could see in my head how his strong arms would cross over his chest. I also knew that warning look in his eyes. Perhaps that had more to do with the number of times he'd pointed it at me, but I digress.

"What's your problem, Geron?" Cruz asked, his stance mirroring Geron's.

"Not a damn thing. Unless you're interrupting Tasha's break. The one Captain Remian approved himself. As you know, he's rather fond of her."

Now, I did roll my eyes. Mitchel was a man to be feared by most, but for me? It was absolute respect and admiration. Friendship.

In the reflection, Cruz straightened minutely. He hated being called out and especially by Geron. At least time in the pod hadn't changed some things. He faced me again, hands falling to his sides. He rolled his shoulders.

"My apologies, Commander." His tone was much more respectful this time. "I'll let Commander Montgomery know you'll be there within the hour. I hope you enjoy your first viewing of Merocius."

"I believe I will. Thank you."

Cruz retreated, and I took the first deep breath since he'd entered.

As if reading my mind, Geron asked, "Is he aware how bad that perfume he wears is? It burns my nose."

Chuckling, I spun to face my old friend. I playfully smacked him in the stomach, then instantly winced when I took in the dark circles lining his eyes. He had been by Mitchel's side, working nonstop, since they'd awoken together. And come to find out, his reanimation hadn't been as perfect a run through as they'd all thought. A few hours in, he'd collapsed, and Dr. Brackett had been called to treat him. Luckily, he was recovering faster than those in Section Nine.

"I don't think he does," I said with a shrug. "Though several of the crew have told him."

Geron grinned. "I'm sure he took that well. And I have to say, I love the way he grimaces when he has to address you as 'Commander.' It's been years, and it never ceases to amuse me. Especially considering he scowls every time."

"He's still angry they promoted me over him and, as is normal, he blames me for the problems with the ship."

"You?" Geron's eyebrows went up. "How? Why?"

I shrugged. "Doesn't matter. He's an idiot."

Geron bumped my shoulder with his, the laughter still in his eyes, and wrapped a brotherly arm around my shoulders. I leaned in, ignoring the sharp, antiseptic smell of his skin. The medicine he was receiving to help him recover was crazy intense. We stood like that for a long moment before he spoke again.

"How long do we have until it's visible?"

"The ship should adjust course in..." I glanced at my armband. I tapped the electronic display, and the time appeared. "Five minutes."

"Glad I made it. I didn't think I was going to." He tugged at the braid that fell down my back. "The captain had me realigning the external dishes, but when we saw Russel stomp by in your direction, he decided I shouldn't wait to see Merocius."

"You haven't seen it yet?"

"No. I was in Medical when the last view cycle passed."

I nodded, then changed the subject. The words were bitter in my mouth. "Have they identified all the systems requiring correction?"

Because the plan had been foolproof, and yet nothing had gone right. With the Elemental Crew missing and presumed dead for over forty years by our count, one failure had led to another until there were cascading system failures everywhere. A vessel like this one was not supposed to be on autopilot for that long. Based on the logs, it was even longer with no active lifeforms reviewing the specs, verifying errors, and maintaining the systems.

"Not yet, but we will." He squeezed my shoulder. "But that's not why we're here. How about we ignore all of that for a little bit and enjoy the quiet? All those problems will be there later."

"Agreed."

We fell into a comfortable silence, one that spoke of the decades of friendship we'd shared. Geron had been my closest friend — save my brother — since I was fifteen. The only thing that had kept my crazy sibling from holding me down and refusing to let me go on this mission was the knowledge that Geron would be right beside me. That and the shuttle crash that took his life six months before we left. Still, I was grateful for both my brother's protectiveness and Geron's refusal to let me go alone.

"I miss Mathew."

He placed a gentle kiss on my hair. "Me too, but we both know he wanted us to take this chance."

"Yeah, I know." And I did. Mathew had understood me better than anyone and supported my dreams no matter what. "I just wish I could speak to him."

Geron's arm tightened around me. I could feel the shift in him that said he was about to respond, but then the ship altered course and the skyline changed.

My gasp at what appeared filled the empty room. "Oh, wow."

The blackness of space was replaced with three glowing objects of awe-inspiring beauty. The Aramitacus Sun was the first to appear. Blindingly bright, it shone blue in ebony depths so dark they took the breath away. It was nearly twice the size of Solis and like nothing I had ever seen. Well, perhaps in my dreams. But even then, they paled in comparison to this. Its color spoke of the hotter temperatures it burned, allowing for more habitable planets within its vast system.

From our reports, four potential options — two moons and two separate worlds. Based on the calculations, Merocius had the best odds for colonization, but there was no way to be one hundred percent sure. Merocius was also equidistant to the other three options as it was one of the moons orbiting Eronis 8, so the placement was perfect should we decide to expand colonization to the others, as well.

The next to appear was Eronis 8 herself. As the ship adjusted its trajectory, she took up more and more of the window. The only gas giant of the system lit up the dark, beautiful and massive in scale.

"Remarkable," Geron said, releasing me and stepping toward the glass.

My mouth dropped in awe. Excitement rushed through me, and I bounced on my toes. I placed my hands against the windowsill; nose pressed to the glass as if by doing so I could take in every detail.

Eronis was beautiful. Pale blue weaved in and out between deeper hues of purple and bright white. Some sections smooth and gentle in their paths, while others swirled with the velocity of storms decades old.

The way the colors stayed separate on worlds like this had always amazed me. It was one reason I'd been so desperate to come. Besides my mechanical and engineering expertise, my passion for aerostatics and aerodynamics made this trip a dream come true. There was so much undiscovered knowledge here, and the opportunities to learn from an unknown world like this was a dream. Who knew what sort of secrets were held within?

"I can't wait to take readings on it. It's amazing."

"Of Eronis?" Geron asked, glancing at her. When I nodded, he continued, "Nerd."

I reached out and pushed him gently on the arm. "Yes, because you aren't as excited as I am."

I felt his smile more than saw it.

"Remember, we have to set up the base first," he said.

"I know," I said in exasperation. Of course, that didn't take away my impatience to be there already. My attention caught on something, and I pointed, then asked, "Hey, do you see that section there? The southern hemisphere, western quadrant?"

There was a massive storm taking up more than a quarter of the hemisphere. It looked like a blossoming flower made of gas and light. From the center poured a deep purple gas. It swept up then dipped down, becoming the edges of the petal. Then, hitting something denser, the gas moved, making the petals look like they were waving in the wind, or maybe the tides of a restless sea? The light that emitted from the center illuminated the gas, making it almost glow.

"What in the heavens is causing that?" Geron asked. "That's not something that's ever happened in the Solis System. We've had some strange storms on Jupiter or the other gas giants, but this?"

I shot him an uncontrolled grin. "Not that I can remember. I'll have to pull up the logs and do some digging. I need to take some pictures before it dissipates. Either way, this could confirm the system plays under different rules. I can't wait to figure out what it is because it's like nothing we've ever seen before. It's so perfect."

"It's..." Geron's head tilted, his eyebrows furrowed as he examined the storm.

Just then, I straightened, gaze locked on the moon making its way from behind Eronis. "Oh! Look there!"

Eronis 8 had ten moons total. Several looked promising for future terraforming, but only one held all requirements for immediate habitation based on the readings we'd received from the probes.

Safely above Eronis's flowing surface, Merocius glided gracefully. Its colors resembled that of our home planet and of the planet Earth from which our people had originated. Huge blue oceans cradled four visible continents and several smaller land masses. From the reports, there were three additional, larger continents present on the moon. A few craters marred the surface, confirming not only its solidity, but the ecosystem's ability to react to change. Clouds of varying size flowed high above the lands, obscuring their view in certain sections — a functioning ecosystem.

I did not know how long we stood staring at the moon that would soon become our new home. All I knew was that it was beautiful, and the hope that bubbled up had me blinking away tears. My hand pressed to my heart. I never expected such an emotional response to seeing this, but here I stood, awe, excitement, and pure joy flowing through me. This was what I'd been dreaming of. A new planet to explore with people I respected and cared about, where I could create a new life.

Soon.

Another moon appeared lower from where Merocius floated, but it was nowhere near as spectacular. It spun, revealing a mountain range that spanned the entire length of it. The colors along its surface ranged from dark reds to a bright green. Perhaps a sign of life we hadn't known about? The idea took my breath away.

I clasped my hands together and pressed them to my cheek, feeling my smile grow wider with each mile revealed. It was spectacular. This entire system was a new adventure, filled with a never-ending list of places to explore. I couldn't wait.

The sound of thundering footsteps yanked me back to the ship and the quiet of the observation deck. I took a deep breath, then wiped away the tears that left trails down my face. A second later, Cruz appeared in the doorway.

"Sergeant, what is the meaning of this?" Geron asked, his calm gone, and fists now clenched at his sides.

But something was wrong. It was clear in the terrified lines of Cruz's expression.

"Commander, my apologies," Cruz pushed out from between heavy breaths. There was truth behind those words in his eyes — this time. "We need you right away. It's an emergency."

I straightened and took a step closer to him. "What is it?"

"We need you. Now. T-there's s-something..." he stuttered.

Cruz stuttered.

Geron and I exchanged glances.

A shiver of dread spread up my spine. This couldn't be good. I'd never seen Cruz look like this.

"Okay, let's go."

As if he could read my thoughts, Cruz's lip twitched. Then he nodded and rushed from the door. Was there gratitude in his gaze?

Geron and I followed him at a jog, our strides quick as we tried to keep up with his longer gait. When we entered Engineering, my eyes widened.

Chapter Four
Commander Patrick Montgomery

"**W**hat the absolute hell? You have got to be kidding me!" I said, cursing the mess of wires behind the panel I'd just removed. "Of all the irresponsible, ridiculous, and asinine things!"

I looked up from my supine position and sighed. Then I shoved my hands into the rat's nest of yellow, white, red, and blue, digging for the problem that must lie behind it. Based on the diagnostics, a degraded chip and a broken connection were causing systems to misfire all over the place. Because of this, I was unable to access my own damn shuttle. Which was just annoying as hell.

Add on that I needed each and every shuttle linked in and ready for the first of five scheduled burns within the next day, and I was about to lose my shit.

"If I find who did this, I'll..." I grumbled from my place on the floor, the shuttle hovering above me.

I spread the wires with one hand and leaned in, reaching for the back where the chip was housed. I could barely see what I was grasping for, but that didn't matter. I knew these ships like the back of my hand. With fifteen years working in Engineering — six under Captain Remian — and the last two as Head of Engineering, I'd better. Plus, this shuttle had been standard order since I was in the academy. Simple.

Hell, I'd helped build *The Aspire*, and she was the best ship in the fleet. Pretty, too.

The ship was made of four rotating modules which spun around a center column which connected each module. The center structure was filled with pathways, research labs, and major systems and expanded out to individual sections of the ship. What was cool about *The Aspire* specifically, was that, when the time was right, each section would detach and land on our new home. This would leave the center column to act as a satellite and research station for those down on the ground — a command center of sorts. We were the fifth mission to use this design, but ours had been upgraded even still.

So, when we woke to find her in absolute and utter disrepair, caused by lack of attention and maintenance, I'd been pissed. Confused, to say the least. It was amazing how one error on top of another could cause cascade failures all over the place. At least some of them had been easy fixes.

Others...not so much.

That wasn't even considering that we were months behind on preparations for the approach and landing on Merocius. If we didn't catch up, there was a high chance we'd hurtle into its surface or be lost in space.

In other words, we were screwed.

All because the crew in charge of maintaining my baby was gone. So far, no proof of where they were. Instead, all we'd found was a burnt-out piece of junk Cruz still hadn't identified the purpose of and this locked-up shuttle. That device was big, though. Big enough to emit a field large enough to encompass the entire ship. And that was after *The Aspire* was thoroughly searched. It didn't make sense. What the fuck was that thing in the lower-level control room of Section Three, and why had the Elemental Crew needed it?

While Mitchel oversaw the investigation as well as countless other projects, and Dr. Connie Brackett oversaw the reanimation of the crew,

I began the work here. Constantly. With less than a hundred of us pulled from simulated sleep so far, our teams were working everywhere, twenty-four hours a day.

"Tasha?" I called, turning my head toward the deck, the sound of the others' footfalls loud in my ears. "Hey, Tash, you there?"

Commander Tasha Evans, my second and one of the most brilliant commanders I'd ever met. Damn, was I glad she'd tagged along on this trip. Smart, funny, and hard-headed, she could fix anything, all while managing a team of hot-headed soldiers and intellectuals alike.

Not waiting for a response, I pushed through the mess of wires, reaching for the board hidden behind it. Whether she was here or not, I needed to find and fix the problem. The other changes the Elemental Crew made could be corrected later.

"Patrick?" Cruz's face appeared as he crouched to see me below the shuttle. "I'm sorry, Commander Montgomery? Were you calling for Tasha?"

A groan of annoyance tried to escape my throat, but I pushed it back. For someone who'd been with the fleet for as long as Russel Cruz had, you'd think he'd be used to using proper titles or at least your surname while on the job. That was the rule, unless you'd earned the ability to use someone's first name. Kind of like the way Tasha, Mitchel, and I were. Yet, Cruz wasn't. I'd never been able to figure out if it was stupidity or a lack of respect. Sure, outside of Engineering, call me Patrick, but here, I was Commander Montgomery — or just Montgomery. Unless you'd been given specific permission by the person, this was how it worked for everyone.

"Sergeant Cruz? Yes, I was calling for Commander Evans," I confirmed. Cruz's eyes narrowed. "It looks like the Elemental Crew made some modifications to this shuttle. I want her to see it before I make too many changes. Is she out there?"

"No, sir. She went to view Merocius, but I'll get her." He stood and rushed away.

"No! Wait," I called, but he was already gone.

There was a quiet *thunk* as my head plopped against the floor. I sighed and fought the urge to roll my eyes.

Shit, I'd accidentally sent Cruz after her while she was on break. She was going to kill me. Or, if Cruz wasn't careful, Tasha would court-martial... or kill him.

I missed the way he used to be. Cruz could be such a good guy when he chose. I shrugged. We never saw that anymore.

As I shifted another collection of wires to the side, a sharp pain lanced through my hand, bringing my thoughts back to my task. Had something bitten me? I yanked my arm back. It caught in the wires for a moment, but I pulled it free. I shook my hand to relieve the pain, instantly noticing the crimson which covered my finger and palm. That computer board must be more damaged than I thought.

Scowling, I removed a rag from my pocket, then applied pressure to the rather-deep cut, which ran along my index finger and down to the crease of my palm. I carefully dabbed at the wound. Removing the cloth, I froze. In addition to the nearly two-inch-long gash, there was some sort of opalescent dust littering the edges of the wound. A shard of something I'd never seen before was embedded in my skin.

"What is that?"

Red welled again. I wiped it clean, took a closer look, and cursed. It wasn't my imagination. A small shard of what looked like crystal was embedded in my skin. It shimmered gold with a pink tint that reflected the light. I grabbed hold of the fragment and pulled. It came out easily, slipping free without much resistance, but just as it lifted from my torn flesh, a shiver of fear ran up my spine.

Something moved. Where the shard had once lain, something was moving. Less than an inch long, the creature — *creature?* — began to wiggle, digging deeper, then disappearing into my skin.

Fuck me.

I shook my hand in a vain attempt to throw the creature off, but that was ridiculous. In less than a second, it had disappeared beneath my flesh. My breaths sped up, and I told myself not to panic.

I'll get Doc to look at it, but first, we needed to finish this. If I didn't, some poor, unsuspecting person would take over and have the same thing happen. I was already exposed. Might as well keep exposure to a minimum.

No longer caring about making the tangles worse, I wrapped the cut with the towel, shoved my hands into the messy panel, and spread them to see what was behind it. A few connections snapped at my force, but I no longer cared. I needed to know what was back there.

My eyes went wide at the sight of thousands of tiny shards similar to the one I'd removed. Gold and pink, they covered the entire backside of the panel. Two of the main control chips were halfway removed from their ports, having been pushed out by the crystals.

"Boston!" I called, attempting to keep the panic from my voice. The young engineer appeared. "Get two full masks, a pair of gloves, and boxes nine and twelve. Then get in here!"

Sensing the urgency, he nodded and disappeared. He reappeared a moment later, crawled in, and slid into place next to me. He placed the requested items between us. I took the mask from his hand, slipping it over my face and mouth, then slid the gloves on over the makeshift bandage. With a click of a button, fresh oxygen filled my nose and lungs. This device would keep any debris I caused from getting into my eyes or mouth.

Specialist Alex Boston followed suit. "What'd you find, Commander?"

"The problem, but I need your assistance."

"Absolutely. How can I help?"

"Hold back these wires for me. Something's growing over the panel. I'm going to take some samples, then change out the chips. Tasha can look at them when she gets back."

"Can do," Boston said. He reached in and spread the wires as I'd done earlier. "What in the..."

I opened the supply boxes and pulled out what I needed — vials, swabs, tongs, and wipes from box nine and various tools from twelve. Working fast, and with as little mess as possible, I chipped off a few crystal pieces and placed them in the vials Boston held steady. Securing the lids, he slid them back into the box. I chipped away the crystals blocking the ports then, using several of the swabs, and wiped various sections of the panel.

When I placed the last sample I'd collected into the tube, I sucked in a breath at the small creature writhing within. It was the same as what I'd seen enter my cut.

Shit. It wasn't a dream. Boston's noise of surprise and disgust confirmed it.

"Sir, what is that?" he asked.

"I don't know, but we need to find out," I said as I pulled the damaged boards free. I cleared away all debris inside. There wasn't much, and I was quickly able to slip the replacements in. With a final adjustment of two loose connections, I said, "You can let go. Give me a moment to make sure I got everything."

Grabbing my tablet, I swiped through the various screens and ran a new set of diagnostics. When the computer finished, it confirmed that all damaged parts had been replaced.

"We're good. Let's get out of here. I need to speak to Commander Evans and the captain. We also need Doc Mendez down here."

We slid from beneath the large shuttle, then headed to the nearby workstation, only then pulling off the mask and gloves. We lined the samples up on a stand against the back wall. In the bright light, the color was even more astounding. The gold crystals shone, small particles of pink glitter littering the inside and giving it that tint I'd noticed before. I picked one up, holding the jar high.

"It's beautiful," Boston said.

"Yeah, but what the hell is it?"

"There's something moving inside this one. It looks like a mix of worm and spider."

I shivered. The thought of that alone gave me the creeps, but knowing one of those was beneath my skin? Bile rose in my throat, but I pushed it down.

"You're right. It does," I said, finally.

"What are they?"

"I have no idea." But it wasn't good. Were these creatures the reason the Elemental Crew was missing? Where did they come from, and what did that mean for the ship? The crew? Me?

Cruz stepped into the room, his expression annoyed. I held back a smile. Clearly, his rushed retrieval hadn't gone well.

"Cruz, good man. I need you to go get Tasha for me. Excuse me, Commander Evans," I amended. Cruz scowled. "I know she's on an approved break, but it's urgent. I found something I need her expertise on now. Boston, call Captain Remian, too. Have him come down here as soon —"

Before I was able to finish my sentence, a high-pitched warning bell filled the room. A second later, the rhythmic beeping sped up. I turned to the control panel above the desk. Things were changing. Sensors across the bay were firing as they indicated an increase in temperature. A whirling began as the monitor showed several systems aboard the shuttle were turning on. Clicking, and then there was a resounding *thunk* as the locks disengaged.

Cold dread had my chest seizing as the hiss of air being released hit my ears. It was like an over-pressurized can was being cracked open. With one glance, terror spread through me as a cloud of fine dust began to fill the air. I spun, then hit the sequence which would initiate a force field to be erected around the shuttle.

Breaths coming in short pants, I spun and prayed that this system was not a damaged one. The powder in the air looked the same as what lined my wound. As we had no idea what it was or what it would do to us, I didn't want anyone else exposed.

Hell, I should be quarantined. What if I was contagious?

All in good time. But first, I had to keep the others safe and stop any direct contact.

More and more spilled from vents. It leaked from any crack in the shuttle hull. It rolled out in waves so thick it blocked our view — every detail of the ship beyond, hidden from our eyes.

My shoulders sagged as the light of the field hit my eyes. It worked. The transparent shield glimmered along the edges, telling me it was active. The noise was still there but muted ever so slightly. With a slow exhale, I scanned the room. Twenty of my team stood staring at the ship and the pale pink dust which floated in the air, brushing up against the force field. It caressed it with a searching touch but did not pass through. A soft glow emanated from the edges of the shuttle door, but from what I could tell, it hadn't opened completely.

"Cruz, I need Commander Evans. Now!"

His eyes were hard, locked on the sight before him. At my words, he met my gaze, nodded, and ran from the room. Boston was only a step behind.

Addressing one of my team standing near the back, I said, "Johnson, how soon until full-ship comms are working?"

"Five minutes, sir."

"Excellent. Thank you."

Johnson nodded and skittered back to his station.

"All right, team," I addressed the rest of the gathered crowd. "Tanaka, Mendez, and Aridas. I need your assistance. The rest of you, get back to work. With this new development, I'm sure you'll all be called upon to help out, but until then, I need you to focus on your assigned tasks."

Each soldier straightened, saluted — I hated when they did that — then, with one last glance at the shuttle, headed back to their stations.

"Team," I said to the three approaching. "As you can see, we have a situation. Tanaka, can you do diagnostics on the field? We need to make sure there are no kinks."

"Yes, sir," Tech Sergeant Alan Tanaka said, immediately plastering himself to the station next to us.

"Doc," I said to Dominic Mendez, the resident healer. I picked up the vials and held them up. "I assume the dust we're seeing is smaller particles of the substance I just pulled from the AFT Port Panel. Although it could be nothing, my gut tells me otherwise."

"Why do you say that, Patrick?"

"Because of this." I picked up the second vial. It was the one with the larger piece of crystal and the creature within.

He took it from me, then tilted it. His harsh curse was followed by a glare shot at the cloud the moment he saw the organism inside. It danced through the air as if a wind blew behind the field. It was creepy and somehow beautiful at the same time.

"Something's alive in there," he said, gaze back on the vial. His attention moved to the bandage wrapped around my palm. "Were you exposed?"

"That's not important right now. I —"

"Answer the question, Montgomery."

I flinched at the sound of Captain Remian's voice, the accent unmistakable. Whirling to the door, I saw the man himself standing next to a very out-of-breath Boston. Behind him, I could see Tasha, Cruz, and Richards. Mitchel stood a few inches taller than all of them. He was handsome. Or so I'd been told by Tasha after a few too many beers. She doesn't remember that night or the conversation, but that doesn't take away my joy of reminding her of it.

With a hard exhale, I explained, "Yes, sir. I was working to correct the panel in question. The wires within were a mess. When I reached through them, I was scratched by some of the crystals growing over the circuit board. The shard was removed, but the dust and one of the small creatures"— I gestured to the vial — "has not. Yet."

Mitchel took the vial and held it up so that Tasha could see into it as well. After a long moment, she faced me.

"Patrick, why is it always you?"

Mitchel snorted, but I didn't dignify it with a response. She was right, of course. This wasn't the first time something strange and dangerous had happened. If someone was going to get injured on a mission, it was likely to be me.

"Sirs," Tanaka interrupted before Tasha could continue. "The shield is at full strength. None of the dust has escaped. However, I would recommend we find a more significant and long-term way to contain it just in case."

Tech Specialist Aridas leaned over him, her dark eyes shifting quickly as she examined the data. Her head bobbed slowly as she continued to flip through screen after screen.

"I agree," Aridas said, straightening. "With failures still happening all over the ship, I think it best we get it contained."

"Ideas?" Mitchel asked.

"Particularly ones without going near any other major systems. From what I saw, these crystals are invasive and can grow through small crevices between parts," I said.

Aridas inclined her head to me. "That's what I figured based on your report. So, since I assume we'll want to test the substance in the future, I've found a secure way for us to pump the air into Section E's axillary oxygen tank. It's currently empty since the system has yet to replenish after so many reanimations. We can hold it there indefinitely, or it can be evacuated at will."

"That's fantastic," Tasha added. "There, we can separate it from the main system and verify no additional connections are contaminated."

Damn, I knew it. Aridas was the right person for the job. She was brilliant.

"Once it's in the tank, yes," Aridas said.

In calm, even strides, Tasha joined Aridas at the console. Her golden hair was pulled back in a braid, which fell over one shoulder as she verified what Aridas proposed. Nodding slowly, she continued, "No other outlets along that path. No risk to any other system. Afterward, we can purge the line to verify all remaining particles are released into space. I think this could work."

Nodding at the schematic, I said, "Agreed. How soon do you think we can get this verified and ready to initiate?"

Doc Mendez spoke up this time, his hands on his hips. "Long enough for me to clean that wound and check your vitals. This should've been looked at right away."

I glared at him. "Doc, I needed to verify the situation was handled first. Would you rather I hadn't, and everyone be exposed?"

His eyes narrowed at me. "Not the point. Tell him, Captain."

"He's right, Montgomery."

"Says the man," I said, "who worked for forty-eight hours straight after passing out from oxygen deprivation after waking up to life support being down."

"That was different."

"How?" I glared at my old friend.

"Because I'm Captain, and I say so." Mitchel glared back.

Tasha chuckled, the sweet sound melodic. For such a hard ass, she had a beautiful laugh.

"You both are a pain in the ass," she said. "Now, let's get to work."

It took an hour for everything to be prepped and ready to go. While Mendez fussed over me, Tasha, Aridas, and Tanaka got everything ready. I hated not being there, but I knew Tasha had it in hand. Plus, Mitchel stayed back, watching over everything, ready to call me back if needed.

When it was time for the transfer, Mendez and I returned. He was reluctant, considering several of my tests had come back strange. He couldn't figure out why or really how, but something was off in both the bloodwork and the scans. He didn't think it was dire, so he warned that, when this was done, I'd be headed back to Medical for a plethora of testing I'd hate.

The particle cloud continued to swirl in midair swept in a breeze that didn't exist. The gold-pink dust glimmered in the artificial lighting. If it weren't so ominous, it would be beautiful. I rubbed my hands together.

"All right," Tasha said. "Let's do this."

Those of us watching braced ourselves in preparation.

In coordinated movements, Aridas and Tasha pressed a series of buttons. There was a rush of sound from the other side of the barrier, and then the powder was slowly sucked from the space. It thinned, the shuttle becoming visible second by second. First there was only an outline, and then the door was revealed. I found myself stepping forward, my mouth dropping open.

Mitchel was next to me, his eyebrows raised.

"Well, shit. I didn't see that coming."

Chapter Five

Captain Mitchel Remian

T he moment that sense of accomplishment settled within me, the universe shifted again. Gods forbid we feel like we were actually making progress. No. The crew didn't need a morale boost, anyway. They were fine. It had been nearly twelve hours since our last near-death experience, so why not?

This was where my internal rambling was already going when Tech Specialist Alex Boston appeared on my Bridge, face stricken. One glance, and I knew things had just gotten worse. How? Didn't matter. He wasn't one to overreact, and neither was his boss. Patrick was steadfast and took things one step at a time. So, although I had no idea what I'd find when I entered Engineering, I braced myself for it to change everything.

The steady, yet frantic rhythm of our boots against the corridor floor was loud, drawing the attention of those we passed. As there were still so few awake, we were all being called to work beyond our expected assignments, which was why I wasn't surprised when Lieutenant Geron Richards fell into step beside me. He'd been working with me from the moment we'd woken next to one another only a few days ago. I'm pretty sure he was the only reason I was still breathing.

The *swoosh* as the door automatically opened was ominous in the sudden silence of the hallway as our footsteps slowed. The first thing that came into view was Patrick arguing with Doctor Dominic Mendez, a vial in the doc's hand. He held it before him, a look of concern on his rugged face.

"Were you exposed?" Doc Mendez's honey gaze was locked on Patrick, his brow furrowed.

"That is not important right now. I —" Patrick started.

Rage and concern for my friend mixed as he once again ignored his well-being for something else. Which was why my words came out harsh. "Answer the question, Patrick!"

He stiffened minutely, and then his shoulders dropped ever so slightly. He knew better than to lie to me. In the past, he had learned that lying did not serve him well. Tasha and I were his friends and would not allow him to risk his life for some misguided sense of altruism.

Stopping just inside the door, I glared at him, arms crossed over my chest. The others filed in around me, Tasha's warm presence appearing at my right, Richards on my left. Tasha's honeysuckle scent filled my nose, and I relaxed a little, lessening my need to chastise Patrick. This was in part because, after working closely with him for so long, she'd developed an astounding skill. She could wrangle Patrick and get him to stop being stupid. In truth, that might just be her. Her calm demeanor, sharp wit, and beautiful eyes tended to trap any aggravated soul and make them behave. I'd seen her work her magic more times than I could count. And far too often on me.

Patrick shifted to face us, and with only one glance, my suspicion was confirmed. He had been exposed.

With a hard exhale, Patrick said, "Yes, sir. I was working to correct the panel in question. The wires within were a mess. When I reached through them, I was scratched by some of the crystals growing over the circuit board. The shard was removed, but the dust and one small creature have not. Yet." He shifted from one foot to the other, refusing to meet my eyes.

At that moment, I was glad for my training because the swell of expletives inside my head would have thrown a hardened soldier. Not an ounce of it escaped, though, my professional façade holding firm.

That was, until I noticed what was behind him. My attention had been so locked on Patrick that I'd missed the real threat — the actual emergency. Where the shuttle should have sat safely nestled in its cradle, a force field glowed, a cloud of gold and pink dust swirling within it. The substance was so thick that only the vessel's outline could be seen as it shifted. Contained only by the field, it arched up, rolling to the side, then down. It danced — that was the only word to describe it — in coordinated patterns which didn't feel random.

Thank the heavens they'd gotten the shield up quickly.

As I watched, the creativity of my internal cursing expanded to words I hadn't used since my field days. My old infantry buddies would've been proud, and from the look on Richards and Tasha's face, they were experiencing something similar. This was why, as the others, including Tanaka and Aridas, created a plan to remove the dust cloud safely, I stayed quiet. If I spoke, I had a feeling they'd come flying out of my mouth. So instead, I examined the vial Doc handed me and focused on holding in the expletives trying to break free.

Bile rose in my throat at the inch-long creature scuttling over the crystal inside. Its long limbs swiveled, lying flat against its long body, and then sliding deep into a tiny cavern within the rock. Before it disappeared, I held it up to the light and noticed that, even with its translucent quality, it held a blue tint to it. I thought it strange, considering the hue of the crystal and powder.

I glanced at Patrick. Damn. One of these things was *inside* him now. That couldn't be good. I handed the vial to Tasha, a conversation passing between us as our eyes met.

Why can't things just be easy? she seemed to ask.

Because it's us, I thought back, the small, amused smile I sent making her roll her eyes. *You'd be bored if it were easy.*

Tasha snorted, then headed over to Aridas's workstation.

I watched the shifting cloud and listened to their plan. It was a brilliant idea. It would remove the risk of release and potential exposure to the substance and allow us to examine the shuttle more closely. Eventually, and with hesitation, Patrick disappeared, leaving Tasha and the others to work.

Eyes locked on where the shuttle hid, I thought aloud, "Once we've cleared area, we'll need to send in a group to evaluate the inside." But we'd need supplies if we were to enter the shuttle safely. I patted the desk next to me twice. "Boston. Cruz. Come with me, please."

They straightened instantly. We went to supply room 45E. It was just off the central engineering platform, where emergency supplies for the main engine bay were held. On the way, Cruz grabbed a drift — a cart that hovered just over the floor and able to carry up to 500 pounds. The underneath reacted to a material in the floor that held the drift a few feet off the ground. These were utilized all over the ship and were invaluable.

We loaded it up with contamination suits, oxygen reserves, and a few other items we thought might come in handy. When we reentered, Doc and Patrick were back, their gazes on Tasha.

"Captain, I think we're ready."

"Good. Then let's figure out what the hell's going on."

She nodded once. "Let's do this."

In coordinated movements, Aridas and Tasha pressed a series of buttons. There was a rush of sound from the other side of the barrier, and a second later, the powder began to thin, being sucked out and into a reserve oxygen tank. Second, after a second, the shuttle appeared. We took a step forward, unable to stop ourselves.

My eyes went wide, my eyebrows rising in shock. "Well, shit. I didn't see that coming."

No one spoke. How could we? What sat before us was not what any of us expected. Or, I didn't think so, anyway.

The shuttle's doors were now open, a spread of broken shards covering the floor around the opening. Larger pieces the size of my arm had broken off as well, settling within that gravel that shimmered like dewdrops on grass. But this was not what stopped us in our tracks.

I blinked as if I could clear the image and make it something I could understand.

"Oh, my lord," Aridas whispered. Similar sentiments filled the room.

A wall of crystal covered the far side of the shuttle entrance. Nearly three feet thick, the deep gold glittered as the lights above shone down upon it. But it was the body fully preserved that hung encased in rock, arms spread wide that took our breaths. Its ankles were crossed, head bent back as if resting. The stone weaved around the body, leaving parts exposed, but most was lovingly held as if it were a resting place instead of a prison. Streams grew up over the face like stripes, keeping the head in place and pulling the lips up to expose its teeth. Somehow, the body was intact and not decaying.

I stepped as close I could without crossing the field. It wasn't breathing from what I could see, and there were no other bodies buried in the rock farther in. But we wouldn't know until we entered and had a look around.

I rubbed my sweaty hands on my thighs. Swallowing hard, I calmed my breath, the need to get in there overwhelming my senses. This might answer all the questions we'd had since awakening.

Patrick appeared at my side, his eyebrows furrowed and jaw clenched. "I think we found part of the Elemental Crew."

"Yeah," I nodded. "I think we did."

He ran a hand over his cropped, brown hair, his hands trembling ever so slightly.

"Commander Montgomery," I said. The official title pulled Patrick's attention, focusing him once more and pushing back his fear. "I need you to pull the logs for the Elemental Crew. I need to know all of those aboard *The Aspire*. I want him identified. We need to figure out when he went missing," I said, pointing to the man in the glass.

"On it, Boss."

Straightening my shoulders, I spun on my heels. It was time to figure some shit out. I was tired of not knowing anything, and maybe our answers were inside that shuttle. Everyone stood as frozen as I had a moment before, the same expression on their faces as I'd seen in Patrick's — a mix of shock, confusion, and terror. I could read their questions and knew that if I didn't get them moving, the fear would grow, and they'd be useless. I'd seen it happen before.

"Evans," I said with authority. I saw as Tasha swallowed her panic, then pushed her shoulders back. "Mendez, Montgomery, Richards, and Cruz, suit up. We're going in. Be ready to run full diagnostics and take samples. A lot of them. Hard suits only. I don't know what we're going to find in there, so be ready!"

"Yes, sir," they chorused. Each of them met my gaze, and I felt their gratitude. Together, they took stance, saluted, then turned toward the drift Boston and I had procured earlier.

"Spec Tanaka," Tasha said in her commander's voice. "I need you to set up the transfer location — a secured area where we can enter without contamination of the rest of the ship. Use the F9 workstation, not G35. It's closer and better ventilated."

One of the more unique features of *The Aspire* was its ability to section off separate stations and energy sources. This guaranteed that should one section go down unexpectedly, another could be sealed off and used without worry. It also allowed for portals between cells providing access to those aboard. Once in place, the crew could go inside just as they could for a spacewalk. Granted, it had its limits, but it was a serious technological upgrade from our previous vessels.

"Yes, Commander Evans. Give me five minutes, and I'll have it up and running." Tanaka hurried to the specified location and began his preparations.

"Aridas," Tasha continued. She grabbed the suit I handed her, pushed off her shoes, and stepped in. "Verify all systems are at full strength. We don't need the shield surrounding the shuttle failing and contaminating the rest of the ship. Keep on it. Then, help Tanaka with the transfer section. It's on a different network."

As they continued their conversation, I turned to my crew. "Boston, you're on vitals. Verify all monitors are functioning, then work with Medical while we're in there."

"Med Tech Julian Verandas is on his way. You met him yet?" Doc Mendez asked.

"No, sir, but I've heard good things."

Doc patted Boston on the shoulder as he slid his suit on.

"Cap," Richards said, pointing to the suit, "your turn."

I nodded and began dressing. The fabric was nowhere as bulky as the previous iterations, but it still restricted movement far more than I liked. That didn't matter; the protection they provided was invaluable.

"Supplies are in these four kits," Richards explained. He placed each kit next to who would carry it. "Medical supplies, two sample collection kits, and general repair equipment. If we need more, we'll request from Boston."

I zipped my suit to the neck and waited as Richards helped Patrick with the seals along the chest, wrist, and neck of his containment garb. The helmet he slid on was sleek, made to be light, and provide a complete range of motion. After Patrick was secured, Richards helped Doc, then approached me.

As the helmet locked into place, I became aware of the oxygen flowing into the suit and the voices coming clearly through the speakers. Boston was talking with Tasha, testing the mics and explaining how the vitals were monitored from the stations — both at the station he resided at and the one which Tanaka sat.

"Richards," Boston said. "You're last up. Finish with the captain, and I'll come check your seals."

Richards inclined his head to him.

After Boston confirmed we were all ready and connected appropriately, we headed to the F9 exchange where Tanaka sat. Seeing us approach, he stood.

"Commanders," he said, addressing us all in one go. "Everything is ready. This is a two-level portal opening. I will drop the one closest to us, you will step inside, and I will close it. Once verified, I will release the other side. On the way back, we will do the same, but with one extra step. F9 is fit to allow for full decontamination procedures, so there will be a two-minute cycle that will be run prior to you leaving the secured area."

"Understood. Keep us updated if any issues arise," I said.

"Yes, sir." He nodded, then pressed the screen, releasing the field. We stepped inside. The sound of Engineering disappeared as we were sealed in. A moment later, there was a flutter of light, letting us know it was safe to walk through.

With careful steps, we approached the shuttle. The suit's boots were generally impenetrable, so we stepped confidently, feeling the smaller shards break under our weight. We carefully moved the larger pieces out of the way, not willing to risk a puncture of either the boot, nor higher up on the suit. With each step, small clouds lifted into the air, only to quickly settle back onto the floor.

I was the first to take the few strides up the ramp and stop in front of the figure. Standing before the figure and taking in his predicament was far more disturbing this close up. With dark hair, he looked to be around twenty-five. If he'd been standing on his own, he would have been five-seven. But he wasn't.

His legs and arms were fully encased to his elbows and knees, holding him more than three feet off the ground. Sections of his skin were exposed to the air above each and stretches of gold wound around his body in four-inch-long strips, reminding me of a candy cane at Christmas. This continued over his torso, up his neck, and then across his face. The crystal covered his mouth, but not his eyes. Instead, they were clear — closed as if in sleep. The crystals crawled over his forehead to disappear over his scalp. A lock of hair fell over one eye in such a way that I wanted to brush it back to get a better look.

From far away, it had looked as though he were asleep, gently cocooned in the crystal. But while standing inches away, it was clear he'd been dead a long time. The problem was, he didn't look like a man who'd been dead as long as he probably had been. His skin still held a radiance you'd expect from a healthy man of his age — perhaps due to the shimmery powder which covered it? — but his skin was leathery and almost dehydrated. His eyelids had sunken, as if the eyeballs behind them were no longer there and his hair had an ashen color to it. Even his lips were a dark blue, like bruises that had never gone away.

"The fuck?" Richards said next to me.

Couldn't say it better if I tried, and I had no explanation, so I just shook my head. There were no words for whatever this was.

A movement within the crystal caught my eye, and I cursed. I leaned closer, avoiding knife-like protrusions which threatened to puncture my suit.

"There are more of those creatures in here," I said, bile rising in my throat. "There's a grouping of them, ten or so, bunched together. Up here, too." I pointed to another area.

Each of my team leaned in, scanning the rock wall. After a moment, they each identified similar pockets all over the damn thing.

"This one looks different," Tasha said. Her tone was filled with both fascination and disgust.

"How so?"

"The one in the vial had a bluish tint to it..."

I'd noticed that, too.

"...but this one doesn't. It's almost red and has antennae."

"There are ones over here that almost disappear into the crystal. They glitter pink just like the rock," Richards added. "And it has a tiny curve at the end of its abdomen. The others don't have that."

"All right," I said, hiding the shiver which ran up my spine and the idea of multiple types. "After the initial examination of the ship, samples from each of these sections need to be taken. We need to make sure each type is obtained. Get samples here and farther into the corridor."

"Yes, sir," Richards and Cruz said. I nodded.

"Um, Captain?" Patrick cleared his throat, then continued, "I...I think this is Major Joshua Samuels. Born on *The Aspire* to Commander Melena Samuels and Medical Specialist Norman Samuels. He completed all training in 457 and moved up the rank quickly. This says he would have been approximately thirty when the Elemental Crew went silent."

We still hadn't nailed down the exact year they'd disappeared. I was hoping something inside would tell us.

"He looks too young for thirty," Tasha said.

"Yeah, I'm sure you can tell with him being dehydrated and all," Cruz said, his tone biting. Tasha shot him a glare.

Before I had the chance to correct the disrespect, Richards spoke up. "Sergeant Cruz, watch your tone, or I'll send you out to pick up every speck of crystal covering the floor."

Cruz's eyes narrowed, but he shut up.

"Come on," I said. "Time to see what's inside."

We followed the hallway. Hitting a *T*, we decided to take the path which had one side completely covered in gold. It curved to the right, and only after a hundred feet or so did I realize something was wrong. I paused.

"Aren't there rooms off this corridor?"

"Yes, but they've been covered or filled with crystal," Tasha said. It was the scientist speaking now, and it made me smile. "I'd be curious to see which."

Patrick scanned his armband and said, "We should note that this was the medical craft of our fleet. This means, instead of a large rec area up to the right, the space is split. Approximately seventy feet up."

"The first door," Richards added before Patrick could, "is the rec area. Then you'll reach the medical bay. I think that's where we should look."

Reaching the first door, I glanced inside to find nothing out of the ordinary. On top of there being no apparent people or bodies, no crystal grew in the space. We moved on quickly, the feeling that the medical bay would hold more answers calling us forward.

The moment I reached the entrance to Medical, I noticed something that had me stopping at the doorway. The lights were on, but there was a green tint to them. There was some sort of additional safety system in place here. I just had to figure out what.

Using my armband, I scanned the space, checking for any harmful radiation. A few seconds later, a white light appeared.

On my screen read: *Radiation levels above normal. Not at dangerous levels. Safe to Enter.*

I typed: *Type of Radiation?*

In response: *Gamma Rays. Unknown wavelength.*

I ran a few more diagnostics, but nothing came back as harmful. When Doc Mendez reviewed what I'd found, he agreed.

"I think it's safe," he said with a shrug.

"Then we move forward. Anyone who is uncomfortable, stay here." And with that, I stepped over the threshold and into the shuttle's medical bay.

To the left was a set of cabinets filled with medical equipment. Floor-to-ceiling coolers stood next to them, every shelf stocked to the brim. Vaguely, I noted two of the shelves were a little less packed than the others, but my attention was drawn elsewhere. It should have hit me as odd, but I was still taking in the space.

This room definitely looked as though someone lived here. Several someones. Unlike other places aboard, which were barren of the messier signs of life, this place had many of them. Stacks of papers covered the desk, an abandoned chair lay in the middle of the room, and even a few food packs were shoved in a trashcan. What was strange was the tub of children's toys shoved in the corner and the large pile of linens stacked from floor to ceiling off to the side. How many had stayed here and for how long?

"Wait, is that a pod?" Cruz asked, stepping through the door. "Why would a shuttle have a pod?"

My gaze swung to where he pointed. Sure enough, there was a pod along the left side of the room. Light glowed from the screen on its side, and a dim brightness shone through the glass of the door. Was it on?

The tables which had once filled the spot had been shoved to the side. Wires which should not have been there ran along the floor, disappearing into a panel that had been ripped open and re-purposed.

"Looks like it. Everyone, spread out, and let me know if you find anything strange," I said.

Richards, Tasha, and I headed for the pod but stopped when there was a gasp behind us. We turned to find Patrick frozen just inside the doorway, his hand pressed to his chest.

"What is it?" Doc Mendez asked, a hand on his shoulder. It was a good question given the look of both pain and relief on his face.

Panting, Patrick said, "This room. When I walked in, it hurt, but then something changed." He looked at Doc and continued, "I told you I was feeling off, right?"

"Yeah?"

"Well, I feel better. Not as tired or sick. I feel like I did hours ago."

Doc Mendez pulled up Patrick's stats on his armband. After a moment, his eyes widened before he clicked a few buttons. "Take a seat. I'm having Tech Verandas run a few tests."

Knowing he was in good hands, and that Doc would let us know if they needed us, we continued on.

The pod had scratches along its side, as if it had been moved here and dropped more than once. A dent on the end had the distinct outline of a doorframe. Whoever had moved it had a hell of a time. The ordinarily clear window was foggy, as if water had condensed along the inside. Strange.

Richards and I exchanged glances as he leaned down to peer inside. "Someone's in there. Female, by the looks of it."

"Can you tell who it is?"

"No," he started but stopped suddenly. He ran a hand down the far side of the glass, then continued, "but, Captain? There's a label on this side. It says, 'Captain Victoria Norris.'"

"What?" I said, skittering to his side. "But that's not possible."

He was right. There on the pod's side, I saw Captain Norris's name in handwriting I knew like my own. I leaned in, rubbing the lid and wishing it were enough to remove the fog and show me what was inside, but it didn't.

"Captain!" Cruz called. "We need you to see something."

I straightened, swallowing down the confusion. Then, with a deep breath, I stalked around the pod and hurried to where the others stood. Doc Mendez and Patrick had joined them, and Patrick was scrolling through something on his armpad.

Addressing Cruz, I asked, "What did you find?"

His face was paler than I'd ever seen it when he said, "Sir." He cleared his throat. "I think we found the Elemental Crew."

He faced the cooler and held a hand out to the two shelves I'd noted earlier as empty. Not empty.

"What do you mean?" I asked. My gaze landed on the shelves, and I felt my eyebrows rise. I leaned in to read the labels evenly placed on the glass door.

Inside the cooler was something that shouldn't be on my ship. I'd only seen something close to this once before, and that was in an unapproved lab, located on an experimental medical base, back on our home planet. But this? This was a hack job build of what I'd seen then.

"Is that what I think it is?" Richards asked.

"If you mean eight fetuses growing from out of the wall?" Tasha asked, her voice dripping with disbelief. "Um, yeah. Yeah, it is."

That's when those colorful curses in my skull returned.

Chapter Six

Commander Tasha Evans

T hat just came out of my mouth, didn't it? My mind replayed the words which slipped from my lips. *"Eight fetuses growing out of the wall."*

Yup, that happened.

I took an involuntary step back, then caught myself. I would not show weakness. I moved closer instead, as if to get a better look.

Strength. I must always show strength. Especially when you're scared shitless. That's a quote, right? A motto? Something? I glanced at the figure beside me.

Mitchel's back and shoulders were stiff, his face blank. He was the perfect picture of a military man, but I knew he was just as affected by all of this as I was. He was just better at hiding it. Not that anyone but those who knew him well would be able to tell he was freaking out. I could, though. His right hand opened and closed reflexively, the muscle in his left cheek twitched, and his eyes had a fire in them that spoke of the anger he held at bay. I fought the urge to reach out. He would not appreciate my sympathy, so I brought my attention back to the oddities before us.

Eight fetuses. Eight partially formed babies sat before us in transparent modules. Though I was confused, disgusted, and seriously rethinking my choice to join this mission, I found myself fascinated with the setup. Each was cradled within thick silicone-like membranes that rested in what looked like hand-cut foam beds. Frayed and uneven, they were of varying sizes, specifically modified for the particular child. A few were so mangled that the maker must've fought against the substance as they tried to shape it.

These had been hand-made, not manufactured. As if against its will, my gaze went to the pod and its sleeping member. Whoever was in there took great care to make them.

I placed my hand against the glass and leaned in for a closer view.

"Woah, I've never seen technology like this," I muttered.

The developing baby was wrapped in its amniotic sac, which was then connected to the silicone outer layer. There was a gel-like substance between the two, but I had no idea what it was. Then, several tubes and wires extended from the artificial sac, reaching to the wall and connecting to travel up the conduit. My gaze followed the collection of lines. Each one had a different purpose, pushing what I would assume was nutrients to the child or pulling its waste from it. They'd created an automated, mechanical uterus.

It was the most remarkable thing I'd ever seen and dangerous as hell. I'd heard about something like this back home, and it had sparked serious controversy. From my understanding, however, it had never been built, only designed. It made me wonder who the person was who made this and where they'd learned it.

"They're not all at the same gestational stages," Doc Mendez said, breaking the deep silence. I'd noticed that, too. With a glance at his arm-pad, he pointed to the three closest to him. "Twenty weeks, thirty-five weeks, twenty-nine weeks..." he trailed off.

"This one down here —" Cruz paused, took a deep breath, and then continued. "It doesn't look human."

I followed his gaze. "No. That's because it has to be less than fifteen weeks."

Cruz shifted back, and my gaze followed him. His fists were clenched, and he was shaking.

"What is this?" Cruz asked, meeting my eyes.

Instead of my instinctive response to dislike him and the need to argue, I saw what was really happening here. A crew member who needed help, and I felt the need to comfort him. For some reason, this had shaken Cruz. In all the years I'd known him, I'd never seen this expression on his face. He was Cruz — broody, argumentative, but willing to work his ass off.

I pressed the pad on my wrist and opened a private channel.

"What's going on?" I asked in a calm voice, stepping closer. His gaze locked on mine. He shook his head, but he was breathing too fast for me to believe him. "Russel, I need you to breathe. Look at me. You've got this."

The use of his first name seemed to settle him. I'd meant it to.

Not breaking eye contact, he did as I asked, then said, "Tasha, this isn't right. What the hell is this?"

I pressed a hand to his chest. "I don't know, but we'll figure it out. Until then, I need you to calm down. You're my best engineer. I need your help to figure out what they did here. How this is possible." I shifted, blocking his line of sight to the cooler. "Can you go examine the pod? You have a lot more experience with those than I do. Figure out how that thing is rigged to the ship. Then search the logs. We need to know if we can wake whoever's inside."

For a few long inhales, he just stared at me. I waited for the intensity within him to abate. Slowly, his shoulders relaxed, his breathing became steady, and the panic in his eyes calmed. He blinked, and with a slight curl of his lip, he said, "Fine, but you owe me."

I snorted, my lips curving at the edges. He turned away, and for once, I didn't want to smack that cocky grin off his face.

Then he froze mid-motion, our eyes met once more, and he said, "Thank you, Commander Evans."

A calm warmth settled in my chest. That was the first time he'd said my title without that underlying current of scorn. Even that bitter sarcasm was missing.

I released the private channel, opening back up to the others. Instantly, I heard Patrick.

"Each of these are labeled with an Elemental Crew member." Patrick's eyebrows furrowed, his cheeks pinkened. I watched as a bead of sweat trailed down his temple. "A few I recognize, but the others? They were born onboard."

"Javier Mendoza," Geron read. "I remember him. He was only a few years out of the academy."

"He would've been in his mid-fifties around the time they disappeared."

Doc Mendez rifled through the medical kit he carried in, retrieving a more advanced scanner. "From the readings I'm getting here, they're in perfect health for their gestational age. No diseases. No genetic damage. They're in the form of simulated sleep just like the pod." He typed on the screen and, a moment later, said, "But there's one difference from our hypersleep. There seems to be a steady stream of radiation being released through the fluid around the sac."

"Is it the same as what I noted when we entered the medical bay?" Mitchel asked.

"Yes," Doc Mendez said. Their eyes met, and he shrugged. "And Captain, they match the profiles we have for the crew."

"You think these are the Elemental Crew?"

"I know so."

"Explain."

Mendez looked back to the cooler. "Can't yet, sir."

"They look to be attached to the pod by a network of tubing here," I said, interjecting.

While they'd been speaking, I'd been examining the complex network of tubes and wires making up the system. Once they exited the mechanical uterine modules, they traveled along the back wall, then out of the cooler and down to the floor. The grouping then split. All but one of the tubes headed toward what looked like an old, makeshift dialysis machine. Fluids were being pumped into the devices and — from my guess — cleansed for impurities. Then, once done, they were pumped back out toward the waiting children. It was a clever and efficient system. There even seemed to be a backup in case there was a failure.

The second grouping, however, led across the ground where it connected to the pod.

"Doc," I asked, wanting to make sure my assumptions were correct. "Can I assume this machine here manages all the fluids and waste they create?"

"That would be my guess, but I'll want to examine it more thoroughly."

I smiled thoughtfully. "I'm gonna help Cruz figure out how these are linked to the pod."

Doc nodded, and I headed for Cruz, who crouched where the wires wove up the side of the unit and disappeared into its depths. He held a flashlight, illuminating an internal panel. I leaned down to gaze into the space.

"What'd you find?" I asked. He didn't look up. "Is what we thought correct? That the connections between the cooler and the pod are allowing both to be in deep sleep?"

"That's what it looks like. But man, whoever did this was remarkable. They've fully integrated the pod and the mechanical uteri system to the shuttle." He pushed to his feet. "You need to see this."

Cruz led me to an open panel along the back wall. This hallway led into a small office where, only then, could I see three large wall panels exposed. Within them was a maze of meticulously organized technology. The complicated patterns within were going to take hours to decode. There were overlapping connections that linked back in and around in crazy brilliant ways.

"Wow..." I said.

"Whoever created this was a genius," Cruz said, awe in his voice. "I want to be them when I grow up."

I chuckled, meeting his gaze. The darkness that was there before was gone now. I was happy to see it. I preferred grumpy Cruz to vulnerable Cruz. All that remained was reverence and a remaining hint of confusion. I could handle that.

Cruz and I had our problems, but when we were working there was always respect. Deep, deep down he was as big a nerd as I was.

"Have you determined if someone's inside?"

"Yes, per the logs, it *is* the original captain of the Elemental Crew, Captain Victoria Norris."

He followed me back to the case. I leaned into the glass, attempting to see through the ice which covered the lid, but it was no use — the figure inside was hidden.

"But, Commander, I'm getting some bizarre readings. I was able to match the genetic code to the captain, but it's altered."

"Altered?"

"Yes. It reads approximately thirty years younger than the last known sample."

"Explain," I demanded.

He shrugged. "I can't yet. All I know is that whoever is inside *is* the captain, but thirty years younger than the last DNA sample we have of her. Which would mean she is five years younger than when she stepped onto this ship."

My head spun. I took a deep breath. "Any luck with the logs?"

"The only report we can access is from right before the pod's systems were initiated. It's limited information, though." Cruz examined his armpad. "The rest of the crew logs are locked up tight. Captain Norris did something to keep us out. It'll take some time to get through her walls."

"Then that's our focus. We need to know what happened here."

It was like the universe heard our plan and said, "Hell to the no. You want answers, you're going to have to work for it."

A deafening *snap* had me jumping. The lights flickered as Geron let out a pained curse. Then he was flying across the room, his body limp when it hit the floor. Smoke flitted from the box mounted up in the corner of the room he'd been examining.

"Geron!" I screamed, my breath catching as fear for my friend paralyzed me.

Doc Mendez slid to his side, taking his charred hand into his and checking to see if it had been breached. He couldn't remove the containment suit, so Doc began taking scans.

"He's breathing," Doc said.

I started toward him just as chatter erupted over the intercom, the team outside calling out. They wanted to know what was going on as alarms blared red, green, and blue. Warnings flashed across panels around the room. Some I recognized; others I didn't. I shared a look with Cruz.

"Doc has Geron," Cruz said to me, meeting my eyes. "You can trust him."

I swallowed back the fear tightening my throat, and then with a nod, we were moving. We stepped up to the nearest workstations and began combing through the warnings. A column I hadn't noticed before came to light above the cooler, and I linked to it. Multi-color bar charts outlined the O2, CO2, and radiation levels for each mechanical uterus. The warnings flashed brighter as the radiation levels began to drop in a steady flow. Cruz and I searched through the systems, trying to find the one initiating the change and shut it off.

An all-consuming *hiss* filled the air.

We froze as water vapor poured from the pod, drifting down to encircle our legs. It kept coming and coming, rising to our waists.

"Evans, Cruz, get back!" Mitchel called.

He didn't have to tell us twice. We backed away just in time for the pop of a soda can's seal to fill the air. The pod door opened, angling up and out.

It took only a moment for the vapor to dissipate and the figure to come into view. She writhed, her body fighting what was a too-fast awakening. Something was very wrong because the sequence was faster than it should have been. We stood frozen as the figure grabbed the intubation tube, and before we could step forward to stop or help her, she ripped it from her throat.

"Good god," Patrick whispered. Patrick's legs were shaking, and his respiration rate had picked up. He looked about ready to pass out.

The woman's dark hair fell over her shoulder as she retched once, twice. She moved with one deep inhale, and her face came into view: smooth tanned skin on a round face with dark eyes. She reached for the workstation and nearly fell from her seat, but Cruz and I steadied her. She started at our appearance but settled — a look of both relief and terror replacing her determination.

"Fix. Field," the woman said, her voice rough with disuse. She swallowed hard and between pants, continued, "quick, or we all die."

My eyebrows rose in question. "What field?"

She pointed to where dark smoke still seeped from the box Geron had damaged.

"Backup is there." She pointed to a smaller unit next to it. "Flip on. Then enter the sequence I give you into this program. Hurry. Please," she begged.

"Right, and what is —" Cruz started.

"Don't you dare use that tone with me, mister!" she snapped. The energy in her retort caused me to step back, and my eyes to go wide.

My knees nearly gave out when Cruz blanched, and he stuttered, "Yes, ma'am. I mean, Miss...C-captain Norris, sir."

What in the ever-loving hell?

Never mind, that was a puzzle for a different time. I nodded and hustled to the box she indicated.

Mitchel met me there, Doc having stayed with Geron and Patrick, who'd collapsed a moment before. He lay next to the still-unconscious Geron.

"Patrick?" I asked him.

He shook his head, fear lining his brow.

"Open the box with the combination oh-seven-niner-two-six," Cruz relayed Captain Norris's words.

"Open," I confirmed.

"Flip the two switches listed 'RAD,' then enter the code two-one-two."

I did as requested. When the last number was entered, I called out, "Ready!"

Not a heartbeat later, a wave of energy spread through the space, expanding in every direction. I felt it in the very marrow of my bones, vibrating deep within. I sucked in a breath. It felt like I was standing beneath an electrical line. Then, one by one, the alarms stopped. The stats monitoring for the fetuses leveled out, and the children inside calmed.

"Whatever that was, the babies have stopped thrashing. Patrick's recovering too," Mitchel said, eyebrows raised, as he walked along the cooler, his gaze trailing along each and every crew member protected within.

With Doc's help, Patrick sat up again. He was a little worse for wear, but his breathing was back to normal. Doc Mendez was speaking softly to him, and it looked like Geron was finally coming around.

"You all right, Geron?" I asked, dropping to his side.

"Yeah, Tash. But don't touch the box."

I snorted and helped him to a seated position. "We got that. What about you, Montgomery?"

"I'm better, definitely better. Whatever that thing is up there, it's helping."

"He's exposed," Captain Norris stated. She sat on the edge of the pod, her eyes locked on Patrick. Even with her sickly pallor, she examined him with the intensity of a scientist. "You might as well take that get-up off, Montgomery. You're staying here with me."

"What! Why?" he asked.

She slid to the edge, then pushed to her feet. The captain swayed, but Cruz was there to steady her, a hand on her back. She placed a palm on his other arm.

"Thanks, Rus, but I'm fine. Just need to get to that chair. Think you can do that without pissing me off?"

"No problem, Captain." Cruz inclined his head, lip turning up at the corner.

"He pisses you off, too?" Damn it. The words were out before I could stop them.

Mitchel and Patrick covered their surprised laughs with a cough. Captain Norris laughed outright. Cruz just glared at me.

She sent me a wry grin, then said, "He does that to those he respects the most."

"Auntie!" Cruz snapped.

My breath caught. Wait, what? If I hadn't stopped it, my jaw would have hit the floor. Even so, if I didn't breathe soon, I might die. Auntie? How could that be? Or better yet, how the hell had I not known this?

I was his commanding officer! Though now that she'd said it aloud, he did have features that...

"Don't worry, Commander Evans. He's harmless enough." She patted his arm again and that motion had me breathing again. "Though you've worked with him long enough you probably know that."

I held back my laugh, but there was no way to fight the smile that crept over my face. She was right and seeing this woman pat Cruz's arm as if he were a child solidified it. Plus, it was just weird. Sweet even. And him? This giant, hulking man doting on her? It made him more human, and I wasn't sure I wanted to see him that way. Cruz helped her into the chair and then stepped back. She leaned down to a fridge mounted below the desk and pulled out a bottle of the post-wake serum we all drank when coming out of hypersleep.

"I'm confused. Are you saying that you're really Captain Victoria Norris?" Mitchel asked, moving closer.

I had a feeling he knew but needed the verbal confirmation. I understood why. We weren't expecting to see Captain Norris again. An eighty-year trip for someone who'd been around forty-five when *The Aspire* left the dock? She would have died years ago, but now she looked to be in her late thirties. It didn't make any sense.

"If he was exposed," she said, completely ignoring Mitchel. She leaned forward to rest her elbows on her knees. "He can't leave the shuttle. Depending on the Cnidramarus he carries, he might not be able to leave this room."

"You have to be Captain Norris," Mitchel grumbled. "She always did ignore me when I spoke."

"Only when you asked stupid questions." She sat straight and met his hard gaze. "You know it's me, kid. I was the one who trained you, after all."

She shot him a teasing smile, one I recognized from when we'd done something unexpected — or stupid — on a training mission and she was assigned to reprimand us. It was half exasperated and all respectful. I remember her telling us once that no leader could abide by all the rules. If we aren't willing to bend them when necessary and cause a little trouble, then our team would die. This unpopular opinion had been proven correct more times than I could count. Looking around the medical bay, I knew we were about to hear another story that aligned with this philosophy.

"I know I look younger, Captain, but I promise it's me. It will all make sense once I explain what happened."

"Yes, can we please move on so she can explain why I can't leave the room?" Patrick asked.

"First, I need to know if anyone else has been exposed. If so, they need to be within the field five minutes ago."

"Not that we're aware of," Mitchel said.

"Good." She sighed heavily, then leaned back in the chair. "What's the date?"

"It's Seronious, the year 2836," I said, as Cruz handed her another recovery drink. "We've been awake less than five days."

Her eyebrows shot up. "Well, damn. What the...what happened?"

Mitchel groaned. "We were hoping you could tell us."

"You locked the logs, Captain," Cruz explained. "We didn't have time to decode them before Richards damaged the field — whatever that is — and woke you up." He leaned against the desk next to the captain.

"Yes, of course. Well, the easy answer is, it was the Cnidramarus."

"And that is?" Mitchel asked petulantly, getting a glare from the captain.

She took a deep breath as if to gather her thoughts. "It was 2785, thirty-nine years into the voyage. Everything was going fine until we came across an asteroid belt. As is necessary, we were collecting the smaller meteorites with elements we required for fuel. One had a significant amount of water crystals on it, so we picked it up. What we didn't know was there was a small collection of something else on the rock."

"The crystals outside."

"Yes. Commander Berkley noticed it first and was the first infected. Initially, we thought it was some kind of illness until we realized he wasn't sick, he was aging. And at an unfounded rate. Within a matter of hours, he'd gained years based on his genetic degradation. By the end of the week, he was gone. Died of old age."

"I remember Berkley; he was a good man."

Captain Norris shrugged. "Most days anyway. But those last days? He busted his ass to save his crew. He was the one that figured out the creature we'd found in the golden crystal shard on the asteroid was a parasite." She played with her hair. Staring off into space, she continued, "Barely a scratch and you'd end up with a Cnidramarus as your new friend. That's what we named it — 'Cnidramarus.'"

"Why?"

"Mostly their physical features. They may not act like the cnidarian of Earth, but they do look like them. Berkley mixed that with the system name and there you got it, a name for the devil parasite."

Patrick stood, beginning to pace while Doc Mendez and Geron, who still sat on the floor, shifted in their seats. Mitchel stayed frozen, arms crossed over his chest.

"A few of his crew were infected too, but they had different responses. Instead of aging, some began to grow younger." She shook her head. "By the time we figured out what was different between their cases, we'd lost more than half the crew."

"But if Berkley figured out it was this creature causing the problem," I said, "didn't he quarantine it? How did more of the crew become exposed?"

She met my gaze and shrugged. "Like any virus. We didn't realize how fast the crystal grew. We had a few vials that we were using for testing.

They unexpectedly shattered while in the hand of someone. Another was a piece we missed while cleaning, and it attached itself to the ship, grew, and cut someone. You get the idea."

Norris rubbed her hands together.

"As long as all of the crystals are still on this shuttle, your team should be fine."

We exchanged glances. Mitchel was about to speak, but I beat him to it.

"Aridas, did you hear that?" I asked through the comm link, knowing they could hear everything happening in here.

"Yes, ma'am. Boston and Tanaka are boxing them up now. No vials breached as of yet."

"Send them in through the shield as soon as possible."

"I'll get it," Geron said. He nodded at me, stood, and headed out the door. I was happy to see his legs were stable beneath him. Apparently getting electrocuted was no big deal. Who knew?

"Richards's on his way to collect," Mitchel added. "Make sure all surfaces are sanitized."

Norris pushed to her feet. Cruz stood, but when she seemed steady enough, he returned to lean against the table. She headed to the nearby monitor.

"They'll need to treat the area just in case. Any location within the ship that's had exposure, including metal, needs to be tended. I'm sending over instructions on what we found worked."

"Treat the area?" I asked.

"These bastards are hard to kill. Not only are they resistant to all chemicals, but heat as well." Norris made a few entries, then pulled up an image of three tiny organisms I recognized. "The only thing that we've found to slow them down is radiation. A very specific frequency of radiation. Unfortunately, the levels required to kill them are not really healthy for the human body. So we need to take care of them before they find a host. Bastards grow on everything."

"So what are they?"

She glanced at the cooler containing the mechanical uteri. Blinking rapidly, she turned back to the screen and pointed to the image.

"These are the Cnidramarus. From what we've determined, they're an invasive species. They feed off the energy of the host and take the time that person, or animal, was allotted in this life. In other words, they eat their life force."

Chapter Seven
Captain Mitchel Remian

These are the Cnidramarus. From what we've determined, they're an invasive species who feed off the energy of the host and take the time that person, or animal, was allotted in this life.

I released a long, slow breath as the complexity of that remark spun in my brain.

The room was silent as each and every one of us tried, and failed, to grasp what she was saying. Cruz's eyes had narrowed in confusion, his head tilted to the side. Tasha played thoughtfully with the braid that fell over her shoulder. And even Doc seemed to be having a rough time as he rested his chin in his hand and just stared at the captain.

"Captain Norris," Cruz said. "You aren't making sense. What does that mean?"

Norris closed her eyes. Her face scrunched in concentration, as if she searched for the correct words. In that moment, Victoria looked exhausted — the bags beneath her eyes dark, her shoulders sagging with the weight of her story. I wanted to tell her to lie down, but my mentor didn't like being told what to do, even if her hands were shaking. So I sat there, listening to a tale that sounded impossible.

"I know it sounds crazy," she started, "but we don't know everything out here."

"Okay..." I said warily.

"I'll try to explain it. So, time is linear, right? That makes sense logically, but what we didn't understand was time goes both ways. It is a concept that we accept as real because we watch it pass. We see people age, trees grow, and the sun rises and sets, but none of us assumed it was a physical thing." She winced. "Well, it's not physical exactly, but it lives around each of us. It affects each of us."

"We're with you so far."

"These things, the Cnidramarus? They can link into these lines of time around us, then they eat the energy their host expends within their lifetime. Not today or tomorrow, but all the days of their life. They do this by creating a small pocket of ..." She paused. The *swoosh* of her pants, the only sound. She rubbed a spot between her eyes. "A pocket of deformity."

"Deformity," Doc Mendez repeated.

"The only way I can explain it is that these things make a pocket around the host and somehow shift time so that the host begins to age extremely fast, or they pull time backward, and the host regresses. That's what happened to the crew there." She pointed to the cooler. It was the first time she'd acknowledged the fetuses since she'd awakened.

"So, by forcing this change on the host," Tasha asked, "these creatures absorb the energy?"

"Yes."

I could've heard a pin drop we were all so shocked by the declaration. I think we were barely breathing. This couldn't be true. If I could have pinched myself through the suit, I would have, because I was beginning to think this was a dream, and I was stuck in my sleep pod.

I rubbed my hands together, focusing on the roughness of the fabric. "Captain Norris, this is..." What was I supposed to say?

"It sounds insane, I know, Mitchel, but it's all true. Have you examined the crew's logs? Or examined the crystals?"

"Not yet. They've been locked up tight, and we just found you and the crystals," Patrick said. His voice was a little shaky, and he swayed ever so slightly.

Patrick was getting worse. He looked sick, but it was more than that. His skin was loose, the gray at his temples stark in the soft light of his helmet. Sweat covered his flushed skin.

I sent a private message to Doc. "Is he okay?"

Doc's gaze was locked on my friend; his eyes narrowed in concern.

Patrick continued, "I was working on the ship to try to get it open. We'd started assessments on the other two shuttles, but for reasons I now understand, this one was locked up tight." He gestured, then said, "I opened the panel and found crystal had grown over the components. I couldn't see them through the rat's nest, so I got cut by one when I was reaching in. They had grown over the hardware, through the breaks in the metal casing, and in the ports. I was exposed."

Norris scowled, then an expression of sheer panic flashed across her face. She spun toward the console. Screen after screen, she shuffled through the computer, opening documents, then closing them. I had no idea what she was doing or why it seemed like she was panicking, but I moved to her side.

"Do you know which one you caught?"

"Which one?" Patrick asked, confused. "Oh, um, no. It was dark under the ship and —"

"Wait." Norris spun on her heels, her eyes latching on Patrick. It was like she searched for an answer to a question we didn't know, and the look scared me. It whispered of danger, trouble that was going to make the next few minutes or hours very interesting. I had experience with that look. It did not bode well for any of us.

"How long ago were you exposed? Exactly. I need to know exactly!"

I shivered. There was something in her tone I didn't like; a warning.

Patrick swayed, holding a hand out to steady himself. In the last few seconds, the color of his cheeks had deepened to a feverish red, and his chest was rising and falling rapidly.

"What's going on?" I asked him.

"How long!" Norris demanded.

"I don't know," Patrick breathed. "Maybe ninety minutes?"

Norris cursed, diving forward. "Catch him!"

Thank the heavens for quick reflexes. Without thought, I responded. I lurched forward, wrapping my arms around his waist just as Patrick's legs went weak beneath him. I lowered him to the floor. Doc and the others stepped forward to help.

"What's happening?" Tasha asked. She shifted from foot to foot, Cruz hovering behind her.

"Ninety minutes? Was his guess right?" Norris asked.

"Yes, why?"

"Because things are about to go to shit." She glanced up at the wall clock.

Well, didn't that just send a chill up the spine?

"Tasha, help me. Boys, you have about a minute to get him up on that bed before the screaming starts. And get the suit off him. Quick!"

That voice. Mother, boss, and mildly erratic friend all wrapped in one. It was the tone of a commander that expected compliance no matter what — a commander who'd saved our asses more than once. Without any hesitation, we listened.

Reaching down, we lifted Patrick, placing him on the table. Cruz removed his boots, Doc his helmet, and I, his gloves.

Tasha followed Norris to the cabinets. When they reached them, Norris said, "Second drawer down, you'll find a black box with four syringes. I need one. In the drawer below is a mouth guard. Grab them both."

"Yes, ma'am." Tasha ran for the supplies as I unstrapped the sides of the containment suit.

Norris, who was already digging in another cabinet, grabbed various other supplies and placed them on a nearby cart. Then she bent, opened another door, and pulled an odd-looking device out. It made a loud *clang* as it made contact.

"What is that?" I asked the others. They shrugged with a shake of their heads.

As quickly as we could, we stripped Patrick out of the containment suit, leaving him in his sweat-drenched uniform. We had to trust Captain Norris and whatever crazy plan she had. If I didn't, he might die.

That was not an option.

Norris fiddled with the device, the cart of other supplies pulled behind her. Tasha added her items; then they joined us. By the time they got to us, Patrick was moaning. I looked to find his eyes open, blank as they stared at the ceiling.

My fingers tingled, and my mouth went dry. I swallowed hard. Doc bent into his line of sight. He spoke but I couldn't hear what he said.

Stop. I had to stop. This was not the time to lose it.

Doc tried again, but Patrick didn't respond. He lay there, eyes glazed.

"Don't worry, Captain. It's normal." Norris picked up one of the prefilled syringes and, before we could stop her, stabbed it into his thigh. "Take the quiet while you can."

Not reassuring.

"What did you give him?" Doc asked.

She set the empty needle down. "For the pain. Now, flip him over."

Pain? She really needed to give us more than just telling us he was going to start screaming, or I was going to lose my shit. She may know what was coming, but we sure bloody well didn't!

With a shared, worried glance, we did as she asked.

"What is that thing? It looks like one of the medical scanners, but...not," Doc Mendez said, gesturing to the first device she'd carried over.

"You're correct," Norris said, slipping between me and the table. She pulled the cart close and shuffled through the pile. "When we realized these things were parasites, Major Bentley and one of the doctors created this. It scans for the location of the Cnidramarus within the body. Gives us a decent picture of it and how far integrated it is."

"And this thing?" Tasha asked, holding up the device she'd retrieved. "This was once one of our laser cutters, right?"

"Correct."

"What's that one for?"

"You're about to find out."

"That's not a good enough answer, Norris," I said with a glare, but she was too distracted to respond.

Patrick began to twitch. When he started to clench and unclench his fists over and over, Norris said, "Ten seconds."

"Until?" Cruz asked, concern tinting his voice. Cruz stood over the table, jaw clenching as the moans from before intensified, and I realized at that moment how much he respected Patrick. They worked together every day, so why wouldn't he? But more than that, they were friends.

"The screaming." She shoved me out of the way, then reached to pull up Patrick's shirt. "Gentlemen, get ready to hold him."

Her fingers brushed his back just above the curve of his spine. Patrick let out a scream that burrowed into my bones and laid a weight on my chest so heavy it was hard to breathe. The sound was so deep and soul-wrenching I had to fight not to step away.

My hands shook as I pressed them into the flesh of his shoulders. My blood ran cold, and I twitched with each rattling intake of breath he sucked in before he released yet another scream.

I leaned down next to my friend. "We got you, buddy. Bite down on this." I shoved the mouthpiece Tasha handed me into his mouth. "Bite down, now."

For only a split second, I saw his eyes darken in understanding, then he was gone again, lost in the cries which tore tears from his eyes. Tasha gasped, face pulled up in terror when his air gave out, and Patrick arched, sucking in a great breath before beginning again.

"This thing's moving fast," Norris cursed. She pushed his trousers down so that she could see the base of his spine.

Bile rose in my throat.

The deep, unhealthy red color spread outward from a nodule about the size of a quarter. It mounded his skin just above Norris's hand, slithering downward in a wave of movement that had Tasha going pale. Darker lines, more purple than blue, snaked out to wrap around his ribs. When his next yell filled the room, I got it. I really did.

Norris pressed her hand flat to his back. Patrick bowed as if trying to curl into a ball. He fought, attempting to roll away from her touch.

Doc, Cruz, and I moved as one. Using all our weight, we held him down. He cried out, unintelligible sobs that I'd never forget.

"Please tell me you have a plan, Captain!" Doc said, raising his voice over the yells.

Norris climbed up onto the table and straddled his hips. Her petite frame strained with the effort, but she didn't back down. She placed her hand to the lump, keeping it within the arch of her thumb and forefinger. The creepy part was how the thing responded. As if sensing her, it gyrated faster, fighting against her touch.

"Tasha, help me. Take your hand and hold it here. You're trying to slow this thing down so I can get him scanned. Then, we'll use the laser cutter."

"On him?"

"If we can see it, why can't we"— Cruz grunted as one of Patrick's legs bent and kicked him in the face — "take it out?"

Tasha slipped closer to Cruz to get a better angle. Her side pressed to his. She leaned in and replaced Norris's hand with her own. "Holy crap! This thing is strong."

"Hold it! You have to. Ten seconds and I'll..." She trailed off as she lifted the scanner and began to take readings. I could barely hear the occasional beep over the noise around us.

"Why can't we remove it, Captain?" Doc yelled again.

"If we try to remove it, we'll kill him. If this thing's gotten this far, it's already placed multiple links into his spinal cord. There's no disconnecting them now."

Suddenly, Patrick's left arm flung out. Tasha lost her balance and was thrown back a few feet.

"What the hell, Patrick!" Her boots squeaked on the floor as she caught herself, then reclaimed her spot. Norris, who still straddled his thighs, was also tossed, but with Cruz's help, she easily righted herself.

"Then what are we doing?"

"Well, depending on which one he has, we either help him and stop the pain or let him ride it out."

"Neither of those seems like good options," Doc said. "Can't we get this thing out of him now?"

"No, we tried that, and it didn't go well. Trust me, this is the only option." The device pinged, and a foul curse burst free of the petite form riding my dear friend.

Everyone's eyes shot to her. That was...interesting and not a good sign.

"He has a red." She dove for the modified laser cutter on the table. Sitting back upright and already flipping the new device on, she said, "All right, Patrick, I need you to stay still. Do you hear me? You're not gonna like me much for the next few minutes, but I promise this *will* help. I just need you to stay still."

She focused her attention on us then.

"This is dangerous. If he moves while it's on, we could cause severe damage to his spinal cord. That won't hurt the Cnidramarus, but it will hurt Patrick. Hold him still no matter what you do."

"Oh, fuck," I said. Meeting the eyes of the doc and Cruz, I tightened my grip. The others did, too. "We've got him, Captain."

Norris shoved Tasha away. "You can't be near this thing. Get back as far as you can go."

"What, why? I can help," Tasha said.

Without warning and no apparent cause, Patrick's screams intensified. His voice was hoarser than before, which made the sound more desperate, agonized.

"You need to get back, now! You will not question me on this, Commander. This thing?" She held up the modified laser. "Will emit a huge amount of concentrated radiation. Your suit will protect you a little, but I have no idea how far the range is on this thing. So, if you ever want to have children, then you will get the hell back."

Oh. Shit. Yup, not good. Definitely not good.

"But —"

"That is an order!" I seconded.

Tasha glared but backed toward the door.

"What about us?" Doc asked with an audible gulp. The sound was over exaggerated, sounding half-real and all amused.

Captain Norris waved her hand in the air. "No one wants to procreate with you anyway."

There was a startled giggle from Tasha. We turned to her, but she just smiled when we glared.

"What?" she asked. "I'm sure you'll be fine."

Captain Norris grinned. "You three will be fine. Tech Spec Clareson said its range was small, but I am not risking her. She's too valuable."

Norris hadn't looked at us once as she spoke because she was busy setting the radiation filter — or whatever the hell it was — while attempting to keep the Cnidramarus from moving too far downward.

"Yes! Okay, Patrick, boys, this is going to suck. I need you to hold him completely still."

"I need you to tell me what you're doing before you do it, Captain. He's under my care, and I am having a real hard time trusting you right now," Doc said.

Norris froze — if that was possible — and looked up at him. Their eyes met, and everything seemed to stop for a moment. Doc didn't back down as we all held our breaths.

Through gritted teeth, she said, "This device emits a concentrated amount of high-powered radiation similar to that of what's protecting this room. And no, they will not interact. But unlike that field, this beam is hazardous. If I don't hit the Cnidramarus directly and get his spinal cord, I could damage him forever."

Cruz cursed. My teeth clenched so hard my jaw popped.

"And if we don't do it?"

"This thing will attach to the base of his spinal cord, and there's a 50/50 chance it will sever it, taking away the use of his legs. This will allow the parasite to direct link into his mind and timeline, killing Patrick faster. And so you know, when he dies, a thousand more of its kind will exist. Reds are nasty little buggers."

Bile crept up and up, burning the back of my throat. Tasha stood back, her eyes on Patrick's face. I saw the plea in her eyes. We couldn't lose him.

Doc's eyes widened with each word out of Norris's mouth. He took a deep breath and said, "Then I guess we don't have a choice. I really hope you know what you're doing."

"Trust me now, and I'll show you everything after he's stabilized."

"Excuse me, Captain Remian?" the new voice interjected into the chaos. The room stilled at Tanaka's voice and the stressed tone seeping through the speakers. "I know there's something strange happening in there, but we have an emergency out here."

"And that would be?" I snapped.

"Lieutenant Richards collapsed. He needs medical attention. Should we send another inside the field?"

"No!" Norris said. "No more exposures. Tasha, get him. Doc, when you examined him earlier, was his suit compromised?"

Doc nodded. "Yes. A small tear where the fabric was burned."

I sighed. Damn it to hell. One thing. Can't just one thing go right today?

"Get him inside the field until we know he's clear."

"I'll get him," Cruz said. "She can't help him; he's twice her size." He gestured to Tasha and removed his hands from Patrick's legs. He began to step away, but Patrick thrashed, nearly sending Norris sprawling. Realizing his mistake, he caught her and returned to his task.

"I've saved your ass before," Tasha growled with a glare. "And if you don't do whatever she tells you to save Patrick, I'll have your ass up for review before you can blink."

With those words, she stomped from the room.

Norris glanced at Cruz, whose cheeks had pinkened with rage. "You really do piss her off, don't you?" She snickered. "Just tell her you're in love with her and get it over with."

My gaze snapped to him, as did Doc's.

Wait, was it rage or something else? Cruz cursed but didn't deny it.

I was snarling when he met my eye and said, "Worried?"

I lost my temper. I wasn't proud of it, all right?

My hands were suddenly no longer holding Patrick and were instead wrapped in Cruz's suit. Doc and the captain cried out just before there was a hard crack to my head. The hit to the helmet was so loud that I flinched, closing my eyes against the booming pressure. Whatever they'd thrown clattered to the floor.

"Not the time, Captain. Quit being a dumbass."

Doc grabbed my arm, yanking me back. "Put your head in the game."

"We're going to discuss this," I growled.

"No. We're not because she'll never find out." Cruz rolled his shoulders, and that's when I realized he'd never released his grip on Patrick. "And you better not fucking tell her. Plus, we have more important things to deal with right now."

Jaw clenched, his gaze returned to Patrick.

He was right. With a shake of my head, I returned to my post, looked at Captain Norris, and said, "Let's get this done."

The next few moments slowed to a crawl. I'm not sure if it was because red had begun to leak into my vision as thoughts of Tasha and Cruz together lingered, or if I'd checked out of what was happening around me, but when the taste of iron filled my mouth, I had to get a grip. I was acting like a child. I was overreacting, especially considering that Tasha and I weren't together. But how had I never noticed? Past missions flitted through my mind, and one by one, I realized I had seen it. I'd just ignored it. Hell, he'd been the one to interrupt Tasha and me from our one and only kiss. Not long after that, Cruz's attitude had declined. Tasha was so upset because, up to that point, they'd been friends. Extremely close friends. He must've had feelings for her even then.

Holy shit.

"On the count of three."

My thoughts snapped back into focus. I'd have to think about that later.

"I'll administer three, fifteen-second bursts, thirty seconds apart. You need to hold him as still as you can while the beam is active. Understand?"

"Yes," we chorused.

She pressed down on Patrick's back, her hand still wrapped around the strange moving thing underneath his skin. My stomach threatened to turn over as she closed her grip, another inhuman scream coming from my friend.

"Three, two, one." Norris pointed the device at the wiggling creature and pressed the button.

A bright beam of light burst from the end of the device. When it touched his skin, his movements became more frenzied, and I had to press all of my weight over him. I counted in my head. The beam disappeared, and Patrick went still, almost limp on the bed. Oddly enough, the movement under his skin settled too. I readied myself for the next treatment.

Norris hit the button again. The skin where the beam touched blistered, deep welts that changed from red to purple to black with each passing second.

"It's burning him!" Doc said.

"Trust me! Please! This will save his life."

Doc looked as though he were about to throw Captain Norris from Patrick and slam her to the ground. He was protective of his people. As the welts spread, I, too, contemplated how to stop her.

I must have moved because Cruz said, "Don't! Remember, she's the only one who knows what's really going on. We have no choice but to trust her."

Fuck if he wasn't right.

The second break started, and with it, Norris shifted. She released her hold of the mass, then prodded along the length of his spine. When she reached about two inches above his tailbone, Patrick jerked. His scream was quieter this time but still agonized.

"Ready?" she asked. "This is the most important one."

As her eyes scanned us, I saw just how scared she really was. We nodded. She took a steadying breath and braced herself. We did, too.

I had to keep myself from vomiting as the beam hit the new area and a popping sound like a wet water balloon filled the air. Never had a sound alone make me dizzy, but Patrick stopped screaming. What the hell was that?

"Thank the gods," Norris whispered. She released the hold on the trigger and hung her head.

At the exact moment, Patrick slumped, his face pressed to the cold metal. The movement under his skin stopped almost completely. Cold fear shot through me. I couldn't hear him breathing. Was he dead?

"Patrick? Montgomery, you stupid bastard." Doc Mendez's face next to his. He checked for a pulse, sighed, then said, "Buddy, are you there?"

Cruz and I stepped back. Norris climbed down from the table, placing everything back on the cart. "He'll be fine. Give him twenty minutes, and he'll be up and running around all over again."

"Are you sure?" I asked. "He doesn't look good." My skin felt heated. My breath came in short pants. If I didn't calm the hell down, I was going to pass out.

"I'm sure, Captain. We got to it before it reached the entry point. He has a much better chance of survival now."

Damn, she was back to speaking in code. I needed to read those crew logs, like now.

"Patrick, can you hear me?" Doc asked again. He patted Patrick's face.

After a long second, a ragged voice said, "Yeah, Doc. I'm here. Can you shut the hell up, please? You're really loud."

A startled chuckle came from Norris. She leaned against the near-by workstation, the confident Captain disappearing underneath an exhausted and relieved friend. She was paler now, a dusting of sweat covering her forehead. She rubbed her face, then ran her hands into her hair. She tugged lightly.

Before I went to Patrick's side, I retrieved a supplemental drink from the cooler and handed it to her. Reaching him, I bent to meet Patrick's eyes. They were still glazed, but they were far more present than they'd been ten minutes ago.

"How do you feel?"

He grimaced as he shifted. "Like I could run a marathon. You?"

"Like I want to beat the crap out of my Lead Engineer for getting hurt."

With a snort, Patrick said, "Like you could take him. I heard he's a real badass."

"That he is." I patted his shoulder, happy he was safe. For now.

From the corner of my eye, I watched Doc's expression darken with rage. He straightened, spinning on Norris.

"What the hell was that?" Doc said. At his tone, Norris pushed upright.

"That was saving his life. Or, at least, extending it."

Doc had probably been about to continue his attack, but those words shocked him. His anger washed away, leaving only curiosity and a hint of wariness behind.

"Doctor, I apologize for not explaining what I was doing before, but if I had not acted, Montgomery would be in significantly worse shape." She pointed to the screen, which still held the pictures of three nightmarish creatures. "He has a red. These are the ones that alter life and make the host age quickly. The problem is, they're also the most violent. They don't care what damage they do to the host in the process of bonding because pushing life forward, making someone age faster takes far less effort physically. Whereas regressing in time seems to take more effort on behalf of the Cnidramarus. The host's body has to change significantly during regression, and that can take weeks. The reds? Days if we're lucky."

"I need to learn everything. I need access to all of it — logs, charts, research. Everything. Right the hell now!"

She nodded solemnly. "Agreed, and I can tell you everything else I've learned since they entered the ship. We tried to document everything, but it was hard. Things moved fast."

"Captains?" Tasha's voice came in over the intercom. "How are you doing in there?"

"We're good, Tash. Patrick's stabilized."

There was a grunt. When she spoke again, her voice sounded strained. "That's great. Then can one of you come out here and help me? Richards's hulking ass is heavy."

Chapter Eight
Commander Tasha Evans

"**G**eron?" I asked, patting the side of his helmet. Through the speakers, I heard the hollow *tap-tap-tap* of my gloves against the plastic. "C'mon, asswipe. You and I both know I'm not gonna let you die here, so you might as well wake up and help me out."

There was a feminine snort, and I looked up to see Aridas standing just on the other side of the force field separating the shuttle from the rest of the ship. Her petite frame was strong, the dark hair and eyes giving her an exotic air. She had a headset linked over her ear, the microphone sticking out toward her mouth. Her expression was amused, but I could tell it was forced.

"Is he breathing? Awake? Do you need help keeping him from stabbing himself with the crystal?" Aridas asked, ignoring my rather unprofessional commentary. "I can suit up."

In between her words, broken pieces of whatever the hell was happening inside the medical bay reverberated over the shared line and through my helm. I was a little glad I wasn't in there. It sounded like they were losing Patrick, but I couldn't handle that. It might kill me. We'd been friends far too long, and the idea of his brilliant mind and calm presence not there to bounce ideas off of? That was not something I wanted to imagine. Then there was his sense of humor and the fact that, next to Geron, he was my sounding board. About everything. He saw through the hard exterior to me. He was my work wife. The one I counted on more than anyone else.

Using the scanner in my armpad, I took his vitals. "Breathing, yes. Awake, no. But he's stable enough. I don't read any spinal injury and since he fell on his shoulder, I think it's safe to move him. And he's already stabbed himself on the crystal, so he's exposed. There's a significant cut on his thigh. I need to get him into the shuttle's medical bay and within the field. I have no idea if what Captain Norris said is true, but I'm not willing to risk it. Maybe he was lucky, and none of those things were in the piece of rock he sliced himself on, or she has some magical way to get them out if newly infected."

"When are we ever that lucky?" Aridas said. The comment surprised me. In general, she was the most optimistic of the group.

"We have to hope," I said, shooting her an angry glare.

Backpedaling, she said, "Yes, Commander."

I didn't care if what she said held truth. Geron was a good man. He didn't deserve to die months from our new home. Seeing him shoot across the room had scared the absolute shit out of me, but hearing he'd collapsed had been worse. Was it the shock that took him down or something else? Had we failed when we'd sent him to retrieve the samples? Probably.

"Call if you need help, Commander. I'll come in if you require it," Aridas said. She flinched as another deep and throaty cry came through the shared line — Patrick's. In a strained voice, she continued, "The vials are there when you're ready."

"We've got this. Please stand by," I said. "And don't worry. Patrick will be fine."

Aridas nodded and returned to the workstation nearby. No one wanted to hear their friend in pain, and we were both close to Patrick. "Commander," she said without looking back, "I wanted to let you know that the teams I sent to work on the list you sent are making good progress.

They have moved on to the shields. They'll provide an update once they've identified the source command problem."

"Any secondary issues identified at this time?" I asked.

"None yet."

Good. With a deep breath, I pushed the worry away. That was one for another moment. Right now, Geron needed me. I shook him gently, digging my fingers into his ribs just enough to get his attention. He moaned but didn't open his eyes.

"All right, old man. If you're not gonna wake up, I guess I'm gonna have to carry you. I hope you realize this means I'll be taking it out of your hide the next time we spar, and I won't be going easy."

Geron lay on his back on the hangar floor just below the shuttle's lowered ramp. He'd fallen five feet to land here, and to get him back on the ship, I'd need to carry him up the ramp. That wasn't a problem. Taking the box of samples he'd collected? That would be.

I sat him up, then threw his arm over my shoulder. With significant effort, as Geron was not just larger but longer than me, I hoisted him into a fireman's carry. I'd practiced this a million times in my life. Used it a few times, too. I was not large, so at only five foot seven, I'd worked to be strong as hell. Being in the fleet this long, I'd learned that if I couldn't lift someone bigger than me, then that put both of us at risk. Especially considering I didn't leave any of my men behind. Ever.

I could hear the taunts he'd throw at me for doing this.

"See, I knew you weren't as weak as that skinny ass of yours claimed."

"For the number of times I've thrown you to the ground, you should know what I'm capable of." I'd respond, *"And quit checking out my butt. It's weird."*

"Ew," he'd say, disgust in his tone. *"I'll admit that from a scientific standpoint, you are hot, but thinking of you like that is gross. You're like my sister."*

I rolled my eyes. I couldn't help it. That is exactly the type of thing that would happen, and all because Geron was an idiot. A brilliant, funny idiot, but an idiot nonetheless. He'd stood by me through some of the worst times in my life, just as my brother had. Lost in thoughts of my brother and Geron together, I missed the fact that the screams coming through the speakers had stopped. I froze halfway up the ramp. My legs shook with Geron's weight, but terror was seeping from every cell in my body as tears filled my eyes.

"Captain?" I said, my voice strained. The next words were hard to get out. "How are you doing there?"

"We're good, Tash. Patrick's stabilized," Mitchel said in that strait-laced way of his.

I let out a heavy breath. Patrick was alive. Stabilized.

Keeping my voice steady, I said, "That's great. Then can one of you assholes come out here and help me? Geron's hulking ass is heavy."

I shifted, bouncing so that I could maneuver his limp weight higher. I continued up the ramp, another unladylike grunt escaping me. I'd reached the top and trudged forward, beginning to think they weren't coming to help. A rumbling vibrated my feet and two figures appeared, Cruz and Mitchel. Mitchel's stride slowed when he saw me carrying Geron, but Cruz's didn't falter. He didn't say anything, but once he was within reach, I bent, and Cruz took hold of one of Geron's arms.

"Took you long enough," I said.

"We were painting our toenails. Figured you had this," Cruz said, voice flat.

"Hope it was a pretty color."

"Black like the color of my soul. The captain chose bright pink. It's so pretty."

I laughed. "Let me guess, you held down Patrick, and his are purple."

"Damn right. On three?" he asked, wrapping the limb over his shoulders. When he got to three, we lifted him together and started forward.

"Here," Mitchel said. "Let me take him. I'm sure you're tired."

"I got him," I snapped, passing him and wishing I wasn't so irritated by comments like that. Because even as we dragged the still-unconscious lieutenant toward the medical bay, I couldn't help but notice how Cruz hadn't taken over. He'd respectfully walked up and assumed I could handle it. This was his typical M.O. Which was why I was so angry with what he'd said before. Cruz never treated me as though I wasn't capable. Even when we argued, it always felt like he was testing me, not doubting my abilities.

But Mitchel? He acted like I was a doll easily broken. You'd think by now he'd know better. Maybe it was because he'd seen me at my worst — after my parents had disowned me because I joined the fleet. That had been the only time he'd seen me cry. Or maybe it was because he believed I was the woman he wanted. I knew that, but he had yet to realize it. The biggest issue was that I was not someone who needed saving, and I sure as hell wasn't the dependent type. Which was what he needed. Someone he could take care of, and I could never fill that need. He was cute, but it would never work between us.

"Situation?" Mitchel asked, following behind, annoyance in his tone.

Unwilling to bend while he was being an ass, I answered his question with a question. "Captain, can you please retrieve the samples? Richards fell while carrying them up the ramp. They're at the bottom on the left side."

With a growl, he said, "Sure." The sound of his boots retreated behind us.

We were hustling past the missing doorways, the glimmering crystal mocking us with each beautiful protrusion. "Aridas and Tanaka think it was a seizure. I'm not convinced."

"Doc will figure it out," Cruz said. He looked down at me, compassion in his eyes. "And, um...sorry about earlier."

I blinked, a little shocked.

"You're right. You have saved my ass. More than once," he said.

I bit my lip to hold back a smile. "And don't you forget it."

The corner of his lip lifted ever so slightly. "Wouldn't dream of it."

Stomping preceded Mitchel's reappearance beside us.

"Is he conscious?" he asked.

"Not yet. And yes, time is being clocked." I twisted my arm, and the screen lit up with the time. "Approaching five minutes."

We fell silent, focusing on getting to Doc and Norris.

The man himself was pulling one of the medical tables, which had been shoved against the far side, back out. It sat parallel to Patrick, who was now on his back, eyes closed and completely silent.

"Status?" I asked over Patrick. Cruz and I leaned against the empty table, lying Geron backward. I moved out of the way as Mitchel lifted his legs.

"Fine," Patrick said, opening his gray eyes. "Tired. What about Richards?"

"Previous tear in his suit. I found dust swirling in his helmet. Not sure where it came from, but per Spec Aridas, he was at the top of the ramp with the samples when he fell. He sliced his leg on the way down to the hangar floor on a crystal. His suit is punctured."

"Damn. We can't catch a break," Doc Mendez snarled. "Let's get the suit off, and I'll do a full exam. He's had a rough day. With his suit compromised, I assume he'll be staying here."

"Yes, he will. At least until we can verify species," Norris said. She stood scanning through documents on the screen. I couldn't see what they were from where I stood, but upon entering, she swiped them closed and came to our side.

We worked as quickly as we could. When we pulled the suit from his body, we found blood seeping from the wound on his leg, a dark crimson against the metal of the table. Tiny shards of gold protruded from the injury.

Norris grabbed his helmet and sighed. "Not a seizure. Direct exposure when his air was contaminated. Doc, this means that he both inhaled particles that could contain the Cnidramarus and has potential infection via the wound. We need to check his lungs first. If he's lucky, he'll expel most of it himself."

"Are there any other effects from inhalation?"

"Nothing more than expected. We only had one infected that way. A few hours of coughing, and he'll reject it."

Doc nodded. "Then let's get him scanned."

We wheeled the table underneath the full-body scanner mounted to the ceiling. Not as nice as the one in Main Medical, but it would provide Doc with a good picture of what was wrong. As he set that up, I grabbed the Cnidramarus scanner and flipped it on.

"I can do that," Norris said, reaching for it. She swayed.

"Captain, sit down. You need to rest. We've got Richards."

She met my eyes, then looked away. "I'm fine."

"You just woke up from hypersleep, and you haven't stopped since."

Her shoulders slumped before she gave in and found a chair nearby. With a vulnerability that was rare for her, she admitted, "It's not just that. Guys, it feels like it did before. For my crew. Things progressed so quickly then, too. One person fell, then another, and then another. We couldn't figure out what was happening. Then Bentley was dying, and Demarco." She sighed, placing her head in her hands. "This time we know what we're up against, but I can't help and feel…"

I had the urge to go to her, but we'd never had that kind of relationship. Which was why I was grateful when Cruz did. He bent down and whispered something too low for me to hear. She nodded, squeezed his arm, and then he returned to stand next to me.

Doc pulled out a wound cleaning kit as I tested Geron. He checked his pupils and breathing, then began his examination of first his palm, then the gash on his thigh. He placed his fingers on either side of the wound, checking to see how deep the cut was. Carefully, he removed a few fragments of gold and began to clean it. I marveled at how nimble his fingers were, especially considering the gloves he wore. I shouldn't be surprised, though. Doc was a medic who regularly traveled with teams off-world in combat situations. This was not the first time he'd had to treat someone while fully suited up.

A reading appeared on the screen that I didn't understand. I moved to Norris's side, holding the device out for her to see.

"It's too soon to tell," she explained. "He has all three. Until one wins out, we won't know."

"They can't share a host?"

"Well." She hesitated. "The red and blues can't. I'm not sure about the others yet."

My face scrunched in confusion. "What do you —"

"Captain Remian," Tanaka's voice cut in. Cruz re-entered the room — I hadn't noticed he'd left — with a plate full of food, which he handed to Norris. "I know you're busy, sir, but we need you and Commander Evans out here."

Mitchel met my gaze over Geron, helmet in hand. He glanced at Doc, who was unwrapping the suture kit.

I could read him like a book. He worried that if we left, with Norris and Patrick weakened, who would assist him if Doc required another set of hands?

Tanaka continued, "Some issues are needing your immediate attention."

"And those would be?"

When he came back on the line, his voice was even more agitated. "Power surges all over the ship. Module Three's rotational systems have failed, complete loss of gravity. The hydroponic systems there have gone down with it, and the garden in Section One is glitching." There was a soft click as he paused, a breath, and then he continued, "Scratch that. It's down. As are the heating systems in Module Two."

"Holy shit," Captain Norris said. "Is anything working on this damn ship?"

"No," Cruz said, his tone a mixture of annoyance and frustration. "Without a crew for forty years, our girl is having some trouble. We're still trying to figure out exactly what happened, and with only eighty-five days until Merocius, we're in some serious trouble."

"Eighty-five days?"

Doc looked up from what he was doing. "I've got this. If I need to, I'll use restraints or request help. We have warning this time around."

I gritted my teeth, not liking that I had to leave. But I did. I trusted Doc to handle this. He was the best we had. And regardless, if we didn't fix the ship, nothing they did here would matter.

"On the way," I said. And, with a final pat to Geron's arm, I headed for the exit.

Patrick, who was now sitting up, nodded to me. "If you need me, call."

We both knew there was little he could do. One, he looked like hell, and from here, there was very little he could tap into. At least until we made some adjustments.

"I'll keep you updated."

Norris began to stand, but one sharp glare from Doc and she settled back in her seat. "Fine," she snapped at him. Turning to Mitchel, she said, "Captain Remian, once we get Richards stabilized, I'll debrief them on everything."

"I expect a full report at"— he looked at his watch —"1600 hours." She nodded.

Cruz fell into step beside me. I opened my mouth to tell him to stay behind, but he beat me to it.

"Don't you dare. I'm coming, whether you like it or not. You need my help. The ship needs my help." His lip curved up into a wicked grin. "I'm your best engineer, remember?"

My eyes narrowed, and my lips pressed together.

"You're also a giant pain in my ass." I stomped toward the door. Forgetting they could all hear me through the intercom, I mumbled under my breath, "Never should've said that out loud. Jackass is gonna let it go to his overinflated head."

From behind me, Cruz had the gall to chuckle. It was dark and teasing. A shiver ran up my spine at the — almost — flirty sound. The words Norris said earlier — the ones I wasn't supposed to have heard but did — flitted through my mind. *"Just tell her you're in love with her and get it over with."* Even more distracting was his response: *"...she'll never find out. And you better not fucking tell her."* I clenched my teeth before I did something I shouldn't. When I glared at him, he only smiled.

I had no idea what to do with that information. We hit the ramp, and Mitchel pushed past Cruz, bumping his shoulder on the way down. Weird.

The last five minutes had not been kind to Engineering. It was in absolute chaos. On the other side of the force field, staff were running from workstation to workstation, attempting to manage the never-ending emergencies hitting the ship. Alarms were flashing, filling up every single screen in sight.

Reaching the corridor we entered from, we found Tanaka. He looked up and immediately dropped the outside field. After a faint flash of light, we stepped inside, and another burst told us we were sealed within.

"Decontamination should take about four minutes," Tanaka said.

Those four minutes were hell. It sucked monkey balls watching my crew running around trying to save the ship while I stood there basically useless. Of course, it didn't help how, in the process, it became even clearer just how short on crew we were. I swear, we'd just had a truck dropped on our legs, and there was no one there to help lift it off. The only good thing to come out of it was that I'd learned that Cruz could speak to me without being a dick. Who knew?

"Commander," Cruz said once Aridas and Tanaka had done a full recap of the issues. "Where do you want me?"

We were standing close, examining the screen on my armpad. His face was serious, ready for whatever I assigned.

"Sir," Tanaka said to me. "Engine fifteen just went down."

I groaned. Cruz closed his eyes and shook his head.

"I guess that decides it," I said to him.

He nodded. "I'll head to the engine room. You're off Module Two to fix the rotational field?"

"Yup."

"Think they're related?"

"Probably. Keep in touch. It might be a good idea to restart them simultaneously."

"They aren't on the same circuit."

"No, but when I was on my break, the lights were flickering. I started digging through all the alerts. The issues are deeper than we thought. We have to be systematic about the repairs." I pulled Aridas into the conversation. "Spec Aridas, please forward the repair findings to Cruz with all updates."

"On their way," she said.

We pulled them up. "There's a common cause. I thought we had more time, but it looks like one of the corrections set off another failure I didn't see coming."

As his gaze scrolled over the document, understanding lit his eyes. "Woah, um, yeah. This...sucks. So, the Solar Array Charge Interface connection into the Power Generator Housing locked up. This would have reset automatically if the ED-NICE system hadn't failed due to lack of maintenance which should have been performed what...fifteen years back?"

"Correct," I said. "And this caused the power payload to initiate these four failures at different times in the last five years which have now caused cascading failures in the systems here, here, and here." I pointed to the map of pure insanity on the screen. "I also identified the trial of failures which led to the collapse of Green House One. It has been sent over to the correct team, and they are working on it."

I glanced up at Mitchel. He was watching us, a scowl on his face. He was a smart man, but complex mechanics sometimes went over his head. Managing teams, verifying overarching processes went off without a hitch because he was amazing at that. His always-professional manner worked well for that type of job, but in-depth mechanical understanding? Not so much.

"What does this mean?" Michel asked.

"That it is going to be a long day," Cruz said, rolling his shoulders back.

"What do you two need from me?"

"People," Cruz said. "And we will need to work with your team during some of the reboot processes."

"Not a problem."

"Are you heading to the Bridge?" I asked.

"Yes." He glanced down to his armpad, then back up. "I have two teams headed to meet you. Use them as you see fit. Another has been sent to Connie Brackett on the re-animation deck."

"Please tell me those haven't gone down, too," I begged.

"No, but dealing with people just awake and with no gravity?"

"Oh, good lord," I said, taking a deep breath for patience. "Those poor people."

"I'll send Robins and Zerkule to help. They aren't on active duty yet," Cruz said.

"When's their first shift?"

"0500."

I nodded. "Good idea."

Cruz and I got in touch with a few of the teams. We assigned them to the various emergencies based on their expertise — or lack thereof. He was a huge help, stepping into the role of my second. It was as if he were meant for it. Probably because he was. Russel Cruz was a damn good engineer and soldier.

Every so often, one of our staff would appear in front of the field, ask a question, then dart away to do whatever we told them. Cruz took charge of his team, already digging into the engine problem. I watched as he read the stats on his armpad, then flashed quick looks up at Aridas, who sat at the far workstation. She'd nod, then click away, her mouth moving a million miles a minute.

"Ten seconds, and you are out of there. Remove the suits in case of any remaining contamination and leave them here," Tanaka said. We nodded.

"Captain Remian," I said, getting his attention. "We've assigned teams to hydroponics, drive systems, temperature control, and life support — since that just went down on deck ninety — and the rotational drive. I'm headed there. Master Sergeant Cruz will be leading the team on the drive system reboot."

"Sounds good. I'll be on the Bridge. They think they've figured out what caused this most recent spike of issues. I'll check it out and keep you updated."

As quickly as we could, we removed the suits and placed them on the nearby cart. As I was about to step out, I nearly fell, my foot getting caught in the leg. Cruz caught me without looking up.

"Thanks."

He grunted. "Comm Line Six if you need me, Commander."

"Updates as they come in, Commander, Sergeant." Mitchel's tone was harsh. I raised an eyebrow in question. He just shook his head.

In response, we said, "Yes, Captain."

Before they disappeared, I called, "Be safe. Don't be stupid." It's what I always hollered before a member of the team left on a mission. Why? Because they are the two hardest things any of us can do.

"You too," he said and disappeared out the door.

Chapter Nine

Commander Patrick Montgomery

The soft cushioned recliner molded to the sore muscles of my back and legs. My feet were up, my arms resting on two pillows. Even then, they felt like they were lying on a bed of nails. I curled my fingers, then extended them slowly, wondering how long it would take for the skin sensitivity to go away. Or for my muscles to stop screaming. I had aches not even basic training had triggered, and that had been the hardest thing I'd ever done. Which was why I avoided movement and sat as still as I could on the lone cushioned chair Norris had brought in for me, listening to Doc interrogate the captain.

My gaze traveled to where Richards slept. Above him, the screen showed the image which confirmed a "blue"— whatever that meant — its long abdomen similar to the one I carried. Its legs, however, were longer, giving it an arachnid feel. Then there was the set of extendable tentacles at both the head and tail of the creature. Those were common to all three types.

I shivered.

"So, you're telling me that these things killed your entire crew in a matter of four months?" Doc Mendez asked, gesturing to the screen. He sat in a chair, leaning back, hands behind his head, and eyes locked on Captain Victoria Norris.

They'd finished treating Richards before it was able to connect and cause any real damage, then settled around him to keep watch. The good news was, it was also done before he came to.

Norris's eyes met mine. "Yes. The infection spread quickly. Unfortunately, most were exposed like Patrick and were matched with a red. Because of this, they only lived a few days after infection."

I huffed. It was insane to see this younger version of Norris. I'd believed it was her from the moment she grabbed that tube and pulled it out of her own damn throat. She'd always been crazy like that. A complete and utter badass who showed her crew what hard work was.

She continued, "At least until we discovered the reaction the Cnidramarus have to radiation and magnetic fields. Then, we were able to slow it down." She stared at her hands, which kneaded together. "It was hard on them. Watching their friends and family die and having no control or way to help. It's why I will make it clear what will and won't work. You've asked me multiple times, Doctor, and I want to stress this again, surgical removal *will* kill them."

My gaze never left Norris. She looked so young compared to the last time I'd seen her. She'd always been interesting to look at. Not quite beautiful — partly because I was terrified of her — but fascinating with her large eyes and high cheekbones. She'd been a knockout in her youth. She still was, in her way, but with scars that marred her left chin and a crooked nose from one too many fights. But now, there was a sadness that hadn't been there before. Losing your crew would do that.

He watched her carefully for a few moments. "Who did you try it on?"

"Sarah." Her gaze dropped to the floor this time, pain filling her eyes. "She was infected by a red. Only eighteen, she had the highest chance of surviving, but while it moved down her spine, the medical team tried to remove it." She shivered, wrapping her arms around herself. "They started severing the connections one at a time. What we didn't know is that the Cnidramarus seriously inhibits the host's response to pain medication." Her eyes met mine. "It was torture. I don't know if you realize this, Patrick, but I gave you one hell of a dose of morphine earlier. Before...everything."

Doc's gaze narrowed and, in a harsher tone than I expected, said, "You did give him something."

She nodded. "It might not seem like it from the outside, but it helped."

"If that was with pain medications, I don't want to imagine without," I said.

She looked away. "No, you don't. Sarah begged them to stop, but they were convinced it would help. They kept telling her the meds were going to take effect. They never did."

A tear slipped down her cheek. At that moment, I saw every terrible event she'd been forced to face, many alone. Every single one of her people had died in front of her, and she could do nothing.

"When the last connection severed, she died. We hypothesized that when the creature reaches the spinal cord, they set links that allow them to connect to the host's timeline. There are several main locations, but the one at the base of the spine is the most important." She spoke to me this time. "That's the strongest connection. The red use their antennae to link in. That pop we heard during your last radiation treatment? That was at least one of the antennae being broken off. It doesn't kill them or take away their ability to force your aging, but it slows them down significantly."

"Why doesn't it stop them?"

"Because the antennae grow back."

My stomach rolled. I shifted in my seat and winced at the pain that lanced across my lower back. I settled again, finding a comfortable position that didn't put too much pressure on the burns marring my skin. It would take a while for those to go away.

When I'd looked at the wounds, the darkened, puckered flesh had caught me off guard. So had the raised section a few inches below the burn, which writhed in slow, methodical movements. They'd warned me, but it was completely different seeing it for myself.

"Like I told you before," she said to me now, "after treatment, the Cnidramarus move significantly slower for a few hours. By the time the antennae grow back, it will already have found its spot at the base of your spine, so it won't hurt like before. From there, the only concern is how quickly you'll age and if we can slow it down long enough to find a cure."

I nodded. How could this be real? Screw the bulge in my skin or the aching in my back and limbs. It couldn't be true. But Norris showed me the scans of the Elemental Crew. I couldn't deny anything after that. The images clearly captured the lobster-like body and the appendages reaching up, around, and into the spinal cord. The picture screamed, *"I am part of you now."*

"I don't believe it," Doc said, shaking his head. "We have to be able to remove it. Maybe they didn't do something right, hit something they shouldn't have."

"Dominic," I said to Doc, his first name demanding attention. "You saw the scans. It can't be removed, but maybe there's something else we can do. We've only begun to dig into the Elemental Crew's research, and we're in a much better place than they were. If I only have a few days, then I want to do everything I can for the ship and its crew."

"You are *not* dying, Patrick."

"We might not have a choice on that one, Doc, but I believe that between the three of us, we can figure it out and make sure we don't lose anyone else."

Doc stared at me for a long time. Then, with a sad droop to his shoulders, he turned back to Norris. He glanced to Richards's sleeping form, then said, "You indicated he has a blue." He rubbed his hands over his face. "Gosh, I feel like I'm back in primary school with this 'the blue one' or 'the red one.'"

That got Norris's lip to quirk. "I'm still not sure if you ever left, Mendez."

He shook his head, then said, "Seriously, what exactly is the difference between the red and the blue, and what does that mean for Geron?"

"That he has a better chance of survival." She shrugged. "When in the crystal, they can be identified by the differences in the body. They have slightly different physical attributes. The red Cnidramarus, or CR3, are the most dangerous. This is the one Patrick has, obviously. You can tell these apart by the antennae attached at the tip of their heads. The blues, we called CB2. They have extra legs on the abdomen, and they're longer. The last ones we called CC1. These are more opaque in color, and they're the ones each of us should hope we're infected with."

"We should wish to be infected?" Doc asked, shocked.

"Oh, hell no. I meant that if you were to be infected, you should be so lucky to have the CC1s. They are, from what we can tell, completely harmless. In fact, we've never had anyone infected by the CC1 alone."

"Then why do they exist?" I asked.

"That's the question we need to answer. We focused most of our research on the CR3 and the CB2, but from the initial research, we think the CC1s are a balance for the other two. We just couldn't figure out how. But back to your question about Richards. The CB2s? Instead of the host moving forward in time, they move backward. The speed varies based on the host, but it is still slower than when a CR3, or red, attaches. Our hypothesis is that it depends on the amount of energy the host had in their younger years. Was the child active versus lazy, sick versus healthy? What is really freaky about the CB2 is that as it shifts the bubble of time, the host re-lives all the emotional and physical changes they ever had. Broken bones, acne, hair loss... all of it. Svesnki was stoked when his hair grew back. He walked around like a peacock for days."

A bubble of laughter escaped without my control. I knew Svesnki. "Hold on. His hair grew back?"

"Yeah. Nearly overnight," she said, grinning. "He couldn't have been happier."

"I can't imagine Svesnki with hair," Doc said.

"The part that sucked, though? Even major medical events are re-lived."

Norris walked to the cooler, running her fingers over the glass, as if she were trying to touch her friends and tell them they were safe. The fetuses contained within the mechanical uteri system just wiggled in their uncontrolled manner. With a deep breath, she gestured to the one on the end.

"Javier, for example. He was in his fifties when he was exposed. Relatively healthy, if a little overweight, but as a child, he had a pretty serious illness. When he began to regress, everything was fine, overall, but then his age hit around fifteen." Her gaze locked on the squirming baby inside the silicone shell. "It slowed the Cnidramarus down. It was like the illness made it harder to connect to Javier. He was one of the earliest to be infected, but because of his past medical issues, he's still alive. It was really hard on him."

Seeing in her face how much the memory of that affected her, I asked, "Captain, how did you do this?" I gestured to the setup. "I looked around a bit, and the tech here is amazing. The way you integrated the pod into the shuttle is a miracle, but the uteri system you made? It's something else entirely. I've never seen anything like it."

"Remian said he'd heard of something like this back home, but it was classified," Doc said.

"By breaking a lot of laws." She tugged on her ponytail, which hung over one shoulder. Her green eyes were wary. "When the first of the crew began regressing, we just assumed that when they hit age zero, their birth date, the creature and the child would die. That's not what happened. We had them in bassinets first. One moment, they were squirming newborns, and the next, they were this."

"That is creepy as hell," I said under my breath.

"Yes, it is. The person you played poker with twice a week was suddenly a fetus in an amniotic sac. And by definition, not technically alive yet. Plus, we had no way to keep them. We didn't know if and how we were supposed to feed them."

"So you created one. You have an outer layer, and I assume that the fluid between acts as the transfer fluid for nutrients, but how is it getting to the child?" Doc asked.

"Look here."

Doc stood and headed to her side. With a lot more effort, I did, too. Norris slid open the glass door to the cabinet, then lifted something along the backside of the sac. She stepped back and gestured for us to look inside.

"Those tentacles are the ones that were once connected to the spine. As the body became smaller in size, they began to release. I assume because fewer connections with time are needed between the tiny body and the CB2. They started to collect and eventually created a makeshift placenta of sorts. If you look right here, there's a bundle of tentacles. From the analysis Dr. Veno did, they act as the parent. Well...sort of. Everything's collected by this section and filtered into the baby from there. Sadly, this regression stage takes the least amount of time, so very little research has been done. That's why I put them in hypersleep as soon as I could."

She looked at her once-friends. The pain in her face made my chest hurt and my limbs heavy. How long had she been alone?

She shrugged, then continued, "They regressed at different speeds, and yet somehow, I ended up with eight kids under the age of ten. Those last two weeks in the shuttle were rough. They were all so good, though. They helped get everything ready, and I was mostly able to have each of the baby pods ready when they flipped. I had to build one at a time, then decide who went in first depending on the speed of their regression." Her smile was sad. "They didn't understand, but they wanted to help even if that meant staying inside the field."

"You look at them like they're your kids," I said.

"At this point, they are. You don't want to know how many diapers I changed in those last four days. Or how many bottles I made. Let alone the number of times they puked on me." She grinned, and then it fell, her gaze turning sad and determined. "Which is why I need to find a way to reverse this. I need to save them."

"How?" Doc asked.

"The CC1s are the key. They're what we need to focus on."

"You haven't told us," I asked, leaning forward, my palms rubbing together absently. "How do they affect time?"

"I'm not completely sure, but I know they're the key."

"You said someone was infected by a CC1. Who was it?"

She licked her lips. "Me."

I straightened, my heart rate picking up. Doc's arms dropped to his sides.

"What? That doesn't make sense. Based on what you said and what you look like, you must've been infected by the CB2, the blue."

She strode slowly away, linking her arms behind her back. "I was. Then, we moved everything into the shuttle, quarantining ourselves and all research inside in hopes of keeping you all from waking up to this. We'd started section-by-section purges, removing the crystal from everywhere it had grown. You were all safe in your pods, and we knew there was no way to save us, but that didn't mean we couldn't save all of you. After the purge, we followed it up by treating each section using that process I sent to Spec Aridas. It worked, didn't it?"

We nodded. She'd confirmed as much an hour ago. Since treating Richards, we'd rested per the doctor's orders, and then dug into the logs.

"There has been no sign of the substance outside the shuttle area," I said.

"Good. So, we were almost done. I was working on getting the radiation field up, and I'd gone back outside to grab some supplies. I tripped on one of the kid's toys. We had an hour before the final sequence, and I fell directly onto a batch of samples. Multiple CC1s entered my bloodstream. Javier freaked out. He was still old enough to help me, and so we did some scans. Unfortunately, I became ill. I don't remember much, but Javier managed to keep the kids and me alive. When I woke up, I found that he'd done regular scans on me every hour. When I reviewed them, I tried to decipher exactly what was different, but I'm not Medical. I have some knowledge, but that's not where my strengths lie. Everyone who could've helped were toddlers. After that first day, we weren't able to do it anymore. It was just too crazy."

"Then that's where I need to start." Doc turned to me. "Patrick, while I am doing a full work-up on the captain, I need you to research something." He rubbed a hand over his close-cropped hair. "A long time ago, before cancer was eradicated, they used something called Seed Implants. They were pellets filled with a radioactive substance that was then placed into the body. While it's in there, the radiation would often shrink the tumor. Obviously, you don't have a tumor, but..."

"You think we could use the concept to treat the parasite?" I asked, my chest suddenly lighter.

"It's possible, but we'd have to modify it. I'm not sure if they could hold the type of radiation needed or if we have the supplies, but it's worth a look."

"I've never heard about anything like that," Norris said.

"That's because the practice isn't used anymore. There were too many side effects, and we've long since discovered better treatments. I don't know much. I just remember hearing about it in medical school and only in passing."

"I can handle side effects if it means I live," I said.

"Don't get ahead of yourself. We don't even know if we can develop them. But it's at least somewhere to start. Captain, can you help Patrick?"

"Of course."

Chapter Ten
Commander Tasha Evans

T he metal of the lockers was cool against my forehead. I pressed my cheek against the smooth door and reveled in the way it anchored me to the here and now. My nerves were fried, my emotions all over the place. It had been a hell of a day. Emergency after emergency, I'd run from one section of the ship to another.

"Hard day, Commander?" Dr. Brackett smiled kindly at me as she exited from the shower room. She held a small basket and a towel. Her hair was wet. "I heard about some of the things your team had to deal with after you helped fix the rotational fields in Module Two. Thanks for that, by the way."

With a chuckle, I nodded, then opened the small door to reveal my personal items. "Glad we got it taken care of. I'm sorry it took us so long."

It had been a bitch. Over an hour to figure out exactly what caused the failure, and then another three to fix it. The hardest part was getting my crew outside. So few of us had been awake long enough to qualify for a spacewalk. And those that had were not really qualified for such a complicated repair.

"You guys did amazing, and with the team Captain Remian sent down to help us evacuate the newly awakened, it wasn't so bad." She paused, grimaced, and then shrugged. "Mostly. Let's just say, I am grateful for the shower and the few hours of sleep I'm allotted. That was a lot of puke."

I laughed. "I heard. Well, enjoy the break. You've earned it."

Grabbing a few of her items, she waved and left the locker room.

I was glad that fix had gone so well. It had required a synchronized reboot with the one Cruz had been working on, which confirmed my suspicions that many of the failures were linked. Afterward, we'd set a plan for repairs. Patrick and the other team specialists had reviewed it as we'd rushed around the ship and added their two cents, too. Now it was about getting ahead of the problems.

Because today did not feel like we had. Instead, the list had only grown. The garden on four had failed twice — *twice*! For different issues, mind you. Then there it was Section Nine, followed by deck forty, the lighting on all of Module Four, and then the heating coil systems on...

Crap, I couldn't remember. One of the decks. And those were only the ones I showed up for. Cruz, Tanaka, and Aridas had been running teams all over the ship, too.

I closed my eyes and breathed in deeply. When was the last time I just breathed? Forever ago. Not since before I'd watched one of my best friends collapse after being infected by a time-altering parasite. I used the breath to release the tension in my chest. Ever since I came awake, it had been nothing but running. It all weighed me down.

I rolled my eyes. I was acting like a child. More so, I needed to sleep.

After the meeting. After I knew how Patrick was and if there was any update on the Elemental Crew, the Cnidramarus, and what in the world we were to do next.

It had been less than a day since I exited the shuttle, leaving Patrick behind to recover. I'd checked on him a few times, even collaborated on some of the issues *The Aspire* threw my way, but I had yet to find a moment to really talk to him. Or sit down. Or sleep.

Always back to the sleep. It was official; I was thinking in circles. Meh. Sleep's for chumps.

I pushed away from the locker I was somehow, once again, leaning against and groaned. I rolled my shoulders. The muscles in my thighs and calves complained as I bent down and grabbed a clean uniform from the bottom shelf. Based on the clock, the meeting would start soon, which meant I needed to get this oil-stained, sweat-drenched outfit off and into a clean one.

I raised my arm and sniffed my armpit. My lip curled, and I reached for my deodorant.

How had Aridas sat next to me for so long?

Pulling my shirt over my head, I grabbed the wet cloth from the bathroom and did what I could to relieve the smell. Then I swiped a generous amount of the bar under my arms. It would have to be enough. I was standing in my sports bra, wiping down my face and arm, when steps sounded behind me.

With a glance behind me, I found Cruz approaching. His head was down, a thoughtful expression on his stern face as he reviewed the tablet in his hands. His wavy brown hair was a rumpled mess as it flopped to the side, brushing his forehead. I grinned, noting he was as dirty as I was. Grease covered his hands, forearms, and even his face.

"You need a haircut," I said, moving to my other arm.

It wasn't a surprise to see him. This shared locker room branched off from the Main Engineering rec space and was reserved for the Command crew. Beyond it, multiple sections allowed for anyone who needed to relax, change, or clean up to do so. Each of the three separate locker rooms reserved for Engineering had sinks, bathrooms, showers, and even a reading area.

He skittered to a stop, his eyes meeting mine instantly. After a long breath, he dropped the tablet to his side and continued forward, heading toward his locker a few feet down from mine. "Sorry, I didn't see you. I was too..."

"Sucked into whatever new disaster we have to figure out next?" I said, rinsing the towel.

He chuckled, releasing the lock and reaching inside. The rich sound was something I rarely heard from him anymore. I felt like I'd just won a prize. Back when we were friends, before he became a snarky asshole, he used to laugh all the time. Then one day it changed, becoming deep scowls and noncommittal grunts.

"Basically," he said. "How did the repair to the dampener go?"

He fisted his shirt over his back and pulled it up and off. The fabric slid up slowly, exposing tanned, warm skin. Without a thought, he rolled it into a ball and tossed it into his locker.

I tore my eyes away, focusing instead on scrubbing a particularly stubborn patch of grease on my neck. I did not bite my lip, and I did not look back to trace the definition of the muscles down his back or the tattoo over his left shoulder blade. Nope. I didn't.

I swallowed hard, then threw the now-blackened, second cloth I'd used into the dirty laundry at the end of the aisle.

I cleared my throat and said, "Fine. It's back up and running. I got to work with that new kid. Robertson something?"

He faced me, and it was like my eyes had a mind of their own. They trailed along the lines of his chest.

Damn it! What was wrong with me? I was checking him out! Wait, no. I was cataloging the change in his physique since being in hypersleep. Yeah, that was it. He'd always been tall and lengthy; he had muscles. Geron and I trained with him all the time, and his physique had never distracted me before. So, it had to be that they'd diminished some while in hypersleep that I'd noticed. Right?

Yup, that was it.

I forced myself to meet his eyes.

"Yeah," Cruz said, thankfully not noticing my ogling. "Good kid. Super smart."

"That's for sure. Did you know he's never been on a real spacewalk? At least not until today."

His jaw dropped. "You have got to be kidding me."

"Nope." I smirked. "So, I had to go out with him since I was the only one with certifier credentials."

Cruz cursed. He made like he was about to step forward but stopped himself.

"You shouldn't have done that with so little sleep. That was dangerous. For both of you."

My eyes narrowed, and the irritation built in my chest. "There wasn't much of a choice," I snapped. After throwing another cloth into the basket, a little harder than I probably should have, I went to grab a clean one from the stack. I wet it, then headed back to my locker. Cruz hadn't moved.

"I know," he said. He held my gaze a moment before lowering his head and turning his back to me. "I have no doubt you got the job done, and I'm sure Robertson appreciates having such a great teacher."

How was I supposed to react to such a comment? Reaching into my compartment, I pulled out a brush to wrangle my hair, which had been a complete disaster when I'd glimpsed it in the mirror. I needed it under control, or no one would take me seriously.

Clearing my throat and deciding it was time to change the subject, I asked, "So, what is it this time? Another engine down, the Hydroengineers freaking out because the filter is growing mushrooms, or let me guess, cannibalistic leprechauns were found in Main Engineering?"

He snorted, walked over to the sink, and wet one of the washcloths. He began to rub it over his neck, across his shoulder, down his arms. Every so often he'd rinse it, then start over again.

"Well, Tanaka got back to me. It looks like you were right. The original failure was caused by a patch of dust hitting the coils along the starboard side. They burned up. I guess he and Oresen — I don't know him —

from Mitchel's crew found it." He rinsed the cloth again, taking a second to scrub his face clean of the oil smeared across his cheek. His back flexed as he moved.

I didn't look. Swear.

"Three of the shields were damaged and require repair. It went several layers deep. He said we're lucky there were no breaches. Anyway, they confirmed there's build-up that needs to be removed and a panel replaced. Maybe more. The cloud also clogged one of the thrusters. From their review, it'll happen again, seeing as we're entering the very outer reaches of Eronis 8's Magnetosphere."

"And let me guess, someone requested additional power to be rerouted to the hangar bay so the external shielding was not at full strength?" I removed my uniform bottoms, pulled on a clean pair of loose-fitting pants, then sat on the bench and reached for my shoes.

I leaned to the side, resting on my outstretched arm. A soft fabric bunched under my fingers, and I realized I still sat in only my bra, the fresh shirt on the bench next to me.

Heat rushed to my face. I looked up to find Russel had frozen at some point, his gaze locked on me. He watched me through the mirror with an interest and longing I hadn't seen in a long time lighting his eyes.

He cleared his throat. "Sorry," he said, a blush rising on his cheeks.

Holy hell, how had I never noticed? I must've been blind. Or his annoyance factor had been so high I didn't want to see it.

He blinked rapidly, then tossed the washcloth into the basket. He approached his open locker and grabbed clean clothes.

"Yeah," he said. "I heard some know-it-all commander who thinks she's better than everyone else ordered it."

Fire erupted in my chest. Better than everyone else? I jumped to my feet, ready to bite back when, shirt in hand, he faced me. His eyes were a challenge, taunting and ready for a fight. He was trying to change the subject. He thought it was funny. I could see it, the joy of getting a rise out of me. Damn, he knew I liked to banter.

"You did that on purpose."

He stepped closer. "Too bad she was right."

My mind stuttered at those words. Maybe I was having a stroke?

"It wasn't your fault, Commander. It was the right call. If you hadn't ordered it, one of us would have." His eyes never left mine, his absolute certainty on the matter clear in his gaze. "But you're always the one to think of our safety first."

Then, as if to shock me again, Russel Cruz, the bane of my existence, reached out and brushed a strip of hair out of my face and looped it behind my ear. His throat constricted as he swallowed hard.

"You need to put your shirt on," he said, voice deeper than normal.

"Because we have a meeting in a few minutes," I stated, gazing up into his face. There was so much emotion written in his expression, but I couldn't decipher it all. Usually, he stomped around, his eyes never truly opening to those around him. Only with certain people would he open up. I'd get glimpses, but it had been over a year — awake time — since he'd shown me any of this.

"Yes, and no," he said softly. "It's because you're my commander, were once my friend, but you're also beautiful and if you don't, I'm not sure I won't spill my secret."

His secret. My heart pounded in my chest, those old feelings I'd had for him so long ago stirring within. I couldn't let that happen. Friend? Russel wasn't my friend anymore. He didn't treat me like he used to. He didn't deserve my affection.

"I don't understand. You've been an ass to me for so long."

He moved closer, but I don't think he knew he'd done it.

"I know," he whispered. "And I'm sorry. Maybe it's better if you keep on hating me, but I don't know if I can do it anymore."

My eyes narrowed on him, taking in his beautifully sculpted jaw and thoughtful gaze. I fought the urge to reach up and touch his bottom lip. "Why?"

He just shrugged.

"Then don't..." The words were more air than anything.

"I can't fix the past, but I will make sure it stops now," he said.

"How can I trust that you —" I started.

"Commander Evans, Sergeant Cruz!" Mitchel called, stepping through the doorway. His shoulders were back, his arms crossed over his chest. He ground his teeth before he sucked in his cheeks.

We jumped away from each other, automatically straightening to attention. Disappointment and regret glowed in Russel's eyes, but inside me, I felt only confusion. It had been a long time since my feelings for him had been anything but irritation. It would take a lot more than one conversation to fix that. In truth, he might never be able to. And yet, in just one conversation, he had somehow transitioned in my head. He was no longer Cruz, he was Russel again. Would it stay that way?

"Captain Remian. Is it time?" I asked with a quick clearing of my throat. I yanked the shirt I held over my head.

From the corner of my eye, I saw Russel do the same. Then he sat and laced his boots before returning to my side.

I shoved all my stuff into the locker, then slammed it shut before I faced Mitchel. I was pulling my hair into a messy bun when he asked, "Yes. Is everything good here?"

"Just discussing the next round of repairs needed. Don't worry, we'll have it fixed and all teams ready to focus on the Merocius approach in twenty-four hours."

"Maybe thirty-six," Russel said. "The thruster might take longer. We'll have to see."

I nodded. Mitchel, however, was shooting daggers at Russel.

"Come on, I'm sure Doc and Patrick are waiting. We're doing this in conference room five, right?" I asked, stepping toward Mitchel. He had cleaned up since we'd last seen him, but I doubted he'd slept. He too had been dealing with problems all over the ship.

"Yes. They should be on in five," Mitchel said.

"Who all besides the three of us are listening in?" Russel asked.

Mitchel pressed up to Russel, and I had to roll my eyes when he said, "I don't think your attendance is necessary. You aren't Command."

Either Mitchel needed sleep, or he was losing his damn mind. The question was, which one?

"Actually," Russel said, his tone surprisingly controlled. "First Lieutenant Samson died during reanimation, remember? All others of his rank have not been brought back on shift. Therefore, I am the next highest-ranking officer. With Patrick out of rotation and Command, this means I am her second. Therefore, I need to know what is happening so that I can cover should she be needed."

A vein in Mitchel's forehead throbbed. He pressed closer, causing Russel to take a step back. Just like that, I was done. Russel had done nothing today other than bust his butt to get the ship functioning again. I stepped between them, and Russel immediately made room for me.

"Captain Remian, I don't know what this is about, but if this continues, I will start thinking you're questioning my leadership. We've been up for days now, but that is no excuse to attack a fellow officer."

"Attack?" His eyes went wide.

"You stopped his progress, invaded his space, and raised your voice. Do I need to have Doctor Mendez order you to your quarters for Rec time?"

He met my eyes, then snarled, "You wouldn't."

I smirked.

"You know I would. I've done it before when you needed it." I placed my hand on his arm. "But we can't afford that right now. We need you. So, get your head out of your ass and go to this meeting. We need to figure out what they've learned about the Cnidramarus. You know, those parasite things killing our friends?"

He growled, spun, and led the way out.

As his figure disappeared, I squeezed the bridge of my nose. I did not have the energy to wrangle any more people today.

As if he'd read my mind, Russel said, "You are way too good at managing us. It's a little disturbing."

It was so unexpected to hear him say almost the same thing I'd just been thinking that I huffed a laugh. Had he always known that was what I was doing?

"Shut up," I said, bumping his shoulder before following in Mitchel's wake.

"What? You did it to me yesterday in the shuttle, and I heard about you handling that young kid who freaked out on his first emergency spacewalk."

"I just told you about that."

With a wink, he said, "Commander, I heard about that long before you told me. It was all over the ship. Plus, my team was working nearby, remember?"

I had to think about that.

"Not really, but he did a good job. Don't make fun. He's not usually one of the crew who works on the outside of the ship, but he sucked it up and got it done."

"First, I'm not making fun and, you're right, he did a good job. But that doesn't take away how dangerous it was for you to be out there."

I glared at him, and he held up a hand.

"I won't bring it up again. And so you know, that's also why I assigned him to Tanaka's team. I thought you'd approve," he added.

I sucked in a breath and smiled at the man next to me. "I do approve. Thank you."

He nodded, then gestured for me to enter before him. I hadn't even noticed we'd arrived.

When we entered, people I recognized from all departments were in attendance —Medical, Research, Climatology, the Bridge, Security, even Ship Maintenance. Three empty chairs sat near the center, and another two at the far end. Mitchel was lowering himself into the seat on the left, so I took the one on his right. Russel fell in beside me.

"Have they let you sleep yet, Commander Evans?" one of the hydroponic techs said.

"What about you, Sergeant?" a kid from Climatology added. "You've both been running circles since yesterday."

Romano, one of Geron's men, spoke up this time. "If they slept, the ship would sink."

"You do know we're in space, right?" I didn't know this speaker, but I had to laugh.

"You never know, Romano, things can get weird out here in space, but to answer your question, no we haven't." I glanced at Russel, then Mitchel. "It's been, what, forty-eight hours? I feel great."

"Naw, the captain got a few hours rest earlier," Tanaka said, entering the room. "Or that's what I heard from the Bridge."

"Yeah," Russel added. "And I took a nap under one of the workstations in the engine bay. I swear I got a whole thirty minutes."

"Quit bragging," I said.

The room filled with laughter and suddenly, I felt better. To me, these few moments of normal were worth everything. They were better than sleep, or so I tried to tell myself. And for these people, I would continue to bust my butt if it meant they survived.

The room fell silent again as the door opened. Doc Mendez walked in, and I had to hold back the urge to hug him. I hadn't known he was out. Granted, I'd been in a very tight bubble of chaos that hadn't let up, so it wasn't that surprising. As he found a seat near the end of the table, the screen above it lit up with the faces of Geron, Patrick, and Norris.

"Geron, you're awake!" I blurted out before I could stop myself.

He smiled. "Have been for a few hours. You've just been busy. I heard a lot of whining from Patrick that he can't be out there helping."

"Yeah, I've heard that too," I said, chuckling. "But I'm sure they've kept you busy."

"Definitely. And we have a lot to discuss."

"That we do," Patrick said, taking the lead. "And as time is of the essence, why don't we get started? Thank you everyone for coming. As you know, I am Commander Patrick Montgomery. Most of you know what has happened over the last few days, but for those who do not, or have just come back on shift, here is the rundown."

I listened as he explained everything that had happened up to this point — the late re-animation of the crew, the timeline to Merocius, the missing Elemental Crew, and the discovery of the Cnidramarus. I kept my face blank as he spoke, finding that his words flowed over me without really absorbing. I was too focused on Patrick and the changes so apparent in his face.

Patrick had aged. There were new lines at the corners of his eyes and mouth. His dark hair, which had only held a light spattering of gray, was now thick with silver at the temples. There were bags under his eyes, and they looked dimmer than the last time I'd seen them, as if he were ill with a fever that had yet to break. Patrick was aging right before my eyes.

I didn't realize I'd been clenching my fists until a hand settled on my forearm. I looked down at Russel's large paw, then up to his face. He leaned in to whisper in my ear.

"He's doing well. The radiation treatment worked. It slowed the CR3 down. Patrick told me that they estimate he's aged between four and seven years. From what Norris says, that's significantly slower than most of the others infected. He told me they have a plan for treatment. That's one of the things they're going to discuss. He wanted me to tell you to stop freaking out. That this more distinguished look is gonna catch all the ladies."

My surprised snort had several of the attendees glancing my way. Russel moved back a few inches so that he could meet my eyes.

"How do you know all this?" I asked.

"I called Patrick an hour ago."

His face was so close. Deep brown eyes watching me from under thick eyelashes. I inhaled the sweet smell of him; sweat mixed with the fresh scent of his uniform. Warmth filled my chest, and I realized he didn't smell of that nasty cologne he always wore. Was that because he'd forgotten to put it on, or was there another reason?

Through a thick throat, I leaned in to whisper in his ear. His stubble tickled my cheek. "You're not wearing that nasty cologne."

The rumbling chuckle so close had me closing my eyes.

"I only wore that to annoy you."

I pushed back, straightening in my chair. He did the same, his lips twitching.

"You did not!" I said, my voice going high-pitched.

His eyebrow arched as if to say, *wouldn't I, though?*

I crossed my arms over my chest like a petulant child and glared. Seriously? I could feel eyes on me, so I schooled my expression and sat back.

With a calming breath, I said to him, "Thank you for checking on Patrick."

He inclined his head to me, the smirk lifting his lip, making me want to hurt him.

Focusing back on the conversation, I was happy to find I hadn't missed much. Patrick, however, was watching me, a curious look on his face.

Chapter Eleven

Commander Patrick Montgomery

It sucked performing this debrief over the damn Comm line. I should be in the room, sitting around that fucking table, with all of my closest friends, and looking into their eyes. Not staring into a screen that only showed me half the room at a time. And not having all the detail and emotion roiling through the air as my words filled the room. It made me feel stunted. I hated it, and yet I continued to outline everything that had happened up to this point for those who hadn't heard it all.

All I could do was take in the subtler movements of those on screen — Doc shifting in his seat, Tasha's flinch, or Mitchel's ticking jaw.

Of course, Mitchel's twitching could be for another reason altogether. Hell, his entire body was tense. My guess was it had something to do with the way Cruz was leaning over to whisper in Tasha's ear. If I could, I'd tell him it was only to inform her about the conversation Cruz and I had had this afternoon — one that had caught me off guard, actually.

Cruz had foreseen the reaction Tasha would have at the sight of the changes in my appearance. Though she'd kept her face blank, she'd gone stark white, and the side of her cheek was trapped between her teeth. Knowing her, her fists were clenched under the desk as well.

The gray hair at the sides of my temples was the most obvious, but it was the excess weight in my midsection that had caught me off guard. I wasn't fat, but I wasn't as fit as I was yesterday.

Yesterday! What the hell happened to make my older self so lazy?

Tasha snort-laughed — my favorite of her laughs — and her eyes shot to the screen. She rolled her eyes, but I knew that teasing glint. She'd get me back for telling her my "new distinguished look would catch all the ladies." It wasn't true. I'd only said that to get a reaction. I looked away from the woman who was the sister I never wanted, and would never admit I'd needed, and focused on the others in the room.

The group we'd gathered were some of the best on the ship, and if we worked together, we'd not only make it to Merocius, but get there with limited casualties. If I was lucky, maybe I'd be one of the survivors.

"Captain, do I have permission to move forward with the meeting?"

"Yes, Commander, everyone is in attendance," Mitchel said.

"Thank you, sir. We've brought you all together because you are essential to *The Aspire* and our team here," I said, taking a moment to look at each face. "We are in serious danger, and it is time to discuss the plan moving forward. That said, there are a few priorities requiring discussion as not only does our ship require years of delayed maintenance, but repair from various storms. Additionally, we are behind on preparations for approach to Merocius. But what we are here to discuss is the new threat to our crew, the Cnidramarus. As you have been told, several of us have been infected. We believe that it's contained, but things out here in space change in a blink."

That was a lot of information to dump on them all at once, but Norris, Mitchel, and I thought it was the best way to start. As those around the table began to breathe heavier, shift in their seats, and look downright ill, my thought on the subject might have shifted.

Mitchel was ready. He lifted a calm hand and said, "I know it sounds bad, and it is, but we have a plan. Please, just listen to Commander Montgomery's debriefing."

That smooth accent and unwavering confidence did what it always did — it sunk into everyone in the room. Second by second, I watched as they took in his unworried expression and relaxed back into their seats.

How did he do that?

Mitchel nodded to the screen, indicating for me to continue.

"As you can guess, this means that we need all hands on deck...um, not that we haven't already been doing that." I shrugged and, mixed in with the quick verbal agreements, came a handful of amused and slightly overwhelmed chuckles. I shook my head, then continued, "We have a few priorities to discuss. First off is the ship. Over the last twenty-four hours, we've made a lot of progress. The captain, Commander Evans, and Sergeant Cruz have been working with teams all over the ship to get *The Aspire* back up and running. She's hurting, and we need to get her stable again. We — and a few of the other section leaders — have set a schedule of repairs, which should get us back on track, barring any additional issues."

Several people were nodding absently.

"With more of the team coming back on shift," Tasha said, "we're starting to get our feet under us. I doubt we've found all the issues, but we're ready for them when they pop up."

I inclined my head to her. "Both you and Cruz have kept me in the loop, and I'm impressed with what you've achieved in the last twenty-four hours, but over the next few weeks, you'll be pulled into some of the projects we're about to discuss. These projects will be of the highest urgency. So, we'll need to review the manifest, verifying who's awake and ready them to step in where possible."

"Yes, Commander."

I ran a hand over my jaw and took a deep breath, praying the next part came out right.

I glanced at the image of Doc Mendez. He'd left a few hours ago when his containment suit needed to recharge. He also required rest. While outside, he planned to access the more in-depth medical archives about the radiation seed implant idea. He'd found some notations which convinced him the plan would work, but he wanted to do some deeper digging. Ultimately, the deciding factor would be if we had the supplies, if we could manufacture them, and if they were safe. He hoped to talk to a few of the researchers and medical staff in this room about the proposal.

My questions were more along the lines of, could we test them? How and on whom?

Doc must've known where my thoughts had gone because he shot me a look that said, *"Well, I guess it's time to sound crazy."*

I grinned.

His words from earlier filled my mind. *"We're in this together. We'll figure this out."*

I paused, swallowing down the worry, then said, "Beyond the ship repairs, which we will discuss in more detail later, there are three main projects that are of the highest priority. The first is to be headed by Doctor Mendez. The initial treatment and spread of the Cnidramarus. Doctor, if you would?"

I flipped the screen to that of the three vials sitting in front of me. The CC1, CB2, and CR3 each scuttled in their jars, moving around and through the crystal shards we'd collected. There was a mixture of disgusted and fascinated gasps from those around the table.

"Thank you, Commander Montgomery," Doc said. He gestured to the image. "The Cnidramarus live in the crystals currently contained within the field around the shuttle in Bay 1. As explained, these parasites attach to the spinal cord of the host and feed off their life energy." He clasped his hands in front of him on the desk. "The Elemental Crew were vital in discovering that certain wavelengths of radiation damage these creatures."

As if unable to sit still, he pushed to his feet and began to pace in the front of the room, hands behind his back.

"Montgomery was infected with the CR3. During his treatment, Captain Victoria Norris of the Elemental Crew was able to properly damage the CR3 and slow its progress. Via scans, we have confirmed that during treatment, both antennae were broken away. This means that it cannot delve into his timeline as effectively. The problem is, these antennae grow back. This outlines the main goal my team will be focusing on."

Captain Norris spoke up from beside me. Her strong, clear voice said, "The Cnidramarus can be hurt, we know this, but the current line of treatment is painful and extremely dangerous to the host. It's effective in the short term, but not long term. We need to find a treatment that will last until we can discover a way to kill them."

Glancing away from the screen and Norris's face, Doc nodded. He rested his hands on the table and addressed the group sitting before him. "When I was in training, we learned about past treatments for diseases that have since been eradicated. During this lesson, they discussed something called radiation pellets as a treatment for cancer. Do any of you have experience with this type of treatment?"

Med Tech Julian Verandas, a man only a few years out of school, shook his head. His education was a little different than the other two — more emergency and combat oriented — so it was doubtful he would've been exposed to this idea.

"I'm sorry, Doctor Mendez, I have not," Doctor Dale Gollie said, his bright blue eyes standing out starkly against his ebony skin. He was a long, lean man in his late thirties with a sharp intelligence and creative mind.

Doctor Verana Pia, a veteran physician with more than twenty years' experience, nodded. Her long black hair fell in tight ringlets to her shoulders, framing her round face. Her accent was hard to place, but it was beautiful. Thoughtfully, she said, "When I was in medical school, I took a course covering various types of retired clinical practices. One of my study groups did a project on something similar to this."

"I remember discussing it with you. I'm hoping we might be able to utilize this knowledge," Doc Mendez said. She sent him a kind smile. "Because I believe that this may be a viable option for treatment. I doubt it will kill the parasite, but maybe we can delay the progression by implantation near the connection sites. With continuous exposure, I hypothesize that the host's time alterations will slow significantly."

"It's possible," she agreed.

"The idea would be to create these implants and have Doctor Gollie, as our Head Surgeon, place them. They're in a very sensitive area, and we need them close, but not so close as to damage the spinal cord."

Gollie nodded and said, "Of course. That shouldn't be a problem."

"After this meeting," Doc added, "I'd like to meet with you two, and anyone else you think might be helpful, so we may determine if this is a viable option. Then we need to see if we have the appropriate supplies necessary for their creation. I also believe we should bring in Research Specialist Simone Renownski. Her research in magnetic resonance and electromagnetic wave manipulation could come in handy. Cruz, we will be contacting you as well."

Cruz nodded.

Doc glanced around, his brow furrowing. "Actually, where is Renownski?"

"The shields were struggling in Sector 65," Cruz explained.

"They were?" Tasha said, her hand flying to the tablet resting before her. Her back was tight, face concerned.

Cruz held his tablet up for her to see. "Already on it. I'm in constant communication with Renownski and her team. They have it handled. This was the emergency I was dealing with when we met up. I was going to discuss it with you, but we got distracted."

"Oh," she sighed, taking the tablet from Cruz and reading through the information. A moment later, her posture relaxed.

"Sergeant Cruz touched base with me about it since you were dealing with something else," I said.

Tasha glanced at me. I nodded. Her attention fell back to Cruz's tablet before they exchanged a few quiet words, and she settled back into her seat.

Doc pulled our attention back to the conversation at hand. "Well, I'd like to bring her up to speed and see if she can help. Richards has agreed to be the first injected."

"I am still not okay with that," I grumbled.

Richards grinned, then, patting my shoulder, said, "I'm less important than you, Patrick."

Chuckling flowed through the speakers, and I scowled. He was joking, but that didn't mean I liked it.

Med Tech Verandas cut in, his expression hard as he addressed Doc Mendez. "Doctor Mendez, you mentioned the potential for future infections. How likely is that, and do we have mitigation strategies in place?"

Captain Norris spoke this time. "Previously, infections came unexpectedly. The Cnidramarus do not travel from host to host. They are impressive little creatures that managed to spread all over the ship before we secluded ourselves. Most of it, we couldn't explain. That's why we came up with the treatment plan we did for the ship. I'll be meeting with a select team to discuss how we can alter it moving forward considering there are people awake and unshielded this time around. Plus, the radiation device we used was damaged during its last usage."

"I think we should include Ship Maintenance in this meeting as well as this will affect them," Mitchel said.

Verandas and the Ship Maintenance group in attendance agreed.

"That sounds great," I said. "As you can all see, Doctor Mendez has been assigned to head the radiation implant project and verify plans are in place to stop an outbreak. Several others on various teams will be brought in as necessary, so if you have any questions, please address them to him."

I linked my fingers together, placing my elbows on the table.

"The next two priority projects link together, and I believe are the most important items." With a glance to Norris, I continued, "Upon review of the Elemental Crew's records, I found something very interesting."

As if sensing my attention on her, Tasha sat straighter in her chair.

"Prior to the Cnidramarus Crystals entering the ship, they were attached to a meteorite that emitted a strong radioactive frequency. Why is this important? Well, from Major Bentley's documentation, the crystal and the Cnidramarus did not begin to grow until after it was removed."

Now Cruz had straightened, as did a few from the research teams.

"Where there was less than five grams initially, after forty-eight hours of being outside this field, it had doubled in size," I said.

"Is this field similar to what you have around the medical bay in the shuttle?" Tasha asked.

"Similar, but not the same," Norris said.

Tasha leaned forward, eyes alight. She shared a look with Cruz, then returned her stare to me. He had a similar manic look in his eye.

"Do we have scans of the emissions? Was the information documented?" Tasha asked.

With a grin, Norris leaned forward and loaded the only screenshot we had of the initial measurements taken.

"When we picked up the meteor, we didn't realize it was important. Only the minimal, required scans were performed. Due to the potential hazard to the crew, the sample was quickly destroyed and used for fuel. It was only after the crystal was removed, and Bentley became sick, that we realized we had destroyed our only information."

"Can you send that to us?" Tasha asked.

"Already done," Norris said.

"There has to be a link between the frequencies emitted and the lack of growth..." she muttered to herself.

"We believe so, too," I said.

"Which is why, we request that you, Commander Evans, and your team review this and see if a common link can be found. It was only after finding this that I realized where the idea for the radiation gun came from," Norris admitted.

Tasha was scanning her screen, zooming in, and reading the notes linked to it. Cruz leaned over her shoulder, his experience in aircraft radiation shielding potentially helpful.

"There are at least seven different frequencies here. Have any of these been tested against the Cnidramarus?" she asked.

"Some, but not all," I said. "I've only been through a handful of the Elemental Crew reports on this. There aren't all that many because, not long after they started, the two crew members working on it passed away."

"That was when the infection rates got so high, we began retreating from parts of the ship," Norris explained. "We need you two to lead a group to investigate what this means. With your backgrounds, and that of several of the researchers present, we believe you are the best team to take this on."

I took over. "There are a few things we need to know." I ticked them off on my fingers. "One, which frequencies subdue the Cnidramarus?

Two, is there a way to use these wavelengths, even by alteration so that instead of subduing them, we can kill them?"

"Without additional harm to the host," Doc added.

"Of course" — I nodded — "and then, three, can we produce these frequencies in enough quantities to treat the entire ship?"

Cruz's deep timbre brought my gaze to him. He looked up from the tablet now on the table between the two, their heads bent together as they reviewed the readings.

"We'll also need to test the three different types to see how they react," he said. "I should be able to make a device that emits these frequencies, but it'll take some time. It will need to be shielded properly. As the captain knows, some of these can be dangerous to us, too. But my biggest concern is, the shuttle isn't equipped, nor big enough, to house the team required for such testing."

"It's also not an easy process to come and go," Tasha added.

"What do you suggest, then?" Mitchel asked.

Tasha turned to the Head of Research and Development, Doctor Michelle Adams. I couldn't remember what specific department or specialty she worked in, but her reputation definitely preceded her. She had only been awake a few hours, which is why I think she'd stayed quiet as long as she had.

With pursed lips, Dr. Adams blinked, pushed a strand of her curly red hair behind her ear and said, "Well, the research labs one section over from where you are, are highly advanced. If I remember correctly, one in particular would be perfect for this."

She stood and walked to the monitor along the wall. A few seconds later, she had the schematics of the lab pulled up on the screen for everyone to see.

Tasha nodded, a slow grin spreading across her face. "I know this area. It *is* highly advanced. It would be easy to create a similar force field around this section to that of the shuttle. I might even be able to secure the corridor."

"Make it happen," Mitchel said.

"Since the three of you can't leave until a long-term treatment is confirmed, maybe one of you can help get us samples?" Cruz asked.

"We can do that. There are also a few tests we'd like to perform," I said.

"I'm in," Geron said.

"Great. But back to Patrick's question." Tasha's voice was thoughtful. "I don't know if we can produce a field large enough to treat the ship like you said. We might have to do something similar to what the Elemental Crew did."

"We don't have the supplies to make another device like they used." Cruz rubbed at the stubble along his jaw as he spoke.

Tasha's shoulders dropped.

"Maybe we can get them from an external source?" Dr. Adams said. "Sometimes stars or planets will emit radiation. We brought in a meteor that did."

"What are the probabilities that we will find another in the same system?" Cruz snapped.

"We have to try," Tasha said, shooting a glare at Cruz.

A few others continued the string of thought, but my attention was still on Tasha and Cruz. It was like Cruz realized he'd done something wrong. His eyes went wide, and then he leaned over to say something only to Tasha. She leaned away, but he reached out and stopped her. Whatever he said had her eyebrows lowering in thought, and her lips pressing together. Her arms crossed over her chest, but she relaxed a little.

That was new.

"Commander Montgomery, we have one more item to discuss, correct?" Mitchel asked, bringing my attention back to the conversation.

Right, the important stuff. Had no one been watching me, I would have rolled my eyes.

"As we begin to perform tests on the Cnidramarus, we need to also prioritize how the three different types interact. We need to figure out why there are three, and specifically what role the CC1 — the clear Cnidramarus — plays."

"May I ask," one of Dr. Adams's team members said, "what does the CC1 do? You never said."

"We don't know," Norris said this time. "And there has only ever been one person that we are aware who was infected with one. Me."

"What?" Mitchel and Cruz said simultaneously. They shot to their feet.

She held up her hand and continued when the conversation calmed a bit. "As we sequestered the remaining crew into the shuttle, I was exposed to a high burst of radiation. Then I was inadvertently exposed to the CC1s. Javier, one of my crew, did a full body scan and bloodwork while I was unconscious. He was fifteen at the time. Because of his regression and...well...everything else, we were unable to perform any more tests prior to my going into hypersleep. But, I can say that before I fell asleep, I noticed a difference. I felt different, but it wasn't until Doctor Mendez did a complete workup of me earlier today that I knew what changed."

Norris crossed, then uncrossed her legs. "I not only carry the CB2, but now also the CC1. It looks like the CC1 has attached itself to the back of the CB2."

Scattered conversations popped up around the room, and questions were fired at Norris from all directions.

"Has the CC1 stopped your regression?" Dr. Pia asked.

"Is this dangerous?" Mitchel asked.

"How? Wait, is the CC1 changing the CB2?" Tasha asked.

"Do you think the radiation burst you were exposed to allowed the CC1 to attach?" Cruz asked.

Doc Mendez held up a hand, and the room fell silent. "This is some of what we need to figure out. It's also why so many of you have been brought in. We need each and every one of you because, as you can see, there are a lot of facets that need to be explored."

"Everyone in this room," I said, "has experience that may come in handy as we begin this exploration, or you might know someone on your team with expertise that could help. We need volunteers from every team. From what Captain Norris said, it is only a matter of time until another outbreak happens. We are less than four months to Merocius. We must stop this infection before we reach our new home."

The room fell silent, a deep thoughtful aura hovering between us all.

With a clap of his hands, Mitchel stood. "All right. We know next steps. Commander Montgomery, Commander Evans, Sergeant Cruz, and Doctor Mendez are leading these studies. As Commander Montgomery stated, and I second, these are of the highest priority. So, unless it's for emergencies, these should be your focus. With so many teams coming back on shift, we have more people to assign to Merocius approach protocols, general day-to-day maintenance, and ship repairs as they come. Contact any one of them if you have questions."

Stepping back from the table, he pushed his chair in, glanced down at his armband, then said, "Thank you. Keep me updated." He gestured to the door, then nodded to those of us on the screen. "Let's get to work."

Those sitting around the conference table stood and headed for the door. The team leads spoke to those who left, letting them know of later meetings which would occur. With a glance at me, Mitchel, Tasha, and Cruz left the room.

I flicked off the camera and spun to face Norris.

"Well, that was fun," she said.

Closing my eyes, I shook my head and leaned back in my chair, hands behind my head.

"We've got a good crew. We'll figure it out."

"Yes, we will," she said. "Now why don't we go get the samples we'll need for the experiments? I think we can handle a few minutes at a time outside the field."

Richards and I nodded. We pushed to our feet, grabbed the sample collection kits, and followed Norris out to the hallway. It was time for the work to begin.

Chapter Twelve
Captain Mitchel Remian

The scans couldn't be right. And yet here I stood, the sensation of razor-sharp rock digging into my palms as I gripped the edge of the desk. I'd been like this ever since Aridas had brought me the report now resting on the wood before me. If I could've shoved my hands through the table, or snapped a piece of it off, I might have tried because maybe — just maybe — it would make me feel better.

Every time I thought we were making progress, something else would go wrong, and we didn't need anything else broken.

"As you can see, Captain" — Aridas pointed to the image — "although we released the remaining Cnidramarus dust into space as per the instructions provided by Captain Norris, and the containment area treatment was started, there are signs that not all was expelled."

"What made you check the section today?" I asked.

She shrugged. "A hunch. After the meeting yesterday, I met with Commander Evans. She's requesting my help with the tests to be performed on the Cnidramarus. With my background, she believes I can manage the technical and research expectations this project requires."

Aridas rested her elbows on the workstation we huddled around. While I stood, she sat navigating through the report and images, pictures taken from within the ventilation systems.

When she first appeared on the Bridge, I told her I didn't have enough time to review her report. Then the normally reserved engineer demanded it. Her outburst had shocked me so much I'd stopped everything.

"While we spoke, I had this niggling feeling like I was missing something. Captain, I'm sorry. I was supposed to be the one that completed the decontamination process of the ejection tubing and air circulation system following the dust's expulsion."

"You didn't?"

She dropped her gaze. "No, sir. The storm hit, and we went into emergency response. With Commander Evans and Sergeant Cruz inside the shuttle, I was required elsewhere. I started it, but never confirmed its completion."

Son of a monkey's... She was right. It wasn't entirely her fault. We were all responsible for following up, but we'd gone into crisis mode. None of us had been able to rest for almost a day — when the first real group had come on shift following reanimation.

With a nod, I said, "You had to cover until they came out."

"Yes. I planned to finish the process and verify its completion, but..." She interlaced her fingers and squeezed so hard her knuckles turned white even as her face remained impassive. "I didn't until today. I performed a full examination of the system, which is what I am showing here, then started the decontamination sequence. It should be complete within the hour."

"You're treating the main system and the tanks?"

"Yes, but I worry about the delay, and that the subsequent growth I see here" — she flipped to the next image — "and here may mean that some of the spores have gotten into the other ducts. There are a few other sensitive systems running through this area of the ship too. I'd like to discuss this with Captain Norris. Maybe she can tell us how far we should extend the treatment fields to verify any potential spread is eliminated before another exposure happens."

Pushing off the table, I walked to the far wall, hands clasped behind my back, and tried to think. I could feel the eyes of the others around the Bridge watching me. They couldn't hear what we were discussing, but they knew me well enough to know this was not good news. How bad? They wouldn't be able to tell. I learned a long time ago how to control my expression.

I spun on my heels and stepped up next to her. "This is not your fault. You were keeping the ship from falling apart, but you're right. We need to talk to Norris." I gestured to the door. "Let's see if we can get her on the Com."

I led her from the Main Bridge and into my office down the hall, which I rarely let anyone enter. This was where I came to think. Having someone else in here was strange. Not large, it held a tiny table and chairs, my desk, and a single filing cabinet. That was it. The cool cream walls were crisp and clean, contrasting against the three oversized pictures of our home solar system. It wasn't that I regretted leaving; it was more that I wanted to remember where I came from and what was at stake should this mission fail. More importantly, I took them as a reminder of who I'd been the day I'd left and the hope I held for my future.

"Take a seat," I said, lowering myself into the chair behind the desk. I reached for the panel embedded along the right side and, with a few flicks of the board, a screen lit on the wall, lighting the space with a bluish glow. I typed in the command code for Norris and pressed "send."

A moment later, her face lit the screen. Her hair was a mess, falling around her shoulders in a way which told me she'd been resting, as did her rumpled uniform and the sleepy eyes.

"Captain Remian," she said. "Do you ever sleep? When was the last time you took a rest period?"

"Captain Norris, my apologies for waking you. We have an urgent matter that requires your expertise."

The slow blink was followed by a yawn. "And that would be?"

"We need to discuss the contamination procedures and the timeline required for completion."

Her fist froze as she rubbed her eyes. Her back straightened as she leaned into the camera.

"Explain."

So, I did. I explained how the decontamination period was interrupted by the storm and not restarted until that day. I shared the pictures of the ventilation system line Aridas had brought and the new growths which had been spotted. As I spoke, Norris seemed to shift into the soldier I'd worked with time and time again, her gaze becoming alert and concerned. Then when Aridas began to explain the vital systems she'd identified as also running through the same area, Norris's shoulders drooped.

"Captain," Norris said. "We need to evacuate the entire module. It needs to be treated in its entirety."

Aridas raised a hand. "Captain Norris, that's not possible. Remember, the device your crew used to treat such a large area was severely damaged. I can only go section by section, but if you believe the Cnidramarus can travel that fast, I may not be able to catch them. Which means it's too late for that."

Norris sighed and shook her head. "No, you won't be able to." Her gaze shifted to me. "This means that the probability of an outbreak is no longer just a hypothetical. This means that it is definitive. We need to prepare."

"There's no other way?" I asked.

"No. The Cnidramarus can travel via the dust cloud. There's no way to know how far they'll go."

"Okay," Aridas said. Had I not been standing beside her, I would not have caught the tremble in her voice. "Then is there a way to predict what they will attach to? You act like they decide where to go, so if that's the case, where should I focus my treatments?"

"I don't know."

Ice ran through my veins at those words. How could she not know? She'd lived this once before, right?

"What do you mean you don't know?" I asked, a little harsher than intended.

Her eyes narrowed, the muscle in her jaw twitching. "Careful, Captain. I do not appreciate your tone."

Heat rose in my chest. I was so tired of not knowing, of having no control over anything! I clenched my fists and pushed down the boiling anger ready to explode.

"Specialist Aridas," Norris said, prying her attention from me. "Has Sergeant Cruz and his team made progress on the Contained Radiotherm Device? I heard he had collected all the parts, but nothing more."

With a hesitant side-glance to me, Aridas said, "His team did examine the Elemental device and was able to salvage some of the parts from it. I heard he was like a kid at the candy store looking over the design. Sergeant Tanaka said Cruz was going to replicate parts of it for the CRD, but with a few modifications. He thinks he'll be able to produce all of the wavelengths Commander Evans has identified within the Elemental Crew's readings of the Cnidramarus rock. This should allow all combinations to be tested accurately and safely."

The Contained Radiotherm Device, or CRD, was planned for two uses. First was the study and verification of the wavelengths, or combinations therein, which were most damaging to the Cnidramarus. And second, for the creation of the radiation pellets.

"Timeline?" she asked.

"Not completely sure. The last time I saw Cruz, the machine was halfway built." A smirk appeared on Aridas's heart-shaped face. "You should see it. It is one of the ugliest things I've ever seen."

Norris smirked. Part of me knew I should too, but for some reason, all I felt was irritation. Ever since I'd seen Cruz talking to Tasha in the

Command locker room, he'd been pressing my buttons more than usual. Which was stupid because I knew there was nothing going on there. Cruz had said it himself. Even if he had feelings for her, he wouldn't do anything about it.

Pushing those thoughts away, I added, "Medical came in today, too. They've verified the two best substances and have been working to collect enough from around the ship. They think this is a real option."

"And the R&D area is nearly ready," Aridas took over. "Commander Evans and Tanaka only had to modify the area a little more to align with the decontamination requirements," she said.

Norris nodded. "That's good news. Has Tasha been able to identify the frequencies?"

"I'm not sure. She was on a mandated rest period issued by Doc Mendez the last time I was in the lab. He found her sleeping at her station. I'll have her check in with you when she's back on shift."

"Thank you. We've collected samples of each type and separated them into test groups. Please let both Evans and Cruz know that they are ready. Once the lab and machine are ready, we can transfer the samples wherever they need."

The emergency com-link pinged, and a red light flashed on the bottom right of the screen.

"I'm sorry, Captain. I must go," I said.

She inclined her head. "Keep me updated."

Ending the call, I pressed the red-light indicator.

Specialist Alex Boston appeared on the screen. He didn't give me a chance to respond before he spoke. "Captain, we have a problem. They need you on Module Two, Level 45, Section Six. We found something you need to see."

The concern in his voice had my shoulders bunching. A wave of trepidation spread through me. Keeping my expression calm, I said, "On my way."

Aridas followed me to the door. As we exited my office, she said, "I'll follow up with Commander Evans and finish the current decontamination program. I'll have a report to you in a few hours."

"Thank you."

With that, she disappeared around the corner. I headed in the opposite direction.

Module Two was what we considered the main module. It was where High Command was housed. Central to it all was the Bridge, which meant that it only took me a few minutes to reach Section Six of the external area and take the lift down to Level 45.

I found Boston in the entrance to one of the crew decks. This was where those off-shift could socialize and spend time out of their domiciles. There were stalls for food, drinks, entertainment, and exercise.

"Captain," Boston said. He shifted from foot to foot, a serious look on his face. "I need you to see something."

"What did you find?" I asked as he spun to lead me through the door to the right.

As we entered what looked to be a viewing room, I caught the sight of three bright crimson spots on the ground. Blood?

"Sir, it looks like the crystal is no longer confined." He pointed to the far wall, where a collection of pink-gold crystals jutted from the ground and reached up to about knee height. A piece had been broken off and now lay on the floor.

"Do we know who found it and when?"

Boston shook his head, his eyebrows scrunching in concern. "No. This area is not heavily trafficked yet as so many are still asleep, but whoever this was clearly was exposed. Especially with the lights low. It's not surprising they missed it."

"We need to find them. Now."

"On it. I have Medical coming down to do DNA analysis," he said, then gestured to the growth guaranteed to kill my people. "What should I do with this?"

I ran a hand through my hair, digging my fingers into the back of my scalp. "Quarantine the area. No one is allowed in this section until we know how far the spread is. Let Commander Evans and Tech Specialist Aridas know that the section requires decontamination immediately."

"Yes, sir," Boston said, his shoulders tall. He spun on his heels and left the viewing room.

I approached the red splotches on the floor. They felt like a warning — an omen — of what was to come. I knelt down, my gaze transfixing on the crystal sparking in the dim light.

Please let us find the poor soul who'd injured himself before it was too late.

"I think it's time to inform the entire crew," I whispered to the empty room. "Let all those awake know about the presence of the Cnidra- marus."

We already had so much going on I hadn't wanted to overwhelm them. I just hoped it didn't cause a panic. Perhaps I shouldn't have waited as long as I had, but it'd only been a few days, and until now, the bugs had been confined to the shuttle.

Chapter Thirteen

Commander Tasha Evans

T he noxious smell hit me in the hallway first. I opened the door and swallowed down the bile that rose in my throat as the wall of pungent fog slammed into my face. Oh, lord, who had burnt popcorn and why in *my* lab? That's when I heard it.

Giggling!

There were grown men *giggling* in my lab, and whatever they were doing was burning away the lining of my nose. With each step, it got worse. Man, I was going to smell that for days. By the time I turned the corner, the scent was so thick that it was hard to breathe. Or maybe that was the smoke filling the air.

"What in the hell are you three doing?" I asked, fists on my hips.

The three figures hovering over the machine — if you could call it that — straightened instantly, spinning to face me. Their smiles shifted into an "oh, shit" expression.

"It was his idea," Geron said, pointing an accusing finger at Russel.

Russel batted his finger away, then lifted his own to point at the other figure. "Nuh-uh, it was Tanaka's."

Tanaka's eyes narrowed at his comrades.

"You both suck." To me, Tanaka said, "I swear, Commander, it was Richards's idea."

I lifted my gaze to the ceiling and tried — *tried* — not to smile. Let's be clear, this was not the first time I'd caught them doing something stupid. It would not be the last. In truth, the only difference was, this time, Patrick wasn't here to egg on their idiocy while he sat safely in the corner. That, and Russel wasn't pretending to be a grumpy bastard the moment I walked in. After a few painful, smoke-filled breaths, I leveled my eyes on them.

"You dumbasses do know this facility is equipped with a ventilation system, right?"

They looked around, and I swear it was like watching three preteens realize they'd messed up. Geron's eyes went wide, Tanaka grimaced and lifted his shoulder in a shrug, while Russel sucked air in through his teeth only to cough.

Praying for patience, I stepped up to the nearest console and initiated the command for the ventilation system.

"All three of you know how dangerous it is to perform experiments in an unventilated space." Okay, I was playing it up a bit. So sue me. The place smelled like the old Smoke Shack on a Friday night. "This is dangerous."

Russel stood from his seat on the stool. "I'm sorry, Commander. I should have been more careful. I was only going to perform one test to verify the shielding had no leaks. There are none, by the way. There would've been no need for the vents, but I was halfway through the test when..." He looked away.

"These jackals walked by and wanted popcorn?"

All three of them giggled, again! And for the life of me, I couldn't hold back my grin any longer. I shook my head and approached them.

I placed a hand on Geron's arm. "Glad to see you up and walking around. I heard we got the field up and running. How are you feeling?"

"Not terrible, not great. I was just here to drop off the samples. Norris wants me back at the shuttle and within the confirmed shield as soon as possible. At least until *she* can verify the one that was erected here."

"She is running diagnostics now," Tanaka said.

"All right, well," I said, rubbing my hands together, "let me see what this bad boy can do."

Russel's eyes lit up. He stepped away from the stool, making room for me.

"Ha! I knew it was an act," Geron said as he took a seat in front of the machine.

Holy wow, what in the fantasy hell realm had Russel built? This thing was a hodge-podge of scavenged pieces all integrated to make it look like the largest, most complicated ray gun you'd find in the backwoods of a shanty town in Jermanis, the largest city in the northern continent. The intricate wiring spiraled together and wrapped around the outside was beautiful.

"Impressive," I said, examining his work more thoroughly.

"I have additional shielding to wrap around the outside, which will make it look better, but I didn't want to encase things before I'd had an initial test," Russel said.

"Were you able to create the frequencies we require? And control the levels?"

"Yes, ma'am," Russel confirmed. "Once the beam is active, we can manipulate the intensity as needed. The beam can be split to allow for multiple samples to be treated at once. We're ready for testing."

That's when I noticed the five giant-sized bowls of popcorn lining the bench. How long had they been at it? I lifted my eyebrow in question, and he ducked his head to hide his grin. The urge to scold them again rose, but then Russel handed me a bag of popcorn kernels. I grinned. Eyes sparkling, he held out a small metal plate. I filled it, and he placed it inside the contraption. Russel explained the control board while I sealed the device. Then he stepped back and gestured as if to say, "all yours."

I tried so hard not to become one of the hyenas surrounding me, but it was impossible. Partly because their child-like laughter filled the air, but more because of how the clear blue beam reached for the kernels, heating them and causing them to expand. The muted *pop-pop-pop* came next as, one by one, the popcorn appeared. Then it was like a wave of activity as the rest decided to join the party. After the laser cut off, the popping sounds continued for a few seconds.

It was awesome. I'd deny it to anyone, but I understood why there were so many bowls on the counter. Some more burnt than others. That was cool. I lifted my gaze to the three men and was about to say something when the sound of footsteps in the hallway reached us.

"What is that scent? It smells awful. Is that popcorn? Who is cooking popcorn down here?"

Oh, crap! That was Mitchel's angry voice. I spun in my seat.

"Get this stuff out of here. I'll intercept," I said, striding to the door.

They listened. In quick movements, Geron and Tanaka grabbed two bowls each and rushed to the opposite doors. Russel scooped the compartment into the last bowl, then shoved the evidence in the cabinet below. I flinched as he slammed the door, choking back a laugh at his hurried movements. It took work to find my professional demeanor because the residual amusement mixed with the panic in their eyes was a thing of beauty. On the way to the door, I picked up my tablet and pulled up some arbitrary stats, nearly running into Mitchel as he turned the corner. I stepped back, feigning surprise.

"Oh, excuse me!" I said, voice a little too loud. "What are you doing here? Is everything all right?"

"Tasha, you're back. Good. Are you rested?" he said, but his tone was so flat, a chill ran through me. Something was wrong.

"Y-yes, thank you," I stuttered, taking in his clenched jaw and the vein throbbing at his temple, but the defeat in his eyes was what had me concerned. Mitchel didn't give up.

"What's wrong?"

He cleared his throat, but what really concerned me was the several-second pause before he seemed to finally be able to speak the words haunting him. "The crystal is no longer confined to the shuttle bay."

My jaw dropped as quickly as my heart did.

"What do you mean?" Russel asked, appearing at my side.

I could tell that wasn't all when Mitchel didn't glare at Russel.

"This morning, Aridas came to me. The decontamination procedures of the air ventilation systems used during the purge of the dust cloud were not confirmed as complete. She completed scans of the entire system, and growths were found in several junctures." He paused as if to gather his thoughts. "Then, about an hour ago, a trail of blood was found on one of the crew decks. After investigation, a significant growth of the Cnidramarus Crystal was spotted within a viewing rec room in Section Two. No reports have come in about the abnormality, nor was there any notification of an injury to the medical staff."

Mitchel's shoulders fell, a quiet breath escaping in a sigh. I wanted to push him to tell us the rest, but it would only slow him down. Clearly, Russel agreed because he stayed silent, his solid presence one of support and not aggression for once.

Mitchel ran a hand over his face, then continued, "We brought Medical down, and they were able to identify the blood. We found his broken body in his quarters."

I pressed my hand to my lips.

"I guess what Norris said was true. The CR3s are violent and can break the host if the integration doesn't go well." His gaze locked with mine. He sounded so young when he said, "Tasha, his body was so broken, the spine bent in half. His legs were at such an odd angle." Mitchel's eyes had glazed over, as if he were seeing the scene over again. "But that's not what killed him. The damn parasite was still able to feed. The poor kid was ancient."

In a gravelly tone hinting at the anger coursing through him, Russel asked, "Who was it?"

"Some young kid named Mikheil Robertson. Just out of the academy. I didn't know him, but I heard he took his first spacewalk a little over a day ago."

A breath forced its way out of my lungs, causing me to squeak. My throat tightened; my diaphragm became heavy.

"Fuck!" Russel cursed. He paced farther into the room, his fists opening and closing as if they ached to punch something. His heavy breaths boomed in my ears. Eventually, he rejoined us, but he was far from okay.

The room spun as I thought back to the bright-eyed soldier willing to risk everything to save his ship and crew. He hadn't needed to. Robertson could have bowed out, but he didn't because I needed another set of hands, and time was of importance. Tears blurred my vision. I hadn't known him long, but he'd had an amazing future ahead of him. I would've made sure of that.

Mitchel reached out, placing a hand on my shoulder. "Did you know him?"

"I was his point on the spacewalk. Lots of potential." My voice cracked; my chest ached as the muscles spasmed without my control. I forced the tears down. I wanted to hide and let them fall, but I couldn't. It was my job to make sure no one else died so needlessly. "Has the spread been contained, the section evacuated?"

"Of course not, Tasha. How would they have?" Russel snapped at me.

I stepped back, feeling as if I'd been slapped. Then, I corrected that automatic response.

Pushing into his personal space, I shoved a finger in his face. "Do not use that tone with me, Sergeant. I understand that you worked with Robertson too and that you're upset, but you will not address me in such a manner."

Russel's lips pressed together. He shook his head once as if he were berating himself mentally, then through clenched teeth, sucked in a slow breath. He swallowed hard as if pushing down the emotion was difficult. I felt the same.

"I am sorry, Commander. Like you, I knew him. He was a great engineer." Russel spun to face Mitchel. "What do you need? Is the area secured? Are we treating the section?"

Mitchel glanced back and forth between us, then, settling on Russel, said, "Is the CRD finished? We need to figure out how to kill these things. Do we have an ETA on when research will begin?"

I glanced away, unable to stop the wave of guilt. Here we were popping popcorn instead of starting testing. Russel's jaw twitched. He must be feeling the same.

"It's done," Russel said, gesturing to the machine that looked like it'd been designed by a mad scientist. "Initial testing of the CRD shielding was just completed to verify safety."

"He made it so that individual frequencies can be pinpointed to allow for complete testing of the Cnidramarus. Multiple combinations can also be utilized," I added.

Russel nodded. "I was not, however, able to save the Elemental Crew's device. Which means we can't treat the ship as they did. We can't stop the growth on a mass scale."

"No," Mitchel said, resigned. "Which is why we need you and Doc to finish the radiation pellets, then figure out how to stop these things from killing anyone else."

"Have there been any other reports of infestation?" I asked.

"Not yet, but that's not surprising. Only a select few have been notified of the threat, but that's about to change. There will be an all-hands announcement within the hour." He crossed his arms over his chest. "But Captain Norris says it's only a matter of time before there are more infections. We need results, Commander."

"Absolutely, sir." With a glance to Russel, I said, "We're ready to secure the section of the ship. We'll start testing immediately."

"I'll call in the team and touch base with Doctor Mendez," Russel said.

"Thank you," I said. With new orders confirmed, he performed an about-face and strode from the room.

"Tasha," Mitchel said, my first name like a plea on his lips. "As soon as you know which frequency combinations affect them, figure out how to create them on a larger scale. We have to treat the ship. I don't want to lose more of my crew."

"I'll do my best."

"It's more than that, though," he pleaded for me to listen. "We can't bring the crystal to Merocius."

Oh...oh, man. The floor disappeared, and I teetered in my shoes. If the Cnidramarus Crystal were to make it to Merocius, it would spread...everywhere. How would we control it then? The answer was, we wouldn't. Wait, now that I thought about it, there had been some mention of this during the meeting, but I'd been too distracted by the engine failure for it to sink in. But he was right; the crystals couldn't get to Merocius.

"I understand, Captain. We'll figure this out." He nodded and turned, but before he could leave, I said, "You know this wasn't your fault, right?"

His shoulders stiffened. A breath later, he dropped his head and said, "Every life on this ship is my responsibility. I didn't share pertinent information, and now a young man is dead." He sighed. "Drop it, Commander. Focus on finding a way to fix this and let me know what you need."

I watched him leave and made a note to check on him in a few hours. Then I pulled up Tanaka's com-line and hit "connect."

"Time to get the shields up and the team moving. I want the new protections active within the hour. All staff should be here in less than that."

The Cnidramarus spores may be out in the ship, growing who knew where, but I sure as hell wasn't going to add to it. We would contain it as best we could, and hopefully, we'd limit the damage.

"On it," Tanaka said. "I'm initiating procedures now. I'll be there in ten."

I clicked off and faced the lab. There was no more time for fun. It was time to work.

Blinking no longer helped. My eyelids had become sandpaper, and the soft tissue beneath now resembled that of ping-pong balls, smooth and dry. Unmalleable. Potentially an exaggeration, but considering the number of reports I'd examined, perhaps not. It had been hours since we'd gotten the team set up and the workflow verified. Once they'd found a rhythm and no longer needed me, I'd retreated to my own part of the project.

I reviewed the scans from the asteroid again, then identified the most likely frequencies controlling the Cnidramarus. I dug through the notes and scans of the systems we'd passed. Read through the medical charts Norris sent over, and even still, I felt I was still missing something. Which was why I'd been combing through everything from the parasite itself to the growth patterns on the ship all over again.

The missing link was here. I could feel it. I just couldn't see it yet.

Rubbing my eyes, I stood and paced the room. I used the movement to stretch the muscles along my back. Then, I headed to the food replicator. As this was the main office and just outside the lab space, it had access to drinks and food. I requested a cup of coffee and made a note to check on the team to verify they've stopped to eat. The warmth of the cup against my skin got me thinking.

Maybe I had to take it back to the basics. The Cnidramarus were living creatures. Their makeup was organic from all examinations, but they fed on something intangible.

Time was intangible, right? I didn't know. From my understanding it was, but maybe humans just didn't understand the truth of this yet. What was time? Was time environmental or something else? It stayed constant but could slow or speed depending on our circumstances. Or was perception?

I was getting a little off course. It was *not* my job to unravel the universe. It was my job to figure out what other factors inhibited the Cnidramarus Crystal's growth.

I lifted the cup to my lips, and again, the temperature caught my attention.

Temperature was one of the most influential factors with any experiment — life or chemical based. I glanced up at the screen, taking in the readings again. Temp was a huge correlator to the activity of these parasites. We'd already seen it in the way they moved far slower while encased in their own crystal than they did within a host. Like most living creatures, heat helped the Cnidramarus grow and thrive. For example, once in the body, they more than doubled in size upon infiltration. They moved faster, extended themselves farther, and were far more active.

Pressure could have an effect. Or air. Were the crystals airtight? Did they need air? My musings continued as I re-read the Elemental's reports for the fourth time.

I did something wrong – or right – I'm not totally sure, but I have no idea what. I was in the lab by myself listening to the Marac Operas. *Wilson always hates it when I listen to them. I treated the first batch of samples with the A6 frequency when something strange happened. The CR3...*

Conversation flowing in from the lab rose in a wave of excited words. The sudden change had me looking toward the door. It sounded different from the last few days. Granted, most of that had been hollering about one system failure or another. This was also not the steady hum the team had found as they'd worked. This was hopeful.

Quick footsteps preceded Russel sticking his head in the doorway. His eyes were wide, his breathing faster than it should have been. "Commander, we need you."

Pushing to my feet, I followed him into the main lab area, where we found the team huddled around a tall woman with curly red hair. Doctor Adams sat in front of her microscope, an image on the screen above her. The parasite filling the screen tilted as she turned the forceps in her hand back and forth.

"Dr. Adams," Russel said as he approached the group. They parted at his words, and the image stilled.

The tweezers released the creature back into its petri dish, and Dr. Adams looked up. Her hair was pulled back from her face in a low ponytail, the ringlets falling to mid-back.

"Commander. I think we figured out how the CC1 was placed inside Captain Norris along with the CR3."

"What?" I asked, rushing to her side.

My gaze landed on the writhing Cnidramarus on the screen. The magnification made it easy to see what was different about this particular one. Instead of the angry-looking CR3, its antennae were missing, and the movements were slow and methodical. Additionally, there was a bump along its back that wasn't normally there. Thin strands of blue wrapped its abdomen, then disappeared beneath.

"Holy shit, that CR3 has a CC1 attached to it." I glanced back and forth from her to the screen. "I...What happened? How did this happen? How was it treated?" The questions spilled from my lips, and Dr. Adams grinned.

"This particular CR3 was treated as Captain Norris was — with two wavelengths in combination with a nearly simultaneous infection of the CC1. We spoke to Captain Norris and, based on her report, attempted multiple time variations and wavelength combination levels to see how they would react. We had to make some assumptions, but it worked." She grinned. "We figured it out. We've confirmed that the CC1 will attach to the CR3 or CB2 if the conditions are right."

One of the other technicians who sat next to Dr. Adams added, "*And that it significantly alters their mobility.*"

Dr. Adams spun back to her station, grabbed another petri dish, and placed it under the magnifier. "But look what happens if the introduction is changed by more than a few minutes either way."

The scene inside this dish was significantly different. The CR3 was thrashing around violently, tiny pieces of what I could only assume were CC1s all over the container. I grimaced.

"The CR3 ripped apart the CC1," Russel explained. "We've seen this anytime they're placed with either the CB2s or CR3s. However, the CB2s only kill the CC1s; they don't eviscerate them."

"Okay, then what happened with this sample?" I pointed to the first dish — the one with the attached CC1. "Is this the only sample that's reacted this way? What other combinations have we tried?"

Dr. Adams pulled the thickly lined gloves she wore from her fingers, placing them on the table. "We have only begun to start combining frequencies. We started with individual ones at varying strengths, then we began to combine the ones the Cnidramarus responded negatively to. Our goal was to focus on those the Elemental Crew identified first."

"Especially considering," one of the other lab techs said, "this particular mix is dangerous to us — potentially lethal. I'm not sure how the captain survived without serious issues. Which means we're missing something."

Russel shifted, bringing my attention to him. "And is also why I'll be treating the next batch with different strengths of these specific frequencies."

"It's entirely possible that there are better and more effective options still to find," I said, looking from one face to the next. "But this is a fantastic start. Provides hope that we will find an option."

"Agreed," Dr. Adams said.

"I found something interesting in the notes that I think we need to keep in mind." I rested my hands on my hips. "So, from all reports, it looks like the CC1s are not parasites that inhabit humans. I've found two other confirmed exposures to the CC1 by the Elemental Crew and with each, there was no infection. Which makes me question if it can survive inside a host's body alone."

"That doesn't make sense. Why wouldn't it infect like the CR3 in the CB2?" Dr. Adams asked.

"What would be their purpose then?" Russel asked.

"We don't know, but I had the doc look at Captain Norris's scans more closely, and the CC1 has attached to the CB2, just like we're seeing here," I said.

Dr. Adams made a gentle humming sound as though she were thinking. She leaned back in her lab chair and stared at the image on her screen. Several of the group hypothesized their ideas, but I was too focused on Dr. Adams. She was on to something.

Eventually, she said, "Could the CC1s be parasites themselves, but only to the CB2s and CR3s?"

This was insane. Could we have found a parasite that was a parasite to its own kind? I didn't even know how to unpack that.

"With how they're so violently killed?" the tech said.

Dr. Monek, one of the research scientists from the back, spoke up. "Perhaps they are intended for balance. To help keep the CR3s and CB2s from spreading too widely?"

"But they didn't before. Until we know what they are doing to the other Cnidramarus, I don't think we can guess."

"Do we have any hypotheses on that?" Dr. Adams asked.

"Not yet, but Dr. Pia and Doc Mendez are coming down shortly to go over the reports. Mendez told me that based on the scans taken of Captain Norris, there have been significant changes in her aging. Apparently, it's slowed significantly."

"Commander Evans," Doc Mendez said from the doorway. "It's even more interesting than that. I just did another scan. Her regression has stopped completely."

Russel's eyebrows rose while Dr. Adams nearly bolted to a standing position, her eyes going wide.

"Are you sure?" I asked, watching them approach.

"Yes. I've reviewed everything and confirmed that Captain Norris was progressing at an increased rate prior to going into the shuttle. This is why she created the field around the medical bay, hoping to slow down the effects of the CB2, which means she wouldn't have been the exact same age genetically as the day she went in. She would have aged some either way, but..."

Doc stopped before me, made an entry on his armpad, and then inclined his head to a monitor over my shoulder.

"As you can see here, the degradation of her DNA has not changed since the integration of the CC1 into her system. Or, at least from the initial scan Javier performed. Which tells me that the CC1 is doing something to the CB2."

"So, you think that the CC1 being attached to one of the other Cnidramarus is what...negating the parasite's effect on the host's time-line?" Dr. Adams asked.

"That's what we're thinking, but we're going to have to do some additional testing to find out. Until then, we need to find a way to kill these bastards because even if the CC1 can negate the others, we don't know the side effects of having these things in us at all. What are the long-term effects of having a conjoined pairing?"

"That, and there's no way we can replicate what happened to Norris. She was lucky it didn't kill her," I said.

"Exactly. It's not exactly safe to implant them," Doc said, inclining his head to me.

"This is fascinating. Thank you for bringing this to us," Adams said. "We will add this to our testing parameters."

"Let me know how we can help."

"So, why are you here, Doc? Was it just to discuss Norris's scans?" I asked.

"No, actually. We've made progress, too." Doc Mendez held up two containers. The first was filled with a handful of small metal beads; the second was a thick, shielded box less than four inches square. "We figured out how to make the pellets. We were able to purify the metal, but we couldn't transfer the radioactive material into the pellets while unshielded, and especially not in Main Medical. So we're here to see if Russel will let us use his new toy. Tanaka said all tests confirmed there were no leaks, and all the other areas with appropriate protection are in use."

"You are correct, and I'm sure that's all you heard," I said, shooting Russel an amused glance.

Russel chuckled. "We can definitely help you. We're at a good breaking point anyway. I was going to re-examine all the samples and set up for the next round of testing. So let's get you set up and get these things made so you can treat your patients."

The group split, excited to continue.

Chapter Fourteen

Commander Patrick Montgomery

"Patrick, is that you?"

Crap. I ground my teeth at the sound of Tasha's shocked voice. It had been thirty-six hours since I'd seen her, and a lot had happened in that time. Though I hadn't been avoiding her, I had hoped someone else would be the one to break the news I was up and about.

She rushed down the empty hallway, the hardsuit she wore molded to her compact figure. When she reached me, she threw her arms around my waist, encapsulating me in a hug.

I grimaced at where she brushed the sore spots on my back. Motherfucker, that hurt, but I returned her embrace nonetheless.

"What are you doing outside the shuttle — outside the field?" she asked, pulling back and scanning me suspiciously.

"Why are you in a hardsuit?"

Her eyebrow raised. "It's never a good sign when you answer my question with a question."

Arms on hips, she just stood there and glared. There was no way she'd let me get away with not answering. Not if I valued my life.

With a crooked grin, I said, "It's fine, Tasha. Dr. Gollie and Dr. Pia implanted the radiation pellets yesterday. I'm fine."

The joy at seeing me shifted in an instant to pure and absolute fury.

"What?" Tasha stepped back, the happiness at seeing me overwritten by anger. Through clenched teeth, she said, "I thought Mitchel put a stop to the radiation pellets after what happened to Geron."

What happened to Geron...

My shoulders bunched and for a moment, it became difficult to breathe.

All I could hear was the sound of that medical bay — the heart monitor, Richards's screams, the terrified conversation as the doctors tried to get ahead of the Cnidramarus ravaging Richards's body. Then there was that resounding snap as his spine twisted in one powerful movement.

No one had expected such a violent reaction from the Cnidramarus. We probably should have, but seeing as he had the less aggressive of the two, we hadn't expected treatment to go so very wrong.

"He did," I said, bracing myself for Tasha's outburst even as my mind continued to play the scene.

It was the intake of breath and then silence from each and every one of us as we stood there in shock that had been the worst, though. Didn't matter if it was only a blip — that second would stay with me.

Her eyes narrowed. Tone dark, stance aggressively leaning in, she said, "You let them implant the pellets knowing that the Cnidramarus would react the way they would! And after Richards was paralyzed because of the procedure! Are you fucking kidding me, Patrick?"

I stared off into nothing as yet another image flashed through my mind. Dr. Pia, Gollie, Norris, and the rest of the medical crew sitting around a destroyed, trash covered, medical bay. Some hunched in a chair or leaning against a counter, but most having slid to the floor with their knees to their chests, exhaustion and devastation written in the very essence of their being.

Tasha shoved me, bringing me back, and I took a step away. I didn't begrudge her this reaction, either. We were her two closest friends, and I'd risked my life moments after he'd almost died.

"The last few days have sucked, I get that. It was a hard decision knowing that Geron was paralyzed, but the doctors are trying to find a way to repair the damage."

Tasha threw her hands up in the air. "And if they do, they risk a reaction from the CB2!"

"Yes," I said calmly, and she glared. "That is a risk, but one worth the shot, and you have to remember that the pellet is helping him. His CB2 is quiet, proving the radiation pellets worked."

If only he still had the use of his legs.

My hands found her shoulders, and I said, "I'm dying. Whether by the Cnidramarus, a random ship failure I don't help fix, or by not reaching Merocius. I need to be out here, Tasha, and you know it. There's way too much on our plates at this point. We don't have enough people to manage it all. And after seeing what happened to Richards, we felt like we knew what we had to do to make sure the procedure was safe."

Tasha pressed her lips together. Her breath came out of her nose in sharp pants as we stood there silently, giving her a moment to calm down. Eventually, she pushed a piece of hair behind her ear and sighed.

"Well, if I know Mitchel's reaction to this — which I do — you won't have to worry about the Cnidramarus. He'll kill you himself."

I snorted, then said, "He'll get fucking over it. Especially when he sees it worked. I guess it could feel the surgery. It didn't like the invasion. All we had to do was treat the already-implanted Cnidramarus with the altered laser before the implantation. While it was in shock, they could implant the pellets without any problem. Now, instead of needing treatment with the altered laser again — which sucks something awful — the pellets should keep the CR3 at bay."

Those soulful eyes examined me as if trying to catch a lie. She knew me well enough to see if I was lying, which is how I knew better than to lie to her in the first place. Tasha could be scary.

Her shoulders dropped in relief a moment before she said, "You're serious? It worked?"

"It did, but the procedure was complicated."

"Is that why you've been MIA for the last thirty-six hours?"

"Yeah, unfortunately."

I grimaced, absently touching the space next to the red blisters along my spine. Seeing as the first batch of blisters hadn't yet healed, the resulting wounds were worse. I'd be seeing Doc Mendez twice a day for bandage changes. He'd told me that if I didn't stop teaching the young med techs bad words, he'd gag me.

I continued, "There was some recovery needed, but we did a scan today and confirmed that everything's looking good. The CB2 is stable, and it looks like my aging has slowed to nearly its normal rate."

"Wow, that's great news." Tasha grinned. "Well, my team is getting closer to figuring out how to kill these things. Sorry it's taking so long."

"There's nothing to be sorry for, Tash," I said, starting back down the hallway toward where I'd heard Mitchel was. She fell in step beside me. "Where are you headed?"

"The hydroponic system in Green Room 4. It's been down since yesterday, but no one knew why." She looked away, sadness lining her face. "I got a call from Mitchel a few minutes ago. They found the problem."

She shrugged, and it was a mixture of anger and resignation. It was a rare thing that caused that particular expression to cross her face. Biting the inside of her cheek, she continued, "The main recycling system was acting up. It's one of the largest growing sections behind the main garden. It's sorta tucked back out of the way. Apparently, one of the techs went to work on it last night at the end of his shift. No one checked on him. They thought he'd confirmed it was good and headed home."

"Fuck..." I rubbed my jaw, the stubble scratching at my palm. A heavy weight settled in my gut. "And let me guess, they found him and some new growth."

Tasha hit the pad next to the main entrance, and the door slid wide. "Yes, and when the morning crew went in to fix the problem that was, well, still a problem, they found him. He was alive, which makes Mitchel think it's a CB2."

"Probably."

"The bigger problem, in the process of getting to him, three more were infected." She met my eye. "They're in the water supply of the hydroponic garden."

I lost a step and almost tripped.

"Yeah. There's a team searching the area. They've found crystals everywhere — scattered throughout all the gardens."

A spot behind my right eye ached as I tried to process this, to visualize the system the Cnidramarus must've infiltrated. Water was recycled section by section, which was good and meant that Sections One, Three, and Four would be unaffected. But even still, there was no way to tell how far the spores had gone. Which meant this area of the ship was no longer safe.

At least we'd confirmed the Cnidramarus spores were rarely airborne. They didn't spread that way normally, as the parasites were heavy and required a larger shard to be carried physically from place to place. But once a chunk had been transported, they had a remarkable way of growing through spaces that they shouldn't be able to, like the air duct systems.

"They know it was in the recycling system? Did they reach the other Green Rooms in this module?" I asked, panic seeping into me.

"Yes, and yes." She sighed and stepped into the main garden space in Section Two, Green Room 4. There were three smaller ones in this module, but they were nothing like this.

The lush dome, which spanned several levels, appeared before me. A thousand shades of green filled my field of vision. There was nothing like the overgrown beauty of the plant life here, nor the awe-inspiring variety of trees and bushes in this one area alone. Intermixed with the larger foliage were food production ladders where the scientists grew everything from lettuce to carrots to squash. Along the far wall, you could even find coffee and tea growing in separate, smaller areas separated by glass. It was in these enclosures where temperature controls were essential to maintain the more exotic plants.

My gaze traveled up toward the even more impressive size of the greenhouse which was filled with weaving pathways for the crew to enjoy. Set up like a natural forest, the large trees loomed overhead, providing an escape from the ship and a much-needed reminder of home. My favorite, though, were the windows along the upper levels, which not only made the confined space seem larger, but allowed those above to gaze down upon it. I loved it here.

We were lucky. Green Room 4 was the hydroponic module that had fared the best, and if it weren't for it, we'd be in even bigger trouble as here was where most of our current food was grown. The other three larger ones were in far worse shape. Module Four's Green Room stopped working twenty or more years back. They were starting from scratch down there.

"What the absolute hell!"

I flinched as Mitchel's angry voice rang out.

The room froze, glancing in my direction as if they all knew the anger was pointed at me. Probably because it was obvious. Those from my team smiled when they saw me until Mitchel stomped in my direction, flames shooting from his eyes.

"Good luck," Tasha said in a sing-song voice. She winked and skittered away to join Aridas, who had stuck her head out from behind the tree where the main controls were. Aridas smiled, saw Mitchel, and disappeared back behind the separator.

"Coward," I shot at Tasha.

She giggled, but moved quickly despite the hardsuit she wore. I looked down at my standard uniform. Damn it, I was out of required uniform. I was about to give him another fucking thing to complain about. At least I already had a Cnidramarus. Can't get it again, right?

"Good morning, Captain Remian," I said, keeping my face serene as Mitchel approached. I ignored the storm cloud of doom hovering over him.

My nonchalance only irritated him further. He clenched his fists. Had we not been in front of others, he might've growled at me and then let loose with his secret arsenal of profanities he rarely let out. It was both terrifying and funny when that happened. It was rare, but I enjoyed how each time I learned a new curse word.

"I heard you were here and wanted to lend a hand," I said. "Also, I understand you're dealing with a situation, but once the teams are in place, I need to speak to you about something urgent."

"Could you please explain how you're here?" Mitchel snapped, completely ignoring my words. "I know you're not stupid enough to leave the shuttle in your current condition. And seeing as I strictly forbade another receiving implant treatment, I can only assume you've had a miraculous recovery, and we should be praying to the gods?"

I nodded, then shrugged. "Sure, let's go with that."

I swear the heat in the air rose with his temper. If I wasn't careful, the captain would blow a gasket, and it would not be pretty. His glare didn't waver as we stared at each other.

Through gritted teeth, he said, "Explain to me how you are here, Commander."

Well, shit. I sighed and crossed my arms over my chest. "You know how, Captain. I bullied the doctors and, as such, I had radiation pellets successfully implanted thirty-six hours ago. Multiple tests have confirmed that the procedure was a success, and the CR3 is in stasis."

Mitchel pushed into my personal space, his face inches from mine. Damn, he was closer to burnout than I'd thought. Mitchel only tried to use his broader form to intimidate me when he was about to crack. The dark circles and the helpless glint in his eyes hit me, and it became clear it was time to intervene.

I stepped back, clapped onto his shoulder, and then led him off to the side of the room. I could feel the other's gazes on us. I glanced to where Tasha had disappeared. As if knowing I needed her, she was there.

She met my eyes and, without having to say a word, she did what I needed, calling out to the crew managing the injured and bringing all attention to her.

"Morning all!" she said cheerily. "So, Captain Norris is ready for the infected. She and Dr. Mendez are awaiting their arrival. Please take them to the new medical facility adjacent to the shuttle bay." Tasha glanced at the two standing behind the gurney holding the young tech who they'd rescued. "They'll be treated and monitored there. A field has been set up around..."

Damn, she was good.

I turned my attention back to Mitchel, who was fuming beside me. The good news was, he seemed to grasp how close to losing it he'd been. I let him take a few breaths before I spoke.

"I understand you're angry that I went against your orders, but it was necessary. *The Aspire* needs me, the crew needs me, and I can't perform my duties in their entirety from that damn shuttle. Captain, you need me out here."

"You should've talked to me first."

I rolled my eyes. "Had I, you would've tried to stop it, and your attention was needed elsewhere. This was *my* choice. Please respect that. Mitchel," I said, as a friend this time, "I'm fine. It worked. We were able to subdue the parasite prior to placement using the altered laser. That was our mistake with Richards."

He nodded. His throat moved as he swallowed.

"Have you talked to anyone since Richards was hurt?" I asked. He shook his head. "Did you go see him?" Again, he shook his head. "Then we are going to go see that surly bastard after this, and you're going to see that he is fine. Still the same pain in the ass as always. Then, we're going to discuss something important."

"You shouldn't have risked it," he grumbled, but I caught the slight rise to his lip at the "surly" comment. He rested his hands on his hips, the movement making the hardsuit creak as it stretched. After a few wears, the fibers would loosen up, and the garment would become as comfortable as a regular uniform.

"Captain, if treating this parasite means we don't slam into Merocius or miss it completely, then it's worth it."

His eyebrows shot down in concern. "What the fuck does that mean?" he whispered.

"That's where I'm at. Let's finish up here and get to Richards. We have something to discuss."

He was still pissed, but now I'd distracted him. He would get back at me for not following orders, but I'd hit at a point he couldn't argue. It was my choice, and I was not the type of man to just stand by and let those I cared about die.

"So, it worked?"

"Yes. I'm sore, but my aging is stable. I can be out of the shield safely."

His eyes narrowed. It was so much like Tasha's reaction that I had to laugh.

"I'm fine, really." I gestured to the greenhouse. "So, what's going on? Really?"

"The Cnidramarus got into the water supply," he started.

Mitchel, now back under control, turned and headed back to where the others were gathered. He gestured for me to follow. We went over to the raised garden opposite where Aridas and Tasha worked. I could see them huddled around a panel in the far wall filled with electronic equipment. It was where the motherboard linked into the pump systems. Their calm exchange mingled with the others that were spread around the space taking samples and helping repair other sections of the Green Room.

"We found crystals throughout the space. They're in the plumbing, the ventilation, and even" — he leaned over, reaching out with his gloved hand to push aside the branches of the small bush — "in the gardens themselves. We've had multiple exposures."

The dark green leaves had barely shifted when I noticed a collection of five crystals, approximately seven inches in length, sticking from the dark chocolate soil. My mouth dropped open, and I cursed under my breath. A few inches past the first was another grouping. The crystals were significantly smaller. And to the right, another set only a few inches tall.

"Yeah, that about sums it up," Mitchel said, dropping his arm. "This confirms the suspicion that the Cnidramarus are in the water supply."

I stepped around him so that I could get a better view of the raised gardens. He was right; they were everywhere.

"We've locked down this area to most traffic, but we can't completely. Green Room 4 is where most of our fresh food comes from. The good news is, it doesn't look like they actually attach or invade the plants themselves."

Maybe not, but they would definitely make it harder on the crew during maintenance and harvest.

I squatted down, examining them closely. They were growing up and out of the soil, which backed the idea that they spread via water. The question was, did they only grow on the surface or below as well? It wasn't something we could risk finding out. At least not right now.

"Are they in every planter?"

"As far as we can tell, yes. I spoke with Norris, and she stated something similar had happened with them. It's what led to the full ship irradiation."

Fuck trumpet! That wasn't good. Full ship irradiation wasn't an option for us. We didn't have the supplies to rebuild the Elemental Crew's device. Tasha and her team were working on other options, but it was a slow process, and the question of what bringing the Cnidramarus to Merocius would be like had just been answered. It would be devastating. They'd spread, killing off every lifeform eventually.

"Have the research teams —" I began.

A high-pitched frequency had me throwing my hands over my ears and pushing to my feet. It filled the Green Room, bouncing off the glass and amplifying it to a painful level.

Suddenly, Mitchel grabbed me by the back of my softsuit and pulled me away from the planter. At first, I didn't understand why, but then I followed his gaze back to the crystal I'd been examining. I gaped.

The crystal was vibrating.

"Turn that off!" Mitchel yelled, spinning on his boots.

"Get back from the planters!" I hollered at the same time to a few of the crew as Mitchel rushed toward Aridas and Tasha, his expression one of pain.

The vibrating was getting worse, each and every crystal now shaking in a synchronous rhythm.

Then, as abruptly as it began, the noise stopped. But before it faded completely, there was a sharp *pop*, and the crystals blew apart.

I jumped. Confusion filled me as I knelt down beside the planter. What were once smooth and beautifully clear crystals had now been broken. The largest of the Cnidramarus Crystals I'd examined had a crack from tip to base and a section the size of my pinky had blown outward and was resting inches away. The smaller crystals, which had previously circled it, were gone, having disintegrated. Dust remnants scattered the ground.

I leaned closer and sucked in a gasp at the sight of the scattered, nearly motionless, creatures mixed in with the debris.

"Holy shit," I said. "Everyone, get back. Don't touch it."

From the corner of my eye, I saw each person step farther away, and I breathed a sigh of relief. Even so, my focus was locked on the fact that every one of the smaller groupings was in pieces, damaged by the sound. Planter after planter, it was all the same.

Whatever the hell that fucking sound was, it had done something to the crystal — it had done *severe* damage to the Cnidramarus!

"Mitchel! You need to see..." Realizing he was too far away, I pushed to my feet and jogged to where he stood next to Tasha and Aridas.

I passed the medical team leading the three injured out of the door. Two of them looked worse for wear — the Cnidramarus clearly taking a toll. The third, however, was showing no effects at all. She stood firm, her color healthy and expression clear. A huge gash ran down her right arm, but other than that, she looked fine. I nodded to them as I passed.

Aridas was speaking when I reached Mitchel and the others. "We've reset the system. It looks like several pieces were damaged by the crystal. That's why the system failed. We replaced and cleared the area out. We'll keep an eye on it so that if they grow back, we can repair it before it crashes again."

Tasha leaned against the wall and said, "This doesn't change the fact that the crystal is in the water supply. The good news is, this is a recycling system, and none of it makes its way back into the drinking water or even out of the green spaces in this section of the ship. That said, it will still spread quickly."

"Please tell me you've figured out a way to stop these things," Mitchel said. "We have more people moving around every day, and if we're not careful, the next time there's an exposure, it will be significantly larger. I don't want to lose the crew, Tasha. Please tell me your team's got something for me."

Tasha put the wrench in her hand back in the toolbox at her feet, then faced the captain.

"We've made progress. We know the two most likely radiation combinations, but we're still verifying the frequency strengths. There's still something missing, though. We've been going over simulation after simulation, and we've yet to figure out what will finally kill these things. I promise, Captain, we're close."

"Wait, when you treat the crystal or parasites with these fields, they don't break apart or die?" Aridas asked.

"No, and I don't know why. It causes them significant harm, but the little bastards keep growing back! It's discouraging."

One of the med techs cleaning up the leftover supplies a few feet away let out a sardonic laugh, bringing our attention to him. "Maybe you should make that awful sound again. That might be what kills them," he said before chuckling and heading away.

"What does that mean?" Tasha asked, confused.

I hadn't interrupted, but that meant I was basically bouncing on my toes, waiting for the opportunity to speak. "The noise from the system rebooting. It caused damage to the crystals. Look!" I said, gesturing to a collection near the lip of the planter to our right.

The crystal was just visible through the leaves of several root vegetables growing in long rows. Even from where we stood, you could see the damage. There must have been two large pieces originally, but now there was only one. One piece had cracked in half, and the other side had blown off entirely. Shards lay like broken trees all around its base.

Mitchel's eyes went wide as he and Aridas bent down to examine them more clearly.

"That's incredible," Aridas said, shocked.

"What in the world?" Mitchel seconded, as surprised as Aridas sounded.

But Tasha? She didn't move. She stood frozen. Her eyes were wide, locked on the planter, and yet I could tell her mind was far away. She mumbled under her breath, which came in tight, quick bursts.

"Tasha, what's wrong?" I asked, placing a hand on her shoulder. She didn't respond. Her scattered words made no sense. "Seriously, Tasha. Are you all right?"

"...Listening... *Marac Operas*... treated first batch ... A6 frequency..." Her gaze snapped to mine. "Holy crap, that's it!"

Without another word, she bolted from the room. Reaching the door, she skidded sideways, nearly colliding with Technical Sergeant Alan Tanaka as he entered.

With one last, "How could I be so stupid?" she disappeared.

Silence filled the space for a long moment, everyone staring after her, mouths agape.

"What was that?" Tanaka asked, scanning the room. Aridas shrugged.

"I'm guessing she figured something out," I said.

"What was it?" Mitchel asked.

"I have no idea, but I have a feeling it has to do with the sound affecting the crystal. She said something about the *Marac Operas*."

Mitchel scowled. "I don't know what that means."

"Captain," Aridas said, "we're fine here. The system's back up and running. The hydroponics crew have been notified of the situation and were told to proceed with extreme caution. I've ensured additional protective garments have been brought down for their use during harvest, but they've been told to avoid the area as much as possible and to never enter alone. Your team will help me secure the room. I'm sure you have more important things to do than to stand here with me."

Mitchel nodded along with her words, but his hesitancy was evident.

"Don't worry, Captain," Tanaka said as he joined us. He linked his hands in front of him. "We'll make sure everyone in this sector knows what's going on. And don't forget, the commander has something to discuss with you. It's important."

Tanaka shot me a look I knew too well. It told me to stop stalling. After covering for me during my procedure and recovery, he was one of the only ones aware of our most recent predicament and the danger *The Aspire* was in. We'd even attended a meeting with Reid earlier where we discussed just how absolutely fucking screwed we were.

"That I do, Captain. Like I said, it's urgent," I said earnestly.

"Isn't everything?" Mitchel joked. Then, with a heavy sigh, he said, "Okay, Commander Montgomery. Let's find somewhere we can talk."

After a few final words with the team, I led Mitchel out.

"Where are we going?" he asked.

"To see Richards. I think he can provide some insight on our discussion. Plus, you need to stop stalling and deal with your damn feelings." I glanced at him sideways, only to receive a glare back. "Don't hate me because I'm right."

Hate me because I'm about to tell you we might just crash on Merocius, and I'm using Richards as a shield. *Fuck me...*

Chapter Fifteen

Commander Tasha Evans

There was no freakin' way I missed this!

How did I miss this? It was right there? So simple — laid out in the notes as if...as if just waiting for me to find it.

The Marac Operas. *The A6 frequency. He had unknowingly spelled it out!*

My footsteps were hard as they pounded against the corridor floor. The few people I passed jumped out of the way, pressing themselves to the walls. Better for them as my mind moved too quickly for their presence to truly register.

The lift came into view, and I rushed for it, skidding to a halt inside the moment the door opened. I slammed my hand on the button that would take me to the research floor and bounced on my toes, barely noticing the two crewmen behind me. They stared as though I'd lost my mind. Maybe I had.

Considering the random phrases slipping from my lips — words I'd read in notes written by those who died for their research — it was a possibility. Had I been minutely aware of their presence, I would've laughed at the wary looks they shot each other or the way they stayed as far from me as they could.

Smart. If only they knew I might've just figured out what would save their timelines from being sucked dry.

Could timelines be sucked dry?

The doors slid open, and without a glance back, I bolted from the lift. I pushed harder, faster, using the excitement of a potential solution to spur me on. Grabbing the doorframe, I used it to make a hard turn into my lab. A figure dove out of the way, his exclamations of surprise doing nothing to slow me. I ran to my workstation, barreling into it. A grunt left me as my hip hit the edge and pain burst through the bone but I ignored it, shoving the papers to the side so that I could reach the inlaid keyboard.

I felt the attention of those in the room focused upon me, but in that moment, I was too single-minded to care. Dr. Adams might have asked me something and nearby, Russel stood from his workstation in front of the CRD to move to my side. Still, I ignored them.

My hands shook as I attempted to enter my passwords, the need to verify my epiphany with the notes, making me clumsy.

Was it true? Had I missed something so simple? Hadn't I just been ranting to my team about testing every factor? Even the most innocuous of them? We tried heat and cold. Pressure, no pressure, water and fire, and various chemicals. Nothing had affected the Cnidramarus! Their outer layers were just too strong. And the truth had been there! In the notes the whole time!

The notes...

"Commander?" Russel asked. "Is everything all right?"

On the fourth try, the screen finally cleared, and the system let me in. Good thing, too. On the fifth and it would have locked me out.

"Are you feeling well?" Dr. Adams asked from the doorway leading into the sample room, her goggles on her head.

Ignoring the questions from my team, I pulled up the notes I'd been reviewing earlier. One after another, the words sped by. I scanned Dr. Ponce's for the passage I'd brushed off as unimportant. Nope, nothing. I moved on to Dr. Marco's notes next.

"Really?" I said, pulling up Dr. Phiri's. "Come on, come on."

"Tasha, what the hell is —"

There!

"Holy freaking shit," I said and placed a hand over my mouth. Conversation stopped, the awe in my voice enough to shock them to silence. Tears sprang to my eyes. I rested my head in my hands, a smile stretching my cheeks.

"Commander," Russel finally asked after a long, hesitant moment. He'd come closer. "What is it? What's going on?"

I faced him, pressing my hands to my heart. He reached out and wiped away a tear that slid down my cheek.

"Tasha, you're scaring me. What's going on?"

I felt more than saw the others approach. I swallowed and said, "I figured it out. I know how to kill them."

For two long seconds, an eternity really, all sound stopped. Only our breathing filled the room, but then it was like the words sunk in and, with them, the tension in air became thick. Hope and fear mixed until it became tangible, weighing against my skin.

"What?" Dr. Adams squeaked, stepping forward. Her eyes were wide, lips parted in surprise. "What are you talking about?"

"It's sound." I was nodding as if the motion would help convince her. "It was in the Elemental Crew's logs all along! I overlooked it, not realizing the connection, but today there was an outbreak in Green Room 4. Crystals got in the water supply. They're growing in all of the planters. Aridas and I were fixing the pump for the watering system when something happened." I met Russel's eyes. "You know when you restart the program, and it lets out that terrible noise? The warning to anyone that there could be a pressure change?"

"Yes," he said. He crossed his arms over his chest.

"Well, when the sound filled the greenhouse, it caused all of the crystals to either crack or rupture. I don't know if it killed the creatures — I doubt it — but it damaged them. They weren't moving like normal. And anyway, half of our problem has been that the radiation can't fully transfer through their crystals or outer layers, right? Well, that's the key!" I spun back to my screen and pointed at the words Dr. Phiri had written in his log. I read them aloud. "*I was in the lab listening to the* Marac Operas. *I treated the samples with the A6 frequency when something strange happened. The CR3 contained within the sample died. Not only that, but the crystal shattered. Not realizing what I'd done, I put it off to the side to re-look at it later. The crystals never grew back, and the CR3s had damage to their outer skeletons.*"

I faced the group again. Each of their faces were flushed with excitement.

"Guys, this is it! We've narrowed down the combinations of electromagnetic radiation we think are the most likely to kill it. Now we just need to figure out the sound wavelength that can break through their exterior."

Was I vibrating? I think I was.

Dr. Adams looked down as if searching the ground for something. She inhaled, a grin spreading across her face. She glanced up, met my eyes, and said, "This makes total sense. How have we not figured that out?"

"That's what I said!" I exclaimed. Everyone laughed. With a smile, I continued, "Guys, we know what to do. It's up to us to figure out how this last piece fits together. Can a few of you head back up to Green Room 4 and take samples? Document which planter they were in so we can calculate the distance the sound wavelength traveled. Make sure to get samples from those in the smaller gardens where glass may have inhibited the sound."

Adams nodded along. "Once back, immediately examine them. See if any damage is visible on the parasites themselves. Check them every ten minutes to verify how long it takes for them to recover. Document everything."

"On our way," a lab tech said. Three others rushed to grab collection kits, and they were gone.

I ran a hand through my disheveled hair. "Guys, I think I have a theory about how we can treat the ship."

"You do?" Dr. Adams asked, eyes snapping to me again.

"I need to check something before I say, but I think it might work. It's crazy, but..." I exhaled slowly.

"Wait, can't we just play the operas or even just the frequency over the comm line?" one of the technicians asked.

I thought about that, then shook my head. "No, I don't think so. We don't have speakers in all corners of *The Aspire*. So, they wouldn't be strong enough to penetrate every inch, and that's what we need since — based on what happened today — we can't verify the location of every spore.

The tech rubbed the back of his neck. "Yeah. I guess that makes sense."

Seeing the kid's distress, Cruz said, "But you have an idea."

"I might. Yeah." I squeezed the back of my arm, the pressure grounding me.

"That's hope. Let us know when you want to go over it. You know we're here to help," Adams said. The remaining team of six all nodded enthusiastically.

"Thank you." I grinned. "Well, you know what to do. I need to start some scans from the main office, but then I'll be out to help. If you need anything before then, just let me know."

"Will do."

Turning to Russel, I said, "Sergeant Cruz, may I speak with you?"

"Of course. Lead the way," he said, gesturing to the office.

Dr. Adams inclined her head, then addressed the team. Before we disappeared down the hall, they were off to their stations, ready to begin our next round of experiments. I took a deep breath, relief filling me. In a moment, the entire energy in the lab had changed. There was hope here again.

Russel followed me into the main office that Adams and I shared. It was where I spent most of my time, even though I had a workstation in the main lab for when I helped with experiments. Adams preferred to be with the others, but I made sure she had a desk next to mine for when she had data to review. It gave us a quiet place for research and analyzing data. It was my safe place and, right now, I needed it.

With the click of the door behind me, I spun and wrapped my arms around Russel's waist.

I sucked in a breath at my actions. Had I just done that? I was about to pull away when his arms wrapped around me. Against my will, my eyes closed as my cheek pressed to his chest. I breathed in deep, taking in the support he was — for some reason — willing to provide. Only then did the panicked excitement begin to subside.

My breathing finally slowed, my heart rate dropping to a normal level. I sighed.

"I can't believe we figured it out," I said, his warm breath brushing my forehead. "I've been working so hard and failing miserably. And then, some kid makes a joke about how the crystal exploded, and it clicks. I bet everyone in the Green Room thinks I'm nuts with how I bolted out of there."

Russel chuckled. "I would've liked to see that."

I pulled back so that I could look up at him. His arms loosened but didn't let me go.

"You really freaked me out when you came running in like that." His voice was soft, vulnerable. Not like Russel, the hardass soldier. "I thought something bad happened. Let me rephrase, I thought something worse happened — with Geron or Patrick."

"Oh. Um...Sorry. No." I rested my palm on his chest, but couldn't quite look at him when I said, "No, Geron is doing as well as can be expected. He's stable."

Russel moved, catching my gaze with his. "They'll figure it out. Geron's tough."

With a sad smile, I continued, deciding to change the subject. "As for Patrick, he is fine. Though he did decide to risk 'death by Mitchel' today."

For a second, I got lost in his gaze, the warmth of his hands on my lower back calming me. Son of a cracker, I needed to get a hold of myself. I could not be growing feelings for Russel. It was not the time. Yes, he was acting like his old self, mostly, but that didn't mean I was ready to forgive him for being a dick for so long. Though it was getting harder every day we worked so comfortably together. Especially as he genuinely seemed to care.

"What does that mean?" he asked, shifting his hands to my hips.

Somehow, that was more distracting. I stepped away from his embrace, his arms falling back to his sides. I felt cold without his touch.

"Well, Patrick decided to get the pellets implanted against Mitchel's orders."

"He did not!" The angry tone aligned with my own feelings on the subject. I still couldn't believe Patrick risked it.

"Yeah, he did. With the way that vein was throbbing on Mitchel's forehead, I was a little worried he was going to kill Patrick. Or stroke out," I said, taking a seat at the desk. I gestured to the other chair, continuing, "Bring that over. I want you to see something." He did as I asked. "Anyway, they treated the CR3 before implantation, and it worked. It doesn't look like he's aging like before."

"That's both reckless bullshit and... great news." The way he scowled almost made me laugh because it was an amusing mix of *"I'm going to kill him"* and happiness for his friend. "So, Patrick's out?"

"Yeah. We should get a hold of both Mitchel and Patrick. We need to debrief them. Plus, Patrick was freaked out about something today. I know he and Tanaka have been working with Lieutenant Reid about the ship's approach procedures. Patrick's the expert on that, so I've let him take the lead from the beginning while I covered other projects. I wonder if they're not going as well as he hoped."

I logged into the computer terminal, then pulled up the readings I'd taken last night. There was something I wanted to show Russel that might warrant another round of scans. If I was right, we might have a path moving forward. The issue was, there was so much freakin' interference in this system, I was having a hard time sorting through it all. Usually, space was a lot quieter.

"I would guess it does," he said, scooting up next to me. "We woke up six months late, and the deceleration procedures take eight. There are scheduled bursts throughout that time. When we first woke up, I worked with him to set up a new plan. It wasn't perfect, but it got the ball moving. When Lieutenant Reid woke up, he took over. I've been too busy to follow up."

"Think we should go talk to him now?"

"No, I think you should tell me your idea for treating the ship. One step at a time. Let's figure this out, then we'll find Patrick, Mitchel, and whoever else we need to. We'll debrief them and figure out what the next disaster is."

I huffed. "Fine. I hope I'm right. I hate that it took me so long to figure this all out."

"We, Tasha. We couldn't figure this out." Russel took my hand, and I jumped but didn't pull away. He was so close, his thigh pressed to mine. "It's because of you that we're this far."

My breath caught as he pressed a kiss to my knuckles. His eyes never left mine, and I swear the universe stopped shifting. All that existed was the tingling where his lips grazed my skin and the emotion in those eyes.

Only a few times over the last weeks had the feelings he'd hinted at made an appearance. Mostly, he'd done what he promised me back in that locker room; he stopped being the jerk he'd been the last year and instead acted like my friend, my partner.

He placed my hand back on the armrest of my chair, then rested his on the desk.

"Russel, I..."

He inclined his head to the screen. "Show me what's going on. You said you have an idea on how we can treat the ship?"

I bit my lip, and his eyes tracked the movement. I shivered at the affection in his gaze. Blinking the haze away, I said, "Over the last few days, I've been scanning the system, trying to find anything unusual or that could potentially be emitting the radiation that we require."

"And?"

"There is so much noise in this system. But it's more than that. Take a look at this."

I pulled up the scans of the region around Eronis and Merocius.

"You've seen how other gas giants appear on these types of scans, correct?" He nodded. "The first thing I want you to look at are the rings around Eronis. Do you see anything strange about them?"

His eyebrows pushed down in confusion. "Yeah, there's a huge collection of metal in the ring. It's a larger amount than documented before, but the meteorites trapped in orbit could have a high content."

"They could, but..." I pulled up the image showing the approximate sizes of each fragment captured in the ring. "When I saw this, I did some high-level analysis of the area, and they don't look like meteorites at all. Or most of them don't. I won't be able to confirm until we're closer, but I think that that is wreckage from a ship."

"That's impossible."

"No, it's not. And if I am right, it would open an entirely new bag of worms. The information I'm getting back looks like pieces of a ship that broke apart. I've only found one larger section intact, but it's along the farther side of Eronis, and I can't get a full image of it. Some of the smaller pieces are very clearly electrical components. And this piece here" — I zoomed in as far as I could on a large cylindrical structure missing the bottom left side. Even with such a grainy image, it was hard to doubt what it was — "looks like something we are both familiar with."

Russel's mouth dropped open. "Is that an engine?"

He leaned closer into the screen. Taking the controller, he shifted the image, examining the area I'd been focused on before being called to Green Room 4. After a few moments, he sat back, his gaze shifting to mine.

"Holy shit," he said, awe in his voice. "It is. It has to be."

"I know, but that is not all I found."

"Do I want to know?"

I smiled. "You really do."

A grin curved the corner of his mouth.

With a few clicks, I pulled up a new image — one that showed all of the radio frequencies flowing through the area.

"Every system, star, or planet gives off a certain amount of radiation that our instruments easily detect, right?" I asked.

"Yeah."

"This system? It gives off vast amounts of noise. Like, way more than I expected. The amount from the blue sun is within normal range of what I'd expect, as are the planets closer to it due to their higher surface temperatures, but what I hadn't expected was the shockingly large amount coming from Eronis itself."

Russel crossed his arms over his chest and cocked his head.

"There is something unique about Eronis." I pressed the button to show the time-lapse video of all scans taken over the last seventy-two hours. I watched Russel's face as it played and knew the moment the storm on the surface came into view.

Russel sat up, his eyes widening.

"What is that?" he asked.

"It's the storm on the southern hemisphere. That day I first saw it on the observation deck, I knew something was off about it. It didn't look natural to me." I ran a hand over my ponytail. I huffed, then continued, "Geron didn't believe me, but he assured me I'd get the chance to study it when we got to Merocius. Looks like it might be sooner than that."

With a grin, Russel met my eyes. "Well, now you get to tell him he was wrong, and you were right because whatever's coming out of that thing is almost as strong as the star itself."

"Yes, it is."

"What are you thinking this means? I don't like that look in your eye. It makes me nervous."

Smirking, I said, "I can't take the readings I want or need yet to confirm — we aren't close enough — but I think the storm is our answer."

"How? I mean, this could be a fluke."

"It could be, but have you ever noticed the color of the rings around Eronis?" I asked.

"No, not really. Eronis is pretty spectacular all on its own. Why?"

I pulled up another image — a simple picture of the star system, Eronis front and center with the Aramitacus Star breaking the horizon. It was an absolute beauty, and it had been in only this image where I'd seen it.

It took a full minute for Russel to see what it had taken me seconds to notice.

"There's no fucking way," he said.

"Right? Again, we're too far out for our systems to analyze it properly or for samples to be collected, but I'm not imagining this, am I? The rings around Eronis glitter red?"

I don't think I had ever seen Russel truly speechless until that moment. His penetrating stare shifted from the screen to me. "What exactly do you think is happening here?"

"It's all speculation, but there's clearly radiation flowing from the eye of the storm. A storm that does not seem natural and never changes in size, frequency, or location. I've been recording it whenever it enters our view, and, Russel, it's perfect. There are no changes in wind speeds or flow. There are no alterations in temperature, no variations in pressure from what I can see, and the computers are picking up something else, too. I didn't know what it was at first, but I do now."

With quick movements, I changed the settings of my program and clicked on the speakers to imitate the wavelength I'd picked up. I winced as loud, high-pitched sounds filled the office. The mixture of tones wove in and out of each other, somehow both beautiful and painful to the ear. I lowered the volume.

"If," I started. "If I am right, then I think we just found a way to treat the entire ship. I don't know if what's coming out of that storm are the frequencies we need or if *The Aspire* could survive the full force of that combination, but it's a place to start."

Hope lit his eyes as he pieced together everything I'd told him.

"Have you sent these combinations to Dr. Adams? I think we should try these sound wavelengths first. It also looks like a few of the radiation groupings are different. We should see what they result in as well."

With a swipe of my finger, I forwarded the information to Adams with a quick note.

"Just did. I wanted to see your response before I sent it over. I knew that if you thought it was nothing, you'd tell me honestly."

He shook his head. "It's not nothing."

There was a squeal from the other room. I grinned. Adams understood. This was followed by her barking orders at the team. Russel shook his head, and my gaze dropped to my hands.

"Russel," I asked, my voice coming out quieter now. "What if the destroyed ship is why the storm exists at all?"

"Wait. You think that storm was created?" he asked. I shrugged. "And that the ship that made it is in pieces around Eronis?"

"I have no idea," I said with a sigh. "But there are a lot of coincidences lining up here."

"Fair enough." He leaned back in his chair, exhaling slowly. I could almost hear the gears in his head spinning as he scratched his jaw. "When are we close enough to get more accurate readings of the storm?"

"A few days. I have scans running every hour at this point. The closer we get, the more accurate they'll become and the more information we can request."

"Then perhaps we hold on telling everyone. Keep this to those who absolutely need to know — the research group, the captain, and maybe those plotting our course."

"I agree," I said, standing. "Although this could give hope, we don't know if it's real yet. With the outbreaks, the few deaths, and now the Green Room contamination, people are scared. I don't want to give false hope."

"True, but we can tell them about the sound waves advancement. Good news is good news. We can't assume anything yet about the storm, but we'll figure it out. Either way, we're making progress both here and on the ship. Did you see the team rerouted the M4-S4 axillary cartistry system, resetting the SRTA for the entire module?"

"They did?" Pride had my chest rising. The team was making huge progress on *The Aspire* repairs.

"They did. We are nearly halfway to setting everything to rights." Pressing his hands to his thighs, he pushed up to standing. He held out a hand to me and said, "Come on. Let's go find the captain and Patrick and tell them what we've figured out so far. I heard they were visiting Geron, who I know you haven't seen today yet anyway, and I haven't been able to give him shit."

I sighed, annoyed. Though he'd been nicer to me, he had yet to let up on Geron. Okay, that wasn't completely true. He'd been kinder since the infection, but the banter hadn't let up.

I reached out and took his hand, allowing him to pull me to my feet. "You better be nice."

"I can't promise anything." But he squeezed my fingers ever so gently. Jerk.

Chapter Sixteen
Captain Mitchel Remian

"Oh, I see how it fucking is. It takes Montgomery dragging your coward ass in here before you come check on me." Richards's tone shifted to something more feminine, and he placed his hand on his heart when he said, "Days!" Then he moved it to his forehead and leaned his head back as if he were a damsel in distress about to faint. "It has been five days and you haven't even called. I thought I meant more to you. And no flowers? How will I heal without flowers?"

Dr. Pia, who knelt next to him, snickered. She shifted his leg up onto the formed foot of the wheelchair he sat within, then turned toward the door. When she realized it was me, she bit down on the reaction and became very interested in getting the other foot placed. By the time she stood and faced us, she'd managed a straight face. I could see through it, the fight to keep from laughing.

"I'll come back later," she said, patting his shoulder. "We'll change the bandage in an hour, and you should head over to PT in the next few minutes."

"We can take him over," Patrick said, shaking Richards's hand.

"Sound's good." With a last glance to Richards, Dr. Pia said, "Don't do anything stupid, and remember —"

"I know, I know, prep at 1600," Richards said.

She smiled kindly; then, with an incline of her head to me, left the room.

I lifted my eyebrow at him.

"Don't give me that look. I'm injured. I can curse at you if I want to. I'm not on shift." Richards placed his hands on the wheels on either side of him and, as if he'd been doing it for years, maneuvered around the bed and over to a small couch.

Patrick laughed, the git. Ugh, now they had me doing it.

I groaned, but approached, entering the spacious room and stopping next to the chair. To my chagrin, I found I was unable to look directly at him and acknowledge the damage that was right in front of me. Which was why I took in the spacious room — the deep blue leather of the couch, the cart of medical equipment tucked within easy access behind it, the bed, and the door off to the side where a small washroom was visible.

I took a seat on the couch next to him, forced myself to finally meet his eyes, and said, "Nice room."

Richards's smile was kind. He knew me well enough. Which was why he'd been an asshat when I'd walked in.

Man...I needed sleep. That was the only way I'd lock this shit back up.

"It is," he said, as Patrick sat beside me. "This makeshift medical wing is pretty sweet. Tanaka, Norris, and Tasha pushed the field they created to include not only the lab they needed, but the one nearest the shuttle bay. Dr. Pia and Doc Mendez have been modifying it so that we can house all the infected. Considering we're up to eight of us now, they figured it was best."

"Eight?" Patrick asked, surprised.

"Before we heard about Green Room 4, two more came forward reporting exposures from crystals popping up in new locations," I said. "That's why we instituted the hardsuit requirement. The crew is doing a great job reporting sightings now. We've been tracking the growth patterns and have been able to predict where they'll show up next. Mostly, anyway."

"Wow! It's great that we can track it," Patrick said. "But the two that came in, did we confirm infection?"

"Yeah. Doc's taking care of it," Richards affirmed.

"And you? How are you?" I finally asked.

"I'm good, Captain. They've stabilized the CB2 and my injury."

I swallowed hard. "And your legs?"

His head tilted ever so slightly, his gaze piercing me. I could feel Patrick's eyes on me, too.

"Oh, you know, Captain," Tasha said, entering the room like a whirl-wind. She strode in, kissed Richards's head, then plopped down on the medical-grade recliner opposite the couch. This must've been a small seating area for a larger office, the coffee table having been removed. "He's playing it up so that he can get all the ladies' attention."

Richards rolled his eyes, then in a sudden shift in expression, waggled his eyebrows at her. "The amount of attention I get hasn't changed."

"Ew, gross. I don't want to know," Tasha said as Cruz glided in at a much more subdued pace. He stopped beside Tasha. "But seriously, how are you today?"

"Overall, good." Richards rested back in his chair and ran his hands down his legs. "We've got the pain under control and the chair fitted properly now, which has made it a whole lot easier to move around."

It was as if my diaphragm had become a brick. It felt heavy, making it hard to inhale. Just imagining what he was going through made my legs tingle. How was he so calm?

"I didn't know we had one on board," Cruz said as I fought to hide my reaction to the words. I sucked in air through my teeth, the cold making them ache. Somehow, the sensation centered me.

"Captain," Richards said. The forceful tone pulled me from my panic and brought my attention back to him. In slow, clear words, he said, "I will be fine. Dr. Pia and Dr. Gollie have a plan. They think that now that the CC1 is connected to the CB2, we should be able to repair the injury to my spinal cord. They're doing some final tests, but it's promising."

"I don't like this," I admitted.

Still, I didn't miss how fast Tasha's eyes lit with hope. How could she be happy with this? It was so dangerous!

"Well, to be honest, I think we've had a lot we could say we don't like about the last few weeks," Cruz said. Heat rose in my chest, and I was about to snap at him when he added, "But it's great news they have a plan moving forward that might return your legs. I hope it does. And we" — he gestured to Tasha — "have some good news, too."

Patrick scowled. "That is? Please tell me it has something to do with why she ran out of Green Room 4 today."

I relaxed the moment the look of confusion crossed her face.

"Of course it does. What else would it be about?" Tasha asked.

After she pulled up some diagnostic information on a monitor nearby, she and Cruz proceeded to explain what they'd figured out about the sound waves being the final factor in the treatment of the Cnidramarus. In the few hours we'd been apart, their team had collected samples from the Green Room and found many of the Cnidramarus were severely harmed by the noise released when the system had rebooted. The team had begun the tests utilizing the radiation combinations previously identified. Those results were not quite in yet, though.

"There's something else." She shared a look with Cruz. "I haven't confirmed it yet, so this information will stay between us, but..."

And over the next five minutes, she explained her theory of the rings, the storm, and a realistic treatment for the ship. It was so much to take in, but as she flipped through the images and readings she'd already collected, it was hard to doubt her. There was too much pointing to this being true. When I looked at Patrick, I was happy to know that I wasn't the only one floored by it all.

"The sound waves are already being used by Dr. Adams. All that's left to verify is what else is coming out of that storm," she said.

"And you think it's what we need?" I asked.

"I do. My gut tells me this is it. My only concern is the strength being emitted. If it's going to harm the crew, it's not worth it, but we needed you to know what we found. I should have confirmation by the end of the week. It's at that point we should be close enough to confirm the frequencies exuded. Commander Montgomery, you've been working on the approach path, and I think that we should consider adding a potential flight plan that passes over the storm." She was pacing the room. "I don't think we should spread the word about this to anyone as it's not a confirmed solution, but I think we should continue reviewing it as an option."

"Agreed." I sat taller than I had in hours. This was hope. The chance we needed.

Patrick leaned forward to rest his elbows on his knees. He rubbed his temples, looked at Tasha and Cruz, and then, he glanced at me. "Captain, we need to begin simulations immediately. Regardless of whether this is a treatment, we must start the calculations. We also need to consider options for utilizing the other moons around Eronis 8 for slowing *The Aspire* during approach."

I eyed him, remembering there had been something important he needed to tell me. How had I forgotten?

Lack of sleep, remember? *Bloody hell, Remian, you're falling apart.*

I wouldn't forget again. "You mentioned earlier that you had something important to discuss. What was it?"

Suddenly, Dr. Pia stuck her head in. We went silent. She pointed at Richards and said, "P.T." Then, she disappeared.

Richards smiled.

"Walk with me. I need to hear this." He reached down and began to move himself slowly toward the door.

We stood, the tension between us thick in the air.

With a deep exhale, Patrick started, "When we awoke, we were approximately five months behind in the deceleration protocols."

"Yes," I said, following Richards from the room and taking up a spot beside him, Patrick on the other. Tasha and Cruz followed behind.

"Over the last two weeks, we have taken a more aggressive approach, which we have discussed previously."

"Correct," I said, wondering when he would get to the point. We turned right at the end of the hall, our steps echoing in the hallway.

"Well, after further calculations, we've confirmed that if we don't take a few more risky, advanced actions, there's a significant possibility we'll miss our target completely and slingshot into space," Patrick said.

We all stopped moving. We just stood silently, the shock of those words tingling against the skin like freezing sea spray as waves crest nearby. Even the roar clouded my senses.

"I've been working with the team to identify options. We've made good progress so far, but we need three large burns — at least — to slow us down enough to land on Merocius. The first one would be tomorrow, if you give your approval."

Tasha spoke up. "If we do additional burns, we won't have enough fuel for the ship sections to separate from *The Aspire* and land on Merocius."

"What?" I asked, voice rising. My fists clenched at my sides.

"Captain." Patrick stepped around Richards, who was watching this exchange with interest. "At this point, I'm not sure there's any way we're landing the sections at all anyway."

"What? What does that mean?" Richards asked.

"It means that at our current speed, the only option may be to crash land on Merocius."

My heart rate picked up. I wiped away the sweat from my brow with the back of my hand. Crash landing? No! *The Aspire* wasn't created for interplanetary entrance. She was a transport vessel, intended to remain a satellite research station upon arrival! Most of her had been assembled in space with only the sections specifically designed and built to detach and enter a planet's atmosphere. The main ship, however, was not meant to withstand that kind of heat and pressure. She'd collapse under her own weight.

"You know the ship can't take that."

"We might not have a choice," Patrick said, voice calming.

Pressure built in my chest. My fist clenched, and I had to focus on taking in a full breath.

"No! That isn't an option," I hollered. I strode down the hallway only to turn and come back. Back and forth I paced, craving the movement and praying it would calm the terror burning through me. Maybe then some of this tension would release, and I'd be able to process what Patrick had said.

"If the burns are successful, there's still the chance that we can slow enough to detach, but we must plan for the worst-case scenario," Cruz said. It was clear he was trying to help. It was in the way he said it, and the fear in his eyes.

But I was no longer rational. "I will not crash land *The Aspire*," I growled into his face.

Patrick stepped closer, demanding my attention. "We might not have a choice."

Before I was aware of what I was doing, I gripped Patrick's collar. My face pressed into his space, and a snarl curled my lip.

"Bullocks! We will not lose *The Aspire*! We will do the burn tomorrow, then recalculate, and every arsebadger on this damn ship will do their fucking job to make sure we make it there safely."

"Captain Remian!" Tasha hollered, her petite frame pushing between us. Tasha's palm pressed to my chest, shoving me away. I leaned away, giving Patrick space to breathe.

Another hand reached out and grasped my wrist. It took me a moment to realize it was Cruz's. I wanted to hurt him, but then his voice hit my ears.

"Captain Remian," Cruz said, voice calm. "Please release Commander Montgomery."

Realizing what I'd done, I did so and stepped back. I dropped my gaze to the floor.

The hallway was silent for a few heartbeats. Then Richards asked, humor in his voice, "Arsebadger? Really?"

Patrick's lips pressed together, twitching as if he were trying to hold back a laugh. I looked to find Tasha fighting a smile. She lost the battle, and a full-blown grin spread her face before she laughed. That had given Richards the go ahead. He let out a laugh that broke both Patrick and Cruz.

"That's a new one, Cap," Patrick said. "I like it."

"I think it's my new favorite," Richards said.

"Shut up," I mumbled petulantly.

"What?" Cruz said. "You call us arsebadgers, and I think you deserve to get a little shit. Especially when I'm the only one who truly deserves that title."

I laughed and met Cruz's gaze. For the first time in a long while, I felt like he was part of our group. It was strange, but nice.

"Ain't that the truth," Richards said, shoving Cruz's shoulder.

Tasha placed a hand on my arm. "When was the last time you slept?"

"I had a rest period six hours ago."

"That's not what she asked," Cruz said. His voice was kind, but regardless, I felt that old irritation build. I glared at him through my eyelashes.

Patrick spoke this time. He'd leaned against the wall of the hallway.

Shit, we were just standing in the middle of the hallway outside what was the physical therapy room.

"I know Doc gave you a sedative," he said. His tone was bland, but his eyes were hard as they watched me.

"I didn't take it. Richards, you need to get to PT."

"This is more important," Richards said, glaring. "Why didn't you take it?"

Yes, Doc had prescribed me a sleeping pill, but I hated taking medications. What if there was an emergency that required my attention? If I'd had the sedative in my system, I would've been too groggy to deal with it.

"Bad decision, Mitchel, and you know it," Patrick said.

With a nod, I said, "Yeah, it probably was. I'm sorry, Patrick...all of you."

Patrick straightened his shirt. "I understand, old friend, but we need you functional. You know what you need to do?"

"Yes," I sighed.

"Do I need to call it in?"

"No." Using my armpad, I pulled up Doc's contact and sent him a request for another sedative, explaining that I had not used the last one he'd provided. Almost immediately, he responded.

"Doc is on his way," I said, glancing between them.

"Good," Tasha said. "Then we need to get Richards to PT. Afterward, Cruz and I are going with Patrick to talk with Reid and finish preparations for the burn."

"What about the research?" I said.

"Our team is on it. The ship needs us today," Cruz said simply.

Tasha agreed. "They can contact us if they need anything, and my first round of scans won't be done until this evening."

"Perfect, because I'll need both of you to help prepare for a maneuver planned for tomorrow." Patrick turned to me, his face serious. "That's if we have your approval to proceed, Captain?"

I inhaled slowly, then said, "You do. Send out an all-hands with the information. Make sure to coordinate with Brackett to verify reanimation is not endangered."

"Will do."

"How is reanimation going?" Richards asked.

"Well, overall, almost half of the crew is awake. She's been working her team around the clock, but it's a slow process," I said.

"I'll reach out to her. We need to make sure her timeline is aligned with all burns and approach to Merocius. I don't want to risk anyone."

"Agreed."

"Get in there, Richards, or Dr. Pia will be on us all," I said.

"Let me know how I can help. I know I'm in this chair, but if everything goes well with the procedure tonight, I should be back on shift in a few days."

I placed a hand on his shoulder. "Focus on healing. That's most important. Once you're better, then we'll get you back on the Bridge, and you can drive me nuts."

He chuckled. "It would be my pleasure."

We left him there, the rest of us continuing on to Main Engineering. There, the conversation picked back up, and Patrick outlined a plan that was, by all accounts, insane. Even in space, the forces he was planning to put the ship under were dangerous and could cause issues we wouldn't foresee until they appeared.

The simulation he ran showed *The Aspire* in all her glory, firing all auxiliary thrusters on the starboard side. The sudden change caused an automatic shift in the angle of the ship. Once moving along in a straight-forward path, the starship now flipped, spinning so that the main engines were now pointed backward, in the direction the ship's momentum still carried us and toward Merocius. Just before the image began to rotate too far, opposite thrusters engaged, and *The Aspire* leveled out.

"Once our new position is confirmed," Patrick said, "we will transfer the fuel to the main engines and perform a three-minute burn. From our initial calculations, this should be sufficient for the first of three."

Tasha's eyes had glazed over. Her face had gone blank as her brilliant mind did the calculations in her head. After a long moment, the light in her gaze came back only to be replaced with fear.

"Wait," she said, her voice shaking ever so slightly. "When we first woke up, we were estimated to be approximately five months from Merocius. But that's not what I see here. I knew it would be sooner because we weren't slowing, but damn...based on our current speed and this plan, we're only eight weeks away?"

"Six," Patrick said. "And that's only if we can slow this bad boy down enough."

"We're going to crash," Cruz said matter-of-factly as he too reviewed the calculations before him. With a curse under his breath, he said, "What do you need?"

"I need your help verifying the calculations. I need you here to help initiate the spin, transfer of fuel, and manage the burn itself. Additionally, we need to recalculate the projected path. With us going this fast, we may need to adjust our direction to give us more time to slow the ship. And now we need to add in the need to pass over the storm."

"Commander Evans," Cruz said, drawing her attention, "is there any reason to believe that the storm would help slow the ship? That the fields emanating from it would affect the ship as a whole?"

Tasha's eyebrows shot up, her lips pursing. "I don't know. Until I can get a full reading, I can't answer that. But I'll look more into Eronis, its gravitational allowances, and, hell, anything else I can think of."

Their voices overlapped for long minutes as ideas were passed back and forth. I asked a few questions or added a few tiny nuggets, but really, this was their discussion. I was just there as an observer. Which was why I was the only one that noticed when Doc Mendez walked into Engineering.

He made a beeline toward me. With a hard smile, he held out his hand, palm open. Inside was a small container with the sedative inside. I reached out and took it.

"Now," Doc said, his voice giving no room to argue. "I have cleared it with your team. You are on mandatory rest for eight hours."

"Doc," I started.

"No, Captain. You were required to rest last time, and you did not. If you do not abide by the rules, you will be pulled from rotation."

Seeing Doc and the way I glared at him, Patrick stepped up to us. "Eight hours is perfect. Estimated time for the maneuver is ten. You should be back on shift before then."

With a heavy sigh, I opened the container and took the medication provided. I'd have about thirty minutes before it took full effect.

Patrick nodded supportively and was about to say something when his lync went off. His face furrowed, and I thought I saw him mouth "Norris." Sliding on his earpiece, he answered, but before he could even get a word of welcome out, Norris's voice came through the line.

I couldn't hear exactly what she said, but the tone was clear enough. She was upset. Panic and fear raced up my spine. Nothing scared Captain Norris.

"I'll be right there," Patrick said. He spun to Cruz and Tasha, who were still in their own world. "Reid and his team are on their way. Get everything started. I'll be back after I deal with something."

"Yes, Commander," Cruz said.

Then Patrick bolted for the door.

Doc and I shared a glance, and then we sprinted after him. We caught up to him at the lift. We peppered him with questions as the doors closed, but he said nothing. He shifted from foot to foot, as if waiting to run the moment the doors opened again.

"Patrick, what's going on?" I asked.

"Victoria," was all he said.

We followed him through the hallways and back into the shuttle bay where the main shield was still intact. Although the air had been recycled again, and the crystal had spread to other parts of the ship, this was still the central location for the Cnidramarus outbreak. But as we were still wearing hardsuits, it was decided that full containment gear was no longer required, so Patrick headed straight for the transfer area. Once we were all in, he locked the first shield in place, then dropped the next one. A moment later, he was running toward the ramp.

Doc and I followed without a word, passing the wall of crystal filled with wriggling Cnidramarus. We were at a near sprint when I ran full force into Patrick's back. He'd stopped in the doorway of the medical suite and barely moved as I collided with him.

"Patrick?" I asked. I leaned around him to see what had caught his attention.

He didn't answer. Instead, he stepped forward, taking slow steps toward the figure who knelt in a puddle of water on the floor. She was curled into herself as she sobbed over her cupped hands. Her body spasmed with each ragged inhale. Patrick lowered himself to a knee at her side and gently pressed a palm to her back. The sound of her harsh cries rose, and she leaned into his side, his arm wrapping around her shoulders.

Doc and I stayed by the door. We had no idea what was going on, but Norris was not one to appreciate an audience.

"Victoria," Patrick whispered. "What happened?"

She choked. After a few heavy breaths, she raised her damp hands and said, "Vincent. He's gone. It didn't work. He regressed too far, and I couldn't save him."

Chapter Seventeen

Commander Patrick Montgomery

Her words didn't register right away. They slipped through my mind like water through mesh. I stared down at the small, cream-colored blob in her hand which had strands of pink yarn-like lengths spreading from it. They threaded through her fingers, hanging limply toward the floor. Near the tips, the color deepened to a vibrant red. A shiny, clear viscous fluid covered her hands and forearms as well as the floor around her. Within it, more pink-tinted sections.

I knelt outside the puddle, but Norris sat directly in the center, as if she had been there when the bubble burst.

"He's gone, Patrick," she croaked, "Vincent is gone. It didn't work. I tried, and he's dead." Tears trailed down her face, slipping from the tip of her nose and falling onto the thing she held.

He? My mind spun, trying to put together the pieces of what she was saying.

Oh, shit. He.

I glanced at the cooler along the wall where eight mechanical uteri were woven into the mechanics of the shuttle. It was technology that still astounded me. Illegal tech back on the homeworld, but that here had saved lives and provided hope for their captain. At the base of each was a panel — lights flickered on each, indicating heart rate, oxygen levels, and other necessary information. Much of which Norris herself had to explain to me. The familiar green lights bounded back as I scanned each one. That was, until I reached the last. That one was red and showed no signs of life.

"Oh, Victoria," I said on an exhale.

My heart broke as I wiped away the tears on her face. She met my gaze, and I caught my breath. The pain there wasn't of a coworker's or even a friend. No, it was the pain of a mother losing her child.

Some of what she'd said over the last few weeks came back to me. She'd explained how these crew members had been her coworkers and friends, but then as they regressed, they'd become more. With each new age — each childhood stage they'd reached — they'd shifted and become her children. It was more than feeding and clothing them. She cared for them.

Refusing to think about what was all over her and the floor — because, eww — I cupped my hands around hers and looked down at the person who had once been so important to her. I managed to hold in the shudder at the feel of the tendrils against my skin — wet and slimy, they adhered to my fingers like the suction cups of an octopus. Barely resembling a human anymore, the pale white creature was curled up, its skin wrinkled, almost translucent.

"Vincent?" I asked. This baby she held was precious to her, and so I would treat it with as much respect and dignity as I could spare.

"Yes. Vincent Demarco," she said with a sniffle.

"I'm so sorry. I wish I'd been here," I said. Her swollen eyes blinked slowly at me. "But I'm here now. Why don't we put him in something to keep him warm? Then we can make sure he has the ceremony he deserves."

Norris nodded, and to my surprise, a silver box appeared next to us. I looked up to find Doc Mendez holding it, a grim smile and kind eyes staring back. Mitchel stood a few feet behind, leaning against the wall. His eyes were drooping, and he was swaying from side to side. I'd forgotten either one of them was there.

Norris blushed when she noticed Doc but recovered quickly.

She had no reason to be embarrassed, but not wanting her to feel that way, I drew her attention back to me. "This should work, and it's pretty."

When she nodded, I took the silver container with one hand and helped her slide what was left of Vincent into it. The tentacles, or Cnidramarus connectors, I had to peel from her skin. Little bastards were sticky.

Once the entire thing was tucked safely away, I closed it, then pulled Norris to her feet. She rose slowly, her position making her muscles tight, and came willingly into my embrace.

Normally, I'd never do this, hug a crewmate like this. But she deserved comfort right now, and I *needed* to give it to her regardless of the fact that we'd always had more of a student-teacher relationship. Because over the last few weeks, our relationship had changed. We'd gotten to know each other. We'd talked about movies and books, our careers, and even discussed personal things. She was a friend now. But even if we weren't, I still would've held her, because at that moment, she wasn't the notorious Captain Norris. She was Victoria, a woman who had to hold a friend, a child, as they died.

Over her head, I said to Doc, "Take Mitchel to his quarters; he's about to pass out. I've got this."

"I'll be back in thirty," he said, shooting a worried glance at Norris.

"No need. I'll stay for a bit."

"I'll need an update."

I could tell he felt bad for saying it, but that didn't detract from my irritation, which was why I said, "And I'll get you one."

He nodded, lips pressed tight. With one last glance toward the puddle on the floor, they left the shuttle.

For long moments, we stood like that, Norris wrapped in my arms, her cheek pressed to my chest. I rested my head on top of hers and had to hold back a laugh. I'd never noticed how small she was. Norris always seemed to take up so much of a room.

"Will you tell me what happened? You said, 'it didn't work,'" I said into her hair. She began to pull away, but I squeezed her tight and she relaxed against me again. "What did you mean?"

Pressing her forehead against me, she breathed deep — a shaky inhale I felt throughout my entire being.

"Did you know that when the sleep pod pulled me out of hypersleep, that the babies were too?" she asked.

"That's what you told me, yes."

"Which means that they were regressing again."

I waited for her to continue, but when she didn't, I said, "Okay."

"Vincent was less than a week away from death," she whispered so softly I had to strain to hear her. "He's been so much to me over the years. My friend, my one-time lover" — she paused — "and then my sweet boy. You should have seen him at five. He was such a troublemaker."

It took effort not to react to her confession, and even more not to ask questions. Norris was in her eighth decade, so of course she had people that played different or many roles in her life. That's how it worked. She and I, for example. But I wondered how much harder, stranger, it was for them to be in reverse, as had been for her and Vincent.

She hiccupped, then spoke.

"After we figured out how to treat you, I started doing some thinking. We've been so concerned about the newly infected — and with good reason — but we've done nothing for what's left of my crew. Then I started to wonder if the treatment you underwent would work on them. So, I..."

When she trailed off, I released her, needing to see if what I suspected happened was true. She refused to look up at me, so I gently placed a finger underneath her chin and raised it so I could look into her eyes.

"What did you do?" I asked.

"I chose the fetus closest to expiration and implanted a radiation pellet along the placental level of the Cnidramarus appendages."

Fuuuck me...

She'd chosen the person closest to death? Okay, I guess I understood that — sort of —especially if they were not likely to survive to a cure. I was aware of the ethical debates, and I would address those soon enough, but then she'd placed a radiation pellet inside the main collection of tentacles? Was this in hope of killing it slowly or something else?

This was so gods-damned reckless. She was playing God, and it wasn't her place. The moment the medical crew were reanimated, her rights as the decision maker had been revoked. That's how it worked.

Which was why I said, "You did what? Victoria! You aren't family, and you know the rules! If someone is injured and doesn't have anyone, then serious medical decisions are left to the doctors. How could you do that?" I pulled away completely. "There are so many things wrong with this, I don't even know where to start!"

Her eyes flared angrily. "No one else was doing anything! He would have died soon anyway, and we both know it. There's no way he'd make it long enough for a cure. If what I'd done had worked, it would've given him time! That's all I wanted."

I paced in a circle, running both my hands over my hair.

"But you didn't have to do this alone. Maybe if you'd added another person to the mix, they could've helped come up with a better plan. Or they could've — I don't know — been here for you when you did it."

"Patrick." Her voice was lost, weak.

"Explain what you did and why. Maybe we can figure out what went wrong."

Her gaze snapped up to mine, eyes going wide. "You'll help me?"

"This may be the stupidest fucking decision I've ever made, but yes. I have one requirement though," I said. Norris winced, waiting for my demand. "We bring Doc Mendez into the conversation before we treat the next person. We need to have a doctor weigh in on this. Can you agree with that?"

She wiped away the remaining wetness from her cheeks. "And if he says no?"

I took a minute to make sure what I said next was really what I wanted to do. If I agreed to this, it could ruin my entire career if something went wrong. But she was right — all the focus had been on the new infestation and finding a cure for those who recently or would become infected. These babies, who once were esteemed members of the crew, had been forgotten.

"Then we do it anyway," I said finally. "We make the decision together, and we both take the fall. Now, go get cleaned up. Then you'll explain exactly what you did and why. I'll call Doc Mendez and ask him to join us, all right?"

Norris nodded, then disappeared into the medical suite that acted as her bedroom. It was a small office with an attached bathroom. While she changed, I cleaned up the mess on the floor, then pulled up Doc's number on my lync.

"Patrick," Doc said by way of answer. "How are things there? How is Captain Norris?"

"She's settled, but, Doc, we need to discuss something with you. Can you head back here? It's important."

"No problem. Mitchel is out, and I'm done with rounds. I'll be there in five," Doc said, and the line went dead.

I leaned against the counter, mop still in hand, and stared at my feet. What was I doing?

Norris cleared her throat. I looked to where she stood in the doorway.

In a sad, but grateful tone, she said, "Thank you, Patrick. Thank you for coming. Thank you for not judging me as harshly as you probably should have."

I shrugged. "I get it, I do, but I'm still mad that you thought you needed to do this on your own." I pushed up and walked to her. I led her to the couch and had her sit next to me. "Come on. Explain exactly what you did and maybe we can figure out how to help the others."

With a heavy sigh, she took a seat at the workstation and pulled up her notes.

"After you were successfully treated with the implants, I began to think that using the pellets on the babies would work to slow the regression — give us enough time to figure out how to cure them. I didn't think they'd freak out like with Richards since it would be on the outside the placenta and wouldn't be near the main body of the CB2. I believed that by placing the pellet within the placental structure created by its tentacles, the CB2's abilities to change the timeline would slow, if not stop."

"Why?"

"Because the majority of the CB2 is located at the placental level during this phase. Plus, I was concerned about how the radiation would affect the development of the babies themselves."

I could see that. Exposing an embryo to high-level radiation was not a good thing. It could cause severe birth defects or even terminate the pregnancy too soon. Perhaps this was what happened with Vincent. It made me wonder if there was a time in pregnancy where the effects would be less severe.

Footsteps sounded in the hallway, and a second later, Doc Mendez strolled in. His gaze latched onto us. He grabbed a chair and brought it over. He didn't acknowledge Norris's meltdown earlier — just smiled sadly and took a seat.

"Hey. I heard you two had a question for me," he said, crossing his legs. He placed a hand on the ankle that rested on his thigh.

"Yes," I started. "Is there a time in pregnancy when exposure to radiation is less harmful to a fetus?"

Doc blinked. "Um, well, radiation is harmful at all stages, but the effects would be much less later in the pregnancy. I would guess the last trimester is best. Preferably as close to delivery as possible. Why?"

"And how could we get the fetuses to that developmental age?" I asked.

Doc Mendez's eyes narrowed as he glanced from Norris to me. "What am I missing?"

With a glance down at her hands, Norris explained everything that happened with Vincent and what she'd done. She explained her reasoning and process just as she had for me. Doc listened, his face impassive, but I saw a tightening of his jaw.

When she fell silent, he said, "Captain Norris, that was not your decision to make. But I agree that we have not focused enough attention on the treatment of your crew." He crossed his arms over his chest. "I warn you, Captain, that should you move forward with any additional unauthorized treatments —"

"Doctor Mendez —" she said, interrupting him. But Doc kept speaking.

"— and without my direct involvement, you will be brought up for review. Do you understand?" he asked. Norris's shoulders slumped, but she nodded. "You should know that I have been thinking about this situation, and I do have a plan. Let me show you something."

Doc pushed in between us so that he could use the keyboard embedded into the workstation. He pulled up a video marked with Tasha's team signature and hit "play."

"We've seen in both studies and host examples that when a CB2 and CR3 are integrated, they will attack each other, correct?"

"Yes," Norris said.

"And yet, when we examine the crystals, they live relatively close together, only a small film separating them. Well, it got me thinking, and with the help of Dr. Adams, they did a quick test for me."

We watched as the two Cnidramarus were placed together in the same petri dish, separated by a thin silicone membrane. First, neither the CR3, nor the CB2 attacked. Interesting, though, once they settled into their new environment, they did notice one another and something remarkable happened. Slowly, the CR3 pushed its appendages gently through the membrane. They entwined with those of the CB2 and began to vibrate ever so slightly.

"What in the hell?" I asked.

Doc nodded. "I couldn't believe it, either. After speaking with Dr. Adams, we think we know what's happening here."

"And that is?" Norris asked.

"They're feeding off each other. They won't share a host, but when a host is unavailable, the two types of Cnidramarus can rely on each other. That's why the crystal was still growing while we were asleep."

"That's incredible, but how does that help my crew?" Norris asked.

"Well, I believe that if we place the CR3 on the outside of the placental structure and not the implant, then it might stop the regression because the CB2 will be too focused on the CR3. But I would like to add one more step to the process."

"And that is?"

"If we were able to treat the CB2 with either the implant or the radiation laser prior, I believe it would allow the CR3 to push the timeline forward."

"What would happen at birth then, considering they can't inhabit the same host at the same time?" I asked.

"We would treat the CR3. As it is on the outside, it would be severely harmed and fall off. Or that's my hope."

"But won't they just start regressing again?" Norris asked.

"Yes, but hopefully by then, we'll have a cure for that."

Norris met my eyes, and hope had replaced the devastation in them. She placed her hand on her cheek as she took a deep breath.

"When can we move forward with this?" she asked.

"Within the hour. I was waiting for approval and for everything we need to be brought here. Once I had that, I was planning to discuss your most recent scans of your crew. I believe that the best to test this particular hypothesis on is Javier," Doc explained. Norris winced but stayed quiet. "From his last scan, it shows he is measuring approximately thirty-four weeks. Even if something should go wrong, I believe he could still be delivered safely."

"Has there been any additional development or hypotheses made in regard to your situation, Victoria?" I asked.

Norris shook her head, but it was Doc that spoke.

"Her last scans showed negligible aging. It seems like the CC1 is negating the effect of the CB2. It's as if she is stuck in time."

"Could this be something to consider for the babies upon delivery?" I asked.

"What do you mean?"

"Well, Victoria told me once that regression slowed once they hit the age of sixteen or something, right? Like it suddenly took them longer to reach the next younger milestone. They assumed this was because of the amount of energy and time it takes to grow physically. Well, what if that worked the same in reverse? What if, upon delivery, we did one final treatment of the CB2 and injected a CC1? It's possible that the babies would grow at a normal speed until they hit a certain age. Then, their aging process would slow to a level closer to that of the Captain's. Perhaps it's because it takes so much more energy during that time to grow, and there is only so much it can ingest."

"I don't get it," Norris said.

Doc tilted his head, thinking. "You think that with the CC1 inhibiting the CB2, the child will have excess energy above what it can absorb and so it will age?"

"Maybe not at the same rate, but yes."

Silence fell as we each worked to wrap our heads around it all. Of course, everything was a hypothesis, but at this point, it was all we had to go on.

Doc leaned forward. He looked at Norris when he said, "Javier was your crew. I need to know if you think he would agree to this."

Norris stared off into space, rubbing the back of her neck as if it hurt. We waited patiently for her answer.

"I-I think he would. He'd want the chance to live, and that's what this is," she said finally.

"Fair enough," Doc said, nodding. "Then we try it. If he ages in-vitro, and we can deliver him successfully, then we know what to do with the others. But I need you to realize what a risk this is."

"I understand," she said.

Apparently, Doc wasn't joking. Within the hour, Dr. Gollie and Dr. Adams appeared, pushing a cart filled with supplies. Some were for the implantations themselves, but the rest was specific equipment meant for the treatment of the premature baby. I hoped it wouldn't need to be needed, but it was better to have it than not.

"Captain, as this is your technology, can you please detach Javier's pod and bring it over here?" Dr. Adams asked.

"Sure," Norris said. "But why?"

"On the way here, we were discussing the potential of a reaction to the CR3 attachment. Considering what we've seen in adults, we want to be ready in case there is a bad reaction. Even half that of what we have seen could be detrimental to a fetus."

It was Dr. Gollie who spoke next. "But I believe that I can calm such a reaction if absolutely required." Gollie pulled out a surgery specific laser cutter from his pocket and held it up. "I have altered this to work similarly to the one you created, Captain. But this one emits the same frequencies identified by Dr. Adams's team, which are known to harm the Cnidramarus."

Doc Mendez pursed his lips and nodded. "That's fantastic. Those are far more accurate than the one we've used thus far."

"It's why I came. I know that this will work far better on such a small patient."

"Thank you, Doctor," Norris said. She placed the small pod, about the size of a medium-sized dog, on the table. Then, with a few flicks of her fingers, opened the outer shell of the mechanical uterus. Its pliable outer layer folded easier to the side as she spread it wide, allowing us full access to the amniotic sac inside. With careful hands, she reached in and turned the sac so that the darkly colored placenta was fully visible. The baby inside twitched, kicking out when Norris's hand brushed his side.

"This is where the main collection is," Norris said. "And this is where I believe we should place the CR3."

Adams reached in and examined the sac and placenta as well. She smiled, then said, "I agree. I also think this will work. This membrane is a perfect barrier."

Doc Mendez placed his hands on the table and met each of our gazes in turn.

"So do we all agree with this plan and accept the risks that might come with it?" One by one, we vocalized our agreement. "All right then, Captain, would you like to do the honors?"

Norris closed her eyes, took a steadying breath, then held out her hand. Meeting his gaze, she said, "Let's get Javier back."

Chapter Eighteen
Commander Tasha Evans

"**L**ieutenant Reid, good morning," I said, speaking over the cacophony that was Engineering. It was the way I liked it — utter chaos.

The room was bustling with activity. Crew members rushed around, readying for the burn scheduled to initiate in less than an hour. The professionalism these people had shown over the last twenty-four hours as we'd double checked the main engines, altered the side thrusters for the maneuver, and secured various parts of the ship, was remarkable. Every day I worked with them, the more grateful I was to be aboard *The Aspire*.

"Commander," Reid said, facing me, expression serious but welcoming.

"How are preparations? Are we on track, and where do you need me?"

"We're looking good. Auxiliary engines will be initiated in thirty to begin the initial shift. You and Cruz will be managing that team." Reid gestured to the figure leaning over a desk off to the right.

The man himself was speaking with someone, pointing to the screen they leaned before. At the sound of his name, Russel looked up and nodded. He said something to the engineer, then headed for us.

Reid continued, "Then, once we're ready, I'll need your help tracking the main burn." He pointed to the schematic of the stern of the ship. "We'll be firing engines two and four to conserve fuel. On the next burn in five days, we will fire one and three."

"Understood," Russel said. He indicated the meter for the starboard back-up tanks. "Overnight, our team drained all excess fuel from one and three as a safety precaution. It is housed in reserve tanks for now."

I'd been part of this, of course, but it was customary to perform an overview and verification prior to completion of the maneuver.

"We will keep eyes out for any issues and misfiring while you maintain the burn," I added. "We have our teams placed all over *The Aspire* ready to step in for repair should one be necessary."

"That's the plan," Reid said. "Any questions?"

"Where's Commander Montgomery?" I asked. I took another scan of the room to make sure I hadn't missed him.

"He's on his way. Apparently, he was held up. He promised to be here for the burn, though," Reid said. "I need to check in with Rodgers." With a curt nod, he retreated, his long strides taking him to a man I'd only met a few days ago. Part of Reid's team, he was known to be a bit of a hot head. I'd liked him from the start.

I shared a questioning look with Cruz. He shrugged and asked, "Coffee?"

"Yes, please."

We stopped short when we found a very haphazard-looking Patrick filling a cup of coffee. His hair was a mess, dark circles marring the skin beneath his eyes. A wave of concern swept through me, and I found myself reaching out to steady myself on the doorway. Was the implant failing? Was the CR3 hurting him again?

"Patrick! What's going on? Are you feeling well?" I asked, making him jump.

"Yeah, man, you look like hell," Russel added.

I ignored him, continuing, "Where have you been? We expected you back last night to help with preparations, but you never showed. What happened? Are you okay?"

He held his hands up. "I'm fine, Tash." His movements were slow, as if he were sore or...as if he hadn't slept at all. He yawned, ran a hand through his hair, then said, "There was an emergency that needed my attention, but I was in contact with Reid and the team all night. I knew you guys had everything in hand."

This wasn't right. Patrick was a control freak.

Russel narrowed his eyes. As if reading my thoughts, he said, "Explain, Montgomery. You don't give up control, and definitely not on something as important as this."

Patrick looked around the small break room. There were a few others sitting or standing around, so he gestured for us to follow. We went back out into the main work area, then into a corner where his main workstation was — one of the more secluded areas of the space. He sighed and took a sip of his drink, then set it atop his station.

"When I ran out of here last night, it was because your aunt called me upset," he said to Russel. Those words set a shock through me. Whether because of the reminder that Norris was Russel's aunt or that she was upset, I wasn't sure. "One of the babies died. She experimented on him. She added a radiation pellet to it without anyone's help or approval."

"What!" Russel said.

"Yeah. I found her holding what was left of him." Patrick gazed into nothing, his expression of grief. A heaviness settled in my chest at seeing that look on his face. My limbs itched to reach out and hug him. Next to me, Russel's concern chilled the air.

In a quiet voice that had me resting a hand on Russel's back, he said, "How is she?"

Patrick breathed in deep. "Recovering. She took his loss hard. We told Doc Mendez what happened. I'm not sure if there will be repercussions since Demarco was close to passing anyway, but what you need to know — and need to keep between us — is that with his help and that of Dr. Adams, we treated another of the fetuses."

"You did what?" I asked, dropping my hand and stepping closer. Our voices had lowered to a whisper. We pressed together in a tight huddle. "What were you guys thinking? Does Mitchel or the other medical leaders know?"

He shook his head. Russel pursed his lips, then rubbed the bridge of his nose.

"Patrick, what the fuck?" Russel asked.

"We have a plan. A good one, too, and Doc Mendez and Dr. Adams have documented proof that this could work. No one has shown concern about the Elemental Crew, and they deserve to be helped as much as the rest of us. When we woke up Norris, we pulled the kids out of hypersleep too, which means they are regressing again. Most of them won't make it to Merocius if we don't do something."

"But don't you think —" I started.

"Listen, it's a two-step process. The first step will stop regression. There is even a chance it will help them move forward to their birth date. This will give us time to find a cure. That is all she wanted — time."

Move toward the birth date? Then what? That would mean they're using a CR3...

"This sounds dangerous. You did this...to one of the crew?" I asked, my eyes widening. Heat rose within me, and my chest flushed with anger.

"Yes, we've been up all night watching over him," he said.

I bit down on my tongue. If I didn't, I was going to lay into him. He was risking too much — the child, himself, Doc, Norris...

"And?" Russel asked. There was a tightness in his voice I recognized.

When Patrick closed his eyes, breathed in deeply, and then smiled, I didn't know what to do. Cheer? Holler? Slap him? Perhaps all of them.

A sense of relief spread over his expression as he said, "The treatment of the CB2 and then the implantation of the CR3 to the placenta went surprisingly easily. Dr. Gollie has a new device for more accurate radioactive treatment, and he somehow managed to do it without harming the fetus." He shook his head, blinking quickly. "I have no idea how. Afterward, the two Cnidramarus linked through the amniotic sac. After about five minutes, they settled. He's doing great so far."

He met my eyes when he said, "The scans this morning show that Javier has started aging. Norris is thrilled. He should be close to his delivery date in a few days. Then we can see if the second stage of treatment will work."

"And if it doesn't, then what?" Russel asked.

He dropped his head and shrugged. "We figure something else out. I don't know...it has to work."

"You care about her," I said simply. The simple respect he'd always had for her had changed into something else, and I wasn't sure if he was aware of it yet. Russel looked from me to Patrick and then back.

Patrick opened his mouth...

"It's time, everyone!" Reid called. "Let's get this thing going!"

Without another word, the three of us were yanked from the conversation of mechanical uteri and regressing fetuses, and our focus was on our ship. Patrick patted us on the shoulders, and we jogged to our workstations.

No thought was required as I entered my passcode and pulled up the diagrams and screens which allowed us to communicate with my teams located all over the ship. I flicked the button behind my ear, which controlled the earpiece I'd put in prior to leaving my suite this morning.

"Commander Evans on comms. Call back," I said. Instantly, I received reports from each and every team situated across the ship. One after another indicated readiness, status, and any issues identified prior to the burn. Once all had verified, I signaled to the leaders of this crazy adventure.

"Commander Montgomery, Lieutenant Reid, all teams ready for axillary burn and rotation of *The Aspire*. Approval for initiation of step one requested."

"Approved," Reid said.

"Approved," Patrick said. "Time to have some fun."

And, just like that, my day got a whole lot more interesting.

We flipped the ship. That was fun. The engines failed once, but we got them back online within three minutes, so it wasn't a big deal. And we only had two fires. We predicted those, and our teams put them out in less than one minute. Apparently, the auxiliary systems needed a bit more maintenance than we expected.

The main burn, however, went perfectly.

"From our initial calculations," Patrick said to Mitchel through the comm link — his face was plastered on the main screen overlooking Engineering. "It netted us more than we expected."

It was much quieter now, most of the crew having gone off shift an hour ago after completion of closing procedures. Reid, Aridas, Russel, and I had stayed back with Patrick to brief the captain.

"We will need to verify our decrease in speed via calculations over the following days to see how they affected our approach, but it's looking promising."

"You should know," Reid added. "No matter what, we'll still need to perform at least one — if not two — more in the following days."

"It'll all depend on what our fuel will allow for," Russel said. His tone was sharp, but not rude. Patrick shot him a look. "Boston has begun an analysis of our fuel supplies and will provide a report at 0800."

Mitchel, who looked much better following his mandatory rest period, said, "Thank you, Lieutenant. Commander Montgomery, please send me the results of the burn, once you have them, and the estimated timeline for the next burns required. We need to get the flight path planned as soon as possible. Thank you again. Now, go get some rest."

And he cut the connection. I grinned at the order. Ever since Doc had the talk with him about taking the time for sleep, he'd been enforcing the mandatory rest periods without exception.

Patrick brushed his hands together, then met Russel's gaze. "I'm taking off. I need to go check on something."

The stare Russel sent Patrick was hard and unyielding. "Let us know what you need and don't do anything stupid."

Patrick inclined his head, then left the room. I watched him go, worried that he would do just that.

"Well, considering everything, I think today went pretty well," Reid said, leaning back in his chair and propping his feet on the desk. He had soot on his forehead from when he'd had to go help with a small fire in the engine room.

He was right, of course. There was just one thing I hadn't liked.

"Yeah...but did any of you feel the tremor when we turned her? *The Aspire* shouldn't shake like that. She should be able to handle what we just put her through. That underlying vibration..." I said to Reid. My hands on my waist, sleeves rolled up to my elbows. Sweat beaded along my brow, and I wiped them away. The movement sent a few droplets down my spine. I pressed my thumb into the spot just above my hip and winced. I was so ready to sit down.

"It was a hard maneuver, though. Plenty of stress on the ship."

"That doesn't explain the —"

Russel was covered in grease. I didn't know why. "We're on a spaceship, Tasha. They shake."

Woah. I glared at him.

"Okay," he groaned. "I know what you're talking about, but I am too damn tired to think about it right now. And if I keep fucking talking to anyone, the asshole in me is going to say something that pisses not just you off, but everyone else."

Aridas didn't even try to hide her laugh. She outright cackled at him. "Should I ask what happened down in Section Ninety-five?"

His eyes flared. "No."

Ah...So there was a story there. Then add what just happened with Patrick and...

"But," he said, meeting my gaze, "tomorrow we can look into it. I don't think it's a dire issue. I can even send a note to Tanaka if you'd like. He's on nightshift."

"Tomorrow is fine," I said.

"All right, guys" — Reid slapped his thighs and pushed up from his seat — "I'm taking off. We've been here for nearly twelve hours. I need sleep and so do you. Great job. Let's hope it was enough."

"Thanks, Reid. Aridas," I said, following him out the door.

Reid disappeared down the opposite corridor as Russel and me. We left together, heading toward the module where our suites were. He was quiet, his scowl firmly in place. Too tired to ask, and knowing he wasn't ready to tell, I reveled in the silence. It had been so loud the last few hours. Talking, computers, alarms, the engines...my favorite part of working was when the silence hit after the long day was over. We reached the hallway where our paths split.

"Good night," I said.

Without looking up, he nodded and walked slowly away. Damn, he really was in his head.

Chapter Nineteen
Commander Tasha Evans

It felt good to rub the sleep from my eyes — not that it worked. In the mirror, my hair fell around my shoulders as I ran my fingers down both sides of my nose to arch over cheekbones and knead my jaw muscles. They were sore. I must've ground my teeth last night.

It was the stress. The last few days had been filled with ups and downs. The burn had gone well, and we'd made great progress with the research. My last scan was due in a few hours. But there were so many concerns and stresses, too. Like the fact that we still weren't slowing down enough, Geron was still in the hospital, or...the call from last night.

"Tasha," Dr. Adams's panicked voice had cut through my sleep haze in an instant. "We need you in Module Three, Section One. I've sent you our exact location. One of the Engineering teams found a new growth pattern. I think we found the reason for the vibration you and Cruz were looking for the other day."

"Shit. Okay...is everyone okay?"

How many times could I say "okay" in a sentence? Freakin' sleep-induced stupidity.

"No. And if we don't figure out how to stop the exposures, the makeshift medical bay isn't gonna hold them all." I squeaked, and she continued, "Don't worry. I've already got Medical here, and the exposed person was smart — they called within minutes of exposure. Dr. Pia had them rinse the wound and treat it as she's requested."

"Will that work?" I asked, pulling my uniform on and shoving my feet into my boots.

"I don't know. We're still trying to figure out how quickly the Cnidra-marus moves. Couldn't hurt, though."

I huffed a laugh. "True enough. I'm on my way," I'd said as I'd run from my quarters, pulling my hair into a high bun.

I blinked at my reflection, then reached up to plait my hair. As I came to the end, the doorbell rang. I grabbed the tie on the counter and secured the end of the braid before heading for the front.

The door slid smoothly to the side the moment I pressed the panel beside the entryway. My eyebrows rose when I found Russel standing there. He never came to my suite.

He looked as tired as I felt, and it made me wonder if his sleep was as restless as mine. His hair was damp, his hardsuit uniform clean. He rubbed a hand along the back of his neck but dropped it when he saw me.

"Good morning," he said, voice still a little scratchy.

"Hello." I smiled, scanning his drawn face.

"I'm heading to Engineering to discuss our findings from last night with Tanaka and Aridas. There are a few other engineers they called in too, but the meeting isn't for a while. I wanted to get a jump on it and figured I'd see if you'd like to join."

"I would. Give me a second." I ran back inside, grabbed my armpad and gloves, then rejoined him. Stepping into the hallway, I asked, "Did you sleep at all?"

"No, not much. You?"

"Not after the call. I can't seem to get enough." I placed my hands on my lower back, arched, and stretched. "Can't say I'll ever catch up."

He fell in beside me, his longer strides shortening to match mine. "It feels that way, doesn't it? What did you tell me yesterday? We'll sleep when we get to Merocius?"

I smirked. We fell silent, continuing toward our destination. Just before we made the last turn that would take us to the entrance, I asked, "We're avoiding the issue, aren't we?"

"That the Cnidramarus Crystals have infiltrated the external bracing of the ship and are making parts of it brittle?"

I nodded.

"Oh, yeah," he said with an exaggerated nod. "I need coffee before I can discuss that."

"Cool. Just making sure. I do, too. Denial is healthy, right?"

He snorted, then scowled. "Probably not, but...coffee. Coffee first."

A few crew members welcomed us as we passed. Sending quick "good mornings" back, we made our way past the control deck, then the offices, and into the break room hidden on this level. It was meant for the Engineering personnel only and was fully stocked. There were ten tables lined up to the left and a long counter filled with various contraptions meant to distribute all types of drinks and snacks on the right. Sadly, nothing more advanced food-wise than what the device in my room could create was available, but in a pinch, it would do.

A small group sat at one of the tables along the back. Tanaka was the first one to spot us. He chuckled when he got a look at us together, and I realized Russel's hand rested on the small of my back as he'd led me into the room. At the laugh, it disappeared.

If I'd been the type, I would have blushed.

Shit balls, how had that looked? We walked in together with him touching me so comfortably, and I hadn't even noticed. A few people had already commented on how we'd been spending so much time together. We were assigned to work together, but...

Ugh, who cared? All that mattered was Russel and I were on the same page. We ignored him, the drinks our focus as we filled our cups. As we did, we shared a glance, and it was as if I could hear his thoughts. *I'm sorry. I shouldn't have done that, but don't worry. He was just giving us a hard time.*

I smiled softly, bumped his elbow, and said, "Come on. Let's go sit down."

"You two look like hell," Tanaka said as we approached.

Tech Spec Aridas and Engineers Jim Angello, Drew Hutton, and Stan Berry looked up. They scanned us, and I swear I was being dissected. What was I missing here?

"Did I forget to brush my hair or something? Because I swear, if one more person tells me that, I'm gonna start thinking I didn't change from yesterday." I ran a hand over my braid. It felt fine.

"You're fine, Commander. You just look tired. We all do," Tanaka said.

Angello huffed and, with the ego I would expect from him, said, "Except me. I look damn good."

I rolled my eyes and took a seat next to Aridas. Russel slipped into the chair next to me. The first taste of the dark deliciousness in my cup had me relaxing back in the chair. I closed my eyes and hoped the caffeine worked quickly.

Drew Hutton, one of my best young female engineers, smacked Angello's shoulder. "Shut up, Angello." She crossed her arms. "Drink some coffee, Commander, and then tell us about this project you have."

"Did you speak to Adams?" Russel asked.

"No. Why? We were just notified to be here."

"Ah, but she was the one that requested you here?"

"She and Commander Montgomery, yes."

Good. Patrick had given his input. I'd sent a request for his thoughts while we were doing our assessment.

With everything going on with Norris, he'd been working, but on an altered schedule. The day before, I'd spoken to him, demanding an update on Javier. The fetus was growing, which meant Norris was handling things better, but the closer they got to the next stage in treatment, the more neurotic she became. Which was why he'd pulled himself off rotation yesterday, and why I'd received the call last night.

I took another sip. "Well, last night, Adams called us down into the structure of the ship after growths were found growing through the struts along the aft section."

Tanaka drew in a breath. Aridas sat forward, her thin fingers moving to rest on either side of her neck just behind her ears. I swear I could see her mind spin with the news, which was why I wasn't surprised when she asked, "You think that's what caused the vibration during the burn?"

Russel's hand lifted, his fingers splaying. "That's what we need to verify, but it makes sense. There are several sections — not many that we saw — where they've eaten away at the metal altogether. Those beams require bracing."

Instantly, each of the members before me shifted into their professional, dedicated roles.

"My team has some of the best welders on the ship," Engineer Berry said. For such a quiet man, he spoke with absolute confidence. From what I'd heard, though, he would back it up with hard work. "I can get them to start a full eval of any areas you indicate."

"We should do a complete exam of the bowels of the ship. See how far they've gotten. Otherwise, there is no way to know how long they've been there," Tanaka said.

Aridas scanned through something on her tablet. "Probably since Norris's time. She thought the treatment with the EC's Radiotherm Device was complete, but I wasn't convinced. I might be able to do some tests to see but...either way, I agree with Tanaka — a full visual exam is required."

"Captain Remian," I said, crossing one leg over the other, "has assigned a team to do that already. They will be contacting us with the information as soon as possible."

"Who is the lead?"

"Boston, I think. But be careful down there and make sure to tell anyone who you send to be extra careful, too. There are Cnidramarus Crystals everywhere." It wasn't a request. It was an order.

They vocalized their agreement.

"How many exposed are there now?" Hutton's hands were in her lap, but they were gripped tightly together. Did she know one of the infected?

"When Doc Mendez showed up last night, he said that we were up to twenty-six. Five from yesterday alone." I couldn't keep the sadness out of my voice. People were dying.

"That's not so bad, considering," Engineer Angello said.

Heat rose in my chest, and the muscles in my jaw clenched. I sat straighter, my back stiff with the anger coursing through me. Russel jerked forward as if to push to his feet and attack the idiot, but I placed a hand on his arm, and he settled back.

In almost a growl, I asked, "Not bad? Four people are dead from our crew and another sixty plus from the Elemental Crew, and that's not bad?"

My fingers of one hand closed around the chair, the other on Russel's muscular arm where it still lay. He shifted, placing the sign of my distress — and his arm — below the table and out of view. I'd thank him later.

Angello's cheeks reddened, and his gaze bounced between us. "That's not what I meant."

"You were in the last group reanimated, correct?" I asked. He nodded. "Then you have absolutely no idea what's been going on or what the Cnidramarus are capable of. You also have no knowledge of our ability to fight it, what options we have for treatment, cures, or even the quantities of supplies being pulled for use on this project. And you sure as hell have not witnessed the pain that these little bastards cause."

With each stern, scolding word, Angello sunk farther into his seat.

Was I being unprofessional? Probably, but the kid needed to understand.

Russel placed his hand over mine on his arm. With a deep breath, I released my grip and instead took his hand. He squeezed gently, knowing in that one move that I was back in control. Yet, he didn't let go.

"I would recommend that you get more information before you make statements like that in the future. This is not a simple issue, and the entire crew is at risk."

"But we have treatments, and —"

My respect for him diminished further.

"Angello, where are we?" Russel asked. His voice was suspiciously calm — murderously so. It felt like eyes staring at me from the shadows. I shivered.

"On *The Aspire.*" Angello's eyebrows lowered into a deep frown.

"So not on our homeworld or Merocius?"

Angello shook his head.

"So, let's use our brains here." Russel threaded his fingers with mine under the table as he leaned back in his chair. I tried not to react. "We've maxed out our supply for the metal used in the radiation implants, which is the most effective treatment we have. Can you tell me what that means?"

He shook his head.

Russel continued his condescending rant. I probably should have stopped it, but I couldn't.

"We also have only two currently functioning handheld lasers that are usable for the treatment of the Cnidramarus. One of which causes severe harm to the host. Ask Patrick. The other broke, and the doctor who created it is infected as of yesterday."

I took over, not wanting Russel to let anymore of his "asshole," as he called it, out.

"So, if we consider the number currently infected and the fetuses requiring treatment, we have enough for about four more people who can receive the implants," I explained. Angello's mouth dropped open. "And no other known and effective treatment for the Cnidramarus."

"We're screwed," Angello choked.

"Welcome to the party. Aren't you glad you woke up?" Russel said.

"I-I didn't know. I'm sorry."

Russel exhaled through his teeth, and I felt the tension release from his shoulders, even from where our hands were bound.

"We know." The kind understanding on Russel's face shocked me a little. "But you have to understand that it's not only the infected on this ship that are in danger. If the Cnidramarus get to Merocius, it will spread. If that happens, we are all doomed."

Angello swallowed hard. Next to him, the others shifted uncomfortably.

"Everything we do in the next few weeks is to get the ship to Merocius in one piece *and* to find a way to treat *The Aspire*. Which is why we are asking for everyone's help."

Aridas drew the attention to her. "And you have to remember, Montgomery and Richards were the first of our crew infected. These two were there, helping treat them, when it all happened. They've seen firsthand what it does."

Angello met both our gazes before he said, "I'm sorry."

As if turning on a lightbulb, Russel's entire demeanor shifted away from irritation to forgiveness. "No apologies necessary. Now let's get to work. Commander, more coffee before we head out?"

"Please," I said, pretty sure I was staring at him like he had three heads.

He released my hand. As he stood, he, as if not thinking about it, reached out and ran his hand up and down the back of my arm. The soft, amused smile had me rolling my eyes. He just smirked and disappeared.

When I faced the table again, I froze. Everyone's stares burned through me.

"What?" I asked. It was nothing! They didn't have to make such a big deal out of something so small. And seriously, how had the whole focus of the group shifted in a split second? I felt like I had whiplash.

Damn it. Okay, it wasn't a tiny thing. I mean, it was, but... Suddenly, I imagined the universe opening up and swallowing me whole. Why couldn't they let it pass?

Aridas pressed her lips together to hold in a giggle, Drew nearly bounced in her seat, and Engineer Berry grinned like a fool. Then there was Tanaka, whose shoulders shook with suppressed laughter.

"So —" Tanaka started, but the gods saved me from embarrassment with something much worse.

Alarms filled the air, and red and yellow lights flashed in rhythm to the blaring noises, which indicated an emergency. Instantly, the drama of a moment ago was gone. I shoved to my feet and bolted for the door — the others right behind. Forgetting our coffee, Russel joined us, and together we rushed onto the main floor.

We stepped onto the Main Engineering deck, and the large screen over the main computer displayed the problem. It was as if cold water were poured down the back of my shirt. I shivered but didn't let it show. Instead, I rushed for the open workstation, instantly taking point. Three of our team were already managing the chaos and outlining the situation.

Engineer Partruce slid sideways as he entered a command for battle stations. "Commander Evans, incoming storm. Three larger objects and a shit-ton of small ones impacting in one minute."

One minute? That didn't give us time to get out of the way. *The Aspire* was a big ship with very little maneuvering capability. She was built to transport us across the galaxy, not complete quick and unexpected adjustments. We could make some, which I would utilize as best we could, but time was limited.

Tech Specialist Boston, who was usually seen up on the Bridge, looked up. With a grim nod, he said, "Two larger on path for direct impact to aft side Module Four and the mark Seven Solar Tower."

Son of a bitch. That was one of the most active sections — where many of the civilians lived. I glanced up to the screen, which showed the approaching onslaught. This was gonna be bad.

"Initiate evacuation of the module, starting with the section most likely impacted. Sound an all-hands brace for impact," I ordered. Stepping up to the command workstation, I continued, "Aridas, seal Seven Solar Tower."

"On it," she said, rushing to her desk.

"I'm on the vernier thrusters. I'll adjust as much as possible to lessen the impact," Cruz said, his hands already flying over his screen. He was Cruz again. Until this was over, he would be.

The computer was already highlighting the path of the incoming projectiles and the best-calculated sequence to keep the damage to a minimum.

I nodded, then spoke to the room. "Partruce, continue tracking. Boston, manage the evacuation. Tanaka, fortify shields. Hutton, Angello, and Berry, be ready to organize repair and rescue teams where needed. This one's gonna be big, guys, so let's be our best. Cruz, get the Module Leads on comms."

"Done," he said. "And the thruster sequence has been initiated." His voice lowered so only I could hear him. "Commander, the impact will be significant, even with the changes."

Yeah, no kidding.

To the room, I said, "When shit hits the fan, Cruz, you know what to do."

From his spot next to me, his focus still entirely on the disaster across his screen, he nodded.

"You and I are at ground zero for repairs while these crazy assholes back us up and keep us from doing anything stupid," he said.

It was the break in the tension and panic we needed. Chuckles filled the room, many echoing through the comms on other levels. I realized in that moment that this was something Cruz had always done. It worked.

"Harder job than you'd think," someone said.

"Cruz, you couldn't live without us," another voice rang.

"I keep you guys alive," Cruz said, initiating a round of snarky comments back.

The tension didn't drop exactly, but it focused us, and we fell into our positions easily, calling out updates, orders, and plans.

My lync went off, and, seeing Patrick's number, I answered. Instantly, his voice said, "Update."

I relayed the stats with our typical efficiency.

"Where do you need me?" he asked.

"Are you still at the shuttle bay?"

"Yes, delivery is expected later today, early tomorrow. Let's take care of this catastrophe, then I can focus on stuff here." In his, *I'm your commanding officer so do what I say* voice, he added, "Now, where do you need me?"

I didn't question him. We needed his expertise and help.

"Work with Aridas and Tanaka for management. Any Module Two repairs are yours. Cruz and I will manage the rest. Act as update for Captain Remian, too."

"Agreed." With that, he cut our direct transmission.

For a split second, I met Cruz's eye. He nodded, hearing and agreeing with my conversation with Patrick.

"Ten, nine, eight," Partruce counted.

Over the main comm, I reported, "Brace for impact."

The rumble that went through the entire ship reverberated through my hands and feet. The desk where I gripped shook beneath my palms.

Less than a breath later, a storm of noise hit our ears. It was hailstorm against a tin roof as the smaller debris passed the shield and hit the hull.

The memory of curling into a ball as a child as I hid under the bed, scared, flashed through my mind. My brother and Geron had climbed in with me and held me as I cried.

I blinked it away.

Then came the crunch of metal. Screams echoing from various parts of the ship. The rush of air through breaches in the hull.

"Seal them!" I ordered. Just like we'd practiced, each of my team fell into place. One by one, the levels were secured, and force fields enacted.

"Round two coming in, five, four..." Partruce yelled.

We braced. This time was worse for us, mainly because the second larger piece hit the Seven Solar Tower, which was only a few levels above Main Engineering. I watched the screen as the object hit the tower, ripping it from *The Aspire* in one pass. The explosion that followed was bright, rushing down the maintenance pathway and toward the main ship. A bright blue shield appeared as it hit the protective barrier Aridas and Tanaka had erected around us.

I sighed, then cursed as I watched the debris of the tower float toward the camera and our module. It was going to hit us.

"Intensify field on Section Two, Module Two," Cruz and Patrick ordered before I had the chance — Patrick's voice coming over the intercom.

"On it," Tanaka said, calm as always.

"Commander," Cruz said, drawing my attention to him. "We're needed in Module Four. The main impact screwed something up bad. The power systems keep going in and out, which means the external fields aren't holding. I think I identified the problem, but we have to correct them manually."

"Can it wait?"

"No. Evacuation was still underway. We have at least a hundred people stuck down there on multiple levels. Captain Remian has them sealing themselves in smaller rooms, as they use less power. It's smart, and they're holding, but they're stuck until we have the levels secured."

With a curse, I said, "Okay, let's go."

As if called from the ether, Lieutenant Reid appeared. "Sorry, I'm late. I was off shift. Where can I help?"

"Cover here. Montgomery will fill you in. We're needed elsewhere," I said.

"I heard. Be safe."

To the room at large, I continued, "Keep us updated."

"Be careful," Patrick said.

On the way out, I stopped to open a door in the paneling. Inside hung a dozen or more fully stocked utility belts. I grabbed two, secured one around my waist, and handed the other to Cruz, who was pulling two of our emergency kits. Cruz took the belt, clipped it on, and off we went.

"Attach your comm," Cruz said, slipping the small earpiece into his ear, and then he began speaking to someone on the other end.

I did as we jogged. There was a whine, and then the swarm of voices as I was linked back into Main Engineering. I listened to reports of damages all over the ship and was impressed at how my team calmly and efficiently organized the crew. I'd catch up with them later.

"Channel fourteen," Cruz said as he opened the hatch that would allow us the quickest way down to Module Four. We stepped inside and started to move. I clicked over, and Mitchel's voice filled my ear.

"— damage on multiple levels with a section torn out along Section Nineteen. We've had visual confirmation that the Stasis Bay on that level was destroyed," he said.

"Was it empty?" Cruz asked.

"No. Brackett had three more groups left. She and her team were working when it hit. Readings state some were able to secure themselves in a small office, but there are no comms in the area, and the power is failing. They're our priority."

"Understood, Captain," I said through panting breaths. "We're three minutes out."

"Good. A team is on their way to meet you. We'll meet you at the point Sergeant Cruz indicated."

Chapter Twenty
Captain Mitchel Remian

Tasha and Cruz came around the corner at a full sprint. I knew they would. In a situation like this, they were two of the best — Patrick and Richards just as reliable. Had Richards been released from Medical yet, he'd be right here, ready to dive into trouble with the rest of us.

Personally, I was glad he wasn't and was still locked away following the procedure Dr. Pia had performed to repair his spinal cord. It had worked, but it would take time to recover from the damage to his legs. So, he was safe and unharmed, if not a little pissed he wasn't able to help.

And Patrick was doing what he did best — keeping the ship together until his team got us back up and running.

Tasha slid to a stop, immediately dropping to her knees and pulling a tool from her belt. With quick motions, she removed the screws along the left side of the panel marking the entrance into the Stasis Bay. It was in there that at least seventeen crew members were trapped. It was also where a giant hole had been ripped from my ship after space debris had collided with the hull.

I leaned against the several-inch-thick window embedded inside the security door. It closed upon the initiation of the emergency protocols — after the fields failed on the other side. As technology could malfunction, we liked to have a physical component that could be utilized should we need it.

Through the window, the damage was terrifying. It took my breath away. What was once a Stasis Bay was now a destroyed, empty shell. Half the room, and its sleeping occupants, were gone. Pieces had been torn away, leaving beams exposed and razor-sharp edges of thick steel reaching toward the stars. The blackness beyond was littered with debris, ripped then sucked from my ship.

A few pods along the far wall were still intact and alight with power. Two teetered on the edge, the cables attaching them to the ship the only thing that kept them onboard. I would save them if it was the last thing I did. Either way, seeing them there, dangling in space, meant we hadn't lost them all. Perhaps there were more, further in, where my view could not reach. I had to hope.

I rubbed my chest, then glanced to the side.

"We need to get this section secure, Commander," I said.

"Working on it, Captain," she said.

Cruz stopped at Tasha's side and began tackling the screws of another panel beneath the door controls. As he did, he spoke to those who had come with me.

"You." He pointed to one of my men. "Head down the end of the corridor. Take a left and then a right. There should be a control panel near the floor."

"The hidden one that manages the links into the power fields on this level?" he asked.

Cruz nodded, his hands never stopping. "Yes. I'll need you to get into the system and identify the shorts. There are probably several. We need to re-route the power from another section and boost any rooms currently housing crew. Can you do that?"

He removed the last screw and pulled the gray panel away, exposing the wires beneath. When the kid didn't answer, Cruz looked up.

The kid, maybe twenty-three at most, looked terrified. Probably just out of the academy back home, and this was his first mission.

"What's your name, kid?"

"Swan, sir."

Cruz nodded, his voice still harsh, but somehow sounding supportive too. "All right, Swan. Do you know how to identify the shorts?"

"Yes."

"Good, get started. I'll be there in two minutes to help with the rest."

Swan nodded and took off. The other two soldiers with me stepped back, staying out of the way and waiting patiently for their next orders.

"Commander Montgomery confirmed those stuck in the Stasis Bay are most at risk," Cruz said to me.

"That's my understanding," I said.

"Captain, can you see the room they're in? Is there a clear path?" Tasha asked, gesturing to the window.

I pressed my cheek against it. Along the wall to the left were offices and labs used for those working to preserve, and then wake those sleeping. The glass which separated them from the main space had been blown out, the contents long gone. From our readings, the crew had gotten to the eighth room down, approximately a hundred feet from where I stood. As this side was built with more of an S curve, it was hard to see the door. I shifted to the right, and a light flickered in my vision just a little. There.

"Minor damage to the walkway. Debris everywhere, but other than that...I can't be sure. I can see their field, though."

"Understood," Tasha said, holding a device which she'd plugged into a port hidden behind the panel. Every so often, she'd place a long tool from her kit on the control board she'd exposed and read the meter. "Those in stasis will be fine until we can secure the area fully — their individual power modules will stay active for up to two weeks — but the ones in that room are in danger, especially with the power fluctuations. I can secure the outer shield for one minute, maybe two. That should be enough to get them out, but we need EPVs for everyone in that room just in case. The office they're in will only have a few."

Emergency Personal Ventilation systems. Small units used to provide breathable atmosphere for up to twenty minutes in an emergency. The hatches that held the EPVs were evenly spaced through the corridors, often holding only two to four in each. In the more populated areas, there were larger stashes of them.

"Well," I said to the two with me, "while they get everything ready here, we'll collect —"

"Brace yourselves!" Patrick's voice boomed across all comm lines just as the floor shifted beneath us.

Noise filled my ears as alarms sounded again, indicating another bombardment of stardust had hit the ship. Tasha fell to the side but steadied herself quickly. I stumbled, managing to catch my footing. I threw out a hand and braced myself on the door.

Through the gaping hole, I watched as a piece flew by, colliding with the already-floating debris. It was like watching marbles bouncing off of each other as they ping-pong'd around, disappearing in different directions. My breaths quickened as several came closer, pushing back into the Stasis Bay. One slammed into the wall, the other making contact with a row of pods — at least two, their lights going out. It became hard to swallow as sparks flew, the base of the pods scraping against metal until they came to a stop along the back wall.

"Everyone okay?" Cruz asked. "Captain?"

I think he could see the fury in my eyes because, with one quick nod of understanding, he said, "We'll get them out," and returned to what he was doing.

"Commander Evans!" Patrick's voice burst through our line. I flinched, wishing I could yank the bloody earpiece out. The others must've felt the same because they winced, too. "You're needed immediately in Engine Room One."

Tasha froze, her grip tightening on the tool she held, knuckles going white. She looked up at Cruz, who'd frozen too, his hands tangled in the wires behind the door.

"Status," she asked.

"Engine one down. Engine two stuck on high. Needs immediate attention or may overheat."

Tasha cursed under her breath. "On my way," she said and grabbed the extra bag they'd brought, but not quite dug into yet. Without a word to any of us, she bolted away, already firing questions at someone on the other side of her comm. Part of me wished I could follow, knowing that without the engine, we were piss out of luck. But Tasha was the right person, and I had to stay here.

Cruz met my gaze as Patrick said, "Sergeant Cruz, get the crew out and join her. She'll need every hand on deck as soon as possible. I've got Tanaka on his way down, too."

"Good," Cruz said, bobbing his head, and I realized I was doing the same. "We're fifteen minutes out. Maybe less. Keep me updated on the engine status."

"Will do," he said, and disappeared.

"If Tasha needs you, you're going," I said to Cruz without thinking.

"No. Tasha needs us both. So let's get this done and rescue our crew. Then we can go back her up and fix our ship."

"Done. So, what do you need from us to get that door open?"

Spec Romano and Spec Bartlet stepped forward. Romano was part of the security team, while Bartlet was one of the flight crew, similar to what I technically was.

"We'll get the EPVs," Romano said. In his late twenties, tall and muscular, he had dark hair and eyes. He was a great soldier — a solid presence in any situation.

"Seventeen," I confirmed the number required. Cruz shot me a confused look. To him, I said, "Boston received a message from the survivors before comms went out. Confirmed seventeen alive, two with minor injuries. Should be an easy extraction."

"Got it," he said in response.

"We'll be quick, Captain," Romano said before they disappeared down opposite corridors.

With a deep inhale to calm my racing heart, I turned back to Cruz. He'd dropped down to where Tasha had been working.

"Good. She was about to... Okay, all I need to do is...Perfect," he mumbled to himself. Intermixed with his words, he'd adjust a dial or enter something into the device he held.

"Cruz." It was a statement and a question. He looked up and gestured to me to join him. I knelt by his side.

"Sorry. Needed to verify where we were. All right, so..." Cruz explained what Tasha and he had done to override the emergency door, and the process I would need to take to open it back up. There were a few steps we'd need to synchronize once he was at the other console and linked into the mainframe, but in general, we were in good shape. My training and years of active duty had put me in positions to learn all sorts of skills needed to keep a ship running and a crew alive. This was no different. I'd done similar things many times over the years and in worse circumstances.

"No problem," I said once he'd explained my part. "Once the door is open, Romano and I will go in. Bartlet will be first contact once they are clear."

He stared into my eyes for a long moment, and it was as if I could hear his complaint.

"I'm going. I don't care if I'm captain. This is my crew, and I'm the most experienced besides you, and we need you to hold the door open and force field intact."

He held his hands up. "Fine. I'll be at the console down the way ensuring just that." Cruz bent and pulled two reels of safety line from his kit and held them out. "I'll have to stay there once you're inside, but I'll send Swan back to help with the survivors and to maintain the door."

I took the reels and secured one to the hardsuit I wore. The other would be Romano's. Although wearing it was more restricting on a day-to-day basis, I was glad I'd made it a requirement ever since the crystals had spread.

"We'll be fast but keep me apprised of any power fluctuations."

"Will do." Cruz stood, rubbing his hands on his thighs as he straightened. "Is this where we tell each other not to do anything stupid?"

I laughed. That was usually Tasha's line for us anytime we went off on a mission without her.

"I think that's fair." I held out a hand, and he took it with a grin. "So, be safe and don't do anything stupid."

"You, too," he said and picked the bag up from the floor, then jogged off.

It only took a few moments for Cruz to reach the other console. He kept his comm open, allowing me to hear him explaining to Swan what he was doing to reroute the system. It made me respect him a bit more to know that even in an emergency situation, he taught those around him. He understood that information like this could save your life.

When he was ready for me, we worked to perform the final few steps and verified everything was in place. We were going over the sequence to open the door one last time when Romano and Bartlet appeared, lines of EPVs thrown over their shoulders all linked together.

I held out the safety line to Romano. "Secure yourself. We'll use two lines to get them out. This needs to be quick."

As he hooked his line to his hardsuit, I attached mine to the support loop in the wall. It made a satisfying click as it closed. He found a spot on the opposite side of the door and did the same. The goal was to keep them from crossing. We wanted two very separate paths for the team to take on the way back — a line that was both directional and a tether to the ship should anything go wrong.

"Bartlet, you and Swan are to help Cruz maintain fields and get the survivors to Medical as soon as they are clear. Understood?"

"Yes, sir," he said.

"Good." My focus shifted again, back to the device on the floor. "Cruz, we're just about ready here. How's it going?"

"Just about there," he said.

That was the sign to get my helmet on. I unclipped it from my belt, where it hung at my hip, and slipped it over my head. I secured it. Lights flashed on the display the moment the latch engaged; my vitals, oxygen levels, and various other stats appearing in my periphery. With its attachment, my suit sealed itself, regulating instantly.

Romano and Bartlet did the same. Romano picked up one string of the EPVs, looped it over his shoulder, then handed me the other.

"Ten seconds, Captain," Cruz said, voice coming through the speakers of my helmet this time. He counted down, and I entered the sequence he'd given me when he hit zero.

A few things happened. First, force fields appeared at the nearest cross-sections of each hallway. They were back-ups in case the outer field fell. Next, a wave of light spread across the open expanse of space where the hole in the ship was. Cruz had increased the power going to the shields in this section while we were in here. And finally, the door opened.

"Let's go," I said, and Romano and I stepped onto the Stasis Bay.

We ran. Time was limited, and there was no reason to wait.

The damage was much worse when seen from the inside. Sections crumpled from the weight of the impact, others torn as if they were paper and not inch-thick steel.

I spotted a few pods that had been crushed, red staining the inside of the glass. I had to look away when I saw a face I recognized — one of the reanimation crew trapped between some debris. It would have been the decompression that had taken her. I swallowed hard and forced myself to focus on those I could save. The coil at my waist spun, its vibration and whirring sound oddly stabilizing, as if it were a reminder I was moving and safe.

We took a straight path, using the curve of the room to our advantage. Reaching the peak of the S in seconds, we got our first true look at both the office we were aiming for and the damage we had to traverse.

"Issue up ahead. Separation in the seams of the floor, but doesn't seem too severe near the wall," Romano said.

"I see it. Maybe three feet. We need to verify the supports around it are stable."

We slowed our approach, taking a few careful steps to test the stability. Near the edge, I knelt, examining the opposite side. Other than one particular spot, the bracing underneath was intact. Those in the best condition could transfer here, taking a larger jump to cross over. Anyone unable to do this could transfer closer to the wall. This would keep us in smaller groups and our lines from crossing. Anything that allowed us to move faster was a good thing.

"Not too bad," I said. "I'll take the outer path. You manage the inside."

"Yes, Captain."

"Cruz, how are we doing on time?"

His voice was calm, sure. "Everything's good here, Captain. All levels are holding steady."

"Keep me updated." I took a step back, then jumped lightly over the crevasse in the floor. There was a hollow *thunk* as my boots hit, and I felt the EPVs swing against my back. It was followed by a creaking that spoke of just how unstable this area was. "Perhaps more in your group if possible."

Romano smirked as he moved to the wall. Bracing himself, he stepped over, pressing down hard on the other side, as if to test it was as solid as it looked. Obviously satisfied, he transferred over and joined me. "My path is fine, Cap."

Good.

It took another thirty seconds to reach the office. When we appeared, most of the crew was waiting. They'd seen our approach. I sighed in relief when I met Dr. Brackett's eyes. We'd been through a lot together, and I was relieved to see her alive.

We pulled the EPVs from our shoulders and detached the clips holding them together. Once they were all separated, I said to Cruz, "Sergeant, we're here. Drop the barrier. We'll get the EPVs on and head back."

"Understood," was his simple reply.

A second later, the force field dropped, and the crew began to file out. Their exclamations of thanks filled my ears, but I was too busy helping them with their EPVs. At some point, Connie had gotten even the newly awakened in hardsuits, which meant we could easily secure them to the safety line.

When I reached Brackett, she looked up. "Thank you, Captain. Thank you for coming and getting us. With comms down, we weren't sure you'd gotten our message."

"Of course we'd come for you." I rested a hand on her shoulder, then addressed the group as a whole. "We don't have much time. Please get your EPV on and then link up to a safety line!"

"Split into two groups. Anyone injured, unsteady, or afraid of heights needs to be on my line," Romano said as we clipped the opposite end of our lines to the wall braces.

The crew did as they were told, quickly lining up. The two injuries were mild, considering — a sprained ankle and broken arm. We made sure they each had a partner, in case they required help, and then we moved.

Tracking along a wire while others were also attached was interesting. It changed the way we walked. With more than eight people on the same line, even a semi-lax one, things got difficult. It took time to sync up and find a way to walk without pulling each other in multiple directions. Romano had the additional difficulty of one of his people being unable to keep a normal stride. Which meant we moved slow, and his group in a more drunken manner.

There was hesitation when we reached the crevasse. Romano's group wasn't there yet, which was probably better. It gave mine time to come to terms with the jump. Slowly, they hopped over the divide. Unfortunately, from the back, I was able to see the damage each person's weight did to the structure below. There was also something else this angle allowed me to visualize. Crystals encased a few of the beams beneath the levels, between these particular sections of floor. That's why it was so much weaker.

By the fifth person, things were worrisome. When the seventh transferred and the floor shivered, dropping an inch, I told them to hold.

Pressing the comm on my armpad, I spoke quietly to Cruz and Romano. "Romano, how's it going over there? You need to get moving; there's a structure problem over here."

"Helping Sarina with the ankle injury over now. There are three after her, including me. What are you seeing?"

"Collapse of the underlying structure. I need your group clear in case there's a failure."

"Will do."

"Captain," Cruz said, a strain in his voice I didn't like. "We may have a problem here, too. With Engine two sucking up so much power, I'm having trouble maintaining levels. You need to get moving. I'm also getting reports of another wave of debris heading this way. We need to secure the bay. Now!"

My gaze spun to where Romano was. His had done the same to me. He'd just handed off Sarina to the other survivors, and his eyes were wide with fear.

I released the private comm and allowed my voice to carry to those nearby. "Move! Now."

Each and every person along my line looked at me with instant understanding, my tone telling them everything they needed to know. No longer hesitating, they ran. With only three of us left, I had to hope the structure would hold.

"Go!" I demanded of the kid in front.

He did, landing with a *crunch*. Not looking back, he moved toward the exit. Good.

I glanced back to Brackett, who'd demanded to be last on the line, and said, "Be careful, the structure is failing. Aim for the left side as far as you can. I'm going on the right. Do *not* go until I'm standing. Understood?"

In truth, it was probably best that she was after me. She was significantly lighter than I was, and I could catch her if she fell.

She nodded, swallowing hard.

The spot I aimed for was a wider section than where the others had jumped, but that was okay; I had long legs. Still, I landed hard on my knees, yanking on the line at my waist and causing several of those up ahead to stumble. I ground my teeth against the sharp pain in my kneecaps and side.

The floor beneath me vibrated. I froze mid-stand. My weight was doing something to the beams beneath. In my mind, I imagined the crystallized structures crumbling like an over-brittle cookie. Bullocks.

Stomping footsteps behind me spurred my urge to yell at Brackett for disobeying my direct orders, but before I could speak a word, the floor beneath me shifted. I slid, falling to all fours.

Apparently, the spot I'd thought was safe had not been.

"Romano!" I yelled.

"Shit! Captain, I'm coming," he screamed.

Falling one way, I was pulled another, my body a ragdoll as the tether tightened and the suit dug into my stomach. My head snapped to the side. I fought to catch a breath and find my bearings, but the floor was no longer there.

Then the line went loose. I slammed against something hard — the floor panel — and my body rolled. I slid once again.

A hand wrapped around my arm. My momentum stopped, and somehow, I rolled to my stomach. Terrified, determined eyes met mine, and Brackett's other hand latched onto my arm. She was farther in on the deck, her body flat on the ground.

"Holy shit, that worked," she said through panting breaths. "Hurt like hell, but it worked."

Too soon. The ground shifted, and we both sank farther into the hole.

Come on, couldn't gravity fail in the one moment we were falling to our deaths? Granted, that would cause all sorts of other problems, but still.

Brackett screamed, and then another set of hands grabbed her waist.

Romano had detached himself from his line and grabbed hold of her hardsuit. Slowly, he dragged her backward until we were both on stable ground. He helped us up and, for a second, all we could do was look back and forth between each other.

"Tie in, Romano," Brackett said. He did as he was told, and without another word, we got the hell out of there.

"Shut the blasted door," I said the instant my foot passed into the hallway.

Bartlet stood guard. He entered the closing sequence and the thick, metal emergency door slid shut with a satisfying *hiss*.

"Stasis Bay secured," I said, clapping Romano on the back. "Well done. Oh, man...well done." My voice didn't shake at all. Nope. I gave Brackett a hug. She'd saved my life, and I was in her debt now. To her, I said, "Head to Medical and get checked out. That's an order."

"Are you coming?" she asked.

"Not yet."

As if on cue, Cruz cut in. "Captain, if we're good here, I'm needed in Engine Room One. Are you coming along?"

"I'm on my way." I gave the order for Romano to secure the area and continue to work evacuating anyone remaining on the level, then hurried to meet up with Cruz.

Chapter Twenty-One
Captain Mitchel Remian

"**I** was told you needed another set of hands, and a line of some wire wrapped in filament. The orange one." I shimmied between the two giant...Um, I didn't know exactly what they were. They were a part of the engines, but which part, I wasn't sure. That was Tasha's expertise, which was why she knelt between a series of tools, panels, and who knew what else spread out around her.

"I do. Can you hand me the screwdriver and the tool right next to it?" she asked without removing her face from beneath a large metal panel. The arm she reached out toward me was smeared with grease, several small scratches present on her pale skin.

"Commander, where are your gloves?"

"Dammit, Tasha," Cruz's voice said over the lync. He was scolding, worried even.

Surprisingly, Patrick spoke up this time. "I told you that if you needed help sooner, needed the tool, we would've had someone bring it to you!"

"You shouldn't have removed your fucking glove!" Cruz said.

She squirmed out from her spot and glared at me, her pale finger shoved in my face threateningly. Funny how I was getting the brunt of all of her anger. "I removed one glove in an area that I verified had no crystals, in an emergency situation that required me to replace a tiny freaking part in order for us to shut down the engine before it overheated." She waved her finger in the air. "I don't want to hear it from any of you. Do you understand?"

Woah. She said all that in one breath. I held up my hands, picked up the tools she requested, and held them out.

She narrowed her gaze, then swiped them from my grasp. With one last warning point, she slipped back into her previous position. I chuckled.

"Cruz, Montgomery, I'd recommend you not push that button right now. Especially if she disagrees to put the glove back on." The exasperated sigh that came from beside me made me smile. She did as I asked.

"Get your ass under here, Remian. We've got some work to do and hand me the damn glove. I can put it on now."

"Hey, Cap," Patrick said. "I have to take care of something else. Make sure she doesn't do anything stupid."

"I'll do my best," I agreed, and he clicked out of the conference.

It took some maneuvering, but I managed to slink in beside her. I was half-crouched, half-lying on the floor and leaning against the back wall.

"So this part burnt up when the engine got stuck on high?" I asked. Commander Evans was detaching the bottom coupling and disconnecting the back wiring that linked it into the internal mechanism when I found my spot.

"Yup," she grunted, "in a moment I'll need you to disconnect the top two bolts. They look just like these two." She pointed to two matching ones on the bottom. "Then you'll need to complete the attachment procedures at the same time I do. This particular reactor weighs about seventy-five pounds. I'm going to need to be out of this position in case you drop it."

"I think that would be best, yes."

She laughed, then continued, "As you can see, it was damaged pretty badly. We have a replacement ready, but I need to clean up some of the wiring in the back. That's why you brought the replacements. I'll need your help with that as well."

"You tell me what to do, and I'll try not to screw it up."

"Cut this wire in lengths about this long," she said, holding her hand up. "Five groups of five. Can you handle that? I know that's a little bit above your pay grade."

"Wait, we get paid?" I asked.

Cruz laughed at that one. "He's got you on that one, Tasha."

I couldn't help but notice the sweet smile that spread over her face as she continued to dig into the panel. It was a smile I recognized. One my sister used a long time ago whenever talking to the boy she liked. It caused me to suck in a breath. A sadness bowed my shoulders, but it was overshadowed by a weightlessness brought on by the realization itself. It was a strange contradiction. I turned off the comm so that no one could hear and said, "You like him."

Tasha froze mid-movement. "What?"

"Cruz. You like him."

She rolled her eyes and continued on with her work. Annoyance in her voice, she said, "No, Captain. And even if I did, it would be none of your business."

It was in that moment, less than an hour after I'd almost died and in a situation where my entire ship could still be at risk, that I saw the truth. I had been acting like a child. A complete and utter bluggard. For years I'd pursued her, but she'd never shown interest. In fact, I'd been jealous, keeping this hope that Tasha and I would become more than friends, but she didn't want me.

"You've never been interested in me, have you?" I asked.

"Captain!" she hissed. "This is not the place, nor the time. Are you serious right now?"

The fury in her eyes would have had me stepping back if a wall of metal hadn't stopped me. Instead, I pressed against it, hoping her rage didn't push her to gouge out my eyes with the tool in her hand.

"I'm sorry! You're right. My apologies. My head is all over the place. The last hour has been a lot."

Her lips pursed, jaw clenched. "Not an excuse. Get it together. I have never seen you this unprofessional." Tasha finished what she was doing. "Sequence starts now, Captain. Cruz, are you ready?"

"Ready, Commander," he responded, far more put together than I'd been acting in the last few minutes.

"Reaction core seven removed. Replacement imminent," she said, leading me to a drift. A far less charred replica of the part we carried sat upon it.

After taking it back, she explained the set-up and process to repair the damage within. She told me how to line up the wire and what she would ask for as we installed it. "Are you paying attention? This is really important. *Sergeant* Cruz and I," she said, accentuating his title to make sure I understood she was still pissed about my overstep, "will be reconnecting the reaction core and verifying power levels. If any of these are incorrect, it could be detrimental to the engine as a whole."

"I understand, and I apologize again."

She stared into my eyes for a long moment, blinked, and shook her head. I stayed quiet as she spoke to Cruz, finalizing the steps. When they were done, she said, "Why was the last hour 'a lot'?"

"The rescue got a little hairy, but I have some interesting news about Module Four to share."

Tasha's gaze flicked in my direction. I secured the bundle of wire together as she requested, then set it on the floor.

"I know something happened in there, Captain, but I didn't get to ask," Cruz said. "Was everything okay?"

"If by 'okay,' you mean the floor fell out from beneath me, and I almost fell into a giant hole, causing Brackett to take a flying leap of faith in order to catch me while tethered to a wall...sure."

Tasha snapped to a sitting position, a muffled "what!" coming from between her lips, which held her multi-tool. Her left hand held the ends of two wires an inch apart, the right a cutter. Sweat dripped down her forehead, and she wiped it away.

"Yeah, I'd say it does." Cruz chuckled. "One of the kids you rescued said something like that when he ran by Swan, but we weren't sure if it was true. But Brackett has always been protective. Tasha, six-nine-nine."

"Shit, sorry. Got it," she said, diving back into whatever she was doing.

"You were glaring at Remian, weren't you?"

"Stuff it, Cruz," she responded, deadpan.

I grinned and handed her the next bundle of wire when she reached for it.

"Was the damage that bad? I'm sure externally, yes, but..." Cruz paused to speak to someone next to him. It was fascinating listening to him have a conversation with others while also having one with me at the same time. "...from the tracker, where you fell was pretty far in."

"Yes, and no."

"What do you mean?" Tasha asked. "Cruz, twelve-Romeo-nine."

"Confirmed."

I leaned back against the wall. "I don't think the damage to the flooring would've been as severe if the Cnidramarus Crystals hadn't infiltrated the flooring structures." When Tasha's eyebrows rose and her mouth opened, I continued, "It was visible. As each person jumped, the compression of their weight broke the structures down."

"We suspected it invaded further, but I don't think we'd heard anything from Boston about the examination yet." Cruz cleared his throat, then spoke to his team again.

"Not before the storm hit." Tasha shifted to her knees. Mumbling something about how she hated the smell of electrical fires and the way it screwed with her engines, she grabbed something and yanked it from the panel. My eyes went wide. Seeing my reaction, she said, "What? It needed to come out."

"Like that?" I asked.

She lobbed the glob of melted wires, and who knows what else, at me. When I fell to the side, she laughed. "Baby." Grabbing two handfuls of connections this time, she shifted the reactor closer and began running lines from the object. "Anyway, so did you see the debris that hit us? Were there crystals in the rock, or..."

I paused to think about it, slicing the next set and spinning them together the way she showed me. Had there been any rock or noticeable debris? In previous hits, if any stayed behind — which there were usually some traces — they were in the scrapes or scratches of the hull. Or they were in the pieces that were thrown into the holes left by the initial impact.

I'd stayed quiet too long.

"What is it, Mitchel?"

"He was focused, Evans. Leave him alone."

"Cruz, that's not it. I...I can't explain it. I don't think we were hit by a meteor or meteoric dust. I think there was more to it."

"Meaning?" Cruz asked, interested.

"As we jogged to the room, we passed the entrance point. I thought it was weird, but I remember thinking some of the metal didn't look right. Like it wasn't from our ship."

Tasha stopped breathing.

"You know something," I said, my gaze becoming penetrating.

Instantly, she locked down our comm link to verify it was only between her, me, and Cruz.

"Tash..." Cruz said.

"I know!" At my glare, she continued, "Do you remember how I told you I thought the storm was made? Well, it was a suspicion until right this second, but if what you said is true, then we have a serious conversation ahead of us."

Oh, man. Was she saying that we were about to enter a solar system where extraterrestrial life was not just confirmed, but from the planet we were headed for? This could be one of the biggest discoveries in our known history.

I swallowed. But the bigger question was, were they still alive or had the Cnidramarus wiped them out before they activated the storm? Or was the storm even a treatment?

"A huge conversation," I confirmed. "Let's finish here, and we can talk more. There are some tasks ahead of us, including a full eval of Module Four to see if we can confirm any of this and getting any active pods out as soon as possible."

Tasha stood from her scrunched position. She brushed her hands on her pants. "Agreed. Good news is it's time to get this bad boy in. Then we can verify it's functional, and we've got two working engines."

"Do you want me to let Commander Montgomery and Dr. Adams know we'll be headed their way for a meet up to discuss?" Cruz asked.

I was grateful for his diligence. Cruz's. Bloody hell, I was going soft.

"Yes. We'll set up a more in-depth planning meeting after the ship is stabilized." Shifting next to Tasha, I helped lift the reactor into position and secure it into place.

Once in, she verified all the connections, then performed the start-up sequence.

"Captain, I need you to step out while I do this part."

"Why?"

"Because if it explodes, I'd like it to only take me out." She placed a hand on her hip, her stained braid falling over her shoulder.

I stepped back, my arms crossing over my chest. "Not funny." I picked up the trash from the project and exited the small space, then walked to the drift and threw everything on the pile. Through the comm, I listened to two of my best engineers finish the process that would get my engines back online.

"That was a little mean," Cruz said, amusement in his voice.

"What? It *could* explode, but more…I'm still mad at him."

"Improbable, and you know it." He paused for a moment.

Wasn't it funny how you forgot everyone on a comm when they were being quiet?

"What did he do, anyway?"

Tasha sighed. "He claimed I like you."

Cruz was quiet for a long time until he asked, "Do you?"

I leaned against the handle of the drift, closing my eyes and waiting for her response. She didn't disappoint.

"No. You're a dick."

Cruz laughed, his amusement bursting out as if uncontrolled. From where I'd worked with Tasha came the sound of tools being thrown into a toolbox and a low feminine chuckle.

She was such a liar, and it no longer sent rage boiling through me.

Weird.

Chapter Twenty-Two

Commander Patrick Montgomery

C aptain Victoria Norris, stubborn woman extraordinaire, was finally asleep on the couch next to me. It had taken for-fucking-ever to talk her into lying down. Her breathing had altered only after I'd forced her head on my thigh, and I'd started playing with her hair.

Yeah, our relationship had changed over the last few weeks. It was still strange, but she trusted me. How I pulled that one off, I had no idea. I glanced down at the nearly full-term baby in the cart next to me.

It was probably because of him.

Javier moved gently in his sleep as the CR3 did its work to help him age. In the next few hours, we expected signs that it was time to begin the second phase of treatment. Though we had no idea what that would look like, which meant we were all on edge, waiting.

Voices carried to me from the hall.

I knew who was coming. Cruz had messaged me, but with Norris only just closing her eyes, I didn't want to wake her.

"Hey, Doc," I whispered. He looked up from where he was doing his hourly check on the Elemental Crew. "Can you tell those jackals to quiet down?"

Doc Mendez spotted Norris sleeping and nodded. He disappeared out the door. Not a minute later, a crowd of people came in, much quieter than before. Cruz, Tasha, and Doc were followed by Mitchel pushing Richards in his chair.

"Son of a bitch! Richards," I said, keeping my voice down. "Decided to come visit me this time, did you? And you brought a party."

Richards grinned, and I noted the way his hair stuck up, as if he'd been running his hands through it. He flicked his head at Mitchel.

"Can't hide it anymore, Montgomery. The captain found out I was released and put back on shift. He found me working with Cruz on the engine restart."

"And no one told me!" Mitchel said in the most irritated whisper I'd ever heard. I bit my lip to hold back a laugh.

Richards lifted his hands, then let them drop dramatically. "I am allowed to be on shift! I'm stable. I told you! Doc, help me out here."

Doc Mendez shrugged. "He's right. His injury is technically healed. He attends physical therapy every day and is working on strengthening his legs. He is not in pain and is getting feeling back slowly."

"Yeah, slowly..." Richards said.

Doc shot Richards a knowing smile, then spoke to Mitchel. "Based on all requirements, he is allowed to be on shift as long as he abides by doctors' orders and continues use of his chair until they say otherwise."

"Doesn't that make things difficult?" the captain asked, hands on hips.

"Not really. I'm a glorified button pusher anyway," Richards said.

I laughed, making my leg jump. Norris shifted. I stilled instantly. Running my hand over her hair, she calmed and settled back into sleep.

Cruz watched the exchange, interested. "Is she doing well?"

"Not sleeping." One shoulder lifted. "It'll be better after Javier's treated. Now, sit your asses down and tell me what's going on."

As this had been made the center for all Elemental Crew treatment, as well as Norris's residence, the medical team had brought in furniture to make it more livable. Several more couches and chairs made up the meeting area, and the back office was now a bedroom. No one needed to know that I'd brought over a fair amount of my things as I rarely left. With so many people coming through to check on them, they never questioned my presence.

Though, I am pretty sure Doc had figured things out.

Mendez came to take a peek at Javier. Then he took the chair closest to me. The others spread out on the opposite couch, Richards pulling his chair in between the two.

Cruz leaned back, his arm resting along the edge of the couch behind Tasha. "Things are finally calming down since the impact. So, we figured a quick recap was in order."

"Probably a good thing. Want me to start?" I asked, noting the way she angled herself ever so slightly toward him.

"Might as well." Tasha crossed her legs. "What happened after we were pulled away?"

"Well, the hit was bad. Other than the hit to Module Four and the one that caused the engine problems you dealt with," I said, giving them a quick update on the sections I'd been in charge of, "we lost Seven Solar Tower. The shields protected us from the explosion, but it made impact with Module Two. The damage was minimal with only two levels impacted. Aridas was able to secure it. No vital systems were affected. Module Three also got hit on the port side, but the shields held. Plus, Tanaka saw that one coming and was able to pull power from other parts of the ship to bolster them. Repair teams were put in place in all sections before I came offline."

Nodding, Mitchel leaned forward, placing his elbows on his thighs. He clasped his hands and let them hang.

"We didn't need this..." Mitchel got lost in his thoughts for a few seconds, his eyes glazing over as he stared into nothing. "...but the sort of good thing that came from it was it exposed some issues we didn't know about. Things we need to take into account moving forward." He scanned the group. "I'm setting up a plan for review and evaluation of Module Four."

He explained his conversation with Cruz and Tasha regarding his findings during the rescue of Brackett's team and her theory about the storm and how she believed the debris that hit us was actually a destroyed ship.

Tasha bit the inside of her lip. "I'm heading over to the lab to review the scans after this. The last set I needed was to finish this morning." She sighed. "We're scheduling a meeting in thirty-six hours to set up the rescue operation of the pods, evaluation of Module Four, and finalize the approach to Merocius."

"Reid is also working to verify how the engine burn during the storm affected our speeds. As we were still in retrograde, we're hoping it was to our benefit." Cruz extended one foot outward, then ran a finger over his bottom lip. "We'll be meeting in the morning to go over everything and come up with potential plans based on Commander Evans's analysis. Either way, we plan to have all data ready at the meeting." He paused, gaze passing over me, Norris, and then the cart. "I know that you have some.... important things going on, but we wanted to let you know."

"Right," Tasha said, taking over. "Our hope is that we can go over every possible simulation and be able to present the final approach plan. We understand if you can't be there."

The breath I took in was long and deep. They needed me. They weren't going to pull me away from everything here, and I knew they could handle it, but they wanted me there.

"You all are fucking idiots," Norris said from my lap. My fingers stilled in the soft hair behind her ear. "Of course he's going to be there to help verify all the fucking simulations."

Every word was said with her eyes closed.

Cruz snorted. Tasha covered her mouth with her hand to hide her grin. Doc looked away, but I saw his shoulders shaking.

"Victoria," I scolded. She looked up at me and rolled her eyes.

"You are. You couldn't live with yourself if you didn't, and neither could I. The ship needs your expertise. Take it as an order if you have to." She rolled back to her side. "Now play with my hair."

Laughter filled the room, and with a low growl, I did as she asked, a mixture of warmth and respect settling within me. That was until an alarm had Norris, Doc, and I jumping to our feet.

Completely forgetting the others in the room, we dove for the cart.

Within his thin membrane, Javier was shifting rapidly as if he were being compressed. The sac around him was no longer twitching gently as before. Instead, the tentacles of the Cnidramarus were contracting, both the CB2 and CR3 reacting to some unseen signal.

"Are they fighting?" Norris asked, not a hint of fear showing.

Doc shook his head. "I'm not sure, but I think we're about to find out what happens next. It's time to deliver Javier." We exchanged glances and then moved at once.

My limbs were suddenly heavy, and my heart was beating a thousand times a minute. Nothing could go wrong, and definitely not because of me. So, I pushed away the sensations and did the one job that was mine.

I lynced Dr. Gollie. The instant the line connected, I said, "Gollie, it's time. We need you."

"One minute out," he said, the echo of his footsteps coming through the line. They were slower than they used to be, and the knowledge hurt. He had refused the implant, choosing to leave it for others.

Doc pushed the cart into what was now the designated medical space. A separate area that was cleared from everything and filled with everything the medical team thought we might need to treat Javier.

Norris was already turning everything on — the heating bed, incubator, ventilator, the scanners that would read vitals...everything. We weren't sure what all we'd need, so we had every piece of instrumentation we could think of.

I grabbed the tray, which held Dr. Gollie's handheld Radiotherm laser. It was the one specific to infants. Placing it on the table next to the cart holding Javier, I met Doc's gaze.

He was breathing as heavily as I was, but somehow, he managed to speak steadily. "Grab the CC1 we collected this morning. We want it ready to implant the moment Gollie treats the CB2."

The petri dish shook, the lid tapping with each of my steps from the cooler to the table Doc indicated. As if it were made of the finest glass, I slid it where he indicated and stepped away.

"Wash up. I'm sure, like Captain Norris, you won't be able to help yourself from getting involved," Doc said as he pulled a full-body cover over the front of his uniform. It was an extra layer of protection for not just the baby, but for him as well. We couldn't afford him getting infected. "But remember the procedure. Both of you."

"They will, Doc," Dr. Adams said, striding in with Dr. Gollie behind her. "Each of us has given them the speech at least twice already." They pulled on their own frocks and joined Doc at the table.

"As have I," Mitchel said from a spot outside the designated area. His arms were crossed over his chest, his jaw tight with tension. He still wasn't sold on this plan.

Truthfully, I'd forgotten they were here. They hadn't left?

No. There they were. All my closest friends watching. Could they see my panic? Tasha met my eye and sent me a supportive smile.

"I know how to follow orders," Norris said. "Now, let's get moving. The CR3 is getting more aggressive. I worry it's going to break the sac."

Norris and I took a step back — not too far, of course — and watched as Dr. Gollie, Dr. Adams, and Doc Mendez performed the strangest delivery in the history of the human race.

It was fast. Scary fast. They'd also decided a few days ago that treatment needed to be performed simultaneously to the CR3 and the CB2 for fear that if we treated one before the other, then the weaker one would be overpowered, and all our work would be in vain.

"The incision to the external placenta has been made. Radiation implant is ready to be placed near the body of the CR3. Estimated time for reaction is fifteen seconds," Adams said, staring into the screen which showed the parasite in question. Her forceps were millimeters from it. "Are you ready, Gollie?"

"Yes. Javier is stable, CB2 is identified and still outside the fetus, and Radiotherm device ready for treatment. We are a go."

"Then let's do this. In three, two, one..." Adams counted.

That was the longest minute of my life. I held my breath the entire time. I also held back Norris, not that she would've really done anything, but when the implant went in, the CR2 went nuts, and she strained forward.

The parasite spasmed around the mechanical uteri violently. And the baby jerked. Norris let out a cry, her eyes glistening.

"Babies are used to this. Remember, they go through labor and delivery. He'll be fine," I whispered in her ear.

I wasn't sure that was true. This was the worst thing I'd ever seen. The CB2's tentacles tightened in ever-increasing fits as if in an attempt to dislodge the implant. Then, as if sensing a worse enemy, the placental grouping unwound, and the tentacles of both Cnidramarus tore at one another. Bile rose in my throat, and I fought the urge to look away. What had we done?

"Twenty seconds. They're slowing down," Adams said.

Holy fucking shit, they were.

"Ten more seconds, and we introduce the CC1." Doc handed Gollie the sample where three wriggling creatures sat. Using a modified syringe,

Gollie collected them and injected them directly beside the now-damaged CB2.

"Look, the rest of the red's tentacles are detaching like we thought...oh!" Norris exclaimed, her mouth dropping open. When she took a step forward this time, I let her. I followed.

Because the CR3 hadn't just fallen off. With CC1 attached to the blue, it had begun to disappear into Javier as we'd expected, and the last of its connections released from the amniotic sac with one last contraction of their appendages. In doing so, it popped. Fluid sprayed the inside of the cart, and a breath later, a strong cry filled the medical bay.

Tears slid down Norris's cheeks. She covered her mouth with her hand, then turned to press her head against my shoulder. I wrapped my arms around her but didn't take my eyes off the newborn as they moved him to the warming table and began to clean him.

"All vitals look good," Doc said as he wiped the baby down with a towel. "The Cnidramarus has receded, and there looks to be no wounds from the radiotherm."

He examined the baby — flipped him over, cut the umbilical cord, and performed general medical checks. It was odd how this was both similar and freakishly different than other births I'd witnessed.

Adams held a scanner over the infant. "Additionally, readings show no side effects from the exposure from the low-level radiation used to contain the Cnidramarus." She smiled at Norris. "He looks to be a healthy baby boy."

"What about aging?" I asked.

The doctors shared a look, but Gollie was the one to speak. "We spoke with Dr. Pia, and we believe that we should know within the next seventy-two hours if he is aging. If he is, then we believe it's safe to move forward with treating the rest of the Elemental Crew."

Norris lifted her head and glanced at Mitchel.

"I agree with that."

She nodded, took a few steps forward, then held her hands out to Doc, who finished swaddling Javier. With a shaking breath, she said, "Thank you. All of you."

"You are very welcome."

Taking the bundle from him, she bent down and kissed his squishy cheek. She pressed him gently to her chest, then to my surprise, approached me.

"Patrick, I'd like you to meet one of my crew. This is Javier Verandas. He's going to be a terror when he is two, but he'll have the most beautiful curls."

I brushed a tear away from her cheek and prayed that this worked both for him, but for her as well. Pulling her into my side, I pressed my chin against the top of her head. I didn't know what we were, but I'd be there for her. She was my friend, and I cared about her more each day I spent in her presence.

"I'm sure between the two of us, and the rest of our psychotic friends, we can keep him and the rest of them in line." After a quick peck to the top of her head, I let her go.

Smiling, she turned to said friends. Mitchel was in front with Richards next to him. Tasha and Cruz stood comfortably side-by-side a few steps behind, her hand wrapped around Cruz's arm.

"I want all of you to meet Javier." Norris stepped forward, holding out the sleeping baby in her arms.

Richards smiled softly. "It would be our pleasure."

Chapter
Twenty-Three
Commander Tasha Evans

"Ugh...my brain hurts." The pressure I placed at the inside arch of my eye socket felt like heaven, my fingers rubbing away the headache that had been taunting me for over an hour.

These scans were so complicated that my mind was turning to jelly. Or maybe it was the fact that I was, once again, at the end of a sixteen-hour day. One filled with the chaos of a meteor storm and a strangely beautiful motherless birth. I still couldn't wrap my head around that one.

Let alone the fact that I'd watched one of my best friends act as though he were in a relationship. He was *never* in a relationship. He tended to keep his love life quiet and never emotional, but his interaction with Captain Norris, that had been all emotion. She had lain in his lap, he'd played with her hair, and he'd even kissed her head!

The world was coming to a fucking end. That was what this meant. Had to be.

"You've got this, Tash. Just take a minute. There's a lot here." Cruz set a fresh cup of coffee on the table next to me. He took a long drink of his, then placed it beside mine. He approached the wall monitor and said, "So in the lab, we confirmed that these three combinations of frequencies were the best at affecting the Cnidramarus, correct?"

"Yes," Dr. Adams agreed. "There are various combinations we tried regarding the strength and length of exposure. We also performed several simulations with the medical team to see what the effect would be on the body."

"And?" I asked.

Dr. Adams pulled up some graphs of their findings. They showed the different combinations, the ranges which showed the best result, and the least adverse effect. It was far more information than I expected, considering the amount of time we'd had for research. I guess emergencies required dedication and results.

"These are our findings so far." Seconding my thoughts, she said, "Of course, we'd prefer to have more and a longer set of data points for verification, but we don't have the time for that."

"This is perfect for what we need and, in truth, gives me hope."

There was a shuffling of papers, and then a high-pitched male voice asked, "Can you explain, Commander?"

I'd worked with Dr. Monek for a few weeks now, and he was brilliant. Odd, but brilliant. Short with a receding hairline of close-cropped auburn hair, he held himself confidently tall. His thin-framed glasses were unique, as most chose to have their eyes corrected instead of opting for wearing eye lenses. But what I appreciated most about him was his candor.

"Well..." Pushing to my feet, I rubbed my hands together, then approached the monitor. I pulled up the scans I'd taken every few hours over the last two weeks. They read decibels of noise, hints of any radiation levels, and everything else our sensors could pick up from Eronis 8. I rubbed my bottom lip. "I'm going to think out loud for a minute. Every system has a certain amount of radio signals, electromagnetic waves, and radiation coming from the star. And we know the frequencies which it emits, therefore we can" — I swiped my hand across the screen, removing the wavelengths from the data — "take them away from our analysis.

Then there are those from any livable planet like the homeworld or Merocius." I glanced at Russel.

Uncrossing one of his arms, he held a hand out, palm out, and said, "That's one of the ways we identified Merocius as a potentially habitable planet."

"Exactly." I removed these as well. "Jovian planets also have a different signature. I can remove some of this, but not all of it, as the storm we're studying resides upon it."

"Now take off the feedback from the debris around Eronis, as much of it reverberates as metal-like substance," Dr. Monek said.

"Did the initial team confirm that we were hit by old alien technology?" Dr. Adams's eyebrow rose in interest as she watched us. She'd come back on shift a while ago and joined in on the debate.

"They did." Cruz rubbed at his lower back and took a seat in the chair I'd vacated. "A few went in and collected samples. It's a metal we don't recognize. It even has writing on it."

"So we remove those from the calculation. What does that leave us?" Adams walked over to me, her hair bouncing around her pale face.

"It means..."

Son of a bitch.

"What?" Cruz asked, leaning forward, attempting to see around me.

I turned to meet his eyes. "It means we have a chance. It means that I think we have a way to kill the Cnidramarus."

"H-how? Ar-are you serious?" Dr. Monek squeaked.

I faced the monitor again. Lifting a long finger, I placed it against the screen. "These are the frequencies coming from the storm. I knew they matched the ones we were testing, but I wasn't sure if they were at levels we could handle. Truthfully, I'm still not. They're right on the brink, but...but based on what you gave me, Dr. Adams —"

Her eyes were wide. "It's possible! I don't know if we should expose everyone, but...holy crap! This might just work!" She bounced on her toes, and I couldn't hold back my grin.

"In combination with the sound waves we picked up from the probe, it might." Tears sprang to my eyes as she wrapped me in a tight hug.

The chair behind me moved, and I released Adams. Before I even had a chance to react, Russel scooped me up in a hug. A giggle escaped my lips, and I pressed my face into his neck. He set me back down on my feet, and I looked up into his face.

"Now, all we have to do is figure out a flight path." I bit my lip. Sarcasm dripped from each word when I said, "Because that's not going to be complicated."

"One thing at a time." He pressed his palm to my cheek, the warmth far more comforting than it should've been.

"He's right," Dr. Adams said, patting my shoulder. "Which is why you two are going to go talk to Reid before you go get some rest. While you do that, Monek and I will verify these radiation levels and their effects so they are ready for the meeting."

"But we —"

"Need to rest? Yeah." She nodded vigorously, a knowing smile on her face.

Cruz laughed. "Then we'll see you at the meeting."

"Actually, I'll be there to help with the evaluation of Module Four in a few hours. The captain wanted another set of hands."

"Perfect." Cruz began to lead me to the exit.

I was picking up my things when Monek said, "Make sure she gets some sleep, Cruz."

My hackles rose. Oh, this was not good. I had definitely been giving the wrong impression to my staff. "What the fuck is that —"

"You will watch your tongue, doctor. The commander is your superior officer," Cruz growled in a tone that had me freezing. Monek looked like he was about to pee himself. "And I do not know what you think is happening, but first, it is none of your business. Second, we are crewmembers and friends. I will be walking her back to her suite where she will go into her suite *alone.* She will rest." He glared at me then, and my lip twitched with a smile. "If I ever hear another comment like that from you again, Dr. Monek, you will be dealing with the 'asshole' version of me. Have you heard of him?"

Monek nodded vigorously, panic in his eyes.

Russel held a hand out to me. "I'm glad you understand. Come, Commander. I've let Reid know we're on the way."

Tucking my tablet into my arm and grabbing my coffee, I left the room. Russel's hand settled at the base of my spine. Through it, his anger vibrated into me.

I had to do something. If I let it, we'd head straight to see Reid, and the tension brought on from that stupid interaction would build until he'd burst. So, I reached back, grabbed his wrist, and pulled him into my office as we passed it.

"Hey, what?" he said as I yanked on his arm, shutting and locking the door behind us.

With a flick of the keypad beside the door, the window went foggy, and I turned to face him. I looked up into his face, only inches from mine and demanded, "Talk to me."

He scowled, confusion and irritation in the way his jaw ticked.

Without thought, I moved closer, my body coming into contact with the front of his. With one hand, I reached up and rubbed at the frown wrinkles on his forehead.

"Commander, what are you doing?"

I shot him a look, and he let out a breath. His shoulders dropped, and the tension on his face lessened.

"Tasha, what are you doing?"

Letting my hand drop to his arm, I asked again, "Are you all right?"

"I don't like people saying things like that about you. Assuming things..."

"Assuming what?"

He rolled his eyes. "Don't give me that. I saw how you stiffened; how angry you got. The idea alone of people thinking we're together bothers you, and it should. You shouldn't want to be associated with me."

My head tilted in confusion. "And why is that?"

"Stop being obtuse."

I couldn't help the way my fingers tightened just a touch. He was trying to piss me off. But realistically, why was I asking these questions? Why was I pushing this? Part of me was still confused about my feelings. He was a good friend, but he'd acted like a child for years. *YEARS.* He wasn't the one I should want, but part of me did. Always had.

I bit the inside of my cheek. "Russel...few men would have read the room that well. Fewer would have said what you did. Even when you were an asshole to me, all those stupid fucking years" — the jerk smirked — "you made sure people treated me respectfully, even when you didn't."

It was as if the guilt became visible; his shoulders drooped, and sadness filled his eyes. "I never should have treated you that way. I'm an idiot."

"I don't think that's what happened, and I think there's more going on here." My voice had dropped against my will.

His hand slipped onto my hip. I leaned in closer, unable to resist whatever was happening here.

"What do you think's happening?" he asked, gaze locked on mine.

"I want you to tell me. I need you to."

Somehow, he'd gotten even closer, his face and lips inches from mine. His breath tickled my cheeks, and the urge to go up on my tiptoes and kiss him was like nothing I'd ever experienced. But could I do that?

"I can't." He jerked back, realizing how close we'd become.

But he didn't step away, so that was something. Right?

"What? Why?" I blinked away my surprise.

"I told you. You deserve better." He looked away. "I made a promise."

"What promise?"

"That's not important."

"Russel, what promise?" I asked more forcefully.

With more aggression than I expected from him, he crossed his arms over his chest, forcing space between us. "Drop it, Commander. You're being inappropriate. We are —"

"Just tell me! You promised me you wouldn't be like this anymore." My arm dropped to my side, my gaze finding a spot on his shirt. I fought to hide the hurt that made my diaphragm heavy. The next words I had to force out. "That we were friends."

My gaze met his as he said, "That any *friendship* we ever had would be completely on your terms." Russel slipped from between me and the wall. "But I was stupid and broke my own rules. I crossed the line. I knew better. All that matters is that I keep my promise because you have better options then a piece of shit like me. So this is over. I'm going back to the way it was before; that's the only way." He slammed his hand on the door panel and stomped down the hall. "You're just not smart enough to stay away."

"Russel!" My shock and hurt at his words meant I was too slow to catch him. "If it's up to me then..."

But he was already gone.

When I stepped into the hallway, I found Dr. Adams standing, mouth agape, watching his furious form leave the lab. Seeing the tears in my eyes, she asked, "Everything all right?"

"Um...I don't know," I choked. "But I think he's been holding in some stuff for a while."

"I think you have, too." She placed a hand on my shoulder and, with a kind smile, returned to the lab.

I followed Cruz, heart aching, chest tight.

Walking into the Stasis Bay that had been hit during the storm was a shock to the system. Mitchel hadn't done it justice. Or, perhaps, he'd been too focused to really see just how bad it really was.

The hole left in the side of *The Aspire* was three levels high — I'd confirmed it — and more than a hundred feet wide. We'd lost thirty who were awake and aware in this section alone, but we'd yet to verify how many who'd been in hypersleep. That was part of why we were here. It was time to get the pods and see how many would be a rescue versus a retrieval.

"How far had Brackett made it through reanimation in this section?" I stepped over a beam that was bent, hinging the floor at a forty-degree angle, then crouched to go under a walkway which had fallen from above.

"She was maybe halfway through," Tanaka said over the comm line in our suits. He was the one monitoring the fields and playing doorkeeper for this Module Four evaluation and rescue mission. "Which means there were about a hundred and fifty people left to go. We believe that at least twenty were jettisoned."

My fists clenched and unclenched.

There was nothing we could do about that. All we could do was try to help those still here.

Specialist Boston, who was a few steps in front of me, asked, "How many do we have to help with the retrieval and evaluation?"

"Captain Remian took in a group of ten initially. A second group will come in later. Right now, he's showing Sergeant Cruz the structural abnormalities he noted. That way, you guys can dive right into your analysis."

The urge to grind my teeth hit me, but I fought it. Whatever game Cruz was playing, I wasn't going to be part of it. Hell, I was still too confused to really understand what happened.

There was a pang of metal, and I looked behind me to where Dr. Adams was climbing over what used to be a workstation. It was in pieces, crushed almost beyond recognition. Behind it was the pod that had done the damage. The sides were dented, the glass cracked in places. The thing must have rolled to be that smashed.

Adams gulped at the sight of the blood which stained the inside. Or, more likely, what was pinned behind it. It was a face we recognized, blank and lifeless; disturbing and painful to witness one we respected now lost so violently.

"Hey, Tanaka. Can you make sure one of the first tasks for Mitchel's crew is to get Brownstone out?" The muscles in my throat spasmed when I spoke his name.

"Someone is on his way now, Commander."

"Thank you." To Adams, I said, "Don't worry, doctor. We'll make sure he's treated with respect."

I understood her reaction. It was a hard thing to see, death.

"The captain said it was bad, but I..." She shook her head, swallowed, and continued forward. "I spend my time in the lab."

I understood and appreciated her willingness to continue, considering this was so far out of her wheelhouse. Everyone on this ship was trained, of course, but that didn't mean they spent their lives in roles where danger was the norm.

"We're almost to the captain. Then we can begin the analysis. I can see the sergeant up ahead," Boston said. "Focus on our task. It makes it easier."

She nodded and moved on, but, like me, I was sure that this was a sight that would stick with her.

When I stepped free of the next pile of debris, I was finally able to round the corner and see the group up ahead. Mitchel was gesturing to the back of the large room, where there was far less damage. There, dozens of the sleep pods were lined up and connected. Additionally, most were still alight. That couldn't be said to the ones we'd passed. Which was probably why, as we got close and Tanaka dropped us into the conversation, Mitchel was saying, "So begin evacuation of the pods starting with those. Tech Specialist Tanaka has a team working on the A564 door. Begin preparations for evacuations from there. He will have a team ready."

"If they are unable to open the door?" one of the soldiers asked.

Tanaka snorted. "Oh, we'll get it open."

I grinned and noted how Russel nodded once, his expression blank.

We hadn't talked one-on-one since the strange argument in the lab, and his actions this morning had been anything but normal. He'd been brisk — inconsiderate and rude, even.

"You heard him," Mitchel said.

The group of six jogged off, careful of the unstable floor in the area.

"Captain," Boston said. He rested his fists on his hips. "Has the team begun analysis of the structure?"

"Not yet," Russel said. He shot a glance in my direction. "We were waiting for the rest of the team to get here."

The muscles in my back tightened. That was a comment of the Cruz from before, not my friend Russel, the man I'd been finding again.

"Morning to you, too." I addressed Mitchel instead. "Sorry I'm late, Captain. Someone moved, then held my morning meeting without me. When I got there and found out, I headed here since he was already with you and hadn't informed me."

Mitchel's eyebrow rose, shifting his gaze from me to Cruz, who continued his examination of the struts beneath the floor. Russel didn't look up or acknowledge the way everyone was staring at him. I waved off the issue, but it was clear Mitchel was as curious as I was about the situation. Not as irritated, though. Which was probably for the best.

"Well, now that you're here, let's get started," Mitchel said. "I've shown Sergeant Cruz the area I first identified the structure weakness." I joined him ten or so meters from where Russel crouched. "This is where the floor gave way. As you can see, the structure below collapsed. It looks like the Cnidramarus Crystal is growing not just through these beams here..."

I'd gotten down on my stomach next to him and scooted so that I could see between the flooring platform and below deck structures. "...but in beams all along the aft portion," I finished for him. "Wow, this is incredible. Boston?"

"Yes?" He knelt near my feet, ready to catch me, but also looking where I was.

"We need to do an in-depth scan between the levels."

"That's pretty obvious." Cruz's low snarl came through the speakers just fine.

The hair on the back of my neck bristled, and I pushed up to look toward Cruz. He was standing, hands on hips, and foot tapping. *Tapping.*

Yeah, I was going to kill him.

Not giving him a response, I walked along the crevasse toward the hole. The floor became more unstable the farther I went, but we were also able to see more of the internal beams of the walls and outer *Aspire* bracing.

"My team had begun the review of this module when the storm hit," Boston said, lifting a metal pole from the floor and throwing it a few feet away. It clanked against the grating of the deck. "We found growths in the major struts in this section — obviously — but also Sections Two and Four. Three is still clear, though we're not done. With the shields down in this section, I ordered my team to evacuate."

"As you should have," Mitchel said.

I pointed to where the wall had been ripped away, peeled back, and exposed. "Look at that. You can see the crystals glimmering. They've completely encased the inside of the wall."

A sense of foreboding grew within me, starting at my toes and climbing slowly like ants crawling along my skin. With every inch, the realization became clearer, my brain taking shape around the truth so big it couldn't grasp it all at once.

Fuck. Oh, fuck! This was terrible. If the Cnidramarus were filling the walls and floors, eating away at the bracings themselves, then could we trust anything in this module?

"Dr. Adams, Sergeant Cruz?" My panic pulled their attention from a crushed piece of something I couldn't identify. My breathing was loud in my ears as the magnitude of what this meant simmered. They joined me, Russel standing behind Dr. Adams as if she were a barrier. Like a complete dimwit, I said, "I'm concerned about what this means."

"Of course you are. You should be," he said, shooting me a glare.

"What is your problem today?" Mitchel held his hands out questioningly. "You haven't acted like this in weeks, and I don't like this, Cruz. So, pull your head out of your arse, or I'm going to send you back to Montgomery."

Instead of getting angry like I expected, Russel sighed, then nodded. "I apologize, Captain."

Closing my gaping mouth, I got myself together. "Let me ask you a question. Our plan is to treat the ship and crystal with the high-frequency radiation waves in combination with sound waves, correct?"

"Yes..." Russel's tone was condescending, the word drawn out, but the light changed in his eyes from one moment to the next. Because, like always, it was as if he could read my thoughts. Understanding lit them instead, then he said, "Oh, shit."

He placed his hand on the mass of debris next to him. Once a wall, it was filled with crystal. He met my eyes.

"You're brilliant, and completely right." Then he remembered he was being an asshole. "Don't let that go to your big head."

I rolled my eyes.

"Can you explain for the rest of us, please?" Dr. Adams asked, but I could tell she was almost there.

So I asked her the most important question. "What will happen to the crystal when we expose it to the radiation and all those sound waves?"

She stared off into space for a second, then she sucked in a gasp, but it was Mitchel that answered. "They'll begin to vibrate until they explode or crumble like they did in Green Room 4."

"Yes. Which means this entire module is going to either explode and become shrapnel, or crumple in on itself." My eyes roamed the already-damaged space.

"That's why this section was so badly damaged from the meteor storm," Russel agreed.

Boston squatted down next to the canyon in the floor to examine something by his feet. "That makes sense. The pieces that impacted here weren't any bigger than what hit elsewhere."

"So what do we do?" Adams was staring off toward the set of sleeping crew still in their pods.

Mitchel straightened his shoulders, took a deep breath, then said, "We finalize this rescue, evacuate all remaining personnel, and get supplies transferred to the other sections of *The Aspire*."

"Why?" Boston asked, glancing from one of us to the next, as if he couldn't track what we were talking about.

Releasing a heavy sigh, Mitchel said, "To save the rest of the ship, Module Four will have to be jettisoned."

Captain Remian rolled his shoulders, and, with his head held high, strode away to join the second half of the team and begin the evacuation of all personnel in one quarter of *The Aspire*.

Chapter
Twenty-Four
Commander Patrick
Montgomery

T he soft cooing and baby grunts which came from my shoulder
was the best thing ever. He was warm and smelled good. I had the
strangest feeling; I never wanted to put him down.

Never had I thought this would be my life.

Yet here I was, sitting at my desk as usual, working, but instead of
having both hands free, one was pressed to the back of an infant who
rested on my chest. When awake, all I wanted to do was stare at him.
It didn't make sense. He wasn't even mine, but I felt a connection to
him — to all of the Elemental Crew in this situation. Perhaps it was the
parasite within us, taking away the control of our lives. Or maybe it was
the woman who cared for each of us with all her being.

A hand glided over my hair. Involuntarily, I closed my eyes, then
looked up.

"Want me to take him?" Norris asked. "You've been working like that
for a while."

I shook my head. "He's out, and I'm about done. Everything's going
well today. Even the prep for section separation when we get to Merocius
is on track."

"Are we going to be able to separate *The Aspire* Sections? I thought we were going too fast."

"We are," I said, running a gentle hand down her side. Stopping on her hip, I squeezed gently. "Doesn't mean we shouldn't prepare. Those systems are used for adjustments in direction, speed, and even evacuation if necessary. I'd rather we be ready for any situation."

"Smart." She yawned.

"Go take a nap. You haven't slept since they treated Nick, Elena, and Tenchi with the CR3. It's been hours, and they're doing great."

"Neither have you, and I thought they were coming back to do the last three today, too. I wanted to be ready for them. I know they're farther along, but I want to make sure they're birthed before we get to Merocius. It's safer that way."

She was right, and I knew it. I felt the same way.

I pushed my chair out from the desk and spun to face her. Keeping my gaze locked on hers, I linked our fingers and pulled her between my thighs. With one gentle tug, she was drawn onto my lap. Exactly where I wanted her. She smirked but did as I requested.

"What's this?" Her grin was teasing.

"I like you, Victoria." Well, fuck me. That was not what I'd expected to say.

Her eyebrows rose, her pink lips dropping open.

I thought I was going to say something about the babies' treatment, or the ship, or her being exhausted, but no...I went all in. We sat there frozen, both of us unsure how to proceed.

With no intonation and her face clear of any emotion, she said, "You can take it back. We'll pretend it never happened. I —"

"Fuck, no." Reaching up, I threaded a hand behind her neck and into her hair. "I don't want to take it back." And I sat taller, guiding her toward me. She came willingly. Our lips brushed, the sensation everything I'd craved for longer than I wanted to admit.

Damn, she was perfect.

She deepened the kiss, shifting closer while still being careful of the baby I held. The kiss was sweet, meaningful, one of her hands caressing my cheek while the other steadied Javier. When she pulled back, she stared down at me.

"I like you, too, Patrick. More than I should for someone almost fifty years my junior."

At my snort, she grinned. "That's not totally accurate, as you're younger than you were, and I am older than I am."

She laughed out loud, making Javier stir. Gently, she brushed his back, shushing him. He settled down instantly. Without taking her eyes off Javier, she said, "But I come with some heavy burdens. I don't want —"

Needing to stop that train of thought right where it was, I pressed my lips to hers again. Her fingers dug into my hair, and I groaned.

A throat cleared somewhere behind us. Norris tried to pull away, but I refused to let her disappear so quickly. I met her eyes and whispered, "They are not a burden, and you are worth it."

Tears glistened in her eyes as I kissed her cheek and released her. She tried to get up, but I wasn't ready for that, either. I didn't want her to hide this, not if it was real. So, I placed a hand on her hip and spun us toward the voice.

Tasha stood there, amusement lining every inch of her face. Arms crossed, hip out, she looked about ready to burst. "Well, well, well."

It was all right. I knew how to distract her. "Want to hold the baby? He's missed his Auntie Tasha."

She'd coined the name, not me.

Her eyes narrowed, but then she dropped her arms, walked over, and scooped the baby up.

"Captain," she said respectfully and without commenting on the way she was sitting in my lap. Then all her attention was on Javier. "Hey, sweet boy. Are they taking good care of you?"

Norris and I shared an amused glance before she brushed my cheek, then stood. "Now that you have a babysitter, I'll take that nap." She pointed at me, then Tasha. "You wake me up if the doctors come to treat the others."

Tasha agreed instantly, clearly still terrified of the venerable captain. I just winked.

Hell, yes. She was gorgeous in that confident way of hers. I may have watched her disappear into the back room.

"Shit, Patrick. You've got it bad."

"We're not talking about it."

"Oh, come on!" Tasha whined. She bounced the baby, kissing his soft hair every few seconds. "Where else am I gonna get gossip with?"

My blank stare did nothing.

"What do you want?" I asked when she still didn't speak.

"Oh, right. Important stuff. Should I lay him down or...?"

I held out my hands, and she handed him back to me. I settled Javier back on my shoulder, and Tasha smiled softly. Tasha connected her armpad to my computer and released the documents for my review.

"It's been forty-eight hours since we identified the severity of the infestation within Module Four. The good news is — or the bad news — Captain Remian has been working nonstop to evacuate and recover everything we can and transfer it to the other modules."

"Is he having trouble again?" I asked, thinking about Mitchel not taking his designated rest periods.

She shook her head. "We've been keeping an eye on him, but I think he learned his lesson. Plus, with Richards back on shift even in just an admin role, he feels more comfortable."

I patted Javier's back and, deciding I needed movement, stood to pace back and forth. He liked it when I did this.

"We've only found minor infestation within the other modules' structures themselves, and mostly in Section One of Module Three. So, we've begun evac there, as well as a precaution for landing."

"Understood."

"Here is my question. We are approximately three-quarters of the way done with Module Four. Which means we've been working on the calculations. We've performed two of the three burns you originally said were necessary, but not in the way we wanted. The first, yes, but the second during the storm which was uncontrolled and not with two engines.

"Because of this, our speed is too high, but we don't have the fuel, nor the time, to do another burn."

"Have you spoke with Reid or Cruz?"

"I was just with the sergeant." It was hard not to notice the bitterness and general frustration in her voice.

"Is he still not talking to you?"

"We're not talking about that asshat."

That would be a no...

"And yes. I came here after meeting with them. I thought he was coming with me, but..." she threw her hands up in the air. "You know what? Never mind. The point is, we came up with a plan. We don't think it will be enough, but it *should* slow us enough that when we begin the orbital transition around Eronis 8, our speed won't be so high that we slingshot past it. Instead, we think it should allow us to maneuver over the storm the way we need, perform a burn *there* to hover long enough to treat the entire ship."

My hands and feet tingled as excitement sparked within me. Taking my seat once again, I looked over the documents, leaning close while taking care to support Javier's head. His snores settled my nerves as my mind calculated each and every step they'd outlined.

The idea was to eject Module Four but do it at just the right position and angle where the thrust of the ejection would help to decrease our speed. The only concern was the fact that in this position, *The Aspire* was likely to be hit by the discharged piece unless we were able to remotely pilot it away.

"This is risky."

"Isn't everything?" she asked.

Fair point. "Have the calculations been verified?"

"We wanted your thoughts first."

"The timeline to get to Merocius went out the window a long time ago. Not only because we woke up so late, but then each time we didn't slow down." I leaned back and pressed my cheek to a head of soft hair. "I see in the calculations you also took into account the number infected and the rate of aging. I assume you spoke to Dr. Pia, then."

Sadness filled her eyes. "I did. As of yesterday, we were up to eighty-one infected —forty-three CR3s and thirty-eight CB2s."

"Did they tell you that something is happening with the speed of aging?"

She frowned and shook her head.

"It seems that the closer to Eronis we get, the quicker the Cnidramarus works. Even I'm aging more quickly, even with the implant. That's why they've decided to treat the infants a day early."

"Patrick, no. I hadn't heard."

"Yes, they think it's best. But in regard to the plan, I think this is the best option we have. The calculations look on point. I'll do a few more simulations to verify, but I think we're there. Have the teams verify and we can begin preparations."

"Will do, Commander."

"Thank you, Tasha. For everything."

My lync went off, and Tasha jumped. Switching it on had Dr. Gollie's voice filling the quiet. "Commander. I wanted to let you know that the team and I are on our way. We want to finish before I am unable. We also wanted to discuss an option of treatment with you."

"And that would be?" What kind of treatment did they have in mind?

"Well, now that we know it worked on the infants — and we've seen it work with Captain Norris — would you want to be the first to get the CC1 implanted? We were going to ask Richards, but considering his CB2's reaction…"

"Yes!" I said without having to think about it.

"Patrick," Tasha whispered. She glanced at the baby, and then to the door where Norris slept. "Shouldn't you speak to Captain Norris first?"

Of course there were risks, but if it meant that I'd stop aging and be given a chance before we got to Merocius, then wouldn't that be better?

"I consent and wish to have the procedure performed immediately. I am off shift for the next eight hours anyway." I locked eyes with Tasha. "But I have one requirement."

"That is?" Gollie asked.

"You can't tell Norris. After treatment of the crew, I will come with you and be treated elsewhere."

Gollie sounded like he was choking on something. This is what confusion sounded like. "Uh, are you sure? You don't want her to be there?"

"I'm sure. Promise me."

He cleared his throat, and with a disappointed air, said, "I will abide by my patient's wishes."

"Thank you. See you soon." I closed the lync.

Tasha was glaring at me. "She is going to kill you. And if she doesn't, I might."

"Tash, she has too much going on right now. She can't handle this too. So, I will go to 'Engineering' for a meeting, and you're coming with me."

"Patrick…"

"I'd like you to be there. Please?"

"Of course. You're such a stubborn ass." She squeezed my arm, then stood. Taking the baby from me again, she said, "Now go wake up the captain. She'll want to be awake for when the doctors get here."

With a sigh, I said, "Poor thing barely got an hour."

Tasha giggled. "You have it bad."

Chapter
Twenty-Five
Captain Mitchel Remian

F or being the captain, it felt strange standing on the Bridge. I'd spent more time in other parts of the ship, then here since I'd awoken. Granted, I checked in at the beginning and end of every shift and was in constant communication with my team, but I had always been the type of leader to lead by example. If I wasn't willing to do the job and fill in where necessary, how could I expect my crew to?

"We've finished the removal of all active pods within easy access. We're now performing the final sweep for any that may have been caught in the blast. Four have already been retrieved." Dr. Brackett leaned over the workstation the group of us were huddled around. The light glistened off her golden-brown skin, accentuating her fine bone structure. "We've confirmed a total of sixty are still unaccounted for."

Cruz, who had been acting like a weasel had climbed up his butt for days, grunted. "Spec Boston and Tasha are down with a team doing one last sweep. Even though it was confirmed by two teams that these were lost to the impact."

He'd been making remarks like that all morning, and I was at my limit. Over the last weeks, I'd forgotten how bad he'd been. I'd also started to like him, but that was quickly going away. If he wasn't careful, I was going to throw him out an airlock.

With a calming breath, I rolled my shoulders and addressed him. "*Commander Evans*, Sergeant Cruz, is down there risking her life searching for crew members who may have been trapped."

For the first time, I saw the irritation pointed at me. He removed his hands from the table and faced me, aggression in every line of his body.

Yup, I was done.

"My office. Now," I ordered.

Brackett's eyes widened, and she stepped back. Aridas and Richards, who'd been watching the exchange, both looked as annoyed as I was.

Richards was leaning back in his chair, a glare outlining everything he'd like to do to the sergeant. It was written in each lowered brow and twitching jaw muscle. Had we not been on shift, I was pretty sure fists would've been thrown by now.

"Now!"

Cruz strode from the room and toward my office. When I entered the code to open the door, he entered without a word. There was no sitting. Instead, he crossed his arms and leaned against the wall.

Fine, if he wanted to play it this way, I'd play.

"Are you going to reprimand me for being unprofessional?" he snarled.

I sat on the edge of my desk. Shaking my head at him, I said, "No."

"Then what?" He pushed off the wall, arms dropping to his sides.

"You're being an idiot. You know that?" When he just stared at me, I added, "I don't know what the fuck happened with you and Tasha, but you need to fix it."

It was like I'd hit him with a two-by-four.

"What? But I thought you were..."

I sighed. "I did, too." I scratched the side of my head. "But then I realized I am not what she wants. You are, and you two are perfect together."

He stuttered, attempting to say something, but I had struck him dumb.

"You make her stronger, are a partner to her. You respect her." I pushed up from where I leaned, getting right in his face. "But whatever you're fucking doing right now is complete and utter hogwash. You're making yourself look like an arsebadger, and you're going to lose her."

His mouth dropped, fully agape as we looked eye to eye.

"So stop being a wanker."

"I feel like I was just cussed out by a toddler."

I smacked his shoulder and stepped back. "You're not as bad a guy as you pretend."

He looked down. "I don't know if I can."

"Then don't, but stop being a prick. You fuck this up, Cruz, and the crew is gonna throw you from an airlock."

Not needing a response — because really, what more was there to say? — I left my office.

"Cap," he said, stopping me in the hallway. I stopped, looking back at a man who was clearly struggling. His lips were parted, and his brow pinched in confusion. He tried to say something more, but nothing came out.

"I know," I said, and walked back onto the Bridge. He followed me back into where the others waited.

They looked up when we entered, and it was clear something had changed. The tension in the room was thick, the air vibrating with energy. Then there was the look on each of their faces. Their expressions were pinched, and lips pursed. It was one I'd seen too many times recently.

Richards was the one to speak up. "We have a problem." The main screen showed an image of Mod Four, where the crew was doing their final sweep — where *Tasha* was doing the final sweep. "The floor collapsed along the port side of corridor nine. The area left of the impact. Boston, Evans, and Romano are trapped."

"Are they in contact?" Cold water spread through my veins. We could not lose more people.

And Tasha...

"Yes."

The wave of emotion that flashed across Cruz's face was both painful and inspiring to watch. His decision solidified, and the determination within him became absolute. "Is she hurt? The others?"

Richards met his stare, and only then did I notice the fear and panic in his eyes. "Boston and Romano are fine, but when the floor shifted, a wall fell. It pinned Tasha. A beam punctured her side, and they're having trouble controlling the bleeding."

The curse that echoed through the Bridge mirrored mine. Cruz closed his eyes and swallowed hard, making a visible effort to push down the pain that news caused him. Then he spun on his heels and bolted for the door. But before he disappeared, he turned, locked eyes with Richards, and promised, "I'll get her out, Geron."

Then he was gone.

Richards's fists were clenched, his jaw ticking. He met my gaze, and I knew what he was thinking. He wanted to be the one helping her, protecting her. Tasha was his best friend. They were all the family each other had.

"We'll get her out," I said, moving to follow. "Aridas, can you notify Medical? Also let Tanaka know Cruz and I are on our way?"

"Yes, sir."

"Be careful," Brackett said. I inclined my head to her and ran after Cruz.

My legs burned as I worked to catch up to Cruz. He'd gotten a head start, but there were still lifts and procedure to follow. When I did catch up, he was breathing hard, adrenaline making his hands shake. I wasn't entirely worried; he'd been in plenty of emergency situations and had proven himself levelheaded. However, this time was a bit different.

Which was why I asked, "Are you good, Cruz?" He shifted from foot to foot but didn't answer. "I need an answer. I can't have you going in there and risking anyone. If I need to—"

"I'm good, Captain. I promise. We're going to get *everyone* out of there safely." His eyes bored into me.

I lynced Tanaka. "Cruz and I are almost there. Can you link us into the situation so that we are up to date?"

"Yes, Captain."

There was a click, and then Romano's voice came in mid-sentence, "...lift the wall. If we do, it'll hurt the commander. We need to brace it first. Can you send a cutter through? I think the pipe's thin enough that we can cut it then slip her free."

"How's her bleeding?" Doc Mendez asked. "And is there enough room to perform such a procedure?"

"Yes," Romano said. "There's about a foot from where the wall is to where it protrudes from her side."

Cruz's breath rushed out of him. I placed a hand on his shoulder. He closed his eyes and nodded. Seeing the number on the lift, we unclipped our helmets and slid them on. When the door to the lift opened, we ran for the entrance to the Stasis Bay.

"Sending the instruments in," Doc said.

We listened to the team's conversation as we passed through the field with Tanaka's help, then began the trek through the debris to where Tasha and the others were trapped. Knowing how unstable the area was, extra precautions were made as we chose our path.

The group of about five rescuers were huddled around a small opening. Doc Mendez was crouched before it, sending instructions and supplies through the hole.

"Tasha," he said. "When they start, they're going to need to keep pressure on the wound. It's going to hurt."

"I'll be fine." Her breathing was labored, the strain clear with each syllable. "How is the exit coming?"

Doc looked up. Seeing us, relief overcame his expression. Turning off all comms but to those of us outside, he said, "We need to get her out. Now. She's losing blood, and we know she's been exposed. The clock is ticking."

One of the structural engineers I didn't know, but Cruz seemed to recognize, spoke up. "We originally considered entering from the side, but this section here is more structurally sound and relatively stable. It's the best option we've got. If we add a brace here and here" — he gestured to multiple points along the debris field — "we should be able to remove the blockage. That should give us enough space to clear the way and get her out. Plus, our movements shouldn't touch the wall they're working on."

"Let's do it," I said, stepping forward. "Tell us where you need us."

"I'm starting," Romano said matter-of-factly. "Boston, keep pressure. Evans, I'll go as quickly as I can."

Of all the crew to get stuck in there, I was glad it was Romano. He was a bloody good soldier.

"On it," Boston replied. "Commander, eyes on me."

The sound of the cutter hitting metal came through the speakers, but it was Tasha's groan and then scream that had Cruz moving.

"While they work, we work. Go!" he ordered in a tone no one was going to argue with.

The structural engineer shouted instructions, and without hesitation or thought, we complied. There wasn't another moment to waste. This was his time to shine, and our time to shut up and listen. Which was fine with us.

The braces were placed, inflated slowly — way too slowly for Cruz's or my liking — and then we began to remove the blockage. That was its own nightmare. Each piece had to be inspected to make sure that there wasn't something else that would collapse or cause an avalanche of parts to come down on those inside. Plus, there was the risk of puncture of our suits and exposures. Everything was dangerously sharp.

It didn't help that through the entire thing we could hear Tasha's cries and Boston's attempts to calm her. It was hard not to picture her; teeth clenched, eyes squeezed shut against the pain, tears seeping from their corners as guttural screams were forced from her when the pipe puncturing her side jerked too much. My stomach turned every time, and I used it to push harder — work faster — to get them out.

The not-funny part was this felt like hours, but it was probably only minutes.

Tasha let out a relieved sound as the noise of the cutting ceased.

"I'm done. We got it." Romano was breathing heavy. "Let's get you wrapped up and ready for transport. How's it going out there?"

"About halfway," the engineer said. He was in the hole, shuffling out pieces to Cruz, who would then hand them to me. I was my job to discard them. "We'll come at you from your left. The scans say we are approximately three meters away."

"There's a wall of steel there," Boston said.

"Yes. Don't worry. We will take care of that."

Five minutes later, we'd cleared a path large enough to bring Tasha through. The last obstacle was the panel that required us to cut through it. It was a structural wall that seemed to be intact.

Before handing the box which held the laser cutter over, I asked, "The structural walls of this module have all contained Cnidramarus Crystal, correct? Do we need to worry about cutting into it? Will it collapse or hold?"

I was surprised when Tasha was the one that answered. She sounded like hell, but it was nice to hear her awake. "It should hold. The Dira...Cindra...Crystal isn't affected by heat or vibration at that level, and we aren't making a large enough hole to affect structure."

"I agree," Cruz seconded. "The biggest concern is puncture of the suits upon exiting, but more than likely that won't be an issue, as they will be smooth after cutting."

"Russel, you're here?" Tasha asked. The emotion in those three words said more than I think she intended.

Cruz gulped and stared off into space. He bowed his head and whispered, "Of course I am. I wouldn't be anywhere else. I'm gonna get you out, and then you're gonna tell me what an ass I am." When she laughed, Cruz's lip turned up at the corner. Meeting the engineer's eye, he said, "Time to get them out."

Chapter Twenty-Six

Commander Tasha Evans

H e was here? Russel hadn't spoken to me in days unless he had to, and he'd rushed down into this maze of death and debris to rescue me. Why?

"How are you doing, Tash?" he asked. Behind him, the sound of a laser cutter was loud, but then was replaced with the sound of metal being moved.

"I'm confused..." I admitted, my gaze staring up at the mangled parts of my ship that had tried to crush me. If I looked down, the pipe sticking from my side reached upward, the second half still embedded in the structure above. I tried not to look at either. It made it more real and the sensation of Boston pressing on the wound was enough to keep me grounded to the here and now.

Romano shifted past me, careful not to jostle my prone form.

"Are you feeling lightheaded? Boston, how is her blood loss?" Doc Mendez asked in quick succession. He shot off a few more questions, to which Romano and Boston responded, but I ignored them.

Waving off the doc's questions, and instantly regretting my movement, I said, "No, no, Doc, I'm fine. I'm confused why Russel came down here. Weren't you helping the captain? You said you had something important to do."

"Tasha."

My name. That was it. It was a scolding and a caress all at the same time. And it made my heart ache for something I wasn't sure was even a thing. Tears pricked my eyes.

"Don't say my name like that," I choked, a sob catching in my throat.

Then someone was leaning over me. His eyes met mine, and the tears slipped backward, falling into my hair as if they never existed.

He placed his hand on the side of my helmet. "That's the only way I *can* say your name. Now, let's get you out of here."

Was he saying? I hiccupped a breath, then winced.

"Romano, bring in the lift as far as you can." Doc tapped on my helmet.

When had he come in? How are they all fitting in here?

"We already got Romano out," Russel told me. Had I said that out loud? "He's taking my spot outside, and Boston's a little scrunched with me in here."

"Yeah, your partner refused to stay outside." I grinned at Doc's irritated grumble.

"And, obviously, Doc's here," Russel said with a smirk. He glanced behind me, nodded, then locked his gaze with mine. "Okay, love, it's time to go. We're gonna do everything we can to keep you steady, but it's going to be rough. The space is tight until we get you on the lift. Do you understand?"

I shifted my shoulder, the protective suit I wore scraping against the floor beneath me. "Yes."

"First, we slip her from the hole, then we can get her on the blanket. Once she's there, the three of us can move her to the opening." Doc shifted around Russel and me. "Here, can you slide the edge beneath her shoulders?"

Russel nodded. "All right. This is gonna suck."

"Shut up and do it. It's weird when you're being nice."

With a chuckle, he wrapped his hands under my arms, lifted me slowly, then placed me back down. He shifted so that one foot was on either side of my torso, crouching in what had to be an ungodly uncomfortable position. One of his arms slid gently around my lower ribs, and the other under my armpit to steady my shoulders.

"Link your arms around my neck, Tash. I'm gonna keep you as steady as I can. We're only moving about four feet, and then I'm putting you back down. Do you understand?" I nodded and did as he asked.

The instant we began to move, pain shot from my side and up under my ribs. At the same time, hot searing heat spread down my spine and into my leg. I bit down on the cry that forced its way from my lips. Black spots appeared at the edges of my vision, and bile crept into my mouth, bitter and strong.

"Russel..." I whined. The floor slid beneath me. My boot got caught on something, and I screamed as the muscles along my side were yanked taut, but Doc was on it. He lifted my shoe, and we were moving again.

"I know," Russel said as he lowered me down. "But we're here. You're on the blanket."

There was no time to recover because Russel had already moved to the side and Doc was saying, "Lift."

The blanket wrapped around me — a full body hug made of thick canvas. They tried to keep me steady, but there was only so much they could do. I watched the crumbled mess of wire and metal pass overhead, the limited view my helmet provided keeping me from looking around and seeing our true coffin the way it was.

"Ow, fuck!" Boston's side of the blanket sunk, and I sucked in a breath.

"You good?" Doc leaned over, his body pressing into my thigh. Boston paused a little too long, and it had all of us looking toward him. "I take that as a no. Did it puncture the suit?"

"Yes." Multiple curses filled the channel, including mine. We didn't need this.

We moved faster after that. Or maybe I began to fade in and out more as the transfer through the cut in the wall jostled me from side to side. Then Russel had to lift me again in order to make the turn. I don't remember much of that.

There was Romano's face.

Mitchel's.

And then we were halfway through the Stasis Bay.

Clearing the force field.

Then Doc was looking down at me. Wait, when did Doc remove his helmet?

"Put it back on!" I said, my heart rate spiraling out of control. The hollow gasps of my breathing were loud in my helmet. "We don't have atmosphere here. Put it —"

Hands pressed me down as Russel appeared at my side, also without his gear. "Tasha, we're in Medical. Everything is fine. You've been out. It's time to get your helmet off too, but I need you to calm down for me."

It took me longer than I wanted to admit. I closed my eyes and forced the panic back; it wasn't doing anything but making my pain worse. Yes, that searing agony spreading down my spine. Catching Russel's gaze, I nodded. He helped me remove the helm and when it was off, I turned my head so that I could see Doc Mendez.

"Doc, something's not right...my back" — I sucked in an agonized breath — "it's on fire...moving..."

He held a scanner over my prone form. Even though he was trying to keep his face neutral, I could see the concern as whatever he read there was not good news. Moving to look down at me, he placed a hand on my head and said, "Tasha, you carry both Cnidramarus. The most we've seen in one person. Probably because what stabbed you was encased in them. I don't know what to do quite yet. Norris is on the way, but until they've...fought it out" — he grimaced, not liking the description, then shrugged — "I can't treat it. All I can do is treat the injury."

"I understand," I croaked, biting down on a moan as the burning intensified for a moment.

"No!" Russel snapped. He stood aggressively tall over the bed. "There has to be something we can do. Doc, Dr. Pia, come on. You're telling me that we haven't figured anything more out?"

Russel put his hands on his head, the muscles in his forearms flexing as he squeezed his hands.

Dr. Pia's kind, calming voice spoke up from somewhere near my feet. "Sergeant Cruz, I understand that this is hard, and she's a friend, but —"

"She's not a fucking friend!" Russel hollered, and I grabbed his forearm, which had dropped to his side. "I love her, gods damn it."

The room went completely silent. Even the noises from those bustling farther off out of my view had stopped.

Russel had gone still, his shoulders tight and face filled with shock. Though he'd meant every word, he hadn't intended to say them quite like that — that was clear.

My pain dulled for the moment, I crept my fingers up his arm and tugged on his uniform, demanding his attention. Slowly, his head turned toward me. He must have seen something in my face because he leaned down.

I placed a shaky hand on his scruffy cheek. "Will you go on a date with me when we get to Merocius?"

The corner of his eyes crinkled when he said, "I have the perfect one in mind."

"I can't wait." And I couldn't. He'd admitted that he had feelings for me. It felt right. "Now, stop being an idiot. Sit here, hold my hand, and let the doctors do what they need to."

He pressed his forehead to mine, our breaths mixing, noses touching. I savored his closeness, taking comfort in his presence and ignoring the rising discomfort.

"I'm scared," I admitted to him alone.

He pressed his lips to my forehead. "You're the strongest person I have ever met. You can do this." He stood and stepped to the head of my bed. After a long shaky breath, he said to the team attending me, "I apologize. Tell me what you need, and I am here to help. If not, that's fine, but I promise to stay out of your way."

He brushed a hand over my hair. I could feel everyone's gazes on us, and I didn't care.

Then, from one second to the next, the high of Russel's words was gone and every ounce of my being was focused on the hot agony shooting through the muscles of my back. I remembered what Patrick had described, a spot of contained fire four centimeters in diameter, spinning downward toward the tailbone. This was not that. From ribs to the top of my hip bone, more than half the width of my body, it felt like a brand was pressed to my skin.

No longer could I resist the urge. The medical team jumped at the cry that burst from me. The lining of my throat became raw with my screams, the muscles in my neck strained with each exhale, and my chest burned with each ragged intake of breath. My back bowed off the mattress, and Doc Mendez jerked forward to press me down as hot fluid slid down my side. I was bleeding again.

The rest — Dr. Pia, Dr. Gollie, and several others included — began to work on me.

Conversation flew, but I couldn't tell who said what and, for some reason, I only got bits and pieces.

"Hold her!"

"The CB3 and CR2 are fighting."

"How do we stop it? Ideas, people!"

"The wound is sealed; we can flip her."

"Attachment is happening. It's a red."

"She's coding!"

"She's back. Thank the gods."

"Stabilizing."

"CR3 treated. Should we insert a CC1?"

"Yes! It might help settle down..."

"All right, CC1 inserted."

To me, it felt impossibly fast, and yet it took a lifetime. It was the paradox of pain — the risk of walking the line of death. Because I know that's what I did.

The only thing I know that held me there were the words whispered in my ear.

"I'll be okay."

"You owe me that date."

"I love you. I just didn't think I could tell you."

"Stay with me, Tash."

I came awake slowly. My entire body hurt. Based on the flashes I remembered, there was a reason for that. The muscles in my back and side were the worst, but I was pretty sure that once I moved, I'd feel every single muscle and ligament I had. Was this what Patrick had felt?

Turning my head, I found Russel asleep in the chair beside the bed. His head rested in the palm of his hand, and there were bruise-like circles under his eyes.

"Tasha?"

I turned my head toward the door. Mitchel stood in the entrance, relief plastered on his handsome face. With a glance at Russel, he came to my side.

"You're awake. How are you feeling?"

My gaze traveled to the glass of water on the table next to the bed. Without hesitation, he lifted it and gave me a sip. Throat aching, I said, "I'm alive. Sore, though."

"I bet. You didn't have a good" — he inhaled slowly — "integration to your Cnidramarus. It was a little rougher than any of us expected."

"How so?"

He shook his head. "Don't worry about it right now. Just rest."

"Tell me."

His lips pressed together. "You had more Cnidramarus in your system then anyone we've ever seen. It's because of the wound in your side. The CR3s and CB2s started battling, and we almost lost you. After we got it out and sealed it up, we had to treat you a little differently. Instead of focused treatment to the parasite, the doctors decided to do radiation to the entire stomach cavity, where the largest grouping of Cnidramarus were. That's why you're so sore."

That made sense, I guess. "And it worked."

"Mostly. Calmed them down, at least. The doctors will explain." He licked his lip nervously before he continued. "They made one other decision."

I waited.

"They added a CC1. Apparently, Patrick was treated like Norris, and it worked. It's stopped his aging. Because you reacted so violently, they thought it was the best option. The moment it attached, everything stopped, and your vitals stabilized."

It was clear he was upset about the whole ordeal, but I was too tired to be. And really, how could I? I was alive.

"It's fine," I said, placing a hand on his forearm.

"Tasha?" Russel's shocked, but warmly happy tone had all my attention moving to him. He'd shot from his chair and rushed to my side. He slid a hand on either side of my face. "You're awake. Holy shit, finally."

"I'll see you guys later," Mitchel said. His footsteps retreated toward the door. "Get some rest. Both of you."

I wanted to tell him *thank you for visiting*, but my throat had become thick, and I was having trouble speaking. Plus, I was too focused on the emotion seeping from Russel. His hands shook, and the terror in his eyes made it clear that what he'd said in that room hadn't been a dream.

"You told me you loved me," I finally forced out.

His lips parted. "I do. I do love you."

So matter of fact.

"And you promised me a date?" He nodded. "That wasn't a dream?"

Smiling sweetly, he shook his head. "It wasn't a dream. I have a lot to make up for."

Damn, whatever wall Russel had erected was officially down. I could see him, the man I'd missed for so long was there in his eyes. He'd told me something else these last few days, too. He needed me to be the one to make the move and for this whole thing to be on my terms. Well, I was finally ready.

I bit my lip. "It's not about making up." I slipped my hand around his neck and pulled him close. With my lips millimeters from his, I said, "It's about creating something worthwhile. And this is."

It was a soft brush of lips at first, but then I pressed closer, demanding the kiss we'd both needed for longer than either of us had realized.

Chapter Twenty-Seven

Commander Patrick Montgomery

I t was the first time we'd been away from the babies, and it was harder than either of us had expected. But the truth was, we had to be here, and we'd left them with people who were more than capable of taking care of a few infants and inactive fetuses. This was the final debriefing before the initiation of *The Aspire's* final approach plan.

Were we ready?

Hell to the fuck no.

But we didn't have much of a choice. Our speed got us here way too fast, the storm inhibited our plan for strategic burns, and then there were all the other issues running wild on this ship. The four months we'd been promised had been cut to eight weeks, but in the end, it was looking to be a bit shorter than that.

Which was why morale was at an all-time low. The crew was stressed, doubting the mission, which was unprofessional for a team of trained fleet. Not that I blamed them. So, the captain thought it prudent to hold a full review of the situation for everyone to hear in hopes of allaying any fears, and he wanted all High Command here to show we were a united front.

Mitchel brushed the front of his uniform, the clean hardsuit immaculate from this distance. As he shifted, the helmet, which hung from his waist, swung from side to side.

Shoulders back, head held high, he addressed Spec Tech Partruce, who would be managing the projection of the meeting across the ship. "Why don't we begin?"

"Almost ready, sir."

As Mitchel stepped onto the small dais at the front of the Observation Deck, the crowd fell silent. I thought it was because Mitchel was about to speak, but then Norris touched my shoulder.

"Patrick," she said.

I followed her line of sight to find Cruz entering the room. No, it wasn't him that was shocking. It was the sight of an extremely pale Tasha in his arms. She looked terrible, her hair dull and eyes sunken, even as her arms were locked around Cruz's neck. She said something clearly snarky that had him rolling his eyes. His reaction caused an evil smirk to appear on her tired face.

When Cruz spotted us near the front of the Observation Deck, he began to weave his way toward us, through the curious gazes of each and every leader on *The Aspire*. Many of the engineers, scientists, Command crew, Medical personnel — anyone who might be integral to the approach to Merocius or the treatment of the Cnidramarus — said hello or wished Tasha a quick recovery. She said, "thank you," but always focused back on Cruz.

A laugh slipped my lips as a very perturbed Doc Mendez followed in their wake. I glanced to the stage. There was Mitchel, both annoyed and happy to see them, his hands linked behind his back.

"I told you to stay in Medical," he said.

"I didn't listen," Tasha said. "And technically, you only said I couldn't walk to the meeting. I didn't. I found my own way." She patted Cruz's chest.

Cruz shot her a droll glare before he lowered her onto the seat next to Norris and me.

"You're such a sucker," Norris said, patting her nephew on the shoulder. "Good man."

Tasha laughed, then winced. Cruz took a seat next to her, placing a protective arm around her back. She leaned into his side and sighed.

With a shake of the head, Mitchel cleared his throat, bringing all eyes back to him. Partruce shot him a nod of affirmative, and the meeting began, Mitchel's soothing accent filling the air.

"Good afternoon. It has been almost six weeks to the day since the first group awoke in the Aramitacus System. From the very first moment, nothing has gone to the plan outlined back on the homeworld." Mitchel glided toward the end of the stage. "But that has not mattered. We have proven why we were the ones chosen for this mission; why we were the ones identified to hold the honor of starting life here on Merocius.

"But this does not mean that we are immune to the hurtles we've had to overcome, nor the stresses of such a journey. What can sometimes help, however, is understanding. Having knowledge of where we are and what is to come allows us to see where we are needed and gives us a purpose." Mitchel looked down, then allowed his gaze to scan the room slowly. "My purpose is to see that you each make it to our new home, and I will continue to do everything in my power to make that happen. So, why don't we dive in?"

As usual, everyone in the room was mesmerized listening to Mitchel. There was something about the way he held the room; a cadence to his speech and an air to him in general. He was confident and brave without being unreachable.

It was nice to see again. Over the last few weeks, he'd been out of sorts — quick to anger, stressed, or without sleep. He hadn't been acting like the captain we all knew and respected, but something had changed.

A weight had lifted from his shoulders, and it was like he'd found his purpose again.

"I am going to start with a breakdown of what has occurred in the last weeks. It is going to seem...overwhelming, especially to those of you most recently reanimated, but I can assure you, we have a plan. I am giving you this information for understanding as to why we are moving forward the way we are."

He gave a concise, but complete, rundown of discovering our new timeline at wake-up, catchup of the approach procedures, the burn schedule, the meteor storm and how that affected us, and the retrieval and rescue maneuver of Module Four. It was a lot, and by the end, you could feel the shift in the room as hopelessness seeped into the air.

"I know how this all sounds" — Mitchel linked his fingers in front of him — "And I haven't even spoken about the Cnidramarus yet, *but* through each and every one of these disasters, I have watched this crew pull together and somehow, we are still on track. Perhaps not on the same track we thought we'd be, but the mission is not over." In slow, even strides, he came to stand before me. "I have requested that Commander Montgomery perform the explanation of our approach."

He inclined his head to me, and I stood, making my way to the far side of the dais, where a monitor filled the large wall. I placed my hand on the sensor next to it, selected the file I wanted to play on my armpad, and it appeared behind me.

I really fucking hoped I didn't ruin his speech. He'd managed to end it on such a high note. I wasn't as good at that. I was a realist, not a politician.

"Thank you, Captain," I said, linking my fingers so that I didn't fidget. "Captain Remian is correct. We have had some setbacks in regard to our approach, but this mission is not over yet. We are approximately a week away from the initiation of our final approach to Merocius, and it is essential that all final preparations are completed prior to this start date." I took a deep, slow breath. "Calculations have consistently shown that our speed is much too high for the approach laid out on the homeworld. Initially, we were to enter Merocius's orbit and detach the sections smoothly, leaving *The Aspire* as a satellite base in space. This, however, is no longer an option.

"The captain mentioned the evacuation of all material and crew from Module Four. The reason is because the Cnidramarus Crystal has completely invaded the module's structures," I said, and Mitchel glared at me. Shit, I wasn't supposed to say that. I tried to save myself. "The storm exposed this issue, and, in the end, this benefits us."

"How?" someone in the back asked.

Fuck, this was going downhill quickly. Why did he ask me to be up here when I was running on so little sleep?

"The storm inhibited our ability to perform the additional scheduled burns planned to slow *The Aspire*. This means that if left alone, at our current speed, we will slingshot off into space."

Panicked cries came from all over the room.

"Why the hell did you have him do this? He's running on, what, two hours sleep?" Tasha asked.

"Yeah," Cruz whispered. "He's crashing and burning."

"Captain Norris, can you grab Partruce's chair? Then, Russel, can you help me up there?"

Tasha stood slowly. Doc was about to say something, but she snapped, "I am not being carried up there for everyone to see. It's less than ten feet."

Doc's lips pressed together, then he nodded.

"But that is not going to happen," I said, holding my hands up. Good lord, I was ruining this. I was never this bad at speaking in public. What was wrong with me?

"No, it is not." Tasha leaned on Cruz's arm as she stepped onto the dais. I rushed over and gave her my other arm. The chair appeared, and we got her lowered into it. Cruz stayed by her side, keeping a hand on her shoulder. Once situated, she met my eye and grinned.

"Let's not give Commander Montgomery too hard a time. He's been helping take care of the Elemental Crew infants and is running on less than three hours sleep today." She winked at me and, just like that, the tension in the room dissolved away. Several chuckles took their place. "Yes, he is correct that if we were to do nothing, the ship would be in trouble, but we are not going to do nothing. The commander, Lieutenant Reid, Sergeant Cruz, all of the teams involved, and I have been working around the clock to identify any possible options to slow the ship and verify that we get to Merocius safely."

I straightened my shoulders and nodded, letting her take the floor.

She continued, "There are several factors we took into consideration. First is what the commander mentioned, the infestation of Module Four with the Cnidramarus Crystal." She scanned the room. "Do not worry, surveys have been performed on all levels within the modules, and any structural growths have been identified, then dealt with as necessary. But, due to this finding, it was determined that it is a danger to the ship, and that Module Four will need to be detached from *The Aspire*."

I wasn't surprised to hear a few gasps.

"In a weird way, this is a benefit," I said, taking over. "This means we can use the module in a very specific and delicate maneuver, detaching it at just the right time and amplifying the amount of gravity assist we receive during orbit around Eronis 8."

Tasha grinned. "Exactly. That is the second factor. Gravity assist, in combination with a timed burn, will additionally slow the ship hopefully to a speed where detachment of *The Aspire* Sections is possible."

"Per our calculations, we will be more than within those limits." I crossed my arms behind my back and nodded.

"The final factor is directly related to the Cnidramarus — the parasite plaguing our crew. Commander" — she looked up at me — "can you pull up the image? Thank you. This is the storm on Eronis 8. From the research Dr. Adams, Sergeant Cruz, so many of the fantastic researchers we have here, and I have done, we have determined that this storm is the best way we have to treat *The Aspire*."

She went on to explain the radiation and sound waves, the real reason Module Four needed to be jettisoned, how the radiation would affect those with and without a parasite, and what was being done to protect those not infected.

"We will be segregating anyone not infected for their protection. Though the wavelengths we are measuring look to be within safe levels." She lifted her hand to Doc and the medical team who sat a few feet behind him. "We are of course abiding by all recommendations set forth by the Medical Command."

Damn, how did she do that? Not only had she provided ample information, but she'd done it with style and grace. All while looking like she was on her deathbed.

I flipped to another screen, the one which showed the projected path. "Commander Evans is correct; Medical Command has been fully involved with research and the analysis of the Cnidramarus and all data collected by Evans and her team. With it in hand, and the help of those on the Engineering and Command crews, we have brought forth the approach path indicated here." I stepped back so that the screen was clearly visible to all.

The path showed *The Aspire* entering Eronis's orbit against its rotational direction along the northern quadrant of the planet. It then looped around the gas giant twice in a spiral formation, allowing us to pass over the storm on the third day of the spin.

"It is here..." I pointed to the spot where Reid's team had verified was the best spot for the release and said, "...that Module Four will be ejected as it will assist the deceleration of *The Aspire*. Afterward, a burn will be performed at this location."

I gave them a moment to take it in, my focus no longer on the crowd, and instead falling on Tasha. She was leaning into Cruz, her body sagging. Norris met my gaze, and I mouthed, "chair." She nodded and disappeared. A moment later, she walked through the crowd, handing it up to me. I brushed her cheek before I took it from her.

Setting it next to Tasha, I gestured for Cruz to take a seat. He did, then half-pulled her into his lap. She was failing, fast. We needed to end this meeting, and soon.

"The closer we get," I said, pulling the attention to me and away from Tasha, "the more information that will be provided, but please realize that we will need everyone's help as we work to complete each and every step ahead of us. This will not be easy, but our new life on Merocius will be worth it."

Chapter
Twenty-Eight
Captain Mitchel Remian

"What if we can't slow the ship down?"

It was a female voice that asked. She sat somewhere in the back, but from where I sat there was no way to tell who'd spoken. I pushed to my feet and joined Patrick and the others on stage.

We knew there would be questions and that people would worry. We just hoped to control the chaos and keep the panic to a minimum.

Patrick looked at me. I nodded and said, "We have other options open to us, ones we prefer not to utilize, but options. Either way, the crew has been working nonstop to prepare *The Aspire*, the shuttles, and the sections for all possible scenarios. Should we be able to perform a separation as planned, then everything will move forward as expected. If something changes and we are not able, then we will approach that situation as we have all the others thus far —thoughtfully, systematically, and together."

One of the lower-level officers from Module Two stood. He was one of the most recent to wake. "Wait, if the sections can't separate? That means...that means you're planning to crash land *The Aspire* on Merocius?" His voice rose at the end.

Shouts erupted all over the place.

"What?"

"No! The ship can't take that!"

"It'll collapse under the weight!"

My bet was this was happening all over the ship. Thousands of scared people realizing just how bad our situation was. We balanced on the tip of a needle — one mistake and we'd fall into space, never to find home.

I held my hands up. "Please! We are —"

"You've been lying to us!"

"Our team is ready for —" I tried again, but the noise had increased to the point that no one could hear me. How in the bloody hell had this gotten out of control? I'd made sure those here were the officers of the ship, leaders who were trained for situations like these. Yet here we were, and they were losing their minds.

A whistle speared through the air, causing me to wince and cover my ears. Turning, I found Cruz, still in his seat and covering Tasha's ears. The noise had been so sharp and shocking the entire room had gone silent.

"Hold her," he said to Patrick. Then he stood, keeping her hand in his. "What is wrong with all of you? Sit your asses down, shut the hell up, and act like the fleet members you are."

Those who had been screaming — hell, even those who hadn't — blinked at him but did as he said. Honestly, I did too, but instead of taking a seat, I stepped back and gave him the floor, interested in what he was going to say.

"How dare you." Cruz glared at the officers who'd started it all. "You're fleet. You were chosen for *The Aspire* because you were the best, and you knew the risks. No one ever said that traveling millions of light-years across the galaxy was going to be easy. If life on the homeworld wasn't, why would this be?" He took a deep breath, glanced down at Tasha, then continued, "Each of you are lucky. You get to experience the complications that come from finding a new home, and when we get there, our new planet will mean more for them."

He cleared his throat. "I have been with Captain Remian, Commander Montgomery, Lieutenant Richards, Captain Norris, Commander Evans" — he kissed the back of her hand, and dammit if she didn't blush — "Reid, Aridas, Tanaka, Romano, Boston, Doc Mendez, and so many more as they have fought every day, killed themselves every day, for you. Each and every person has given everything they are to make this work. Some have even given their lives whether via the Cnidramarus, the storm, or another way. We have lost people — our family.

"But still we fight. If you need examples, think of Engineer Mikheil Robertson, who took his first spacewalk to fix *The Aspire* only to be the first to die from an exposure to the Cnidramarus...alone. Montgomery lives during the day for *The Aspire* but spends his nights as the acting father to the infants of the Elemental Crew. Do any of you help? No. Boston, who got hurt saving Tasha, who was trying to save those in Module Four. People she has never met. Or Dr. Pia and Doc Mendez, who supervise the care of all the Cnidramarus infected at all hours of the night, risking their own health and safety."

He paused, his gaze locked on nothing. I stared at him, amazed at this person who was usually a total pain in my arse, but was showing he was far more than anyone knew.

"And then there is Captain Remian." He turned to me.

The muscles in my back stiffened as I braced for an insult.

"He's the one who nearly died turning on life support, ran himself into the ground trying to save the ship until we — his friends — had to force him to sleep, and he continues to support our stupid asses as we do dumbass things even when we shouldn't. He led us, and *he* is going to be the one to get us there." Cruz turned back to those who'd doubted the plan. "So my question is, what have you done?" When they stayed silent, he nodded. "That's what I thought. So shut the fuck up and get to work.

You're fleet, be what the captain believes you are — the best, and we'll be at Merocius before you know it."

There was a snort from somewhere close by. It was so quiet, anyone more than a few feet away wouldn't have heard it. So maybe from Tasha or Norris?

Without another word, Cruz wrapped Tasha's arm around his neck, slipped his hand under her legs, and swept her into his arms. He walked proudly from the room, the woman he loved draped against his chest.

Norris and Patrick stood, Doc following and whispering to them, "Take out the curse words and that would've been perfect."

"No," Norris said, "the way he said it *was* perfect."

Bloody hell, this meeting had not gone the way I'd expected. It had gone better.

Chapter Twenty-Nine
Captain Mitchel Remian

Richards grunted, then said something too low for me to hear into his lync. Though it was nice to see him at his normal station on the Bridge, I found myself far too aware of everything he did. I didn't like it. My friendship should not affect my reaction to him, yet the chair he continued to use while on shift was hard to ignore.

"Captain," he said, drawing my attention. "It's official. Every section on Module One and Two have been verified. The teams have confirmed that all mechanical systems are in working order and all processes have been scrubbed for malfunctions. We are good to go."

"Module Three?" I asked.

"We're waiting on Sections Two and Four. I will let you know immediately when word comes in."

"Thank you, Lieutenant."

Which meant, if everything went perfectly, the separation sequences could be completed, and we'd be able to travel down to Merocius as planned, utilizing each of the remaining modules of the ship. One step forward. That's what this was.

"Spec Boston, are we ready to begin the ejection sequence?"

Boston spun in his chair, meeting my gaze. Behind him an image of *The Aspire* — or more specifically, Module Four's connection point to the main shaft — filled the screen. "Sir, we are T-minus fifteen minutes. Commander Montgomery and Commander Evans are in position. Their teams are ready and have reviewed the procedure for the release and the plan for maneuvering should we need to evade."

"Good. Have they vocalized any concerns?" I asked, leaning to the side and reviewing the specs on the tablet on my workstation.

"No. All is looking good so far."

I nodded. "Thank you."

"Captain," Specialist Zeran said. I turned to face her. She was a small woman with deep brown eyes and chestnut hair pulled up into a high bun. An unassuming figure who kept to herself, you'd think she would disappear into a room, but Zeran didn't. Her brilliance didn't allow for it. When she spoke, people listened. Which was why she was our communications expert. "Dr. Pia's calling in. She says it is an emergency."

"Put her on the main screen."

Zeran nodded and did as I asked.

Dr. Pia's face appeared before me, the image of Module Four shrinking and then shifting to the far right corner.

"Dr. Pia, what can I do for you?" I asked.

She looked exhausted, and her eyes were swollen and red. "Captain, Dr. Gollie has passed."

The Bridge went silent, a heavy weight falling across the entire space. I gulped, my throat suddenly going dry.

"What?" I collapsed back into my seat.

"Yes, Captain. Dr. Gollie died this morning," she confirmed, clearing her throat. "His CR3 officially reached the end of his timeline. I can confirm that what I told you the other day is true. The closer we get to Eronis — to Merocius — the faster the effects of the Cnidramarus become. People are aging or regressing at a faster rate." She wiped a hand down her face. "I've lost two in the last twelve hours, sir. I don't know what to do."

Richards moved to my side, appearing in the doctor's line of view as well. "I send my condolences, doctor." He bowed his head. "I have a question, though. Have any received a CC1?"

"No. After the severe reaction Commander Evans had, the Medical Board decided it was too risky."

I pushed to my feet, ready to say something, but Richards beat me to it.

"What? But that was a totally different situation. She was severely injured," he said. Richards leaned forward, his hands rubbing up and down his legs. "These people are doing well. They won't react the same way."

The doctor glanced away. I placed a hand on Richards's shoulder.

"I agree, Dr. Pia. If they're dying, they should be given the choice if it will save their lives."

Richards took a breath to calm himself before he said, "And you know Tasha would agree. It has been days since she was hurt, and she's nearly back to normal. And like Patrick, she's not aging. Do you think she regrets it? Do you think she would change it?"

"I know. The additional concern is that we do not know what the long-term effects of having both Cnidramarus will be. We have nearly a hundred and fifty people infected at this point, gentlemen. What are we risking for them that they don't understand? How can they give an informed consent when we don't even understand it?"

Richards's expression softened. "That's a fair point. They don't know, but life is a story of unknown risks. And, doctor, take it from someone who knows, it's worth the risk if it means you live."

"It should be their choice," I seconded, "even if that choice is complete faith in the fact that they don't know. Give them a chance. I don't want to lose anyone else."

She sucked in a long, hard breath, and a sense of resolve hardened her face. "Neither do I. Please excuse me. I've got some work to do."

"Do you need assistance?" I asked.

"No. All staff are in clinic readying for the approach. Some of Dr. Adams's team is as well. I have a plan." She nodded, then cut the transmission.

I exchanged a look with Richards.

"Do you think she can treat them all in time?" The worry in his expression had me rolling my shoulders to relieve the discomfort in my chest. He'd known Dr. Gollie well, had been treated by him, and seeing others fall because of the Cnidramarus had to be even harder than it was for the rest of us.

"She has Doc Mendez to help. They're both too stubborn to fail."

He smirked, then said, "Ain't that the truth." Richards placed the palms of his hands on the wheels of his chair and expertly spun back to his workstation.

"Geron?" He turned back to me. "We will give Dr. Gollie and the others the goodbye they deserve."

Richards pursed his lips and looked away. With a nod, he said, "Thank you, Captain."

Boston cleared his throat. My eyes stayed on Richards for a moment more, then I scanned the rest of my team, and I strode to his side. We'd lost too many already. It was time to finish this trip, get to our new home, and start our new lives. And without any more loss of life.

I reached Boston's side and he said, "Commander Montgomery requests approval to move forward with the ejection of Module Four of *The Aspire*."

The screen was back to showing *The Aspire* in all her glory. A pang of regret hit me at the idea of having to release a quarter of my ship. Was this my failure? No, it wasn't, but that didn't mean it didn't feel like it.

"Open channel to Engineering so we may begin the sequence." Boston did so, and I continued, "Commanders, this is Captain Remian. You have my approval to initiate the expulsion of Module Four due to the complete infestation by the Cnidramarus, deeming it a risk to *The Aspire*. Are we ready to proceed?"

"Yes, Captain," Commander Montgomery said.

I began the standard checklist required before a process like this could begin. "Wonderful. Please confirm all life forms have been evacuated."

"Confirmed, Captain." His voice was steady, professional. Ready.

"Verify external shields are in place?"

"Verified, sir," Tanaka responded.

"Secondary fields?"

Aridas's feminine voice came back this time. "Active and strong, sir."

"Auxiliary thrusters ready?"

"Ready and capable to maneuver, Captain," Evans said.

"All right, everyone, then I guess it's time to get started." I took my seat, clicked the all-hands comm and spoke to the entire ship. "Attention crew of *The Aspire*. Jettison of Module Four is to commence in T-Minus three minutes. Please find your seats. Update to be provided to you in fifteen minutes. Until then, expect possible turbulence."

Once I'd clicked off the main comm line, I entered my code into the screen, which had appeared on my personal console. This level of ship alteration required multiple approvals. I scanned the list of names who had already signed off — Montgomery, Tasha, Reid, and Adams. I was the last and final one required.

"Approval sent," I said, hitting the submit button.

Montgomery's face appeared at the corner of the Bridge's main screen. He sat in Main Engineering, the rest of his team surrounding him. "Cruz, begin the release sequence. Evans, fire aft thrusters to initiate whole *Aspire* spin. We want Mod Four to catch just a bit of Eronis's gravity."

"Got it," Tasha said. "Aridas, watch the angle. When I'm at 0.056 exactly, we'll fire nine and thirty-two."

My fingers tightened on the armrests of my seat. Although I understood what was happening, I also had limited knowledge on some of the steps. This was where being the captain was a miserable experience. Yes, I was a pilot and had moved my way up, but at some point, I'd chosen to lead and trust those in my command. That meant my training has shifted. I'd become less hands on, and so every working element of the ship and the processes we underwent had become more overarching knowledge. The worst part was in moments like this when Boston and others around the Bridge worked in tandem with those in outside teams. They helped with the separation, monitoring the crew, maintaining communication, and all sorts of other tasks, all while I sat here completely useless.

I ground my teeth and crossed my legs.

"Five seconds, Evans," Aridas said. Then she began to count.

Even though *The Aspire* was massive in size and scale, we felt when Mod Four was caught in Eronis 8's gravity. It wasn't as strong as the last burn, but there was a definitely a jerk as the force of the planet began to play even more against that of our acceleration.

"Now, Cruz! Release," Montgomery said, glancing toward Russel.

Behind him, Cruz's fingers moved quickly over the keys, his face scrunched in concentration. Unable to sit still, I stood and approached Boston, who was working in tandem with the sergeant. I watched over his shoulder as they shut down every port and lock between the sections and walkways, then released the connections between each section and the supports, therefore officially separating the module from the main stem.

The ship wrenched at the same time that the screen showed Module Four pull roughly away from *The Aspire*. I stumbled, throwing a hand out to steady myself on the back of Boston's chair. As if in slow motion, the module moved, peeling carefully toward the planet with only a few remaining wires still connected.

"Release power supply," Montgomery ordered. There was a puff of vapor, and the wires dropped, following the part of the ship we'd deemed no longer ours. Then he asked, "Rotation progress report?"

"We need to adjust, Commander," Tasha said, a little more concerned than I liked. "It looks like we might hit. Port side, Mod Three."

"How close?" I asked. The diagrams were already up on the screen, and it didn't look good. *Might* was not how I saw it. "Can we adjust?"

"Trying now. Aridas, Cruz, I'm sending you a sequence. We'll need to be perfect. Confirm calculations, please."

Even though the conversation around me was loud, those moments where the engineers reviewed what she'd sent seemed unbearably silent. The entire time, my gaze was locked on the image of Patrick leaning over Cruz as they reviewed the data.

When Cruz finally spoke up, I released the breath I'd been holding. "Minor alterations to plan submitted. See attached. Do you agree?"

"Agree with adjustment. I came up with the same modifications," Aridas seconded.

"Damn, I agree. Thanks, guys. Sorry about that," Tasha said. She shook her head.

Patrick was back at his post. "That's why we're a team. Initiate immediately."

"Captain, you should sit down," Richards said.

I nodded and rushed to my seat, lowering myself just as the first burst of power caused *The Aspire* to rumble. The walls shook, the floor vibrating beneath our feet. Our girl was not happy with this one. Another blast was followed by yet another.

"Two hundred feet," Richards reported.

Zeran squeaked. She gripped the edge of her workstation as if it were the only thing keeping her to this universe. Her eyes were closed, but I could hear her continuing to relay messages professionally to those across the ship.

"One fifty."

I focused back on the viewscreen and listened to the frantic discussion coming from Engineering. It was amazing how they communicated — the trajectories, angles, thruster numbers. Each brilliant mind communicating in perfect harmony, all while my breathing sped with each foot that was lost between my ship and the discarded module.

"Ninety." Richards's chair shifted against the carpet.

Spurts of vapor, larger this time, appeared on one, two, a dozen spots along the bottom end of the ship — only a few of the auxiliary thrusters Engineering were controlling to push us away.

"Fifty."

I held my breath, my finger tightening once again on the armrests of my seat. An outlying branch of Module Four made contact, and sparks appeared in the image. I flinched, but then they stopped.

Richards sighed. "Eighty. One hundred."

The angle became shallower. The image shifted with the rotation of *The Aspire* to show the next section at risk, and suddenly it was obvious that our team had done it. We were clear. The Engineering team had pulled off the impossible.

"Five hundred feet!" Richards confirmed.

My shoulders, back, and limbs went heavy as my breath shot out as *The Aspire* swung free of the debris that was once Module Four.

The conversation over the comm slowed as they finished the procedure and verified we were back on course. Once there was a break, I said, "Well done, everyone. Well done. I owe you all a drink after this."

There were cheers, a few laughs, and then we signed off. I grinned and looked around the Bridge.

"Are you going to start brewing beer when we get to Merocius, Cap?" one of my other staff asked. "You don't seem like the type, but I think a few of us would be willing to help."

"Having a rough time not having alcohol on *The Aspire*, are we, Johnson?" Richards joked.

Johnson laughed. "Naw. I'm just sayin' that he'd have some volunteers if that's the profession he decided to go into."

I chuckled and relaxed back. Step two done, and one more win for the day.

Chapter Thirty
Commander Patrick Montgomery

The captain strolled in, stride purposeful.

"Montgomery." He inclined his head to me. "Dr. Adams. I wanted to discuss the sequestering of the crew to the designated areas."

I leaned my hip against the table and crossed my feet at the ankles. Next to me, Dr. Adams swiveled in her chair, and the four others looked up from their screens. Cruz leaned back, Reid ran a finger over his lip, and Tanaka lifted an eyebrow.

"Absolutely, what's your concern?" I asked, resting my hand in the pockets of my uniform.

Mitchel opened his mouth, but before any words were able to form, Tasha came through the door like a tornado. It was nice to see her looking so much like herself. Though she still favored her side and became weak whenever she stood too long, she'd mostly recovered from her ordeal, the doctors having healed the stab wound remarkably well, considering. Her color was back, and she was acting more like herself every day.

"I don't think segregating the staff is a good idea. It's not going to work," she said, ignoring the obvious meeting and Mitchel standing there. She pressed a hand to her side and swayed.

I rolled my eyes. What had I just been thinking? Granted, she was not one to slow down when she really needed it.

Cruz sighed and stood. When he didn't say anything and instead just gestured to his seat, she narrowed her eyes but then nodded. As she continued her thought, she lowered herself into the chair. "I had Spec Aridas do another scan of the areas we deemed clean of the Cnidramarus. It got me thinking." Mitchel joined me next to the table, interested in Tasha's rant. "Yes, they are clean, but they aren't taking everything into consideration."

"What do you mean?" Reid asked. "What are we missing?"

"First are the air duct systems. Like before, we've tried to limit spread and have been successful for the most part, but some we cannot stop. But there are other, more important aspects that are really concerning." She glanced from one of us to another, taking her time as she scanned each of us. "We're not requiring decontamination of hardsuits as people pass from one section to another. Not only that, but we did find some infestation in Section One of Mod Three, remember? It wasn't bad, but... Are you getting what I am saying?"

That was a lot of rambling in a very short amount of time, but I had gotten her point. My breath stopped, my shoulders drooped, and my jaw dropped wide open. A few of the others had, too.

Cruz was the first to speak. "As we've been moving around the ship, repairing it and just living, it...we could have been spreading the spores unknowingly?"

"Yes," she confirmed with a shrug.

"But we do decontaminate when we leave contaminated areas," Reid said, head tilting to the side. "I've done it."

"In places like the medical wing, shuttle bay, or Module Four, yes. But in less significantly spread areas, we don't." Tasha rested her elbow on the armrest and pressed a hand to her side. Cruz rubbed her shoulder gently.

Dr. Adams stared off into space. "She's right. Although the crystals are, in general, not out in the open or accessible to the normal population, those who do go into areas that are contaminated could have them on their suits. And there is no way to tell if they've been tracked into one of the safe zones."

"Is this what you wanted to speak about, Captain?" I asked Mitchel.

His jaw ticked, the muscles along the side flexing as he clenched and unclenched his teeth. Mitchel shook his head. "There was something not quite right about that particular part of the plan; I just hadn't figured it out yet."

"Well, it looks like Evans figured it out," Reid said.

"That she did. So, what do we do about it?" Mitchel shifted from foot to foot. When that didn't satisfy his need for movement, he began a slow path around the table.

Tasha met my gaze. "We need to treat the entire ship." The statement was so simple, but there were so many things buried within it. "That's the only option."

"But that exposes everyone to the radiation," Dr. Adams contested.

"I spoke to Doc Mendez and Dr. Pia about that. We knew there were going to be a few who would need to be outside the field in order to maintain the ship, as not all of it is in unaffected areas." She shrugged her shoulders. "There are medications they can give to lessen the effect of radiation exposure. With your approval, they can begin production and have enough for everyone," she finished, eyes locked on the captain.

"Let me conference Dr. Pia into this conversation." I sent her a message, letting her know what was happening. She immediately agreed, then I pulled her into the main comm lync. "She's on."

Mitchel linked his hands behind his back and continued his turn of the room. He must not have heard me because he asked Tasha, "How did the last scans of the storm look? What do the doctors think the effects of the radiation will be?"

"Hello, Captain," Dr. Pia said calmly. "I spoke with Commander Evans earlier and from our review, we confirmed that the levels are not as high as some of the tests performed in the lab, but we had hoped to keep anyone who was not exposed from being treated with the radiation at all. However, considering the revelation the commander had, I believe she is correct in assuming that we need to treat the entire ship. That said, we would request that exposure to the radiation be kept to a minimum."

"What does a 'minimum' mean?" the captain asked.

"Well —" Tasha moved to stand but winced and fell back into her seat. Pressing her lips together, she tried again, and with Cruz's help, made it to her feet. She pointed to the image of *The Aspire* hovering over the table as she spoke. "The areas we deemed the most infected are to be treated for the entirety of the time we are over the storm to verify that all Cnidramarus are destroyed. What if we can control how long the areas the non-infected are getting the wavelengths?"

My eyebrows shot up. Leaning in, I highlighted the planned safe zones and said, "We drop the shields in those areas for only a certain amount of time? That would work. Allow us to verify that anything that *might* have made it into those areas is destroyed."

"I would ask one thing," Dr. Pia spoke up.

"Yes?" Mitchel rested his hands on the desk and stared at me through the hologram of *The Aspire*.

"We have ten women who are with child, and they are all late-stage. This number was limited due to the potential risk to the fetus during hypersleep. I ask we sequester these crew and any high-risk in a pretreated area and *not* drop shields."

My heart rate sped up. "The Elemental Crew infants need to be included in that. They are all still so weak."

"I agree, Patrick. I've been working to set up a space for you, Captain Norris, and the babies to use closer to the medical wing."

"Thank you," I said, then looked to Mitchel.

He nodded, then said, "If the area is pretreated, that is acceptable, but that means we have less than six hours to get them moved. Commander, can we get these changes completed in time?"

I glanced to Tasha, then Cruz and Tanaka.

"Of course we can." We'd do whatever was necessary.

"Do it." Mitchel nodded, then headed for the door. "The Bridge has been deemed a safe zone. My team and I will be there, ready to fill in wherever you require." He bowed his head and quit the room.

I became lost in the image of *The Aspire* twirling before me. She was beautiful, even in her altered and damaged state. The three remaining modules spun in alternate directions around the main shaft. The balancing outcroppings looked like hammers on each side but were actually engines built to accelerate the vast ship.

"Commander?" Dr. Pia's voice pulled me from my thoughts. "There is one other thing I wish you all to consider."

"Yes, ma'am?"

"Each person will react to radiation differently. Though some will not have any effect, this is rare. Most will not do well, especially at these levels. Headaches, dizziness, nausea, and even unconsciousness are highly likely, even with the prophylactic treatment."

"What do we do if this happens?" Cruz shifted next to Tasha.

"The initial symptoms should be mild. I'll give you some hydration options to help hold off the effects, but that won't last long. If it gets bad, then you should find a place to shield yourself."

Cruz and Tasha exchanged a look, and it was like I could read their thoughts. So when they turned to me, I was already nodding. "That's a great idea. Do it. Set up secure areas around the ship where we can run a decontamination. Safety areas close to where we know crew will be working."

"Do we know how those with a Cnidramarus are going to react to the storm waves?" Dr. Adams asked, her brow drawn down in worry.

"I mean, we know what happens to the crystal. I worry for all of you carrying one."

"As was I, Dr. Adams. As was I," Pia agreed. "But with Sergeant Cruz's help, we were able to perform a few extra tests. The good news is, those with a Cnidramarus in a steady-state, or already attached, should not be severely harmed by the storm. It won't be pleasant, mind you, but it shouldn't harm them. In fact, it may act as a treatment for those who do not have a CC1 yet injected and will probably slow its effects. For those with a CC1... I don't know long-term. But either way, it looks as though having a Cnidramarus will actually provide additional protection against the radiation."

Dr. Adams closed her eyes and sighed. When she opened them again, she refused to look at any of us.

I narrowed my eyes but didn't ask what that was about. We were not close enough for that. I clapped my hands together. "Okay, everyone. Then I think we are good to go. We know the plan, verified the trajectory, and even before Evans caused a scene, added a few things to the docket. Get moving."

They chuckled, pushed to their feet, and headed for the door. Before Reid disappeared, I handed off the remaining items on my list and transferred over control. With a grin, he said, "I've got you covered. See you in a few hours."

Just as the last of them exited the room, my lync went off. The moment I saw Norris's name, I clicked my tablet to accept the call, needing to see her face.

"Hey," I said. "Everything all right?"

Those beautiful eyes narrowed in suspicion. "I can tell the meeting's over. Which means you have a six-hour rest period."

"Victoria," I chided her.

"That's Captain Norris to you, sir."

I snorted. "Playing the captain card on me, huh?"

She winked, moving back from the camera so that I could see the baby resting on her shoulder. Kiho's dark skin made a beautiful contrast to her pale complexion. She patted his back in a constant rhythm. His little foot extended, and he crooned.

"Come home and rest. You've wrapped up the last meeting, I'm sure added a billion things to the to-do list, but your team is on it, and you know it. Tenchi has been refusing to go down. You know the only one she'll fall asleep for is you." The warmth in Norris's eyes had me shoving to my feet.

"I'm on my way. I could use some baby time."

"Rest. You could use some rest," she said, glaring, but there was no heat behind it. Or, at least, no anger behind it.

"I will. I promise. We have a team there to help. I'll help get the babies to bed and then you and I can take a nap. Deal?"

Her cheeks went pink. "Deal."

Chapter Thirty-One

Commander Tasha Evans

"Thank the goddess ejection of Module Four slowed us as much as it did. If it hadn't, this burn and readjust would be so much worse." I entered the new sequence into the keyboard of the workstation and hit "send." "On the way."

The tiny image of Russel in the corner of my screen smirked. "No kidding. Just shows you how big of a badass Patrick really is."

I raised an eyebrow. "Hey, I was a part of that."

He looked up and grinned, eyes sparkling.

Heat like I'd never known before bloomed within me. I had feelings for him. Big ones I didn't fully understand yet. And while Russel had been watching after me like a mother hen ever since I'd been hurt, making his feelings for me extremely clear, he'd been nothing but a gentleman. Other than the one kiss that I'd initiated while in the hospital, nothing else had happened.

"My apologizes, mistress. You are also a badass."

"Damn right." I bit my lip and grinned.

Aridas leaned into the screen next to Russel, a look of disgust on her face. "You two flirting is both cute and really, really weird."

I covered my face with my hand, feeling the heat rushing to my face. "Cruz! I thought we were on a private channel. I am going to throttle you!"

He laughed, the asshole.

But then he did things like that, and I had this urge to beat him... then kiss him.

Aridas sent me a droll look. "Technically, if I weren't in this tiny hole of a room we're in, he would be, but here I am." She held her hands up in the air. "The labs in the safe zone that are powerful enough to connect into Main Engineering are split up a little strange, and since I don't mind Cruz's surly ways, I got stuck with him."

The glare he shot sideways made me chuckle. He respected her more than most, and I couldn't blame him.

"Tanaka and the others are right outside in the big room, and since we do everything over comm anyway..." She shrugged.

"Well, I'm sorry. Had I known you were there, I would've yelled at him for his professionalism and sent you the calculations, too."

"Don't worry, I forwarded them to her."

Now, I glared. "Hit him, please."

It was Aridas's turn to laugh. She shook her head, reached out, and extended the view of the camera to include them both. "Have you seen this storm? It's amazing."

"I know..." I lifted my gaze to the livestream image of the Eronis storm. What I'd thought was awe-inspiring before was a thousand times more impressive close up.

A light burned from somewhere deep within. I didn't know if this was the planet itself or something held inside the storm. An artifact creating the funnel, perhaps? And that's what it was, a funnel, but one that moved in multiple directions.

"It looks like a living flower," I whispered, lost in the way the deep purple gases swirled upward from the center to pour up and over a ring of white.

"It does. It's so dark on the inside, then thins to that gorgeous lavender. Uh...I had a dress that color once." A sweet smile graced Aridas's face.

"You wear dresses?" Russel asked, then grunted when Aridas smacked his arm.

"Gah!" I barked. "You smack him for that, but not for me. I see how it is!" I crossed my arms over my chest, and she chuckled.

Russel held his hands up. "Okay, okay, let's get to work. We're getting a little distracted here."

"Don't start, Cruz," I said, grinning. But he was right. "Hey, I sent over the new listing from Reid. Did you get it?" Russel winked, then started scanning it.

My attention turned to Aridas when she said, "Burn calculations look good. Auxiliary firing for additional connection to gravitational assist match initial estimates. They should provide ample time for treatment of the ship."

"And Tanaka is managing the shields?"

"Yes." Russel pulled up the list of assigned duties. "He'll be working in connection with the Bridge, specifically Boston and Richards. They'll bring down the secondary shields as discussed."

"Main shields are staying intact, correct?" I verified.

"Yes. As we can control the limits more succinctly, and they are intended for more physical items, they will be altering them instead of bringing them down in their entirety."

A request pinged our channel: *Connect with Bridge and Main Engineering?*

I glanced around the much emptier Main Engineering than I was used to. Patrick, who had joined me a few consoles down, nodded. The three others who had also been exposed over the last few weeks gave him a thumbs up.

"All right, you two," I said to Russel and Aridas. "We're starting here. Get ready on your end."

"Confirmed on three," Engineer Partruce, the kid who'd helped during the storm, said, and my heart sank. I hated that he'd been exposed. During one of the rescue missions, he'd contracted a CR3, and you could see the effects in the salt and pepper splattering at his temples. Although it looked good, he was also ten years too young for them to be there.

The others reported back similar sentiments. They weren't as familiar to me. Major Gern and Tech Spec Darnell worked on different shifts and would act as our hands-on team outside the safety areas for this adventure. Everything else was to be controlled remotely from inside the safety zones.

"Ready on one," I told Patrick when my time came around.

"Tasha," Russel said, and I looked down at his face on my screen. His expression was pinched with concern, his eyes filled with the pain of not being nearby. "Be careful. Show them what you can do, but don't do anything stupid."

My lip lifted in a smile. "I won't. You owe me a picnic, and I'm not letting you get out of that one."

With absolute seriousness, he said, "I love you, Tasha. Now, get to work."

Before I could say anything else, he switched back to the main line and began speaking to Patrick, reporting on the status of his team. I trailed my fingers over my earpiece and let out a slow exhale. Never had Russel pushed for me to say those words back. Never had he asked for more, but if I was honest with myself...

"Commander Evans, we're entering the outer ring of the storm," Patrick said.

All thoughts of Russel and my love life disappeared, and instead I was once again Commander Evans.

"Stabilizing thrusters ready." In quick movements, I initiated the series of scans which would cycle while we passed over the storm. There were so many opportunities here. Not only were we treating the ship, but we were traveling over an extraterrestrial-created storm. "Adams, I've begun my scan. Are yours initiated?"

"Yes. Uploading and adjusting timelines now. Initial calculations for treatments still holding."

"Perfect. Keep on them and let me know if anything changes. If necessary, we can alter treatment times. Commander Montgomery, we'll be over the first waves in five minutes. At that time, we —"

The ship began to shake. Not violently, but with a quiet hum that had everything vibrating.

"Captain, are you feeling this on the Bridge?" Patrick asked.

I looked up at the large viewscreen, which showed images of every group we were in contact with; the Bridge, Russel and Aridas, Tanaka, Reid, and his team, Adams, and a few more.

"Yes." Mitchel nodded, glancing around the Bridge, as if he could see inside the structure itself. He clicked his tablet, and his voice played over the ship's speakers. "Crew of *The Aspire*, we are entering the range of the storm. Remain in safe zones at all times and remember that treatments to the ship will be performed incrementally. Safe zones will be the last to be treated, as they will require the least amount of exposure."

As he spoke, the vibration increased, the hum becoming more of a rattling. I felt like I stood on a rock shifter, the belt shaking violently beneath me, attempting to throw me through the holes beneath my feet.

Mitchel's voice didn't waver. "Remain seated as effects to the radiation will vary from person to person, even with the pretreatment given. And remember, additional doses are there should you need them. Stay safe, everyone, and send your thoughts to those risking their lives as they perform this task." He cut the transmission, then inclined his head. "Commander Evans, you're lead. Get us through."

"Yes, sir," I said, then began shouting orders. "All right, everyone, it's going to take a little more than thirty minutes for us to pass over this bad boy. We know the plan. Let's execute *Aspire* treatment. Partruce and Boston, Module Three. Darnell, Richards, Mod Two. Montgomery, Aridas, Mod One. Monitor crystal response."

Verbal acknowledgments came back immediately, their conversations picking up and signals of their processes showing up on the main screen.

Perfect. Next step.

"Captain, approval to perform assisted pulsed burn requested." I pinged Reid, sending the request for his approval first. As before, multiple level signatures were required. I got a response back immediately.

"Approved," Mitchel said, signing off as well. "Continue with plan to utilize the storm's waves of energy to slow the ship."

Entering my code, I puffed out a breath, cheeks poofing. Yup, the waves coming from this thing were that powerful, and Reid's team had come up with a plan to use them to slow the ship even more. It was needed, because even with the help from the Module Four release, we were going too fast. And if this didn't work, there was no way we could separate the sections.

"Sergeant Cruz," I said, glancing at his image for only a second. "Begin initial auxiliary burn when the next wave comes. Reid, are we ready to open and fire the main engines?"

"Yes, Commander." We'd set up a safe zone near the main engines. A small, pretreated room where he and his team could be and only go out if absolutely required, but two exposed engineers were assigned as their hands-on workers in a pinch.

I rolled my shoulders and wiped the sweat from my forehead with the back of my forearm. I blinked at the sound of Russel's voice. "Next wave, thirty seconds. This one is going to be strong."

It was.

The viewscreen, alight with so much information, flickered but immediately settled back into place. My eyes unfocused for a second. I shook my head and took in the updates from all over the ship — energy levels, warnings, and step in burn process. The hologram of *The Aspire* I'd activated, which floated just below the screen, showed that the shields to our section had been taken down.

Ah. That made sense.

"Commander, are you holding up?" The words were far away.

I glanced at Patrick. He leaned toward me, sweat beading on his temple, his skin flushed pink. Had he asked me a question?

His lips moved again. "I need you to answer me. How are you feeling?" He must've not liked my answer because he held out a flask of water. "Drink."

I did as I was told and immediately felt better. The restorative additives the medical team had added would also help me. "Yes, I'm good. The effects are calming down." I pushed away the sensations, swallowing down the swirling tide of vomit. With a settling breath, I forced the winds attempting to knock me over to calm and to instead find my balance again. "It just caught me off guard."

He nodded. "They said it'd be strong but..." He lifted a shoulder in a shrug.

I straightened in my chair, totally unaware I'd slouched. "Everyone else all right?" My gaze ran over my console. I had to blink a few times for my eyes to focus. They did, and I sighed. "What did I miss on the burn procedure?"

"We're good," Partruce said. "All got hit like you. Sorry if it caught you off guard. We reported the shields were down in our module, but you were speaking."

I waved off his concern.

"And the team has you covered." Patrick lowered himself carefully into his seat. "Now, let's get back into it."

Taking a quick moment to recenter my thoughts, I listened into where the team was and caught up on the steps I'd missed. The impulse pulse burns had commenced, and we were less than five minutes from the main burn, which would hold us over the center of the storm and where the focus of the sound waves was.

"Well done, team," I said when there was a break in the conversation. "Reid, can you confirm you can hold the main burn for four minutes thirty seconds?"

"Yes, Commander Evans."

Patrick spoke up. He'd been listening, of course, but working on other projects as well. "Remember, Commander Reid, that much time is *required* for treatment to the main sections of the ship infested by crystal. *The Aspire* isn't going to like it. She's going to fight back. Hold strong as long as you can. Evans and I will manage as many failures as we can from here. Tanaka and Richards will be managing shields for the safe zones."

Dr. Adams clicked into the conversation. She sat on the Bridge behind Richards. "We're aiming for only ninety seconds while in the eye of the storm. Anymore, and those without a Cnidramarus may be too affected. Dr. Pia and I are in contact with Tech Sergeant Tanaka in case we notice any issues."

"Understood," Reid said. "We will keep in touch."

The next wave hit, and the ship jerked. I slid, barely catching myself from falling from my seat. Holy shit, what the hell was coming from that storm?

A crash came from down the hall. I met Partruce's eye.

"Looks like we forgot to secure a cabinet," he said with a smirk.

I huffed a laugh, then nodded. "Probably not the only mess we'll find."

The closer we got to the center, the quicker the cycles became. The more violent, too. With each one, I felt my limbs become heavier, my chest harder to expand. Was the air thicker?

I ignored it, continuing to monitor and push forward the process of the auxiliary burns.

On the viewscreen, we watched the crystals across the ship vibrate. Lightly at first, and then as we hit the center — and Reid initiated the main engine burn to hold us in place — they began to shake.

All over the ship.

In the green house, the movie theater, vents, recreation area, internal bracings — each and every one of the cameras showed Cnidramarus Crystals responding to the radiation and sound waves coming from the planet below. Soon they vibrated in a harmonic rhythm, releasing a noise that filled the air. It became louder, rising higher until I had no other choice than to throw my hands over my ears.

Still, it continued, becoming even more piercing, breaking through my skin like an icepick. Those around me did the same, tears gathering at the corner of our eyes or trailing down our cheeks.

Then, there was a blast of noise — a *pop* — and the harmonic note stopped abruptly. Or maybe, that was my eardrums giving up the fight.

I opened my mouth, moving my jaw as if to clear my ears of water. Perhaps if I popped them too, sound would come back. Slowly, it did. There was the muffled roar of the engines, the beep of an alarm, and the straining groan of metal.

"Engines struggling," I screamed at Reid. Even so, it was as if I spoke through glass. "Failures due to crystal eruption within vital systems on deck one-oh-three and two-nine-seven."

"Confirmed," Reid said, putting a finger in his ear and shaking it. "Pulling power from back-up systems. Engines stabilizing. Holding. Two minutes to go."

"Montgomery." Richards's voice held a hint of panic. "The crystals have exploded all over the ship. On top of the failures reported, we have multiple structural collapses: one in Mod Two and two in Mod Three."

"Are there people in those areas?" Captain asked.

"The Mod Two failure was below a safety area. They are requesting immediate help."

I glanced at Patrick. "There is another issue," I said into my lync. "When the crystals exploded, the spores were aerosolized. They're spreading." I examined the area with the structural failure. It was between two levels; one we hadn't known was infested and had caused the safety zone to fall into the one below it. I continued my previous thought. "The vibration of the ship isn't letting them settle, which means that if any of the air is able to make it through the shields, or if any of the people fell into the infected area, then they're now infected. We need to get them out. Now."

"We're closest," Patrick said. "I'll head —"

"No," I interrupted. "I'll be going. Commander Montgomery, Lieutenant Richards, I need you to calculate and add a new step to the plan."

Patrick's eyes narrowed, but it was Mitchel who asked, "And that would be?"

"As long as the Cnidramarus are airborne, we can't guarantee every spore is killed. Yes, we'd like to believe that the storm is going to take care of them all, but unless we get them off the ship and *then* treat, we can't verify it."

Darnell and Partruce's heads snapped to me, and Patrick's mouth dropped open before he said, "You can't be asking me to do what I think you are."

"We have enough air to replenish what we'll lose — to last us the twelve hours until we crash on Merocius. And we all know that's what's happening." I never looked away from Patrick, but from the corner of my eye, I could see Mitchel's face go pale in the viewscreen. "We need to expel all the Cnidramarus from the ship. Every. Last. Spore. Eject the shuttle, too, just to be safe."

"Holy shit." I don't know who said it. It could have been one of the fifty people on the line, but the breathy, terrified plea held every emotion we each felt.

I shifted to look at Captain Remian. "You know I'm right. It's the only way to guarantee we don't take the Cnidramarus to our new planet."

"We'll have to drop secondary shields completely. No protections can be in place unless decontamination can be performed," Patrick said warily.

I pursed my lips, then said, "I know."

Mitchel took in a long, slow breath. Then nodded. "I give approval for the vacuum of all Cnidramarus Crystal remains from the ship and eject the shuttle. Commander Evans, you have five minutes to help secure those in the Module Two collapse. Partruce, go with her."

"Yes, sir."

A harsh breath escaped my lungs. My gaze shot to Patrick. He swallowed hard, then nodded. With one last look to Russel on the screen, I spun on my boots and ran for the door.

Chapter Thirty-Two

Captain Mitchel Remian

"This has to be level by level, section by section." I shoved to my feet, pacing the Bridge, the eyes of every crewmember on me. "We have several sections where crew have been evacuated. Perform a scan to verify no one has gone into those areas. We start there. That should give us time to warn the other rest, verify crew have time to secure themselves, and have alternate air sources."

"On it!" Boston and Richards chorused. They spun, fingers swiping over their stations, activating the scans for their assigned modules.

"Adams, please contact Medical and notify them. They need to begin securing all patients. Masks should be provided to anyone not in a hard-suit."

"Yes, Captain."

"Commander Montgomery, team, we have a lot to do in very little time."

Patrick shook his head. "I swear, Evans really likes to complicate things, doesn't she?"

The noise on the Bridge spiked as each person dove into notifying levels or starting the sequences for the dropping of shields, release of secured hatches, and emergency refresh of the oxygen systems.

I couldn't help the laugh that slipped out. "That she does. Think she does it to keep things interesting?" I moved from one team member to the next, helping where I could.

"You know I can hear you two, right?" Tasha said between panting breaths. She was running through the corridor, the life indicator with her name tracking her movements on the screen above Boston. "Just because I'm not in the room doesn't mean I'm off the line."

I grinned, but instantly felt foolish when Doc Mendez's voice came over the line. "Oh, he knows. Hey, Commander, how are you doing? Your vitals are a bit higher than I'd expect."

"I'm fine, Doc. Or I will be. This radiation is no joke, though."

"What effects are you feeling?"

"Sweating, mild headache, and my limbs feel heavy."

"Dizziness?"

"Not since the shields first went down. And when I put my helmet on, it increased the O2 level automatically. That helped, too." Her footfalls reverberated through the line, the sound changing when she hit the grating.

"Your side?"

"Sore, but stable. I'll baby it. Promise. Entering the damaged area. Fifteen seconds to where the crew should be. I can see the collapse up ahead."

"Stay safe, Evans. The goal is to get them back to the safe zone and strapped in. We're going to give you as much time as we can," I explained, looking over Richards's shoulder as Doc continued his evaluation of those outside the protected areas.

"Montgomery, Darnell, are you having similar experiences as Evans?"

"Yes," Patrick said.

"I'm dizzy and nauseated as well." Darnell looked much worse off than Patrick did. He was red in the face, his eyes drooping ever so slightly.

"Montgomery, you need to get Darnell into containment immediately. There's an injection —"

Patrick had already moved. The moment Darnell had mentioned being sick to his stomach, Patrick had rushed around the table, flung the man's arm over his shoulder, and begun to drag him to the room off the far side. It was the space they'd set up in case of an emergency. He dropped Darnell to the floor.

"You need my help," Darnell protested.

"I need you to live. Strap in." Patrick pulled a face mask from the wall, slipped it over his engineer's face, then secured him using the emergency seat embedded into the wall. This was one of the most secured sections of Main Engineering, the spot crew went to tie in when needed. Before he left, he grabbed the injectable needle, opened an emergency panel in his suit, and slammed it into Darnell's thigh just as Doc Mendez had taught them. The poor guy had little to no warning and yelped. "Stay here and don't take that mask off."

He initiated the shield around his crewmember and bolted back to his post.

"Damn, Montgomery." Doc laughed.

"I'm not losing anyone else," he stated simply. Patrick was already back at his station, calling out orders. The whole exchange took seconds. To his team, he said, "Approved. Opening hatches A339, A456, B593, and F253. Vacuum for fifteen seconds."

The hologram lit up as each hatch opened. The cameras placed along the pathways showed a chaotic mess of air being pulled from the ship. Crystal shards, dust, and air was sucked out violently, swirling in a hurricane of danger. I held my breath, the shock of what we were doing finally hitting me.

"Close A339. Close B593...." The process continued, each section being cleansed by space. Though my brain heard it and recorded it, my focus was pulled back to Tasha.

"Four injured. Additional two trapped. Partruce, here's what we're going to do. See that spot up there?"

"Yes!" Partruce said. She didn't have to say more; he was already on it. "I'll find a good path. Here, take the end of the line. I see a spot to secure it."

"Perfect. Let me know when it's secured, and I'll send the first ones up to you." Her tone changed as she spoke to one of the injured. "We're gonna get you out of here."

"Does this mean I'm exposed?" a female voice asked. "I don't want to get old."

"I'm not sure yet, honey, but we'll figure it out. First, we'll get you back up to the safe zone and get that leg taken care of, all right?"

"Okay...it hurts." The girl groaned.

My chest tightened. She couldn't be more than sixteen. "Do you need assistance?"

Tasha declined our help, then switched off the main line conversation, saying she needed to focus on what was in front of her. "Lync me if you need me."

"Keep in contact with her," I told our comm specialist. Zeran nodded.

"Um...Captain, I think we have a problem," Tech Aridas said unexpectedly.

Another one?

I glanced down and realized she'd lynced into a private channel, including only me, Richards, and Patrick.

"Cruz isn't here."

Those words sent a line of dread racing down my entire body. "What do you mean, 'he isn't here'?"

"He said he had to talk to Tech Tanaka in the other room. That he'd identified a malfunction in the main shields. I was too distracted at the time to think anything of it. He hasn't come back."

"That stubborn son of a..." Patrick stopped himself, trailing off. He held his hand out before him, curling his fingers as if he were imagining strangling the man himself. "We know where he's going. We need to get someone —"

Alarms started firing, filling every inch of the ship with flashing red lights and the telltale screeching. In three quick strides, I was back to my seat, staring up at the main viewscreen.

What the bloody hell was happening now! My pulse was beating out of my chest, and I no longer filtered the swears from my thoughts. There were too many other things to care about.

"Reid, what's happening?" Yes, I could see by the red lights highlighting the engines, proving there was something wrong with them, but the exact issue...no idea.

"Cruz lynced me. He identified a malfunction in the main shield caused by one of the relays being damaged. Apparently, there was a crystal deposit close to it. When it exploded, a large section was thrown into the relay and destroyed it. He's on his way to complete the repair."

"Why didn't he have one of those close and already exposed go?" Patrick asked with barely contained fury.

"Do we know where he is?" I asked.

"No," Aridas said. "His tracker isn't working."

At almost the same time, Reid said, "He's the closest besides us, and my guys were already fighting to keep the engine from overheating. Plus, once he exchanges it, he'll need us to reset the system and reengage it around the engines." Reid spoke so quickly, I swear I was missing words. "Evans is the next closest, and she's detained."

Patrick choked. "These are the shields over the main engines?"

Reid nodded, never looking up at the camera. "Yes, Commander. We need this up. Now. If we don't, the engines' temperatures are going to hit critical mass."

"They're going to explode?" Several eyes shot to me.

Bloody fucking hell.

Yup, all internal filters gone.

I ran a hand through my hair. "How much time left on the burn?"

"One minute, and I'm not sure she'll hold. The temperature's rising, the struts are buckling on the aft side. I'll run them as long as I can, but we're nearing the end here, Cap."

I stared at the image of my ship for two heart beats, then said, "Can Cruz repair the relay on his own? Realistically?"

Patrick's slow grimace and then shrug was followed by, "Normally, I'd say yes, but with the radiation? I don't know."

"Richards, get a hold of Cruz. Find his location." I clapped my hands, then bent to pull the gloves from the compartment next to my chair and slip them on. "All right, people, here is what we're going to do. Montgomery, you, Richards, and Boston will continue the evacuation of the Cnidramarus from *The Aspire*. Get that shuttle gone. Keep the areas where Evans and Cruz are headed for last. Reid, your team is going to hold that engine together as long as you can and then cut it. With that said, Tanaka?"

"Yes, sir?" His voice was focused, ready to do whatever I needed. I could count on him.

"I need you to take down all shields but the main shields in fifteen seconds. Put a counter on so that they go back up automatically at the time set by Dr. Pia. It's possible some will lose consciousness. In case that happens, we want those bad boys back up."

"I'm on it. Boston..." Tanaka said.

I clicked off his line and turned to Richards. "Cruz?"

"He's not responding."

"Send me his most likely path. I'll find him."

"Captain, you can't go out there," he whispered.

"We both know Cruz has to finish this. If I can get him there and set up a field so that he can fix the damage, that's what I have to do. Keep things running here. Send me updates and let me know Montgomery is close to opening the hatch close to us."

The muscle in his jaw ticked, but he nodded. Without another word, I grabbed my helmet and jogged toward the door. When I reached the separator between the defined safe zone and not-safe area, I waited.

"Five, four, three, two…" Tanaka said.

I slipped the helmet in place and readied myself for the wave of discomfort I knew was coming. I'd seen how it had affected the others. It was so much worse than I expected.

I threw my hand out to steady myself on the wall. The room swam, and I squeezed my eyes closed, then peeled them apart. Why were my eyelids so heavy? Bile burned the back of my throat. My ears rang, and I swear there was water rushing in my ears.

I shook my head, reminding myself it was just the radiation. I needed to push it down and find Cruz. He needed help. Putting one foot in front of the other, I forced myself forward.

"Richards? Any word from Cruz?"

At first there was no response, but then he coughed. "Uh. Yeah. He, um…he came back. Sending coordinates. Sorry, Cap."

"Status?"

"Cruz is down. Lost consciousness and reports hitting his head. He says he's fine, but I'm not sure. Comm in his suit is down."

My steps quickened to a slow jog as I pulled up the coordinates. The muscles in my thighs burned, but as the oxygen levels in my suit adjusted, the vertigo started to abate, and I was able to move faster. "No problem. I'm almost to him."

"Sir, you would know that I'm getting reports of crew down all over the ship. And, when the shields dropped, more than half the Bridge lost consciousness. Only Zeran and I are awake. Reid is down. Tanaka, too. Adams and Pia. Half her team."

"Aridas?"

"I'm fine, Captain," she said, voice pained. "Montgomery and I are covering. Darnell is helping from the secured area, and we've pulled in a few of the others still awake. Don't worry, we're good for now."

"Remind everyone to put their helmets on. It'll help," I said, ducking into the service tube, which ran down to the next section. I placed my feet on either side and slid carefully, using my feet and hands to slow my descent. "Any updates from Commander Evans?"

"They've gotten the first few to safety. She's working on the two injured now," Richards reported. He was starting to sound more like himself.

"Good," I said, completely out of breath by the time I came around the corner to find Cruz on the ground. "When she's done, tell her to head this way. We'll need some help. Cruz isn't looking good."

He was on all fours, crawling in the direction of the substation which held the array. I couldn't see his face, but even through his hardsuit you could see how hard he was breathing. His shoulders rose and fell, his back fighting against a gravity that wasn't there, just to take a breath.

Finally close enough, I saw the reason for his lack of communication. Not only had his armpad been destroyed, but his helmet had been damaged. There was a crack in it.

"Cruz, buddy," I said, tapping on his shoulder. He rolled to the side to look up at me.

Squinting, he asked, "Remian?"

I knelt on one knee and grabbed his arm to help steady him. "What the hell were you thinking coming out here alone? And what happened?"

He frowned and tapped his helmet next to his ear.

Whoa, he must be disoriented. I flipped the switch, which would transition the helmet to speakers only and repeated the question.

A slow blink was followed by him clearing his throat. "Oh, floor came down on me. Hit my head. I think my ankle is broken."

"You shouldn't have come out here alone. That's not how we do things." And he sure as hell shouldn't have done it without letting anyone know.

"I was in contact with my team. Making sure they stayed on task."

I growled. Yeah, he'd made sure everything was moving forward, but he hadn't kept himself safe. My lip lifted in a snarl as I threw his arm over my shoulders. If Tasha didn't kill him, I would make sure his arse was hit with some sort of reprimand for this.

I grunted, and with a bloody hell lot of effort, I pushed us both to our feet. "Come on, we need to get that thing fixed."

"I'm sorry, Captain." Cruz leaned on me, unable to put weight on his right foot. "It was supposed to be quick. I didn't want to risk anyone else."

Though I respected that, I also wanted to beat him for it.

We moved slowly at first, eventually finding a rhythm. Even so, each step was miserable. Cruz had trouble balancing, his head scattered both from the head wound and the continuous stream of radiation. One second it would sweep up from the floor, taking our stomachs with it and causing every nerve in our legs to tingle. Then it would shift, and a heavy blanket would slam down on us. Whoever the cruel toddler was that kept whipping it at us like that, I hated him.

When we finally made it into the mechanical room and computer bay, Cruz indicated where in the maze of vital system electronics, small engine rooms, and other various controls we needed to go. I followed his instructions, half carrying him to our destination. When we entered the space, I spotted the issue instantly.

A spear of golden-pink glass an inch in diameter and more than a foot long stuck out from a large piece of what looked like extremely important equipment. It was vibrating, but not yet at the harmonic frequency which indicated its destruction.

"We have to get that out first," Cruz croaked.

Sifting through the cloud of golden shimmering mist, I lowered him onto the floor and told him to stay. "I'll take care of it. Tell me how to do it and then what you need to fix it. When we get to the hard part, we'll drag your arse over there and get you working. Understood?"

With a smirk, Cruz nodded.

"Montgomery, how close are we to expelling this section?" I asked, knowing that we *had* to have this piece loose before we evacuated the area.

"You have two more sections before you. Does that give you enough time?"

"I'll make it work."

Cruz explained the process, and I got to work. Being as careful — and as quick — as I could, I removed the damaged array. One step at a time, I detached connections, removed panels, unplugged entire sections, and threw away crushed metal and circuitry. I did everything Cruz indicated, listening to each step and making sure not to screw up anything around it. I wasn't gentle, and although I may not be an engineer, I'd been known to take apart plenty as a child. My mother would attest.

When the last piece was out and all pieces were removed, I lynced Patrick. "Commander, I think we're ready for Cnidramarus removal. How are we doing?"

"We're ready when you are. The hatch is on the end of the bay. Being so close, it's going to be rough. You *need* to be secured, Captain," Montgomery said. "Twenty seconds."

Mother of the goddess....

I glanced around, searching for the tie downs, which were located at intervals all over the ship. When I couldn't see them, I called out to Cruz to see if he knew. He lifted a weak arm.

Bloody hell! They were on the other side, through the maze, nearly two hundred feet away. I ran to Cruz and yanked him from the floor.

Without any preamble, I dragged him with me, my body burning with the effort. My back spasmed, but I continued on.

"Ten seconds, Captain. Tie in!" Montgomery said.

We were almost there. The instant we reached it, I slammed my hand on the corner, and it popped open. I yanked the line free, the reel of wire unspooling just enough for me to attach it to the clip at my belt. There were straps to slip my arms into, but I needed to get Cruz attached first. He'd slipped to the floor, so I went to attach it to his waist.

But his harness wasn't there.

"Where's your clip?" I asked as Patrick counted — passing four.

"Cut off to get out..." Cruz whispered. He was sagging, his eyes slipping closed as unconsciousness took him.

I bit back my curse, wove the wire around his waist, and clipped the clasp to its own line just as Patrick hit one. But this was *not* going to be enough to hold him, and I knew it.

I flung my arms around him, grasped my own forearms, and prayed.

Chapter Thirty-Three
Commander Tasha Evans

"**H**e did what?" I screeched. The poor girl I was helping up the pile of rubble flinched, jerking away from me. "How could you let him do that?"

"Let him do it, Tasha..." Patrick said. In my head, I could imagine the glare he'd be sporting.

Yes, all right. I knew I was being unreasonable, but still!

"You know what I mean."

"The captain went after him. They've made it to the mechanical room, but they need you. Cruz isn't going to be able to install the new array alone, and the engines are approaching critical mass."

"Why?"

"Uh...the radiation," Patrick said, but his tone sounded off. The girl sucked in a breath, and I wrapped my arm tighter around her waist.

Are you fucking kidding me? I'd ask what else could go wrong, but I'd learned long ago that was bad luck in situations like this. So instead, I let loose a string of mutterings that had Partruce chuckling, and me rethinking being the one assigned to the teenager.

"I kind of wish we recorded that one," he said, helping crewmember Strewser the last five feet up the bank of debris. We'd gotten him free, discovering only a sprained wrist; lucky bastard that he was. "Cruz and the captain would be impressed."

"Well, she's underage. I can't say what I want to." I growled. My patient leaned on me, her leg badly broken. I'd thrown a shotty, makeshift splint on it, and now I hefted even more of her weight onto my shoulders as I carried her up the maze of crumpled mess and back up to the level above.

"Are we there yet?" The poor girl was swaying, the muscles in her neck standing out as she bit down the pain.

"Almost. One more big climb and then Partruce will pull you up? Then it'll be flat."

My hands shook; my breaths came faster with each passing moment. In my head, I chanted to myself to move faster, but to her I kept up my stream of gentle support. Still, I think she heard the panic in my voice. Who cared? We didn't have much time before Patrick would be opening the hatch to clear this wing. So anything that got us there was a good thing.

"Do you have her?" I asked, balancing on two separate bent flooring panels. I straddled a gap that opened to a hole twenty feet deep, then led my patient over the crack and to the spot where my teammate would take over.

"Yeah. Got her!" He grunted, and she shifted her weight forward, allowing me to stand straight once again. I moved behind her, ready to catch her if she fell backward.

The girl did amazing, listening to my prompts and understanding the severity of the situation. When she could no longer use me to lean on, she found a secure railing and to keep the weight off her injury.

"Evans and team, you're up next. There's a…" His speaker cut out.

I shot Partruce a concerned look. "Go!"

His eyebrows drew down. He wrapped his gloved hands around the girl's arm; then, in one strong tug, he pulled her the rest of the way up.

She cried out as she landed against his chest. He didn't give her enough time to adjust before Partruce picked her up and ran down the hallway.

I scrambled up after them, my boots slamming against the floorboards of the hallway before I knew it. They shifted beneath me, but I didn't care. The floor would hold until I was clear. It was more important to get out of the damaged zone before Patrick opened the hatch anyway. Up ahead, Partruce took a sharp turn. I was only a second behind, but it felt like forever before I, too, was grabbing hold of the wall and using it to change direction.

By the time I cleared it, Partruce was with the others we'd rescued, securing the girl and slipping an oxygen mask over her head. I slid into place, attached the lead, and dove into the straps.

Then, all hell broke loose.

The pressure in the corridor changed. My hair, limbs, and body were yanked violently as everything was sucked toward the exit we couldn't see...or the hatch Patrick had opened. Air, Cnidramarus, crystal shards, and anything not tied down flew past us with terrifying speeds. We covered our heads as the roar of air rushing past became deafening.

Several of the others screamed as they swung in their harnesses. Tears gathered at the corners of the girl's eyes before being sucked away themselves. I tried to brace her leg, but it was hard. This was not the first time I'd been through a breach, but that didn't change the fear that went with it. Once I braced myself around the girl, holding her still, I held my breath. My back stiffened, and my throat closed as I waited for it to end.

Fifteen seconds is an eternity in situations like that.

We swung in mid-air, our hair whipping, cheeks stinging.

Then from one second to the next, it stopped. We fell back to the floor. The noise disappeared, and only the sound of our ragged breaths and stuttering heartbeats were left to us.

"Hatch closed," Patrick said over my comm. "You're safe to unstrap. O2 levels rising."

I glanced around, happy to see our group intact. A little worse for wear, but intact.

"Evans," Aridas said worriedly. "If you care about Cruz, you need to get moving. He is *not* okay, and Captain Remian needs help."

"Why? What's going on?"

She told me everything, and heat welled in my chest. Patrick hadn't told me he was hurt! What in the ever loving...I bit back the thought. If I let that one go, it might never stop. I understood needing me to finish my current task, but lying to me?

"Montgomery?" I said, irritation lining every inch of my voice.

"Your area is clear," he said, totally unaware of my ire.

I spun to Partruce. "Get them to the safe zone. Shields are going up. There's a team waiting for you."

He nodded, unstrapping. "Yes, Commander."

I slipped out of my restraints, pulled up the schematic of the ship, which showed the quickest path to where the captain and Russel were, and scanned my options.

"Patrick..." My tone was dark and threatening. "Is Sergeant Cruz hurt?"

His silence told me everything.

"Gods damn it!" I took the quickest path to where Mitchel and Russel were. The issue was getting there without passing into areas that had collapsed or were about to be treated. Or... "When are you treating their wing?"

"They're next. Thirty seconds." He sounded upset. Was he worried? Or sorry he'd lied to me?

"What's going on?"

"Nothing."

"I swear to everything I am," I threatened between each forceful stride, "if you don't tell me what's happening, I will kill you when I see you. You already didn't tell me Russel is hurt! Now, what the hell is going on!"

Patrick released a heavy sigh. "Cruz has a head wound and...hurt his leg? He's going in and out of consciousness. The captain is removing the array, but they're pretty far away from the tie down." He paused. "Shit."

I was sprinting at that point. When I hit the center column, I barely slowed, jumping onto the ladder that would take me between levels. I slid down, my boots squealing against the metal along the outside. "What now?"

I went down two, then took a turn as fast as I could. Down again. A right this time. My arms pumped; my chest burned. Who was I kidding? Everything burned. There wasn't a part of my body that didn't fucking hurt at this point. Between the radiation and the exertion, forget it. But I was not going to let either of them die.

"Patrick, open the line so I know what I'm walking into," I demanded, officially leaving all decorum behind.

He did, and part of me questioned my request.

"Ten seconds, Captain. Tie in!" There was definitely panic — for Patrick, at least — in his voice.

"Where's your clip?" Mitchel asked Cruz as Patrick counted, passing four.

"Cut off to get out..." I could barely understand Russel's garbled words.

"Well, then, Cruz, we're about to get real friendly..." Mitchel said.

Wait...did that mean? Oh, gods.

Didn't matter, I was there. I could help. Without a connection, Russel was...

I started to shake.

"Tasha, you can't go in there!" Patrick screamed into my line. He must've been watching me over the cameras.

"Aridas, erect a secondary field!" I screamed as I slammed my hand on the door panel, took the line attached to my suit, and readied to clip on the moment I swung into the room. There'd be an attachment just on the inside, recessed into the wall. The door slid open, but as I tried to dive through, I rebounded against an invisible barrier and bounced back. Grunting, I fell to the floor.

My breaths came in quick, panicked bursts. I crawled back to the doorway, my hand resting on the frame as I pleaded, "No! No, no, no. Patrick? Aridas, no. I can help!"

"No, you can't," Patrick said, his face appearing on the small screen above the panel. His eyes begged me to understand, but I didn't want to hear it.

The next instant, the same violence I'd just experienced occurred on the other side of the force field. Only this time, I had to watch as my friend and the man I clearly had feelings for were lifted from the ground.

Mitchel's guttural cry made me wince as Russel's limp form was yanked against his hold. I jumped to my feet. His grip tightened, and Mitchel tried to wrap his legs around him, but he was unable. The safety cord around Russel's waist — a smart idea, but only if it held — slipped, moving higher up onto his chest. The problem was, Cruz's arms were hanging loosely over his head, removing the rigidness Mitchel and the line needed to hold him.

"Russel..." I whimpered.

"I'm sorry, Tasha," Patrick said. "I can't."

"Please," I begged, my throat catching on a sob as Russel slipped farther in Mitchel's grasp.

"You know I can't." So sad...so resigned.

I fell to my knees and counted.

"I will not lose you, you bloody jackass. Even when you were a bastard, you were essential to this crew," Mitchel said through clenched teeth. "You make Tasha happy, whether she knows it or not. And she's my best friend. So, wake the fuck up and help me!"

I chuckled. I couldn't help it; my heart warmed at words he would never say otherwise. Aridas and Patrick's laughter echoed in my ears as well.

"Five seconds remaining," Patrick said through the comm.

And as if he'd heard Mitchel's threat, Russel's arms moved, wrapping around his friend, fingers digging in.

"Come on, guys," I cheered. "You've got this. We're here for you. When it's over, they'll let me in. I'm here. Don't give up." I didn't know if they could hear me over the noise around them. I couldn't care less. The words flowed from me without my control.

Then it was over. Their bodies lowered to the ground, the safety lines went slack, and the two men lay there, wrapped around each other as Aridas and Patrick returned the pressure levels to normal.

My gaze never left them as I attempted, and failed, to get control of the way I shook. When the field finally dropped, letting me in, I ran to the two men.

"Guys?" I dropped to one knee by their side. I rolled Russel off Mitch, taking stock of him. Russel was awake but looked like hell. Definitely a head injury by the way his pupils were a little too big. Mitchel was red-faced, covered in sweat, and exhausted.

Mitchel panted. "I didn't lose him."

I pressed my forehead to his, the helmets *bonking* as they touched. "You did well, but you're done. You don't look good, Cap. Hey, Aridas, where is the closest safety space you can create? We need to shield these two."

She was quiet for only a second before she said, "The room next to you. Can you get them there?"

"No problem."

I unlatched them, then dragged first Mitchel, then Russel into the small space as quickly as possible. Mitchel tried to help but saving Russel had taken the last of his energy. Even lifting his arms was an effort. Russel was worse. Though he was awake, he was dizzy. Eventually, I just grabbed the back of his suit and pulled him across the floor by his shoulders. It only took a few moments, and then Aridas had the shield up, and they were sighing, the radiation blocked.

Part of me didn't want to leave them. I wanted to curl up next to them and rest, my body craving the relief of no more waves coming from the storm.

As if hearing my thoughts, another a wave of nausea hit me all at once. I threw my hand out to steady myself on the wall as I strode through the mechanical room toward the missing array. The new one Mitchel had already moved sat on a drift nearby. How the hell had he done so much in such a small amount of time? Desperation was an amazing tool.

"I don't have the injection to give them," I said, grabbing hold of the drift and pushing it forward.

"We'll get it to them as soon as we can. One thing at a time." Patrick paused, then asked, "How are you holding up?"

I stumbled but caught myself before I fell. My shaking had slowed, but...

"Meh. I'll feel better when I know they're safe, the engine isn't about to explode, and we're safely on Merocius."

Chapter
Thirty-Four
Commander Patrick Montgomery

T ech Spec Darnell had recovered some and managed to link into the main system from the secured area I'd locked him in. This meant that when more than half the ship went down, he'd picked up the weight. At first, he'd only backed Aridas and Richards, managing the shields and the Cnidramarus Crystal evacs, but as the last one finished, he jumped in and really started managing things with the engine. It was a relief that he was doing so well.

Reid was still down, and I was getting no response from any of his team.

"Commander" — Darnell leaned far to the side so that he could see me — "I finally got imaging working in the engine room. The team is down. One looks injured; the other passed out. Possible gas release. Levels are a bit high, and with the radiation levels..."

I finished his thought. "They would've been more susceptible." *Shit!* I scratched my head, digging my nails into my scalp. "Which means that when Tasha gets the array in, there is no one to work out the reset."

Darnell nodded. "Yeah."

"That's not true." Captain Victoria Norris's voice came through the line, and I froze, my entire body suddenly and completely not in control of itself.

"What do you mean?" I asked.

"You didn't think I was just going to sit back and wait, did you? Really, Patrick?"

I choked, a gurgling sound the only thing coming from my throat.

"I have been the captain of *The Aspire* for eighty years. Yes, I've been a bit distracted for the last few weeks, needing to take care of the most vulnerable of my crew, but that doesn't take away my need or responsibility to watch over and protect the rest of my ship and those aboard it."

As she spoke, I pulled up her locater beacon to find that she wasn't where she was supposed to be. She was in the engine room, moving toward the panel which sat just before the core controlling the three main engines. Red lights littered the screen above her.

"And although you all are beyond capable of running this ship, I am a useful member of the crew who just happens to be used to radiation exposure, less effected due to my Cnidramarus, and trained in Engineering. I've been watching over you all and was ready to step in. So, Tasha, I heard my nephew has passed out, and it's up to us to fix this bad boy. How are you doing over there? Are you ready?"

Tasha let out a hysterical giggle. It was littered with exhaustion, but even so, had me cracking a grin in response. There was a clang of metal on metal, then she said, "Absolutely, Captain. I am almost...hold on" — she grunted — "get in, you stupid piece of junk...ready." More noise. On the screen, Tasha was bent over, reaching to connect the array into the computer behind it. The sound of the drill filled the speakers, and then she stood. "Okay, we're good. Let me link in."

"And don't worry, Patrick. The kids are in good hands. All fed, secured, and watched over."

"I..." Yup...there were no words. I was at a loss.

Tasha connected her armpad into the computer beside the array, then removed the panel to expose a keypad. She started entering her passcodes, navigating into the system and beginning the process of connecting her end of the ship to the engines. This would initiate the shields to reengage and lower the exposure to outside influences.

"Talk me through the setup, please," Captain Norris asked.

"Captain," I said, knowing in this moment I had to separate my feelings for this woman and think of her only as Captain Norris because if I didn't, I'd be lost in the fact that she was standing next to three extremely explosive items. "Follow my steps exactly."

I explained each step in precise and exacting detail, watching on the screen as she followed my instructions to a tee. Norris moved quickly, her graceful hands strong and sure as she entered codes, restarted systems, and initiated cooling processes. When it was time, Tasha and Norris synced their steps, each press of a button performed as I called them out. Then a light would shift from red to yellow, and eventually the measurement ticks would lower to green.

Minutes passed, and the temperature began to decrease. We continued, and I heard Darnell speaking to Richards, "Clearing the storm in ten seconds."

"Warning, one last wave coming from below. This one looks stronger than most," Richards warned us, but we were too lost in the process of resetting the array and cooling the engines. We were almost done, and there was no stopping now. "Should we raise shields?"

I gave the last two instructions to my team. "Temperature normalizing. Reducing speed to half power. Once stabilized, enter the following..." I provided them with the fifteen-digit code to end the burn and simulate a total shutdown. They did it as instructed, and the ship shuttered as the burn finally disengaged. The exhale was one of absolute relief.

"Commander?" Aridas bit out, voice a bit higher than normal, but I didn't notice. My thoughts and eyes were still locked on the engines and them returning to normal.

Damn, that had been the longest burn in the history of the fleet. Only...thirty seconds longer than planned. Would that be good or bad?

"Wave coming in five, four, three..."

I glanced up to the monitor, and Richards's question finally clicked.

Aridas squeaked, "Shields, sir?"

Oh, shit. The wave was huge. It measured larger than all the others we'd experienced thus far, and the levels of both radiation and sound were at astronomical levels. Far greater than anything we'd been hit with so far. I wasn't sure our even full shields would completely protect us, but with only externals...fuck.

"Raise the shields!" Norris and I both screamed.

But it was too late. The wave hit, *The Aspire* shuttered, and everything went black.

Chapter Thirty-Five
Commander Patrick Montgomery

A hand brushed down my cheek, pulling me from the darkness. I groaned, then rolled to the side, my head pounding as bile climbed up my throat.

"It'll pass," Norris's voice filled my ear, and I fought to urge to vomit. "You're good. I gave you the injection. It'll start working here in a moment."

I pressed my head to the metal grating of the floor. "What happened?"

"The wave knocked everyone on board out. We've been asleep for hours, but the good news is shields are back up. Tanaka's automatic reset finally kicked in."

My mind was mush. The world spun, and her words mixed, not making any sense. Hours? That can't be.

"No!" I shot to a sitting position and regretted it immediately. My head felt like it was going to explode, and the urge to vomit became real. I bent to the side and released the contents of my stomach on the floor beside me.

Norris stepped back, grabbed a cloth, and then pressed it to the back of my neck. It was cold against my skin. "I know, but there's nothing we can do."

I closed my eyes and waited for the universe to stop spinning.

"I told you he wouldn't take it well," Tasha said, entering the room. She and Reid had Cruz between them, one arm over each shoulder.

"You're awake?" I asked, taking in their bedraggled states. Their helmets were off, which told me that life support and oxygen levels were back to normal in this module.

"Yeah, after waking Reid and his crew, she came to check on us first," Cruz said as they lowered him to the floor. Tasha squeezed his shoulder, then walked to the workstations. "Brought us the radiation treatment, then came to get you."

Tasha pressed her finger into the arch of one eye as she examined the screen. "Mitchel's on the way to the Bridge," she said, reading something that had her expression pinching. "Good news, life support is up everywhere."

"Walking in now. And thanks for letting me know," Mitchel said, his voice coming in over the main speakers. We all flinched, and Norris smiled.

"Perhaps we turn down the volume a bit. Thoughts?"

Everyone nodded.

"Do we know anything else?" I asked.

Reid had joined Tasha at the workstation and was scanning through everything as Norris helped me to my feet.

"Not really." Tasha opened the line to the Bridge and the groups which included Tanaka, Aridas, and even Medical. "Report. Is anyone there?"

Some quiet moans and grumbles came from Tanaka and Aridas's rooms, but it was clear they weren't fully conscious yet. We'd send someone there soon to check on them and help with recovery.

"Richards is waking. Boston too," Mitchel reported. "I'm having Boston treat the others. Adams is the worst off."

"Um...guys, we have a serious problem." Reid's face was paler than I had ever seen it.

We rushed to his side to look over his shoulder. On his screen was a nightmare — the flight path to Merocius. Where we'd been almost twelve hours away, we were much, much closer now. In fact...

His throat bobbed as he swallowed. "We've already started our descent into Merocius. We'll be *landing* within the hour."

Had I not just puked, I would have then. The terror had sunk so deep into me that I couldn't move. I met Tasha's and then Cruz's eye. Norris's hand slipped into mine and squeezed.

Then it was like our training clicked in all at once. Almost as one, we moved. Tasha ran to Cruz, pulled him up and planted him in a chair in front of a workstation. Reid began calling out to Aridas, Tanaka, and his crew. Norris was waking Darnell and getting him up to date, then assigning him tasks before claiming a workstation. And I found myself calling out to Mitchel. "Crash landing imminent. Decline begun."

"Any way to enter orbit?" Mitchel appeared on the large screen, one hand clasped on the arms of his chair. The other was swiping along his monitor, no doubt reviewing what we'd already seen.

Richards was behind him. His head rested heavily in one hand, but he was awake, taking measurements and relaying information to Tasha as I could hear her speaking with him. Boston sat in his chair, hair a mess and eyelids heavy. A textured pattern was pressed into his cheek, but other than that, he was all professionalism.

"No, Captain," Reid replied before I could. "The gravity has already taken hold. We're crashing, and there is no way to stop it. Firing auxiliary thrusters to adjust angle and verify tilt as per appropriate entrance perimeters."

"Approved," Cruz said. "Let's do this in four steps, Boston."

Mitchel took a deep, steadying breath. "Commander...Patrick, fortify shields toward the bow. Put everything you can into them. Do we know where we will land?"

My fingers were already moving, my focus absolute as I did everything to solidify the ship for the crash we could no longer avoid.

"Yes, Captain." Cruz displayed an image of the northern continent.

There was a small bay to the west, a large mountain range, which ran down the center of the continent, and plenty of fresh water via streams and lake littering the area. It was one of the two continents we'd hoped to settle. Though the optimum location was the eastern side.

"We are set to land about here" — he indicated just north of the bay — "but with a few adjustments, Tasha and I think we can use this lake here to buffer our landing. It's deep enough."

"It's risky, though," Tasha added.

"Do it," Norris said.

"Do it," Mitchel seconded, speaking at nearly the same instant.

Cruz, Tasha, and Boston's voices weaved in and out of each other as they bounced back coordinates and fired thrusters in small bursts that would shift our angle just enough, they hoped, to get us to the massive lake. We'd still do some serious damage to the land mass, but at least we wouldn't destroy everything on this side of the equator, because let's be clear, *The Aspire* was a big ship, and its direct impact could do some serious damage.

We hit the outer atmosphere, and the ship shook so hard my teeth vibrated.

How the fucking hell we were already here, I had no idea. I had never expected it to play out like this. We hadn't even been able to verify if the Cnidramarus treatment had worked.

"Brace for a crash landing!" Mitchel said over the all-hands speakers. "Strap in if possible!"

I released the belts hidden in the chair and slipped my arms through. I clicked them into place in between each of my entries. The others did the same as alarms blared all over the ship.

"Heat shields holding," I reported. The external cameras were going red, the fire of reentry burning against our mass. "One minute until we break through the atmosphere."

The entire ship was shaking now. The joists rattled. The engines heated once again. New alarms fired, indicating that pieces of the ship were falling off. Previous damaged sections were peeling away with the force of the atmosphere.

"Sections Ninety-four, Seventy-one, Twenty-three, secondary shields now! Lock down all sections and initiate bracing procedures!" I hollered over the cacophony of noise radiating through Engineering.

"Come on, baby. Hold together," Mitchel said. The image flickered then went out, but we could still hear him calling out questions to Richards. Plus, Cruz was still in contact with Boston.

Tasha's words were a little more flamboyant. "You can do it. Come on, you piece of junk. We put too much into you for you to fail us now!"

Cruz laughed at her words, shaking his head, but he didn't look up from what he was doing.

The ship jerked to the side. My head snapped, and the impact against the straps caused pain to shoot through my shoulder. A beam buckled nearby. The sickening crack had Darnell releasing a terrified scream. He ducked his head.

"Can we fire thrusters on the sections to slow us down?" Reid's hands gripped his straps so tightly his knuckles were turning white.

"They're within the ship. If we do, they'll burn up *The Aspire*. It'll cause more problems," Tasha said.

"Not if we fire those of Section Three only," Cruz hollered over the noise. A few of the wall panels shook loose, falling to the floor. A pane of glass farther down the hallway shattered.

I blinked and thought about it. "He's right. If we use the section thrusters along the bottom side only — the ones used for the maneuvering out of *The Aspire*. Holy shit!" I looked from Reid to Tasha to Cruz. "We each get a section in Mod Three. Do it now!"

It was the best we could do. It had to be enough to slow us down, so we didn't break up the moment we hit land. Thank the gods we'd prepped as if we were still going to detach from the ship. If we hadn't, we would've been completely screwed.

"Based on the computer's calculations," Norris said, "it should be."

"On three." I counted down, and in tandem, we fired the engines. We felt a minor shift, but at this point the shaking was so violent, it was hard to even see straight. I licked my lips. "That's it."

They nodded, and I could feel the resolve settle into the room. They knew as well as I did that we'd done all we could. Either *The Aspire* was strong enough to withstand the planet's gravity, or she wasn't. Ships like this were built in space — created for space travel — and not meant to enter a planet's atmosphere. Although those secured within parts of the module were protected, it wasn't guaranteed. Especially considering the damage done over the last few weeks.

I met Norris's eyes. Her lips pressed together, her brow drawing down.

I took in her serious, but beautiful face. The gorgeous eyes and crooked nose. Her long silky hair. I had come to adore her more than I'd ever expected.

"Thank you," I mouthed, knowing she'd never hear me. There was too much noise — alarms, grunts, rattling, the rushing air of a burst pipe somewhere nearby.

Her eyes glistened as she pressed her head against the headrest.

With one last look to the screen, I watched as the ship I'd built crashed onto our new home. The world around me turned into chaos.

Noise and movement.

Pain.

Warnings as parts were ripped from my hull, or chunks separated completely. Fires started. Engines went missing. Cries for help through the comm as people came awake. Up was down, left was right. Objects around us broke off and went flying. Glass shattered. The world spun, and we knew nothing as the ship made contact with water. Then land.

We bounced, skidded, and eventually came to a stop.

Chapter Thirty-Six

Commander Tasha Evans

M y chest rose and fell in rapid pants. I hung from the straps of my seat, the belts digging into my shoulders and the blood rushing to my head. When we'd come to a halt, our section was at a sharp angle, nearly upside down.

I glanced around to find everyone in a similar positions, though I was the only one actively moving. Blood trickled from Reid's ear, and something about him looked off. Norris and Patrick looked better, though they had their eyes closed. Probably lost consciousness. We'd been thrown around pretty good, and it wasn't just my neck that hurt.

"Russel?" I called, terrified that he'd also passed out. Another head wound so soon after his last one wouldn't be good.

His arm moved into my field of vision. "I'm awake. Fine. Are you all right?"

"Yeah." The word was more an exhale than anything. I released my straps and swung myself down, feeling like a kid on a playground as I twirled over the bar. I lowered myself to the ceiling, then moved to Russel. "Can you reach the release?"

"Yes, but I won't be able to land on this leg."

"You know what? Give me a minute and let me get Patrick and Norris down." He nodded, and I moved to my other friends. I walked along the uneven roof to where they were, then called up to them. It took a few moments before they opened their eyes.

Norris rubbed at her chest where the binds pressed in. "We made it?"

I nodded, looking around at the destroyed mess that was Engineering. It looked nothing like our workspace. Glass was everywhere. Beams littered the space and the screens were shattered. A few were bent into shapes completely unrecognizable. Based on the damage around us, we barely survived.

What did the rest of the ship look like?

"We did," I said. "Let's get you down. Then I'll need your help with Russel and Reid."

"Are they awake?"

"Russel, yes. Reid, no." I was worried about that, actually. I'd made a lot of noise, and Reid hadn't twitched. "It'll only take us a second to get Russel down, though. We just have to catch him."

Patrick got down pretty easily, his movement similar to mine, but Norris was a different story. Apparently, she was a bit afraid of heights. Who knew? So, getting her to detach the straps had taken some prodding. Then, she'd basically fallen into Patrick's arms.

Then, it was Russel's turn.

"All right, kid. You kick me in the face like you did as a toddler, and I'll spank your butt like I did then," Norris said.

Russel choked. "It is so much weirder when you say that while looking only a few years older than me."

I cackled, and he glared at me.

Norris nudged me. "Can we get this over with? I want to get out of here."

"Yeah, and we need to get Reid down, then find Darnell." Patrick shook his head and held his arms out, ready for Russel.

"I'll lower myself down as far as I can." Russel flipped himself from his seat, controlling his fall as best he could with his arms. He straightened his elbows, lowering himself farther, then when we had his legs, released his hold. He fell into our waiting hands, only letting out a small hiss when we hit his injury.

We grunted.

"Damn, Cruz. How much do you weigh?" Patrick asked, and I laughed.

"It's the planet!"

"Uh huh. Sure it is." We set him on his good leg, then moved on to Reid.

I walked a circle around him, examining him carefully. It only took one spin for my stomach to cramp, and my throat to tighten. "Oh, no."

The others' attention was suddenly on me. I could feel their gazes, but I was still staring up, searching for movement of his chest. Then I shook my head and turned my armpad on. Thankfully, it still had the ability to connect to his suit. That was... if he was alive, it would transmit his vitals to me.

Nothing came back, and I swallowed hard.

"Reid, buddy." Patrick's steps were slow, but his voice was urgent. He glanced over my shoulder. I shook my head, and his head dropped. Then he spun in his boots, calling out, "Darnell?"

Norris and Russel had moved closer to the downed beam that blocked our view into the protected section where Tech Darnell had sat. Balancing on one leg, Russel leaned down and lifted it. Norris narrowed her eyes at him but didn't argue, as she was also moving debris out of the way.

"I'm getting vitals," I said, rushing to their side. I shimmied Russel out of the way and worked with Patrick and Norris for a few minutes before we saw anything.

"There he is," Russel said. He knelt on one knee, the other out to his side, a grimace on his face. "I can see his chest rising, but it looks like something's pinning his hip."

"I see it." Norris was in front of me. She'd taken point, assessing the damage and identifying the items to remove first and then handing them to us. "I have one more, and then I think I can get to it. Good news is it doesn't look to be supportive."

"We can remove it without this whole thing coming down on us?" Patrick asked.

Norris nodded. "Looks like it."

Russel ran a hand over his head.

"Darnell? Hey, soldier." Norris patted the tech's face as she hovered over him. He groaned, then blinked his eyes open. There was a collective sigh, and then she said, "Good to see you, kid. We're gonna get you out of here. Does anything hurt?"

"N-not really? Well, my hip where this beam is, but other than that..."

"Can you move your toes?"

"Yeah."

"Good. That's good. So, Patrick and I are gonna lift this, and you're going to slide out. And then we are gonna haul ass out of here, okay? Are you ready to see Merocius?"

"We're here?"

She grinned. "We are."

"Hell yes, Captain."

That was all she needed. Patrick slid in, and together they lifted the beam just enough for Darnell to scoot free. I grabbed his shoulders and pulled him far enough out for him to pull his legs the rest of the way free. Then, they set the beam down and got clear from the rubble. It shuttered, and we waited for it to collapse. Once done, we caught our breath. We were quiet, tired not just from the rescue, but the day.

Sadness washed over me as my eyes strayed back to Reid's body just hanging there. How could we make it this far and lose him here? It wasn't fair. He deserved to make it to Merocius. To feel the air on his skin and touch the dirt.

There was no way I could leave him like that.

I pushed to my feet. Going to Patrick, I held out my hand. He met my eye, handed me a knife, then stood, understanding in his gaze.

"We will do this together," Patrick said.

I slipped the knife into the waistband of my suit, then jumped up onto the underside of the workstation. It creaked, but Patrick knew what I wanted. He stepped up, his back to me, and I easily stood onto his shoulders. The padding of his suit protected him. We've done this in the gym too many times, so it felt natural, and he only had to take one step forward before I could reach Reid's hanging arm to steady myself.

"Norris and I are here to catch him."

I glanced down to find Russel below me, ready for me to release Reid's body. "I'll have to pull myself up to cut the waist strap, then I'll do the arms."

It wasn't pretty. It wasn't kind, but once he was down, we could put him in a more dignified position. Plus, it would be easier for me to come back and get him. Because if it was the last thing I did, I would make sure that he rested on Merocius. I refused to let him be forgotten.

I stared down at his prone body, fighting to control the tightness that pinched my throat when Patrick cleared his. I didn't look up. I didn't know if I could. None of them would judge me for crying, but I wasn't ready yet.

"We need to find a way out. We'll come back for him. I promise you, but we need to find the others and by now, they'll be heading outside."

"I know." I took one last moment before turning away and following them toward the door. "Darnell, how are you feeling?"

"About as well as the rest of you, I think. Though my side hurts. Doc needs to take a look once we find him."

There was one hell of a bruise and a sharp pain when we pressed on it. We weren't sure it if was internal bleeding, but either way, we needed to get him and Cruz help. Until then, we'd track his vitals.

And help was outside. So, we made our way through the broken bowels of *The Aspire*. A maze of debris and pathways we once understood that were no longer as they once were. Some had collapsed from the weight above becoming twisted or too unsafe to travel, especially with injured. Then others were in perfect form. Oddly, those were the ones we didn't trust.

I squeezed through an opening in a wall, which took us into a hallway far more intact than the one we'd been traversing.

"It's clear. Come through," I said as I helped Russel slip his much larger frame past, then led him down the hallway. "We can take this past the lab. There is a small medical suite. We can get some supplies."

"There's an airlock not far from there, right?" Russel asked.

"Yeah. A456. Based on our angle, it should be above ground." I lifted my armpad to look at it. Though the ship was pretty well shot, not all our tech was lost. "The measurements I'm getting say it's clear and not underwater."

We passed the lab, and when we reached what I thought was the med unit, I leaned Russel against the wall. "Stay here."

He shot me a droll look, then hopped after me. He glared, grabbed my hand, and pulled me close. We were alone, the others farther down the corridor. He brushed a piece of hair behind my ear, then rested his forehead against mine. I placed my hands on his hips and closed my eyes.

"I can see it," he whispered, finger rubbing along my cheekbone. I opened my eyes, unable to resist his gaze. "You're holding it together, but you are not okay. With the ship and Reid...but you're being cold to me, too. It's because I scared you, isn't it? I'm sorry."

My face twitched, my body spasming with a sob attempting to escape. My eyes filled with tears, but I held it all back. I pushed it all back down. For now. All I allowed was a nod. Because it was all of it, and he was pressing on the wound.

"Too soon," I admitted.

His head tilted, a gentleness filling his eyes so dear it made my chest tighten.

"I understand." He leaned down and kissed my cheek right where his thumb had grazed only moments ago. "But we will talk about it soon, and I promise to make that last one up to you if it takes the rest of my life."

I sucked in a shaky breath and, with all the bravado I could muster, said, "I'm going to hold you to that."

His grin was sad. "I look forward to it."

A completely different emotion spread through me, even with him covered in dirt and grime. Shit, even the sweat was sexy. "Aw, hell," I said, releasing him and spinning to the room at large.

I hurried to the cabinets and began pulling out medical supplies. Russel did the same, finding a bag to put it all in. Patrick came in a moment later and started helping. When we found a cabinet of nutrition bars, we grabbed another bag and took them all. We'd need them.

"Are we ready to take our first steps onto Merocius?" Norris asked. She stood in the doorway with Darnell, her arm around his waist.

"Is it strange that I'm nervous?" Darnell shifted his knees, bending.

"I am, too." It was true. I was. "But my excitement of being here is making it hard not to run."

"Right?" Norris laughed. "Bowl over the men and leave them to fend for themselves?"

As the men glared, I laughed. Seeing as we were the ones lending them a hand, literally half-carrying them, they had to know she was joking. I slung the bag over my shoulder and looped my arm back around Russel's waist. "Come on, big guy."

We reached the hatch, which would take us outside, and I stood back as Patrick worked to open it. Russel slipped his hand into mine, and I held my breath. When it swung open, I squinted, the light blinding in its beauty.

Patrick held out his arm as if to show me the way. "Welcome home."

Chapter Thirty-Seven

Captain Mitchel Remian

I turned from the light, squinting against the glare, and raised my arm to block the brunt of it. Pulling up to my full height, I stepped the rest of the way through the broken panel, then reached back and helped Brackett through the door. Once she was clear, we moved forward, drawn to the outside with its sight and scents. The exit was just ahead, calling to us, telling us that we were safe, officially on our new home.

Part of me was still in shock — my mind muddy, shaken from being rattled around my skull like a blender on high. I adjusted the bandage wrapping my bicep and bit my cheek at the pain, which shot through the wound hidden beneath. It was deep, but we'd managed to stop the bleeding for now.

The fresh, clean air blowing from the crack in the hull cooled my skin, reminding me of mornings back on the homeworld. It felt as it did when the sun peaked over the mountains first thing in fall. It smelled like salt and pine with a hint of moss. It had been nearly eighty-five years since unfiltered air, not cleansed by an engine, had filled these lungs, and it was heaven. All I wanted to do was close my eyes, sink to the floor, and breathe it in. But I knew there were too many waiting for us. Plus, those in my care needed me to get them out.

Who was I kidding? I wanted out. I wanted to see Merocius. It was need, crawling along my skin like a million tiny spiders.

"Are you ready to see it, Captain?" Dr. Brackett asked as I ducked, reached back, and took her hand once again to help her through the small space I'd just squeezed through.

On the way from the Bridge, we'd passed Main Medical. There'd been a blockage keeping them locked in, but our strange and roundabout path had meant we were able to help them find a new way out. They would've found another way free eventually, but with our help, it had been quick and easy.

To my surprise and relief, Brackett was one of the ones standing in for Norris after she'd left to help us save the ship. She, Doc Mendez, and two other crew members had kept the infants safe and protected during the entire ordeal. Every one of us had teared up when we'd found them happily cooing in their cribs.

"I've never been more ready for anything in my entire life," I admitted. She blinked up at me, surprised. "I know how much is to come, the struggles and trials, the people we need to pull from the wreckage..."

Connie straightened to her full height, looking up at me with curious eyes.

I finished my thought. "But we made it, and all I can think about is taking my shoes off and putting my feet in the dirt. Is that weird?"

Her hair fell to the side, eyes crinkling. She smiled sweetly. "No. I think that sounds wonderful. Would you mind if I joined you?"

My fingers tightened on hers. "I would like that very much."

She stepped past me, dropping my hand and placing it against the infant resting against her chest in the carrier. "But I would add one caveat, if possible."

"And that is?"

Doc Mendez came through, two babies slung across his chest. I'd watched in fascination as he's tied them so expertly. The babies? They'd settled instantly, loving the close contact of the big, burly man.

"That we find a stream to sit beside."

I grinned. "Deal."

She waited off to the side as I helped the rest who carried the children through the low, small opening.

Dr. Pia headed the next group, a section of infected seemingly reacting well following the treatment of the storm. "Go ahead, Captain. I've got the next group."

I inclined my head, then moved back to the front as the rest followed. It would take a long while for those of our group to exit, considering there were more than two hundred and fifty people in this section alone. I hoped that those of the others were having as easy a time finding a way out as we had. If not, rescue would be next on the agenda.

Brackett and I led the pack, approaching the crack in the hull, which leaked light into the dark ship. I met her eyes, and I found myself drawn to the way her lips pursed and the sweat dripping from her temple had me recognizing just how hot I was, too.

"Let's go," she said, "I don't want to be in here anymore. It's sad seeing her like this." She scanned the corridor as if seeing the ship in its entirety.

A huff of air and I licked my lips. I knew exactly how she felt.

We got closer and realized it was a hatch that had broken open during impact. With a little bit of prodding — that was a lie; it was a lot — Doc and I were able to slide it open. I refused to look through, instead letting him exit first. When he did, I watched his face morph to absolute amazement the moment he took in the world outside.

"We're good," he said. "Oh, it's beautiful. So...the side of Mod...I don't know, one of them provides plenty of room to walk on. There's even a way down to the ground. Anyway, it's safe to come out." He paused, taking in a breath and turning to look behind us. "Oh, wow. You have to see this."

I couldn't resist any longer.

I closed my eyes, pressed my hands against the edge, and stepped out. Once my feet were on the other side, I stood. I felt the heat of the sun against my skin. The breeze was like a dream I had waited a lifetime for. What I'd craved from the moment I'd walked away from the homeworld. Slowly, I opened my eyes and gasped.

Merocius was beautiful. No, that wasn't enough. It was everything I'd ever dreamed.

Mountains lined the horizon so tall they kissed the sky. Huge peaks topped with bright white snow that glittered in the morning sun. Down near the bottom, deep green trees covered the landscape. They resembled pine trees, but they were purple tipped with hints of gold. Off to the right, a waterfall more than 200-feet tall cascaded down in multiple tiers, falling in beautiful rivulets and creating rainbows of color scattering the sky.

So beautiful.

"Captain?"

Turning to Doc's voice, I found him staring off in the distance. The west perhaps? What I had thought was beauty at first glance was nothing when I took it all in. In every direction was something new, clean, and untouched. Mountains, hills, and valleys filled with vegetation and wildlife of all colors, happy and healthy. A world undamaged. One filled with potential.

And watching over it all was Eronis 8, large and glorious as it hovered above.

"You know, I knew it was going to be amazing," Brackett said, "but I didn't expect this."

She stood next to me, her arm lightly brushing mine.

I chuckled. "I feel the same way. It's remarkable." I climbed higher onto the ship, joining Doc where he stood overlooking the crash. She came with. "What's up?"

He pointed. "Am I seeing things, or are those ruins?"

I did a double take, first to his face, then to the place where he pointed. My mouth dropped open. We couldn't be sure from here. It was along the far mountain range near the base, but from the layout, they sure as hell didn't look natural. The crumbling wall-like structures were too organized to be anything but made. "Looks like we have one more piece of proof pointing to Tasha's hypothesis of life on Merocius being true."

Doc nodded slowly, his eyes wide. "They're too far for me to get a scan of them, and the ship's power is down."

"That's a long trek, too. We'll put it on the list. Let's focus on rescue first."

Doc nodded.

"Mitchel! Doc!"

Doc scowled. I did, too. We turned in the direction of the voice.

"Holy shit, Tasha!" Doc called, waving his arm in the air. "Did you hear us talking about you or what?"

She laughed. It echoed over the wreckage, and something settled within me at seeing her, Patrick, and the others trudging along the ship toward us. They were safe. They'd made it.

"Brackett!" Norris said, her speed picking up. She said something to Patrick, and suddenly they were all moving faster, finding the quickest way to us. Even Cruz was hobbling faster. Poor guy looked like hell.

We met them halfway.

Tasha wrapped me in a hug, her tiny frame strong and familiar.

"I'm so glad you're all right. I was so worried," she said into my shoulder.

"Me too." My eyes were closed as I held her.

Patrick and Norris were next. They squeezed me tight, thanking me for not just landing the ship, rescuing Cruz, but for getting the others out. I waved them off and moved on to Cruz.

At first, we hesitated, then laughed.

"I think we've passed this," I said, lifting an eyebrow.

He nodded. "Probably true." He patted my back hard, laughing. "Thanks, Cap."

From behind me, Doc Mendez told Norris, "Don't worry, Javier and the rest are doing just fine."

He let her peek in on the babies tucked into the slings on his chest. She grinned at Javier, who was snoring softly.

"He is in heaven right now. Look at that." She glanced up. "Do you babysit?"

Doc snorted. "Anytime, Captain Norris. Anytime."

"I think we have passed the point where you can call me Victoria." She pulled him into a hug and laughed.

"Everyone," Tasha said, grin wide. She got the attention of those who had already made their way out of the ship. "We've found an easy path down to the forest floor over there." She pointed in the direction they'd come from. "There's a field with a stream that runs through it. We think it's a perfect place to set up camp for the night. I've already set a beacon for those who make it out. Once we've settled, we'll start sending people in to help the rest find their way out. Sound like a plan?"

There were smiles all around.

Joy radiated from her. "Then all I have to say is welcome to Merocius! Isn't she beautiful?"

This time cheers erupted from everyone. It was loud, filling the air and causing the animals nearby to go silent. From somewhere down the ship there was a responsive call.

"I think more have gotten out," Cruz said, lip twitching. He pulled Tasha to his side and kissed her temple.

"I'll send a few to find them and bring them to the identified field. Can you give me the coordinates?" I asked. She transmitted them to me, and I asked for volunteers.

Doc stopped me before I decided to join them. "You need stitches. Come to camp first. I need to check you out, Cruz, and Darnell. Once you're all good, then you and I can head out to help the others."

For once, I didn't argue. My arm hurt and in a situation like this, I knew he was the expert. I was no longer the one in charge, and it was time to lean on my team. Hell, it had worked so far. In the end, it had been Norris, Tasha, Patrick, and the others who had landed the ship. Well...crashed it.

I was just a side character.

Chapter Thirty-Eight

Captain Mitchel Remian

The steep incline, which led from the crash site to the first of two encampments we'd set up, ran along the side of a cliff. The walkway was fifteen feet wide in most parts, allowing us plenty of room to move supplies from *The Aspire* to our new homes. In others, it widened, allowing for those who needed to rest to take a seat and gaze out at the remarkable landscape below.

The lake below was a sight to see, the sun glimmering off it and casting rays back in hues that could make even the most unimaginative believe that fairytales existed. Trees that resembled pine but produced a maple syrup-like substance lined one side, casting shadows along the path. It was appreciated, considering the heat of the day and the humidity that had peaked early.

As I adjusted the straps of the large pack on my back then continued forward, pushing the drift full of supplies up the embankment, I found myself distracted by the violet glow coming from the tips of the needles.

"Morning, Captain."

I nodded to the crew member on his way down, heading back the way I'd just come from. I'd tried to get them to stop calling me that, but it had yet to work. Even after weeks of being here, they'd refused to let old habits die. In their eyes, they said, I would always be their captain, the one who led them and got them here safely.

Well, most of them.

I paused, looking back at the remains of my ship. The modules stuck from the ground at angles, the lower sections either embedded in the dirt below or covered by the lake. Metal shot into the air, curled and burnt from reentry.

Although I had a sense of pride knowing that we were here with so many safe, my heart sank each time I thought of those we'd lost. The ones lost due to the Cnidramarus or jettisoned during the meteor storm, or even those taken in the crash.

I glanced toward the destruction that led off to the west. One of the sections had broken free and skidded to crash into the mountains there. Our rescue team had only found thirty alive out of the nearly two hundred. It had been a hard loss for all of us.

My grip tightened on the drift. I forced myself to look away and start back up the hill.

The medical team needed these supplies. They were in the process of setting up the new hospital. We'd just finished building it — half the town had chipped in — and we'd been toting supplies all day.

"Hey, Cap?" Boston said from behind me. "How close are we to getting the first section removed from the rubble? I heard Evans and the others were working on it."

He'd been my partner in this adventure, having told me I was too old to take on such a job myself. The snarky kid looked like he could do this all day.

"Another few weeks, I think," I huffed. "We're close, but they're having some issues with power. Something was damaged in the crash, and they're having to manufacture some parts by hand."

"Well, with Montgomery, Evans, and Cruz on it, I'm sure they'll figure it out." He stopped to breathe and wipe his face. "It'll be huge with transporting stuff. Hell, getting the shuttles and off-road vehicles out would be a huge help."

"I know. Soon."

Reaching the top, I sighed, then lifted my shirt to wipe at the sweat dripping down my face.

There was a sharp whistle; a catcall I hadn't heard since I was a young man in a back-alley town. Shocked, I glanced up to find Tasha cracking up as she elbowed Brackett in the side. Brackett's cheeks were a deeper shade than I'd ever seen them before. Unsure what that was about, but not surprised Tasha was the instigator, I approached them, pushing the drift up next to the town meeting house.

"Hey, Boston. Can you let them know this is here?"

"Definitely. Thanks for the company," he said and headed inside.

"Are you all right, Connie?" I asked Brackett, concerned. Then I glared at Tasha. "What did you do to her?"

Tasha smirked, her mouth opened, but Brackett clapped a hand over the commander's mouth. I scowled.

"Nothing. She's done nothing. She was just showing me the new whistle she learned from Cruz. Apparently, it was used back on Earth, but was considered *inappropriate"* — Brackett glared at Tasha — "on the homeworld and is *still* considered inappropriate here on Merocius."

Tasha's shoulders began to shake, but Brackett's hand remained over her mouth, so she just nodded. Brackett turned the commander and pushed her away.

"Hurry up, Tasha, or they'll plan the expedition without you!"

That got my attention. "Expedition?"

"Yeah." Brackett faced me, far more composed than a moment ago. "They're finally planning to go to the ruins or debating the options, anyway. Tasha says she's waited long enough. Don't worry, they assumed you'd want to be a part of the conversation. That's why I'm here."

I smiled. "My expression tells you I wanted to go?" She nodded, and I gestured for her to join me as I followed after Tasha. "There's so much we need to learn about this planet, but even more we need to do to get set up."

People moved around as far as the eye could see. Some worked on the new buildings going up along the main square, others on ones farther down in the grasslands. New fields for growing crops had been started both in the valley here and on the other side of the river. Several groups of hunters were just coming in from their day's hunt, the oddest-looking creatures hanging from their backs. As they did, people cheered them on, proud of their effort.

It was a dream.

We'd even set up another town fifty or so miles east of *The Aspire* crash site. From our daily contacts, it was going as well as this one.

"What do you think happened to the people of this planet?" she asked, looking up at me. We weaved toward the outskirts and to the small cabin erected for Norris and the horde of infants she and Patrick were looking after. Eventually, they'd be split between couples able to take care of them, but until more homes were built and their conditions verified, it was a community event. That was except for Javier, Tenchi, and Kiho. Patrick and Norris had made it *very* clear those three were off limits.

I shrugged. "I don't know, but it'll be interesting to figure it out. Are you going to go to the ruins?"

Shaking her head, she opened the door. I held it so that she could enter first. "If you head out today? Nope. I'm on baby duty. I have spent the last two days working the fields and building a house. Then my nights digging through *The Aspire* to help build circuitry for Tasha. I'm tired. I want to feed a baby, set it on my chest, and take a nap. If another time, hell yes." Brackett winked, and I laughed. "But I expect a complete report when you return, Captain."

I grinned. "Yes, ma'am."

We followed the sound of Cruz's voice into the main room of the cabin. The far wall held a line of eight bassinets removed from *The Aspire* wreckage, each with a hand-painted nametag hanging above it; Tanaka of all people having made them. But the cribs currently sat empty, for each of the children sat propped in the arms of one of my crew.

Around a massive table sat Cruz, Tasha, Patrick, Norris, Richards, and Doc Mendez, squirming babies in each of their arms. As this was often a regular meeting space for us, we'd built a huge dining table and chairs to congregate around.

"This doesn't look like a planning session," I said, cracking a grin. "It looks like a playdate."

Six faces turned to me.

"You're jealous," Doc said.

"Damn, right. Give me one." I held my hands out to Norris, who held both Tenchi and Elena.

Elena's sweet face brightened when she saw me. I slipped my hands under her chubby arms and lifted her so I could kiss her cheek. She giggled. Then I found an empty chair.

"You're such a sucker," Cruz muttered.

"Like you can talk." I glared at the hulking man sitting pressed up next to Tasha, baby Trae in his lap.

Cruz shrugged. "What? He's a cute kid, and I remember what a good poker player he was."

Norris pointed a finger at her nephew. "You will not be a bad influence."

"Oh, yes, I will. That's what adoptive uncles are for, and you can't even argue that fact. Do I need to share the stories of the trouble you and I got into?" His eyebrows rose in question.

Norris leaned back in her chair, her posture relaxing. "Um...no. That is unnecessary. Thank you."

"Hell, no! You have to tell us now!" Tasha said, scaring poor Trae. She soothed him as we all laughed.

"Anyway," Patrick said, smiling at Norris. "So you know what you walked in on, Mitchel. With the help of Dr. Brackett, we were able to get the long-range scanners up and working. We had to do some modifications since they were damaged and the ruins are so far off, but we confirmed that our scans during the identification of the planet as a potential home are still correct. There are no humanoid or advanced lifeforms on Merocius."

"But there were." Tasha smirked.

Patrick nodded. "There are signs of multiple cities in ruins; the one closest to us is the largest."

The room had gone silent except for the quiet baby gurgles, shifting, and the sound of our breathing. I met Brackett's eyes. She'd taken the seat next to me, her posture relaxed, legs crossed.

"What you should know" — Cruz's tone was serious, but excitement vibrated in each word, too — "the scans show that the ruins are just the top level. There are underground caverns as well."

Something settled heavily in my stomach.

"Can we wait until the section is evacuated to go, or do we want to make this trip the priority?" I asked.

We exchanged glances, as if by doing so, we could read each other's minds. Perhaps, by now, we could.

"Setting up camp is priority," Norris said.

Everyone agreed.

"Then we focus here, and we plan for a full exploration trip once the section has been removed, and we can fly there."

"Agreed," they seconded. Good, a group decision.

"Well, then, if we aren't going to go on a death-defying trip to explore an alien city, what are we doing today? I'm off from the fields and building duties until tomorrow," Norris said.

"Me too," Cruz and Tasha seconded.

"Same." Richards nodded.

Brackett touched my arm. "I have an idea." When I raised my eyebrow, she continued, "We could go down to the riverbank and see how these little munchkins take to the cool water. Dig our toes into the sand."

She tickled Elena's pudgy feet. Elena smiled, pulling them away.

"They could use a bath." Norris hummed.

"And it is hot out," Tasha said, gazing up at Cruz, who smiled down at her. "It'd be a great way to cool down."

I smacked my leg and stood. "That's it, then. We have the day off. Officially."

"That's a thing?" Patrick asked.

"We're on our new home now, Patrick," I said. "Anything is possible."

THE END

Thank You for Reading *The Secrets of Eronis 8*!

I hope you enjoyed getting to know the crew of *The Aspire*! If you did, I would greatly appreciate it if you'd consider supporting me by leaving a review. Reviews help authors more than you know by letting other readers know how you feel about the book. I enjoy reading them, too! It would mean the world to me if you did! To leave a review, head to your vendor's website and/or the GoodReads book page. I would greatly appreicate it.

This is the first installment of the Merocian Saga. Which means, book 2 is planned and in progress! If you'd like to stay up to date on any of my new releases and giveaways, then please head to my website at Tra ceyCanole.com and join my mailing list to keep updated on upcoming projects and check out my short stories! Thank you again for all of your support!

Interested in other works by Tracey Canole?
Then check out the Source Rising Series, a complete meteor impact adventure scifi trilogy!

Source Awakening, Book 1
Source Ignited, Book 2
Source Evolution, Book 3

SOURCE AWAKENING

It's funny how being trapped in an avalanche can make you rethink your past mistakes. They said the world was safe. I guess they were wrong.

Reena Novak was just a normal girl until the rogue planet Goliath entered the atmosphere, ending the world as she knew it. Now, the mysterious ash trailing after Goliath has absorbed into her skin, and she's seeing things she can't explain — images of an ethereal swirling liquid and ever-changing landscapes. They haunt her, just like the powers developing within her.

Tension is high as she and her ex-best friend, Jaxson, must work together to reach their families. But it isn't until he saves her life with new abilities that she realizes she's not the only one changed by the ash. What are these powers and why do they only appear in some?

After meeting Remy, a stranger with powers both like and unlike hers, Reena is determined to find the common link. But the only clue she has are the dreams and the pull she feels in her chest to some unknown force called The Source and the power it wields. It calls to them all, but why?

Is this another test, a punishment for the way she's treated Jaxon, or something else? Reena must restore her relationship with Jaxson, protect those she loves, and stop anyone who might use the power of The Source for personal gain. Or what's left of this world will disappear forever.

About the Author

Tracey L. Canole is a Science Fiction and Urban Fantasy author. Her stories take you on an adventure to far off worlds, drawing you into characters and their experiences as they navigate their extraordinary lives. Tracey loves both stories based in reality and those that bend our understanding of the universe. Her favorites are those that have a fantastical element, allowing the reader to go somewhere they never expected.

When not writing, she enjoys reading and dabbling in many different art forms, such as painting and ceramics. But her absolute joy is found in exploring the world through hiking and camping with her husband and two children.

For more about her, and her other projects, head over to her website at TraceyCanole.com. While there, sign up for her newsletter and keep up to date with all her upcoming projects!

Printed in the USA
CPSIA information can be obtained
at www.ICGtesting.com
JSHW010854060823
45926JS00005B/89